SLAVES, SAINTS AND SOLDIERS

DAVID CLAIRE JENNINGS

Slaves, Saints and Soldiers

First edition - first printing June 2017

Southern Heart Publishing Co.
Author's website: www.davidclairejennings.com

ISBN-13: 978-0-9974601-8-6
ISBN-10: 0-9974601-8-0

Also by David Claire Jennings:

After Bondage and War

Hanna's Promise: A Story of Grace and Hope

The American: A Man's Life

The Goodness of Alzheimer's

Collected Essays on Americanism

The Men Who Gathered Together: An early history of SURC

For Edith, Mom and Dad –

Would that they could have known

Foreword

Following my historic fiction novels *After Bondage and War* and *Hanna's Promise, The American* is the completion of a trilogy. I had not set out to write a trilogy but only knew the purpose of each book as I wrote it, often knowing the beginning and the end clearly even as I began.

My characters taught me their story – like a human history lesson. Unlike William Faulkner who claimed he often knew precisely what a book of his would be right down to the last period at the end, these books revealed themselves to me as I wrote them. I doubt that Faulkner ever outlined his books as he began them and I have not either; he because he believed he did not need to, me because I did not know what each chapter would be.

The writing of them showed me that there would need to be three to tell all the stories within them and that there would be a unity in the totality.

The structure of that last book will appear to the reader as a novella with a central character telling a personal story in linear time progression from beginning to end. At least that is how it will appear throughout most of the book, with the exception of some looking back by the story-telling character.

At the end of the book, the reader learns that all that appeared present was past. At the final moment the alert and engaged reader will see that the structure was indeed circular and that the end curved around to meet the beginning.

My earlier novels, particularly *After Bondage and War*, brought me to this. It became apparent David Wexley's story needed to be told. He was an American for his time and place in the American story. His life informs us of what it used to be like – how it was.

Since *The American* is a novella, its style contrasts with the two proceeding novels. Its focus is narrower and is concerned with just thirteen years of the central character's life. For that period, the sub-title of this work might also be – A Man of the Gilded Age.

When the work was completed, from a historical perspective, I had covered all of the 19th century with some overlap back into the 18th and forward to the 20th. I was satisfied with the effort.

If the fictional character in this novel had been a real historic figure, this work would have been an academic work with the figure as a primary source telling a first person history as a personal biography of what he had seen, experienced and done. It could have been so because in either case, he tells the reader just how it was in his time.

And even those authentic non-fiction historiographies have perspective because as Shelby Foote has reminded us "the truth is the facts we love."

- DCJ

Part One – After Bondage and War

An Historic Fictional Novel

Contents

Foreword

Slavery was a stain on our country. It deeply falsified our founding ideals and was a longstanding shame for us in the eyes of the world. In the first hundred years of our history, we developed as two divergent societies and cultures based on two different visions in interpreting our founding ideals. Adams had a vision for a country of enterprising merchants and property owners with emerging industrialism in small towns and cities bound together under a central government - a system of Federalism. Jefferson had a vision of an agrarian society of independent small farmers with slavery under more localized governance in states. The North and South grew apart.

The period of the Civil War and its aftermath of failed Reconstruction was a watershed moment in our history, and perhaps its most important moment. As the regional and sectional issues heated up beyond reconciliation, the country blew up. The Union was preserved and slavery was abolished. But the South was devastated and the country's wounds have never completely healed.

What if the Civil War had not been fought? Would slavery have ended a couple decades later as the rest of the country industrialized? What would have happened if Lincoln had not been assassinated? Would the subsequent century of racism and sectional divide have been lessened? What would have happened if Eli Whitney, or anyone else, had not invented the cotton gin, or the boll weevil had been successful, or the world market for cotton as a raw material had declined 50 years earlier than the early 20th century?

While the backdrop for the story covers a century of our history, beginning with the antebellum period, progressing through parts of the Civil War and failed Reconstruction, and ending around 1900, the characters resonate with thoughts and feelings we all share today: frustration, hopelessness, loneliness, spiritual longing, friendship, and love. Like all of us, there are parts of our being that we can define as evil, or morally corrupt, and parts that are pure and good. As Shakespeare once said, "There is nothing either good or bad, but thinking makes it so." In addition, as peoples' lives progress with time, the fundamental nature of their character may change. We readers may start out rooting for one person that we believe to be a morally good person, and end up feeling that he or she has fallen short or utterly failed in his or her growth, or even has become corrupt and evil.

As I have come to re-know David after more than forty years apart, I have learned that he cares about and feels these things deeply. Through his extensive study, reading, and writing, he has developed a great sensitivity for our history and country and has gravitated toward a care and concern for its South.

I was the consummate Yankee, having been raised outside of New York City and having lived 10 years in Upstate New York, who knew nothing about the South. However, for the past 44 years I have lived in Georgia or Alabama. From metropolitan Atlanta to the most rural area of northern Alabama, I have come to know and understand the South as it has become. The New South rose from her ashes when she was rebuilt after the war. The South began to industrialize. For the rural Deep South however, much remains the same as it was in the past. Many of the positive characteristics of the southern culture embodied in this book are alive and well today, particularly in the rural areas.

A deep abiding faith in the love of God, family and country still prevail in most of the people I know. And for many southerners, the Civil War continues to be a deep wound in their hearts.

The people of the South that I have come to know over the years are steadfast in their views and willing to lend a hand to anyone needing help, be it friend or stranger.

I am an educator by calling and a story teller by nature and David is a feeling historian. Several months ago, David asked me if I would read the book he was writing as a favor. It only took one reading for me to become intrigued by the characters and their story. Since then our old friendship has come alive in a new way, now that we are much older and have lived our lives and careers. Though a thousand miles apart, we have mentored each other and labored together to produce this book. With our care and concern for all the American people, we believe *After Bondage and War* to be a sensitive and important statement about this period of history and the people who lived through it.

Not since Stephen Crane's *Red Badge of Courage*, has this story been told with such emotional intensity and pathos. I feel we have treated it with a broader reach, dimension and poignancy. Through its personal recounting of history and its very human characters, it is our intention that our readers will feel this way also.

We hope so and hope you enjoy the story.

- Joan Austin

Prologue

The old man paused in his daily walk to rest on his favorite bench on the quad of the Miami of Ohio campus. He enjoyed the energy of the young students, their passion for civil rights and to end an unjust war. It was the 1960's.

He told them about his grandfather and his struggle 100 years ago. He told them about the Civil War and his grandfather's friend David whose name had been chosen for his father. He wanted them to gain a perspective that can only come from knowledge of the past.

Josiah was tired, not in his muscles or bones from a hard day's work, in his soul for the loss he had suffered and the apprehension of what was to come. He slowly walked down the hard-packed and rutted red clay dirt road leading away from the Savannah Oaks plantation. He felt old beyond his years, and the simmering sultry heat and humidity of the southern Mississippi summer added to his fatigue the longer he walked. The massive live oaks, with their curtains of hanging Spanish moss provided some shade, but held the humidity so close to the ground that he could feel the droplets of water floating in the air around him.

He remembered the last time he had traveled this road, as a young man 13 years ago, when he was brought to Savannah Oaks. This time the journey was for a different purpose and under different circumstance.

Now he was traveling away from the place - his forced home for those last arduous, grueling and cruel years. The farther he walked, the further he remembered that bitter past journey on this road from Natchez. His thoughts drifted back to that earlier time, to his brief happiness with Josena and his accomplishments then.

The live oaks with the hanging moss became less oppressive and brought him a sense of calmness and peace he had not felt earlier. Hope began to fill his heart. Now he would have the chance to find his beloved Josena. He began to walk faster.

This long day had begun with the arrival of the federal authorities at Savannah Oaks. They had come to broker the release of the plantation's slaves. Although the war had officially ended in April when Lee surrendered at Appomattox, the fighting didn't stop immediately, but continued in the western sections of the country.

The South had been so completely devastated and crippled by the war, communication was almost non-existent with virtually no functioning telegraph service. While communication in southern cities had been difficult, the southern plantations, which had always been spread far and wide in the Deep South, were more isolated than ever. It had taken from April until July for federal authorities to finally arrive at Savannah Oaks.

With the arrival of the government people, the plantation's slaves were gathered together. Some came from the fields, some from their cabins, the rest from the mansion. They assembled in the big yard in the front of the main house. They stood in groups and alone, anticipating a change but not knowing what it would mean. Some of them stood near the pole where they had been bound and lashed on so many occasions.

The government men explained to them that they were freed. This pronouncement was unprecedented, unfamiliar, but joyously welcome for the human beings who had always been enslaved, always been the property of some other human being, in one place or another. The authorities explained that there was hope for government programs to help them. They assured the emancipated people that the Freedmen's Bureau would make its best effort, with limited funding and political support, to provide for them.

The ideas they were considering were for better education, land provision, legal rights, and a societal readjustment to a free labor agricultural system. These noble plans for reconstruction had not been worked out and could not be guaranteed. A free labor system was a concept the South had no experience with or knowledge about. The many governments involved would debate and contend for authority.

But on this day, their message was received as both hopeful and frightening for the former slaves who were just now released. In the end, the politicians in the South and Washington looked out for their own interests and little was done to help them, despite the best intentions of the Freedmen's Bureau and some in the government.

As the former slaves stood there not quite knowing what would come next, they were told that for now they could leave as they wished and go where they wished. The younger ones were anxious to go and face a new future. The older ones were hesitant to leave their familiar life and more frightened of the unknown. None of their ancestors had traversed this free world before them.

They must be on their own and care for themselves. Their security and sustenance would be their own. There was no place to live, no food to eat. No one would provide. This was the end of a co-dependent society, a cruel security, where some would be forced to work for others and the others would provide for their care. The enslaved and the enslavers would part their ways.

They could search for their families, travel freely throughout the country and contract for their labor as best they could arrange. For the first time in their lives, those gathered in front of the main house realized that they owned their own selves.

This was both an exhilarating and worrisome revelation, for they were homeless now, they had nowhere to go, and their life was going to become very difficult in new and unanticipated ways. They were going to have to deal with a world in which they had no experience and, as it would turn out, with little help from the federal government that had just given them their freedom.

With the loss of the Confederacy, the southern whites were embittered toward the federal government of the North for the devastation of their land and loss of their way of life. A bitter white aristocracy would look for ways to gain back their way of life and win their lost cause. They would find new ways to economically enslave the freedmen despite the passage of the 13th Amendment.

When the embittered South could not accomplish its mission, it would resort to other means of taking out its anger on the freedmen through many acts of violence. While the two races had formerly lived together in a form of a co-dependent society, now whites would set the former slaves apart from southern society and enact laws to deny the new freedmen their individual rights.

None at the Savannah Oaks plantation that day could foresee all the problems or know how it would end as the slaves were gathered on the front lawn of the main house. They began to move away from the yard, some returning to their cabins not ready to leave. Many, like Josiah, decided to leave the plantation right away.

For Josiah, there was the realization that for the first time in his life, he was free from bondage. But how would he go forth? What would he do now? He had never known anything other than bondage his whole life. Now that he was free, he would have to apply his keen mind to begin to understand what this newfound freedom would mean to him. More importantly, now he would have to find out how he could make a good life for himself in this new different reality.

Without looking back, he walked away from Savannah Oaks and began his search for understanding and a new life.

Illustrations

Fountain in Forsyth Park - Savannah, Georgia

Savannah Oaks plantation mansion - near Natchez, Mississippi

Battle of Antietam - September 17, 1862

Andersonville Prison - Ft. Sumter, Georgia

One - Marcus

Now, wherever the stars and stripes wave, they protect slavery and represent slavery... This then is the final fruit. In this, all the labors of our statesmen, the blood of our heroes, the lifelong cares and toils of our forefathers, the aspirations of our scholars, the prayers of good men, have finally ended! America the slave breeder and slaveholder!

- Seth Grahame-Smith

Marcus Taylor was born in 1807 in Savannah, Georgia to a wealthy family. His people were of Dutch ancestry tracing back to New Amsterdam in the 1600's. His father Hendrick made his fortune as a cotton factor before Marcus was born. Accountants and brokers were in demand.

He was one of the earliest to prosper from Savannah's role as a major seaport for the cotton business. Shortly after his death, his work, and that of the other early successful factors, would require the completion of the Savannah Cotton Exchange. As the South's king cotton continued to boom, it was built there on Bay Street. Savannah later grew in 1880 to become known as the "Wall Street of the South" before the boll weevil and falling world markets decimated cotton agriculture. Savannah's heyday and decline would come after his day, but Hendrick was one of its pioneers.

Savannah's bustling business hub was perched on a ridge facing north and overlooking River Street and the brisk seagoing activity on the Savannah River. Stone steps were built along the way to descend the steep bluff serving as a levee to the river front.

The Taylor family - Hendrick, his wife Jane, Marcus, and his younger sisters Marcy and Constance - lived in a mansion on Columbia Square, originally laid out in 1799. This was one of Savannah's historic squares developed over several decades. They eventually became miniature parks, beautified by live oaks, and with historic monuments and sidewalks running north-south through their centers.

The squares south of Bay Street grew to 24, but began as 4 originally laid out by British General James Oglethorpe in 1733, the same year he founded the colony of Georgia and the city of Savannah. His original plan was to provide space for the colonists to practice military exercises and as vegetable gardens to feed his troops stationed there as a "border" defense in case of invading Spanish from St. Augustine, Florida. James Oglethorpe also established the first Masonic Lodge in America on Bay Street in 1734 at the site that would later become the Savannah Cotton Exchange.

The city was undergoing growth in every direction as expansion tried to keep pace with its commercial successes from king cotton. At the east end of Bay Street, a new road and bridge were under construction to open up Tybee Island to wealthy leisure seekers.

Savannah preserved its history. Fort Pulaski still stood on Tybee with its long history dating back to Oglethorpe and the French and Spanish before his time. Bonaventure Cemetery lay along the Wilmington River to the east of Savannah on the way toward Tybee. Its old graves dated back to the end of the 18th century.

West of the squares, and south below Bay Street, a new city market was opening for outdoor sale of fresh produce and social gathering. At the west end of Bay Street, the bridge over the river to the north led to South Carolina low country, its Sea Islands and Beaufort, the quiet village in the tidewaters.

The beautiful 30 acre Forsyth Park was under construction south of the squares. Neighborhoods south of that were being built for the poorer working folks. These would become the neighborhoods for freedmen after the war. Savannah was a unique city in that it was not as driven by the passions of racism or views of social class as much as most of southern society. As a bustling seaport, Savannah's people were exposed to visitors from European countries and, perhaps more than other southern cities, held a more international perspective. Their very nature was more friendly and inclusive.

More than Savannah, Charleston typified antebellum southern culture and defined the old South. Nearby Savannah, in Georgia, would never reach Charleston's size but would develop its own character. The contrast in societal view between Charleston and Savannah was stark. This was simply understood by the way people greeted strangers. If you visited Charleston, the greeting was "Hi. Where y'all from?" In Savannah it was "Hi. What y'all want to drink?" The Charleston people needed to test your social worthiness by inquiring about your origin and family. The Savannah people weren't concerned with that. They wanted new people to join the party. To say that they were colorful, eccentric, and humorous was to begin to describe them.

People believed that, while Grant struck at Richmond as the capital of the Confederacy, Sherman struck at Atlanta to destroy its heart and soul. But this was not true. Sherman knew that Atlanta was a major strategic target as a railroad hub for Confederate transportation and logistics.

Incorporated as late as 1837, Atlanta didn't participate in antebellum culture. Slave plantations were all over the South, but people would consider them and southern society with an eye on Atlanta. But back then the city was just forming and the region was a frontier with dirt roads and Andrew Jackson's contentions with Cherokee people. The Cherokees were expelled in the sad Trail of Tears. Atlanta would rise from its ashes after the war.

The southern cities on the coast - Charleston and Savannah - had a longer history dating back before the Revolutionary War. They were more developed and the places of southern refinement.

Given the circumstance and nature of the three cities, perhaps Charleston was the seat of southern culture - the notions of chivalry, nobility, aristocracy, gentility, smooth southern charm, courtliness and refined manners - the southern way of life if you were white and wealthy.

Sherman struck Atlanta and burned it to the ground. He followed with Savannah and spared it. He spared Savannah the devastation he had wrought on Atlanta in his march across Georgia to the sea. He left it intact and offered it to President Lincoln as a Christmas present. His troops occupied Savannah and entered unopposed. They seized their cotton, guns and artillery and set up a prison camp on Bay Street. They stayed for several weeks before continuing their scorched earth policy northward to South Carolina.

But long before the war, Savannah was a place of prosperity and gentle indulgence. Marcus grew up with a life that was privileged. His parents provided him the finest education available for his time. But he was not a serious student. He took his unearned position of birth for granted. The work he did with his father gave him a working knowledge of the cotton business - at least from the broker's end of it.

But that did not interest him and he had no passion to follow his father's path for his career, or live under his shadow. He wanted success, to make money, but on his own, his way. He was an ambitious dreamer with delusions of grandeur.

The sailing ships and bustling business activity in Savannah fueled his dreams. But he came to the belief that he would need to seek his fortune elsewhere - somewhere where the competition would favor his own enterprise, where he could exert his own power and autonomy. He witnessed the slave auctions and thought he might strike out to the west and build his own plantation as a cotton producer. That was where the real money was to be made.

Marcus kept his ambitions to himself. He continued to work for his father. For the longest while, this was the easiest way to make a living. And it gave him a freedom to wander about Savannah and think his private thoughts - dream his private dreams.

He enjoyed the city and courting the young women he found. His position in the Savannah society offered him many opportunities to sample the many young women who were looking for a suitable mate to marry, and settle down with, and raise a family. He found them wanting. The truth was that they never found him worthy of marriage. If asked, most would have said that they felt he was a shallow self-centered person, although pleasant enough company.

Hendrick had watched his son grow to manhood. He surely loved him as a man does his only son. But he doubted he had the ability to be successful based on a feeling he had that something was missing. Maybe his ambition was misplaced or unrealistic. He wasn't sure what it was. Somehow he seemed to lack the drive and perseverance.

Hendrick was unaware that Marcus had great ambitions, and so could not know what they were. Marcus continued to work for his father and enjoy the relaxed social life of an eligible bachelor. He continued to dream his dreams.

He met Rebecca Stanley in the riverside park at the east end of Bay Street. He was attracted to this young woman for her elegance and patrician manner. She was tall and thin with beautiful blue eyes and long auburn hair in soft curls. She was the quintessential product of Charleston society and a model example of fine southern womanhood. Her father and brothers had built a manufacturing dynasty in Charleston, supplying the South with work wagons, replacement parts, plows, and hand tools for farming and workshops.

Rebecca was visiting Savannah with her brothers to develop marketing alliances for their products. With her upbringing in the family, she had proven to have a keen head for business and understood how the social graces could win orders and contracts.

She was exercising her foxhound in the park when Marcus approached her. When they began their courtship, Rebecca's older brothers vetted Marcus and found him a worthy companion for their younger sister.

The couple soon formed a comfortable loving relationship and decided to marry. With the blessing of both families, they took their vows in the new First Baptist Church on Chippewa Square. It seemed as though the two rival societies had married and it was a big day for Savannah.

As a boy, Marcus revered his father and wanted to make his own fortune someday when he was able. When he was 28, in 1835, his father staked him in a venture to buy rich land in the west for cotton production. Speculation for new land was competitive by then.

Marcus found his opportunity in Mississippi near the port of Natchez. It was 57 miles east of the port and a one-day trip by horse drawn wagon. It was an ideal location and he bought 650 acres for $7,800.

After he purchased the deed to his plantation, he remembered home and named it Savannah Oaks. Savannah was a major center for slave trade, but practicality demanded he purchase his slaves locally. The Mississippi river was a conduit for the internal slave trade from the upper South to the deep South. He immediately visited Natchez again with the purpose of inquiring about the slaves.

His immediate challenge was labor. Compared to the cost of land, this would be the biggest expense. He talked to local people and learned that slaves could be purchased separately or in lots and conveniently at the same auction with horses, mules and cattle. He found the going price at auction for a prime Negro averaged $1,000.

He learned about an upcoming auction and pondered how to begin. He would eventually require fifty or more slaves for a plantation the size of his. At about $1,000 per head, there was a lot to consider before spending $50,000 all at once for fifty humans.

But to get started, he would have to determine the smaller number needed for the initial work. For right now, the swamp forests would need to be cleared. The timber would be milled for lumber to build the barns, cotton processing buildings and slave cabins to house his human property. He would build a primitive house for himself until the plantation could get started. Sod would need to be broken before the first crop could be seeded. He would need mules and horses. There was a great deal to do.

He returned to Natchez for the scheduled auction he had seen posted on his earlier visit. He had seen slave auctions before in Savannah but *The Forks of the Road* auction here was on a much larger scale with auctions offered more frequently on a continuing basis.

He looked again at the signboard posting the human commodity available for this day's auction. The asking price and the bid price were hardly ever the same. He had to bargain well and spend his father's stake wisely.

Sale of Slaves and Stock

The Negroes and Stock listed below, are a Prime Lot, and belong to the ESTATE OF THE LATE LUTHER McCULLOUGH, and will be sold on Monday, July 20th, 1835, at The Forks of the Road auction, intersection of Liberty Road and Washington Road in Natchez, Mississippi, at 1:00 P.M. The Negroes will be taken to the grounds two days previous to the Sale, so that they may be inspected by prospective buyers.

On account of the low prices listed below, they will be sold for cash only, and must be taken into custody within two hours after sale.

No.	Name	Age	Remarks	Price
1	Sarah	27	Prime Field Hand,	$1,275.00
2	Violet	16	Housework and Nursemaid,	900.00
3	Lizzie	30	Hand, Unsound,	300.00
4	Minda	27	Cotton, Prime Woman,	1,200.00
5	Adam	28	Cotton, Prime Young Man,	1,100.00
6	Abel	41	Cotton Hand, Eyesight Poor,	675.00
7	Tanney	22	Prime Cotton Hand,	950.00
8	Flementina	39	Good Cook, Stiff Knee,	400.00
9	Lanney	34	Prime Cotton Man,	1,000.00
10	Sally	10	Handy in Kitchen,	675.00
11	Ned	46	Prime Man, Good Carpenter,	980.00
12	Dorcas Judy	25	Seamstress, Handy in House,	800.00
13	Happy	60	Blacksmith,	575.00
14	Mowden	15	Prime Cotton Boy,	700.00
15	Bills	21	Handy with Mules,	900.00
16	Theopolis	39	Cotton Hand, Gets Fits,	575.00
17	Coolidge	29	Cotton Hand and Blacksmith	1,275.00
18	Bessie	69	Infirm, Sews,	250.00
19	Infant	1	Strong Likely Boy,	400.00
20	Samson	41	Prime Man, Good with Stock,	975.00
21	Callie May	27	Prime Woman, Cotton,	1,000.00
22	Honey	14	Prime Girl, Hearing Poor,	850.00
23	Angelina	16	Prime Girl, House or Field,	1,000.00
24	Virgil	21	Prime Field Hand,	1,100.00

25	Tom	40	Cotton Hand, Lame Leg,	750.00
26	Noble	11	Handy Boy,	900.00
27	Judge Lesh	55	Prime Blacksmith,	800.00
28	Booster	43	Fair Mason, Unsound,	600.00
29	Big Kate	37	Housekeeper and Nurse,	950.00
30	Melie Ann	19	Housework, Smart Yellow Girl,	1,250.00
31	Coming	19	Prime Cotton Hand,	1,000.00
32	Uncle Tim	60	Fair Hand with Mules,	600.00
33	Abe	27	Prime Cotton Hand,	1,000.00

There will also be offered at this sale, twenty head of Horses and Mules with harness, along with thirty head of Prime Cattle. Slaves will be sold separate, or in lots, as best suits the purchaser. Sale will be held rain or shine.

Marcus had to prioritize and determine what he needed first and most, while pacifying Rebecca's needs. He decided to buy nine Negroes to get started.

Rebecca stayed back in Charleston with her family until Marcus had completed a rough temporary house and begun the major work on the mansion. When this much was ready, he sent for her. When she arrived, she was not happy. The roughness of the land, the oppressiveness of the heat and humidity, and the lack of refinement of the people didn't measure up to Charleston. This place was crude and backward. This was not what she had expected when she married Marcus.

He had promised her, "Rebecca, we will have a great plantation with all the refinements you had known in Charleston." She hoped so.

"When I was growing up, I always wanted a fine home and family of my own and an important place in society."

There would be a strain in their relationship as time went on.

After Bondage and War

Two - Rebecca

Rebecca Stanley was born in 1809 in Charleston, South Carolina. All the years she was growing up, her family had participated in the high society there. Her father had risen through the degrees of the Free Masons, as had Mozart and Virginians Washington and Madison before him. The social and business connections had enhanced his position and station in society. Her brothers had joined De Molay and would join their father's fraternal Order of Scottish Rites when they were old enough. Her mother belonged to the sister Order of the Eastern Star as she would one day.

The parents belonged to the 1748 St. Andrews Society which met at 70 Meeting Street. They shared this same hall with the 1737 South Carolina Society. There were many other societal organizations in Charleston, including the most prominent St. Cecilia Society. They were all involved in philanthropic causes. The history of their society and its culture was rich and old and deep.

There were gay parties, coming out debutante galas and balls for the upper crust families, seasonal cotillions, celebrated engagements, big wedding affairs, receptions for all the important people on grand lawns with white canopy tents and flowers everywhere. There were mint juleps, merry cheers and toasts, flocks of pretty young ladies twirling in their finest long dresses, older men standing straight and proud, arms crossed, smiling with contentment, watching over them smoking their cigars, and handsome young men excited to begin the courting game.

The splendid architecture, the galleries, the cobblestone streets basked in sea breezes, the wonderful low country food, all brought a fulfillment and great satisfaction to Charleston's people. They loved their lives, filled with gentility and refined courtly manners.

Rebecca had completed her social etiquette training lessons, paid for by her old-moneyed parents. When she was 16, she was presented to Charleston's bachelors and their families at her cotillion. There were escorts, flower girls and pages to attend the grand affair. She had been paired with her beau escort by her parents in agreement with the committee of elite members of society. Her father had formally introduced her to the audience from the stage. She wore a white gown and satin kid gloves and curtsied in the St. James full court manner to receive the invited guests in the line. They had paid for their tickets and this event had charitable benefit for those unfortunate poor souls who weren't invited.

She was eligible to marry. But that was not what she wanted then. She wanted to enjoy her youth and the many beaus who would come to call. The attention and the grand life was the best she could have imagined. Charleston was a joy.

After some years had passed, things changed. She was older. She began to reconsider her life, thought about herself, looked back at and inside of herself, 'Then Charleston was stuffy - saw past this - as after youth began to fade, the courtship game grew tired, boring, too easy, had lost appeal, win was loss, many loves played and forsaken, too many young men's love's lost, while not the right gallant man had come or been found, for too long, it's late, time running out, still none proved strong to make me lose, and put me up high, and cherish as deserved because intelligence was the impediment, no gentlewoman to gentleman man who would do all these things and still make a woman partner, trust and rely on her, let me free to judge, free to decide, rectitude, righteousness and fair, alone love's trials had run its course. I'll inform father, carve out my own path, join the brothers in business, travel, see new places, start new, bide the few years left before spinsterhood is the answer, maybe lower sights, take better aim, settle and lose to win the game in the end.'

That's what she did. Strong-headed she was. Made up her own mind. She traveled through the South with her older brothers to build marketing alliances with distributors of farm and workshop equipment to further develop the family's business. She worked smart and hard, sharing the marketing efforts with her brothers. But the South was a place of ease for the genteel and successful. She often enjoyed its leisure and took respite.

She arrived in Savannah, a short trip from Charleston, and took in the sights of the city. It was different than Charleston. Savannah had grown rapidly at the turn of the century and had more diverse architecture, monuments, statues, refined art, and shops along the riverside quay. There was more of an international flavor to the area with the busy seaport activity on the Savannah River. She had brought her dog and they enjoyed all the beautiful parks and historic squares there together.

She often turned off Bay Street and walked south to St. James Square on the corner of State Street. This was talked about as the most fashionable neighborhood in Savannah. There was a new mansion there she always stopped to admire. The old woman, matron of the estate, was often tending her vegetables on the side yard or flowers in the front. The home was stately, beautiful and imposing.

The morning air was still cool. The flowers sparkled with the dew and soft sunlight rising toward its glorious mid-day brilliance. She took a few moments to compliment the woman on her beautiful Gloriosa daylilies, gardenias, petunias, and Floribunda wild roses.

The woman took pride in her garden and appreciated Rebecca's admiration.

Each time, by habit, Rebecca strolled further south to the expansive Forsyth Park beyond the squares. The new fountain there was splendid and a wonder. The whole city was a place of peace and beauty - an urban city yes, but abundant in gentle earthly comforts.

On other occasions, she walked her dog in the park at the east end of Bay Street, looking at the sailing ships moving in and out of the port. She noticed a handsome man watching her from the sidewalk and smiled to herself. She was flattered that she still had the looks to turn heads. And she was amused and gratified - still confident of her charms. She thought, 'Now there's a man I'd like to meet. I mustn't approach him. That wouldn't be proper. I'll bet if I smile at him, he will come over here'. Sure enough, she did and he did.

Marcus approached and smiling back said, "Good day Miss. I saw you and your dog standing here. I wanted to ask if that is a purebred foxhound."

"It is", she replied smiling sweetly with the convincing unbeatable charm that melts the heart of the savage beast.

Struggling for a way to keep the conversation alive, he said, "Do you hunt with him?"

"We have taken him out, but he is mostly a companion in the household."

"Are you from Savannah? I thought I knew all the pretty girls in town."

'Oh, he's a smooth devil', she thought.

"No, I'm visiting here. I'm from Charleston. How about you?"

"I'm born and bred here in Savannah. My name is Marcus Taylor."

"My name is Rebecca Stanley. It's a pleasure Mr. Taylor. Maybe we will see each other again. Good day."

As she moved away, Marcus thought, 'I hope so. I'll see to it.'

Marcus was enchanted with Rebecca, as so many others had been before, and even more, he was smitten. He looked for her in the park every day. She was never there, but he continued to hope they would meet again.

Then one day, he thought he saw her next to his father's office, near the site the city planners were developing for the future Cotton Exchange. She was descending the stone steps with two older young men down to River Street. The men looked about his age. He couldn't help but wonder and worry whether one or both were her beaus. He was jealous without any justification or earned right.

He thought, 'I must catch her, but cannot appear like I'm following or chasing her.'

He surged ahead with a flimsy plan, and didn't do it well.

He rushed down the stairs and caught up to the Stanleys slightly out of breath and puffed up with his face flushed.

He said, "Rebecca Stanley is that you? I was rushing to meet that incoming ship to discuss the cotton cargo with the captain. But then I saw you and wanted a chance to meet you again."

She didn't believe him but smiled and said, "It's good to see you again Mr. Taylor. These are my brothers, William and Francis. We are traveling together for our father's business. It's good fortune we saw you. We're leaving soon for Charleston. I love your beautiful city. The customers here have been receptive to us and we will be back again."

When Marcus recovered his composure for his awkward advance, he said, "Pleasure to meet you gentlemen. I'm sorry to hear you are leaving. I was meaning to ask you Rebecca, and now you William and Francis as well. Could y'all come to our home for dinner and meet my family?"

Rebecca looked at her brothers and winked.

She smiled at Marcus and said, "Thank you Marcus. May I call you Marcus? We would love to come. It will give us excuse to dally a little longer and enjoy the hospitality of the kind people of Savannah."

He looked too pleased and said, "That's wonderful. Where are you staying? I will send you word."

He said his goodbyes and, as he walked away, thought, 'It will help things go smoother when William and Francis catch a glance at Marcy and Constance.'

Marcus walked toward the dock, pretending to meet the sailing ship.

Rebecca watched him leave, turned toward her brothers, pointed and said with her hand covering a grin, "Looks like that ship is heading full sail out to sea. Marcus won't be able to meet it after all."

They all laughed.

When Rebecca received the embossed linen invitation, she opened it and it read:

Dearest Lady Rebecca and Gentlemen William and Francis:

Our family requests the honor of your presence to accompany us for dinner on Tuesday eve next at 7 o'clock.

Our coachman will pick you up at 6:45 and bring you here to Columbia Square.

Without your regrets, we look forward with anticipation for your acceptance and appearance.

Warmest Blessings,

The Taylors

She smiled. Another courtship, maybe the last one, had begun.

The dinner party went well and was a great success. The brothers talked about the family business. Rebecca chimed in. The Taylors were impressed that these young folks, with their tender experience, had such confidence, savvy and ambition. Hendrick wondered if a confident poised young woman like Rebecca would be a good match for Marcus - or even if he would qualify for it. They got to know each other better.

The young men and women enjoyed each other's company and the parents were pleased. The Taylor and Stanley siblings expressed a desire to maintain a cordial friendship. They all noticed Marcus and Rebecca exchange furtive glances when the conversation was at a lull. With warm feelings, the Stanleys left with the coachman and returned to their lodging shortly before midnight.

Rebecca and Marcus met often on Bay Street, in the parks and in the squares. Savannah was a compact city and a pleasure for strollers taking in its beauty. This was Marcus' home and he was proud to squire her around town, showing off Savannah and himself. It didn't bother him a wit - he was flattered for himself as heads turned when they saw them arm in arm.

They often walked south from Bay Street, through the squares, to the gorgeous Forsyth Park with its great fountain. Here they sat and talked long hours about everything - their childhood lives at first, then their hopes, dreams and aspirations. He wanted to impress her with his dreams of being a bigger success than his father. But he was careful with that, didn't want to reveal too much just yet. He feared he might put her off and spoil his chances with her.

Marcus grew fonder of Rebecca and recognized that she was an exceptional woman - intelligent, poised, and an elegant lady with a surprisingly wry sense of humor. But he thought, 'She has high expectations. That will be a challenge for me. She is so lovely and full of life, it will be worth it. No one has ever made me laugh as she has. I can't imagine the rest of my life without her companionship.'

Neither of them was truly young anymore. Time was short and they felt it pressing down like the August humidity in the South. It was time - time to make decisions and move forward. Their courtship was brief.

They sat down on a bench next to the fountain, clasped hands, looked into each other's eyes and sweetly smiled. They had come to a place of mutual love and understanding and decided to marry. He proposed to her on one knee and she was touched by his heartfelt appeal.

She had some doubts but believed it her best choice. She didn't want to lose him. Maybe he would let her lead, maybe not. He didn't seem too bright. With his head in the clouds, he didn't seem too practical. Still maybe this was her best choice - her last choice.

When she didn't answer immediately, Marcus became worried she would say no.

Finally she smiled her Rebecca smile and said, "Yes, I will marry you. I am happy. We must tell our families at once."

He smiled and looked away when it occurred to him, "I know William and Francis, but I have never met your mother and father."

She said, "They will love you, Marcus. We must go to Charleston so that you can meet them. We should stay for a while. They will want to arrange a party to celebrate our engagement."

"Of course, we will go as soon as we visit my folks and tell them our good news. As for the party, I expect they will require it. That's what our folks do."

She laughed and remarked, "It's the only life I have ever known." They both laughed.

They immediately made plans to have dinner with Marcus' family. At the dinner table, so many smiles and furtive looks were exchanged between Rebecca and Marcus that his folks reckoned they had some news to share.

When Marcus told them that Rebecca had agreed to marry him, they were surprised, but acted overjoyed. From the moment they had met her, they had hoped that a romance would blossom between the two young people. Hendrick believed Rebecca's business sense would help Marcus shape his dreams to practical reality. They listened closely, and cautiously, as the couple explained that Rebecca would be sharing the happy news with her family as soon as they could arrange it.

She laughingly told them that she was certain her parents would want to have an engagement party in Charleston right away. The Taylors were delighted to hear this and hopeful Marcus would prove worthy. They were certainly curious about her folks too. They knew the brothers, and the only piece of the puzzle left was the parents. They were sure they would find them delightful. Everyone waited in anticipation.

William and Francis were the first of the Stanleys to hear the news. They were happy for their sister and pleased for the couple. They returned to Charleston soon after the congratulations and told their parents the whole story with enthusiasm. The Taylor elders anxiously awaited the visit from the couple. They were excited for Rebecca and wanted to meet her best beau.

They hoped that Rebecca had finally found the man of her dreams, or so they hoped. There were undercurrents. They had secretly feared that she was bound to end up a spinster. Her independent and strong-willed nature would deny them their grandchildren. The mother had particularly endured the gossip and murmurings about Rebecca's unconventional behavior - taking too long to marry, working as a marketer (little more than a drummer) gallivanting all over the countryside.

When they arrived at the Stanley's estate, William and Francis were the official greeting party. They rushed down the steps to meet them.

Rebecca threw her arms around them and said, "Willy, Fran, I missed my big brothers."

They were happy to see her too.

William smiled at Marcus, kept his eyes on him, while turning his head toward Rebecca and teased, "This man you have brought with you, have you disarmed him?"

"Yes, of course I have. I have completely disarmed him. He is at our mercy."

Marcus finally caught up with the fun and they all laughed. He added for their instruction, and with a grin, "You men will learn this for yourselves one day."

Rebecca's parents were warm and charming and made Marcus feel welcome and comfortable. While they had heard the engagement story from Willy and Fran, they were anxious to hear all the details from Rebecca and Marcus themselves. Before long they were all telling amusing stories and having animated conversations. The young ones recounted their courtship together. The old ones told Marcus delightful and revealing stories of Rebecca's privileged childhood. Marcus thought 'I see where Rebecca had developed her appealing nature from this family.'

After dinner the second evening, the old man spoke to Marcus, "Marcus, let us retire to the study and enjoy some cigars and old Bourbon."

Marcus thought, 'I'd better be mindful' and followed him into the man's sanctuary.

They sat in easy chairs, surrounded by books and fine pieces of art to a man's taste, puffing and sipping, eyeing each other in reflection.

The old man Taylor said, "Marcus, what are your plans for the future after you and Rebecca are married?"

Marcus nervously replied, "Well, I expect we will enjoy some time together in Savannah. I have worked with my father in the cotton business for many years. I could work for him as a factor and take over some day. But I have been thinking about maybe striking out more on my own, something big, maybe in cotton production."

Taylor looked at him askance and said, "I hope you figure it out and get settled before you raise a family. She might be able to help you. Good luck, son."

It was the early spring and Charleston's finest were anxiously awaiting the beginning of their social season. The engagement celebration party fulfilled their expectations. It was splendid, of course. The Stanleys spared no expense. After all, Rebecca was their only daughter and they had waited patiently a very long time for this event.

The house was filled with fresh flowers, the caterers had provided a wonderful buffet and there was a five-piece ensemble playing dance music delightful to their southern heritage. All the cordial finest came to celebrate the planned nuptials of this well raised and bright young couple.

Marcus's folks and sisters came up from Savannah a few days before the important social event so that the two prominent families could became acquainted. With everything they shared in common, they fell into friendship with ease. The Taylors touted Rebecca's virtues and the Stanleys surely approved of young Marcus. They surely hoped he'd be the husband their daughter wanted, deserved and waited for.

Rebecca remained in Charleston for a time to plan her wedding. It was going to be a short engagement. There was a great deal to do in such a brief time. The Stanleys, as the bride's parents, were expecting to hold the grand affair in Charleston. That would be traditional.

But Rebecca was headstrong and favored Savannah. She wanted to make her own decisions - had spent the last few years making her own decisions. This was her affair and the most important day of her life. She was determined that everything about her wedding would be exactly the way she wanted it. She loved Savannah and wanted her wedding there. Her parents graciously conceded and agreed to share the planning with the Taylors.

They married in the late summer of '34. The newspapers in Savannah and Charleston ran articles about the important affair.

The service was held at the First Baptist church on Chippewa Square. The August weather was hot and sticky. It felt close in the church and the people grew impatient. The ladies demurely fanned themselves; the men tugged on their collars. There were tears of joy and lots of perspiration masked with sweet perfume.

Rebecca wore a strikingly beautiful white wedding gown. It was in the Spanish style with lace and a tiara and an ornately beaded bodice followed by a long train. Standing with her father, looking into the church, she prepared to walk down the aisle, and marveled that her wedding was so much like her debutante experiences. She thought, 'This is just like my cotillion. Now I see that was a dress rehearsal for my marriage.'

And poor Marcus, overwhelmed with possibility, stood nervously waiting at the front of the church for his bride. He couldn't believe how lucky he was to have found someone like Rebecca to spend his life with. He gasped with awe at his first view of her walking down the aisle towards him. She was more beautiful than he could ever have imagined.

The reverend instructed them to take their vows and repeat after him, "Do you take this woman ...." "With this ring, I thee wed ...." "I now pronounce you man and wife." The happy couple left the church in a horse drawn carriage, decorated with white flowers and streamers, and headed for the reception.

The layout of the historic district was a unique feature of Savannah. The squares each had a miniature park at its center, surrounded by only four mansions. This made for intimate small neighborhoods. The residents of the mansions would often use the small parks for their own private purposes - neighborhood parties, social gatherings with friends and family affairs, picnics and wedding receptions.

The two families held a large reception - large as they could - in front of the Taylor home. It was hosted together by the Taylors and the Stanleys. The park was decorated with streamers and flowers. Having the wedding in the groom's home town wasn't traditional, but it surely wasn't a problem for Savannah. After all, the thing they loved best was a great party, and this promised to be one of the best. The problem was fitting all the people in the small park in front of the mansion on Columbia Square.

It would be attended by all the important Savannah elites and three neighbors on the square, all the Taylors of course, and all of Rebecca's folks, the Stanleys, and important friends from Charleston. While the cost didn't matter, the family planners struggled to keep the size manageable with the small park in front of their mansion. But with great effort they managed the struggle; the embossed linen invitations were sent out once again, and it was a great affair for both families and Savannah.

Rebecca knew how important her wedding was to her family, so in a spirit of cooperation, appreciation and love for her folks, she agreed to have a second reception back in Charleston. Her father had so many business associates and other socially prominent friends who had known Rebecca all her life and had not been able to come to Savannah due to the restrictions.

After a short honeymoon, the new couple stayed in the big mansion with Marcus's folks and spent the remainder of the summer and most of the fall enjoying Savannah. Marcus continued to work for his father and learn more about the cotton business. There were visits to Charleston and the Stanleys occasionally joined the Taylors for their visits to Savannah. Their lives were happy. They enjoyed their refined southern life with its congeniality and grace.

Rebecca relaxed for a time. This was close to her vision for her adult life - temptingly comfortable, but she missed the excitement of business. There was a lot to consider - partnership as a wife, children, fulfillment in work, and a fine and grand social life.

But the news of the nation's politics was disconcerting. The sectional issues over slavery had fomented troubles in the west. There was growing talk of South Carolina and other states seceding from the Union. There was passionate language and hints of war in the future.

At the end of summer, with the bloom fading on the rose, Marcus told his bride about his ambitions and plans. He told her clearly this time - no hints or equivocations. He had been awkward in the past, and this time was no different.

At a quiet moment he sprang it on her, "I've bought land in Mississippi and will build a plantation."

Her mouth fell open in astonishment, "I thought it was just a dream you had. I didn't think you would do it."

"Early this summer, when you, Willy and Fran were finishing your sales trip back to Charleston, I located good land near Natchez and purchased it. I wanted to make us a fine life with wealth of our own. I promise you I will do that. You will have the grand life with me that you want."

With his father's investment support making it possible, he had pursued his dream on his own, without conferring with her - without her blessing. He entered into their marriage with this deception. He had bought good land far away near the Mississippi River. He would buy slaves and grow cotton.

She was astonished at what he had done and said, "Marcus, how could you? What about Savannah? I thought we were going to establish ourselves here. A cotton factor is one thing, this is another."

He looked at her, saw her concerns and said, "Rebecca, I promise you, it will be all right. When I go to Natchez and begin my work, you will have to stay with your folks in Charleston until I send word for you to come join me. I'm not sure how long it will take, maybe a few months, but I want to have a comfortable place for you first."

She had heard him dream out loud about schemes like this before, while they were courting, but now it was an imminent reality. She grew concerned about the effect this would have on their lives.

Rebecca pouted, looked resigned and said, "I see that is for the best, but I'll miss you dearly."

She knew her life would be ruined.

Three - Josiah

Out of the night that covers me,
Black as the pit from pole to pole,
I thank whatever gods may be
For my unconquerable soul.

In the fell clutch of circumstance
I have not winced nor cried aloud.
Under the bludgeonings of chance
My head is bloody, but unbowed.
Beyond this place of wrath and tears
Looms but the Horror of the shade,
And yet the menace of the years
Finds and shall find me unafraid.

It matters not how strait the gate,
How charged with punishments the scroll,
I am the master of my fate,
I am the captain of my soul

- William Ernest Henley, *Invictus*, 1888

Josiah Ashford was born in 1829 on a plantation in Missouri. By that time most slaves had been born in America from slaves born here also. In most cases it had been generations since they were brought from Africa. The direct link with their heritage and culture had been severed.

His ancestors lived in the West African country of Gambia which was surrounded by the country of Senegal. Well before the 14th century, Muslim merchants had established commercial trade in slavery of its people through trans-Saharan routes. The Arab culture by the 14th century defined the area as the Mali Empire.

The first Europeans to arrive in the area were the Portuguese in the 15th century. They provided slaves captured in Gambia to Brazil. Dutch, French, German and British came there in the 17th century. Africa sold its people to Europe. Ultimately, the British established the trans-Atlantic slave triangle routes to the Caribbean and the British colonies in North America later in the 17th century. This enterprise lasted for two centuries.

For its indigenous African people, a human was defined by his will to survive. His courage was tested by his bravery to hunt and provide. The symbol of his strength was the heart of the lion. For the human spirit to be human, it must be free. This core belief of humanity would pass on through the centuries.

By the 19th century, America had grown from a country with slaves to become a slave country. By custom, they were given their names from their owners, from biblical or white family sources. Often they had no last names but would gradually be given, or adopt themselves, the family names of the slaveholders.

Josiah's grandfather had been brought from the Caribbean to a plantation in Virginia. He labored there as a tobacco planter under the task system. His son, Josiah's father, had been born there. Years later, Josiah's father was sold to a plantation owner in Missouri. When Josiah was born, the owner had named him Josiah from his recollection of the Old Testament in the Bible. He didn't remember that Josiah had been an ancient Hebrew king of Judah whose name meant "Jehovah saves".

The agriculture on Missouri plantations was a mix of tobacco and hemp crops like the Upper South and short-staple cotton like the Deep South. The slave labor system was also a mix of the more benign task system and the harsher gang system. Josiah's father worked the task system and labored to produce tobacco. But life was not easy for the Negro slaves all the same. They found their solace in worship services on Sundays.

Josiah grew up attending the services which blended the hope for salvation of the Christian belief with the African traditions of the ancestors. The gospel songs they enthusiastically sang were unique Negro spirituals plaintively expressing their angst and sorrow. He sang *Swing low, sweet Chariot* which expressed the longing to be free, and *There is a Balm in Gilead* for the comfort that Jesus heals all who come to him. The congregation stayed after the service for the "ring shouts" which were a carryover tradition from African dance, very expressive, and animated. There was hand clapping, foot tapping and blissful moaning.

He had an insatiable curiosity about life and an African respect and reverence for the wisdom of elders. His father, however, was fully resigned to his station in life and did not look in a forward direction to change his fate as Josiah did. There wasn't much of substance or hope he could learn from the older man. So Josiah watched as time passed and his father grew older and remained resigned to the fate of the enslaved. Salvation did not come in this earthly life. He would have to wait for the next.

His father had long ago given up and, in a contradictory way of reason, inspired Josiah to hope and prepare for the future. When the time came that his father passed, he mourned his father's death but vowed that he would never give up hope or faith in life. His life would be better.

Josiah had strong faith in Divine Providence - that God had a plan He didn't reveal to man. There was a guiding force. The Lord required Josiah to relinquish his will to Him, while God gave him free will for good or ill. As an adult, he came to the view that he was the master of his fate. Free will permitted him to take charge of his life and strive for his own betterment. God's Providence would do what it would do.

The Missouri Compromise of 1820 under President Monroe had sanctioned slavery for the proposed new state. The practice had been established before that. Henry Clay's Compromise of 1850 seemed to offer temporary relief to the growing tensions over slavery in the new territories. But Steven Douglas's Kansas-Nebraska Act of 1854 provoked bloody conflict over the idea of popular sovereignty in those territories.

As the strife over slavery grew in Missouri and surrounding new territories, the plantation owner decided to sell some of his human property and move south. He believed the Deep South would be more secure and protected. He would have to start over. To make that possible, he would have to sell many of his slaves to pay for a smaller parcel of land with the few he kept. The owner bound his slaves with neck collars and shackles and chains on their wrists and ankles and transported them down river from St. Louis to the Mississippi port of Natchez.

Josiah was put up on the auction block there. It was 1852 and he was 23 years old. On the day of the auction, Marcus Taylor bought him as a prime field hand and fair carpenter for $1,150. Many of Marcus's slaves were getting old. In his view, few of the second-generation bred slaves had come into their own to his satisfaction. He regularly visited Natchez looking for an exceptional slave to fulfill his needs.

Marcus made this trip to the auction to look for a Negro that could help Ned, now that his master carpenter was getting older. The plantation was prospering, growing and expanding. He needed more cabins, out-buildings and upgrades. Ned would not be able to keep up single-handedly as the plantation continued to flourish.

He brought his new slave back to Savannah Oaks plantation by horse drawn wagon. The 57 mile trip took all day and they arrived after nightfall.

Marcus pointed over to a cabin and said to Josiah, "You will stay in there with two other field niggers for tonight. Tomorrow morning there will be food for you. The first rule is that you will always speak to me beginning with 'Massa Taylor'. Do you understand nigger?"

Josiah answered quietly, "Yes Massa Taylor."

Marcus smiled cruelly and said, "Good. Don't ever try to run away. Our dogs will catch you and we will bring you back and punish you hard. You will be tied up and lashed until your back is all blood and flayed skin. We will treat your wounds with salt and vinegar if you are still alive after 100 lashes. You will feel more pain than you have ever felt in your life. Do you understand?"

Josiah dropped his head and said, "Yes Massa Taylor. I have the scars on my back from before."

"Let me see your back boy. Make sure you ain't lyin' to me."

He took off his rough cloth shirt and turned around. Marcus looked at the thick scars from his shoulders to the small of his back. "You must have done something bad."

Josiah had been just a young man back at the plantation in Missouri. One of the overseers drove him to town often to help load the wagon with supplies. He overheard two men on the street corner having an animated argument about abolition. With his sense of curiosity, he started walking over toward them. When he drew closer to listen to them, the overseer saw him and became very upset. He didn't want his nigger to take part in these discussions and get thoughts in his head. Just to be certain, he bound Josiah to the pole back at the plantation and gave him twenty lashes.

The lashing was painful, but it didn't change his desire to understand the world outside his isolated existence or his view to improve himself in any manner he could fashion and control. His spirit would never be broken. But he was smart and instinctively understood how to avoid fruitless confrontation and protect himself.

"It was a misunderstanding. I ain't done nothing wrong."

"Let's not have any misunderstandings around here."

Marcus warned him, "Tomorrow overseer Benjamin will set you to work in the field. Obey him always or you will be punished. He is not as kindly as me."

Being a slaveholder for so long had changed him. When he thought about it, he recognized that he was not the same as the young man back in Savannah. His demeanor had taken on a role of arrogant ease and leisure. He took his view of his niggers as matter-of-fact - just as he did his horses.

Marcus had Josiah work the cotton fields for a while until he put his plan in place for him. It helped him establish his authority and achieve submission from his human property. He used the hardship of work in the fields as a device to mold his tool into shape. But he had brought Josiah there with a more important plan in mind. Once he was satisfied with this effort - Josiah gave him no sign that he had failed - he moved him in to live with old Ned. He would now begin his plan to bring more value to the plantation operations.

He said, "Josiah, I want you to apprentice under old Ned and see if you can learn some skills to benefit me."

Josiah responded, "Yes Massa Taylor, I would like to try that. Maybe I can make furniture for you too. That is something I have always wanted to do."

So Josiah began to serve his apprenticeship under old Ned, the plantation carpenter. Ned and Josiah lived and worked together every day. With his father long passed, Josiah soon began to regard Ned as a father. Ned became the elder, dearly respected in the African culture, and someone he could talk to and be free to be himself with. While Ned was completely illiterate, they had many close heartfelt talks about life and faith.

Ned saw intelligence and a thirst in this adopted young son. He became proud of Josiah and hopeful for the young man's future. There might come a day when God would bring his wrath on man and end this sinful shame of bondage.

One of Josiah's duties was to mill timber at the plantation saw mill. He enjoyed this work much and, with Ned's guidance, became expert at making the best cuts to get the most lumber out of each log.

Josiah's practical intellect and interest in self-improvement motivated him to learn everything he could about the nature of wood. He had a pride that searched for affirmation. Ned became his mentor and affirmer. Josiah's thirst for knowledge was quenched by Ned's patient tutelage.

Ned was pleased that Josiah's knowledge of the local wood species - southern pine, pecan, walnut and white oak - had advanced so quickly. With an eye for detail, Josiah studied the grains and figures of wood and aspired to become a fine furniture and cabinetmaker someday. Ned taught him.

One day Josiah was running the saw mill and Ned came out to check on his progress. Josiah saw him approaching and disengaged the conveyor drive and turned off the saw. As the machinery coasted to a stop, it became quiet enough that they could speak to each other.

Josiah said, "How are you today Ned? I'd like you to look at this board on the pile over here and answer somethin' for me."

"I'se doin' fine. What do you wants to know?"

"Well, I look down the edge and lay it down flat liked you showed me."

Ned smiled and asked, "And what's wrong with it?"

Josiah explained, "It's not flat across its width. See the curve?"

"Yep. Sho is not flat. That's called cuppin'. What else you see on them boards?"

"Sometimes they have a big belly along the length like a banana. Sometimes they have a twist along the length."

"That's 'nuther problem. It's called warpin'."

"I think these ain't good enough to make furniture Ned."

"You right 'bout that. But they good 'nuff to make cabins. We can pound 'em flat with nails."

Puzzled by the non-uniformity and inconsistency, Josiah asked again, "Why does wood do this? We mill them all the same."

"When we stack 'em fresh, they are wet. We leave 'em to cure 'til they dry 'nuff."

"But they all don't dry flat, do they?"

"No they don't, we choose 'em for what we need. Some's so bad we hafta scrap 'em for firewood. Some's good for carpentry. The best go into makin' good furniture."

"Thanks Ned. You always help me understand."

Josiah learned. He understood that the artisan could bend wood to his will only so far. As a thinking man, who thought much deeper about things, he knew that this was the same with the master and the slave.

Over the years, he worked with Ned who became like a father to him. They did carpentry repairs to maintain the slave cabins, barns and outbuildings. They built new cabins and did new work upgrading the mansion.

Ned was old and grew sick. When he died, Josiah became the master carpenter of the plantation. Over the years he had learned the many basic skills from Ned.

After Ned's passing, he taught himself the fine points of cabinetmaking and became a skilled furniture maker. This became his passion and fulfillment. He was a valued asset to the plantation.

He wouldn't let his life ebb away as his grandfather and father had done. He knew there was much he did not know, could not even know what there was to know, but was determined to learn and find out what he needed to know.

Despite what others thought and did or controlled, God's Providence, his intelligence, courage, persistence and hard work would prevail in the end. In time, life would get better and he would succeed. Josiah believed that.

Four - Josena

Josena was born in 1837 on the Savannah Oaks plantation. Her mother was Sarah, the feisty field hand that Marcus had bought at his first slave auction in Natchez. He hadn't recognized how much trouble she would be. He only saw her youth and strength. Sarah was one of those slaves that couldn't suppress their resentment. Her nature and spirit would not submit. She couldn't keep her feelings to herself. She always found ways to rebel and show her unwillingness to heal.

Marcus Taylor had begun his work developing his new plantation - an enterprise that was new to his experience. Sarah was a problem. At the beginning, he had left his new bride Rebecca behind in Charleston until Savannah Oaks was sufficiently ready for her to join him. Marcus was busy with all there was to do and lonely without her. As for Sarah, he decided to break her spirit and make her an example.

He stole into her cabin often at night and raped her repeatedly. In this way, he punished her behavior and enhanced his pleasure with his cruel dominance. Josena would be born as the outcome of his authority and his vile, cruel acts.

When she was born, he gave her the Dutch name Josena and favored her. Once she was weaned, he kept her in the plantation main house and raised her as the little mulatto girl of his affection. Everyone on the plantation had known the truth about this. Little needed to be spoken. It wasn't unusual.

Before, when Marcus had completed a rough house as a temporary measure, he had sent for Rebecca. She was immediately disappointed with what she saw. In a short time, she heard gossip and understood what had happened with Sarah and why she was pregnant. There were few secrets at Savannah Oaks.

When Josena was born, Rebecca knew that this light skinned, yellow girl was the scion of her husband Marcus. She knew where Josena had come from. She seethed with anger, embarrassment, and jealousy and cruelly took out her hatred on little Josena. Confronted with this uncomfortable and disturbing truth every day, she intended to get back at Marcus with a vengeance for his acts of disloyalty. This would become a constant source of pain and their relationship would never be a loving one again as it had been in Savannah. Nevertheless, Josena grew up in the mansion.

When Marcus brought Josiah to the plantation, he quartered him temporarily with two other field hands in one of the slave cabins. The first morning he was to start to work in the cotton fields, overseer Benjamin brought him out to the yard in front of the main house to gather with the group of slaves. As a new arrival, his wrists and ankles had been shackled the night before. Everyone noticed.

Josena was on the veranda hanging up clothes and saw this new man right away. She noticed how strong and ruggedly handsome he was and the intelligent look about his face. She heard that his name was Josiah.

Once Josiah got over the initial shock and adjustment to his new surroundings - the harsher heat and humidity, the harder work - he noticed the young girl working around the main house as a servant. He heard her name was Josena. Everyone on the plantation called her Josie. He noticed her watching him too and hoped for the chance to see her everyday as he happened by the mansion, or better still, had a carpentry task to do inside.

They took to smiling at each other each time they passed. They got to giving each other a shy little wave. The attraction between them grew. They dreamed about each other - her beautiful face and delicate body, his rugged handsome muscularity. She was coy and flirtatious. He had a sweet smile. She had her mother's spirit that often got her into trouble. He had his resolve to improve his lot in life. The first time they spoke a few words to each, they knew the attraction they felt was real and mutual.

But there was danger in this for both of them. She was Marcus Taylor's daughter. Late one evening Josie carefully and quietly left the house and went to Josiah's cabin. When Josiah opened the door, she stood before him awkwardly and neither of them knew what to say. Their hearts began beating rapidly. This was no dream. This was real.

He backed away and she came inside. They looked at each other a moment longer until she threw her arms around his neck. They kissed passionately. She pressed her body tightly against his and let out a soft moan. They felt his manhood responding. They kissed again, more deeply and urgently. The passion grew quickly for both of them. Their passionate feeling of love turned to lust.

She looked deeply into his eyes, trying to be sure of his trust. Convinced of his goodness, she flashed him a passing glance, looked away and stood back. She slipped her shoulders out of her gown and let it fall to the floor. Josiah gasped and stood back gazing at her naked beauty. He couldn't have imagined how beautiful she looked.

He reached out to her and took her tenderly in his arms. He gently ran his strong hands up and down her arms and strayed to her small perfect breasts. She shivered from the delight of his touch and struggled to breathe.

He picked her up, light as a feather, and placed her gently on his bed. He lay over her looking into her eyes, their eyes locked together. She wrapped her arms around him and caressed his strong back. She winced as she felt the ridges of his deep scars and felt saddened for his suffering. Her instincts were to help him and protect him from pain if she could.

Josiah turned to his side and his hand found her most tender places. Every nerve in her body was on fire and she was overcome with desire. She had never felt this way before. His steady caresses brought her excitement higher and higher. Her breathing grew faster and faster until she gasped and groaned at her completion.

He knew at that moment that he loved her beyond doubt. It was more than he cared for himself. He wanted to continue but wanted to protect her from harm. As the Massa's daughter, she had not seen or felt the cruel reprisal that he had known. She was young and sheltered from the true harshness of slavery.

She looked at him as he grew quiet and gently caressed his strong body. She knew she loved this good man and wanted to be with him always. His honor compelled him to act.

Kissing her tenderly on the lips, he said, "Josie, we have to stop. I don't want to, but we must. You must leave right away. I don't want us to get caught and see you get punished."

She responded, "Don't worry, Marcus won't punish me but I will go because I love you and don't want you to get whipped."

Josie slowly put her gown on as Josiah watched in wonder. After this passionate encounter, they knew that they needed to find a way to get together somehow. And stay together always. They missed each other already.

As Josie walked quickly across the yard, she saw a movement to the side in the shadows. Benjamin had been outside and saw her leave Josiah's cabin. He would report this the first chance he got. He was resentful of the special treatment Marcus gave Josie.

The next morning, Marcus summoned her into his office. He asked her to explain what happened last night. She was never fearful of her father, but feared for Josiah.

She said, "Father, I love Josiah and want to be with him. Please give me your permission to see him."

Marcus couldn't bear the thought of whipping Josie for her transgression. He decided to punish Josiah instead. He knew as master of the plantation that he had to keep control of his slaves and the respect of his overseer.

He instructed Benjamin, "Bind him to the pole in the front yard and give him 25 lashes. Don't punish him with salt and vinegar in his wounds. I need to teach the nigger his lesson but want him to get back to work tomorrow."

After he had thought about it a few days, Marcus saw benefit in permitting the union of Josie and Josiah. She was almost 16 years old and he could not keep her as a little girl anymore. The marriage would provide future offspring and some contentment among the slaves. It might reduce some of the relentless pressure and attitude from his wife Rebecca regarding Josena's irritating presence. The more he thought about it, the more sense it made for the plantation and his marriage.

If he decided they would marry, he would officiate over an informal ceremony. It would not be a church wedding and would have no standing in law as a civil marriage either. He would have them perform the simple African ceremony of holding hands and jumping over a broom placed on the ground. To them, this would symbolize their union. Marcus would always be free to sell them individually in the future should that benefit him.

A few days after he had punished Josiah, Marcus spoke to Josie and Josiah together. He said, "Josie has told me that she loves you and asked me for permission to be with you Josiah. What do you want?"

Looking tenderly at Josie, he said, "Massa Marcus, I love her and want to be with her too."

Marcus asked, "Do you want to get married? That is the only way I can permit you to be together."

They both were overjoyed and said excitedly in unison, "Yes."

Marcus explained his conditions and told them, "After I marry you together, Josie can stay in your cabin at night but must come to the house early each morning to do her work. If she becomes lazy and doesn't do her household chores, I will forbid her from staying with you at night."

That Sunday, Marcus gathered all the slaves and the household together and married Josie and Josiah. The yard was decorated with a trellis of flowers and, for a few moments, everyone on the plantation shared a feeling of happiness for the new bride and groom. Almost everyone.

Rebecca wasn't certain what to think. She had mixed feelings and hoped that this change would take Josie more out of her husband's life. They jumped the broom and everyone applauded.

After their lovemaking, Josena loved to lie with Josiah at night, snug in their cabin. Their old bed was small but he cradled her in his arms. He stared at the ceiling in the little room, dimly lit from the glow of the oil lamp on the table. His thoughts would wander with imagination and notions about the future.

He asked Josena, "I have a favor to ask you, it is important to me, but dangerous for you."

She turned and looked at his thoughtful face, "If it's somethin' I can do for my lovin' man, I has the courage to do it."

"I know you are brave and love me. I have been thinking. Could you bring me some books from the house without nobody knowing? I have been wanting to do this for a long time."

"I thinks I can. There's some in my father's office. There's more in the empty nursery. Miss Rebecca has some. They's old ones she brought from Savannah. She got new ones sent to her from Charleston. I seen her readin' em."

"If you can do it, without getting caught by her, I'd like to learn to read better. I learned a little bit in Missouri, but we are not supposed to know how to read. Look for a reader not used by them often. Might be able to sneak them out of the empty nursery when she's not around. Be careful. Please bring me one at a time."

She brought him books to read at night, starting with McGuffey's old primary reader, *The Eclectic First Reader*. As his reading improved, he advanced to the popular new books - Hawthorne's *The Scarlet Letter* and *The House of Seven Gables*. Eventually he read Emerson's *Representative Men*, Melville's *Moby Dick* and Stowe's *Uncle Tom's Cabin*.

He learned how to read and learned about the world of ideas. He learned what the world was like outside of plantations and for other people. With a fertile mind like Frederick Douglass, he became self-educated. Unlike Douglass, who expanded his mind as a freedman, Josiah was still a slave.

The year was 1853. Dark clouds were gathering in the southern sky and the storm was coming.

Five - David

It is not the critic who counts; not the man who points out how the strong man stumbles, or where the doer of deeds could have done them better. The credit belongs to the man who is actually in the arena, whose face is marred by dust and sweat and blood; who strives valiantly; who errs, who comes short again and again, because there is no effort without error and shortcoming; but who does actually strive to do the deeds; who knows great enthusiasms, the great devotions; who spends himself in a worthy cause; who at the best knows in the end the triumph of high achievement, and who at the worst, if he fails, at least fails while daring greatly, so that his place shall never be with those cold and timid souls who neither know victory nor defeat.

Theodore Roosevelt from the "The Man in the Arena" section of his speech at the Sorborne in Paris, 1910

David Wexley was born fighting. His people had originated from the same place as Andrew Jackson's and Francis Marion's. They were born and raised in the Carolinas, he in Baltimore, Maryland. But their people came from Ulster in Northern Ireland. They were not Irish. They were the lowland Scottish troublemakers and cattle thieves King James VI sent to Ulster to rid his border of the problems they were causing him. They married with Irish and became the Ulster Scots. In America, they became the Scots-Irish.

They had a long history of hating the English but would pick a fight with anybody if the cause was right. In America, there would come to be differing views of the Scots-Irish. For those who knew, there were two - the racist evil of the KKK founder, Nathan Bedford Forrest II, and the goodness of the tragic hero of freedom at Stirling Bridge, William Wallace. David would embody the second.

He was born in 1832 in Baltimore where his father's folks had settled. Many of the Scots-Irish had settled in the Ridgely's Delight neighborhood during the growing city's first period of expansion in the early 19th century. After they grew to prosperity, the Wexley family had built a grand row house there and moved in next to the many professional people who populated the area. It was a beautiful spot just a short walk to the harbor front, but away from its view.

His father Morgan had been born there also in 1802. Morgan made his money in banking as had his father before him. When David was two years old, his mother suddenly died from an unknown illness. Her heart had simply stopped beating. Morgan never remarried and did his best to raise David without a mother in the household. They were always close and discussed everything together. David revered and respected his father.

They attended Presbyterian Church service together all of David's formative years. Morgan believed in helping the less fortunate and contributed generously to the church's missions. Their faith was kind but without a passion for God's direction or presence in their lives.

But for David there was always a void in his life. He lacked for no material comfort, or support from his father, but there was an emptiness. Morgan knew it but couldn't change it. He grieved for their loss himself. There was a prevailing sadness that never went away.

As a young boy, David was a good student, attentive and eager to learn. He received a good grounding in the classics and shared his father's passion for history. Morgan discussed with him the significance of the long history of the European old world and its impact on the brief history of the new world here in America. They enjoyed their Socratic debates about the value of history for its ideas and meanings for mankind.

Morgan told him about witnessing the British naval attack on Baltimore harbor when he had been a young boy. The citizens of Baltimore watched the bombardment of the British ships and Ft. McHenry, back and forth, into the night. The British were defeated and the harbor was successfully defended. The flag still flew over the fort in the morning. It was named after James McHenry, a Scots-Irish immigrant and surgeon-soldier.

David grew up a restless boy who always longed for adventure. In his youth, he read all the great epic works - fiction and non-fiction - of action, adventure, exotic foreign places, the great military men and war. He was imaginative and lonely. He thought about becoming a writer, or a traveler or a soldier. He talked to his father about history and politics and would later become a journal writer. He was one of some young men who would leave the quiet life of the privileged father for life on his own terms. He wanted to strike out on his own and see the world. Morgan understood that David would not follow him in the banking business.

When David was 16, and with Morgan's blessing, he joined the Merchant Marines and sailed topsail schooners - Baltimore clippers - out of Baltimore and along the Atlantic coast to ports in Boston, Charleston, and Savannah. He learned about the societal views and culture of southern people in Charleston and Savannah, and how they differed from Baltimore and even from each other.

At sea, British impressment of American sailors had continued long after the War of 1812 and he saw some naval battle action himself. With an abundance of time at sea, David began keeping a journal of his experiences and thoughts - sometimes expressed very personally and poetically. Life at sea could be very lonely; it brought back memories of his childhood.

He wrote of sadness and how it had become a warm companion. It was something he had become accustomed to. At ports-of-call, he often posted letters to his father to continue his lifelong habit of sharing his views with him. But his journal entries were mostly his private thoughts he kept to himself.

Journal entry, July 12, 1849-

Made port-of-call to Boston Harbour. Much more than Baltimore, this old city housed the first American rebels - the Adams's, Revere, Hancock and Paine - patriots all. Massachusetts was surely the colony of troublemakers for old King George. The place still reverberates with the ghosts of these great freedom fighters.

I feel a strong kinship with these great men. Somehow injustice, whether it was in the past or in the present, seems to stir feelings of rage within me. I can't explain the strong hatred of injustice I feel, where it comes from, or how I can abide with it. Sometimes I imagine myself to be like my ancestors

- the clans in the Highlands in their tartan kilts with their sgian-dubh short knives in their hose fighting the English with their broadswords and pikes.

The people are serious minded merchants with some of the Puritan blood still flowing in their veins. They are honest, decent and forthright. I'd be proud to be like them.

Journal entry, September 4, 1850-

At sea, we have to keep a close lookout for trouble. We are charged to protect and secure the safety of our cargo and the important passengers we often carry. We met a British privateer off Cape Hatteras.

Our lad in the crow's nest on the focsle saw them with his spyglass and reported they were flying British colors. When she closed to 100 yards, she struck the skeleton and crossbones and we knew she was up to no good.

As the privateer closed in, she fired a warning shot over our bow. We answered with a flurry of our cannon shot through their sails. They took our intent and sped off. After the powder smoke cleared off our cannon, the boys on the main-deck cheered our victory for this very short battle.

Journal entry, August 4, 1851-

We sailed into the port of Charleston for a two-day layover. The town has beautiful neighborhood areas, away from the wharfs, where the old Revolutionary War homes are preserved. There is a lot of southern colonial history in this place.

The South Carolina people hold a very independent view and I expect they will cause trouble for America before long. They have their own elite view of high society I find noxious to my taste. Their refined airs remind me of strutting peacocks showing off their colorful tail feathers.

Journal entry, October 16, 1851-

Made port at Savannah, Georgia. To my surprise, the people here are more down to earth than their neighbors in Charleston. Like Charleston, there is Revolutionary War history here as well. There is an old fort out toward Tybee Island and unique squares below the main street next to the river front.

They love their southern culture, but have more of a humor about it. They don't take themselves so seriously or think themselves so self-important.

I delighted in visiting their fair city and enjoyed some mirth and drinks on their river front. I felt at home in the taverns. Sailors are sailors and people are people everywhere that you go in the world.

I also witnessed a slave auction near the city market and could not believe that human beings could sell other human beings as a commodity in such an unfeeling and nonchalant manner. The prices were posted on the building for the buyers to shop for their humans and farm animals. The South is a different world.

Journal entry, March 12, 1852, after visiting Charleston and Savannah -

The southern way of life includes an affectionate flavor of courtly manners. I find it endearing and a comforting delight, and can find nothing wrong with it. The manners are related to the language. It goes way back, like we were in the North during colonial times. It's old and elegant the way we talked and behaved.

On the return leg to Baltimore of his final voyage, October 14, 1853 he wrote-

The vast ocean is a cold and selfish mistress.

She deceives with her lies that she makes me free. She roils and crashes in angry rage or lays in quiet passive calm.

Her two moods are only for herself. She gives no comfort to me. I have only myself as my warm companion for this life's loneliness.

The open sea had once appealed to his nature, but after a few years he resigned his commission and came back to Baltimore, ready to move on to something else. He stayed with his father in the row house in Ridgely's Delight, but valued his independent spirit too much to work for wages in a factory. He had learned as a shipmate that he enjoyed creating and building things with his own hands.

David took an apprenticeship as a carpenter and soon practiced his new skills working with a crew that build houses in the growing city. Their crew built the frames and did the roofing for new construction of residences and businesses throughout Baltimore's urban neighborhoods. Other crews followed after them and did the lighter finish work.

The boss of the crew, who trained him, was a man named Geoff Braxton. He was a master carpenter and from Baltimore also. He was a big beefy man of medium stature, but hard muscled from many years of heavy-frame carpentry. His appearance was a contrast to David's taller, more wiry frame.

They hadn't met before and Geoff was five years older than David. As was customary with many tradesmen, they started the job early in the morning, just after sunrise, to accomplish as much as possible while it was still cool. They picked up their tools and knocked off work mid-afternoon when the heat grew most oppressive.

Most days the crew spent the late afternoons in the local taverns and enjoyed each other's company over several pints of beer and tavern food. This had been a customary way for working-class men to socialize that dated back to the earliest American colonial days and before that in the English pubs. Men from all the trades - the carpenters, the masons, the shipbuilders, the coopers, the riggers - gathered together and shared the male companionship at the taverns. It reminded him of his brief visit to Savannah.

Geoff was affable, always smiling, and liked to talk. He led the conversations and soon learned that David was intelligent and more worldly-wise than his younger years would have suggested. They became friends and respected each other's views. They talked about everything - women, politics, religion, and of course building construction. Usually the talk came around to the state of affairs in America. The subject was on everyone's minds. In Maryland, like the other border states on the Mason-Dixon Line, not everyone agreed where the country was headed or what should be done about its problems.

On occasion, Geoff came over to David's home for dinner with him and his father. He quickly learned from the dinner conversation with the old man where David's intelligence and knowledge of the country's politics had come from. He listened in amazement as they exchanged the latest news circulating in the newspapers and on the street. He recognized they were more aware and informed than many on the street.

One afternoon, when they were picking up their tools for the day, Geoff told David, "There's trouble in the country. The southerners are goin' to pick a fight before long."

David agreed, "I know it too Geoff. You've heard me and my father discussing it. I read the newspaper articles and it don't look good."

"If it comes to it, we will lick 'em easy and put down any rebellion they try in short order", Geoff concluded.

"I hope you're right. We can't know how deep the resolve of the southerners will go. The folks I met in the South won't give up their way of life easily. I think the aristocrats, and I suppose the poor folks, will fight for their rights to the death."

David enjoyed the work, his friendships with the crew, and the freedom to move around the neighborhoods of Baltimore and work outdoors with them. But for him, this was still a confinement. The city wouldn't hold him for long. He had seen other people in other places and couldn't stand still forever.

He had a problem with authority. It didn't come from Morgan. His father had always given him free reign to become what he would become. David's worldview would serve him well throughout his life, but in the end, it never brought him happiness.

Morgan Wexley was sitting in the old leather chair behind his big mahogany desk in his front room study. He was working on some papers and had been watching out his window at the sparkling morning sun in his beautiful neighborhood. The flag over Ft. McHenry was visible on the harbor in the far distance.

Morgan had become concerned, and then despondent, about the country's politics. David came into the office to greet him a good morning.

Morgan looked up and responded, "There is going to be war, David. It's unavoidable. The moderates of the North and South have been silenced by the roar of the firebrands."

"I know father. I have been following *The Liberator* and Garrison will keep pushing for abolition without compromise. Emancipation with no plan for the aftermath."

"Worse than that David is John Brown. That wild-eyed madman caused bloody violence in Kansas and a foolhardy attack on Harper's Ferry Arsenal. He is plum crazy."

"The southerners are no better father. They are committed to their system of slavery and their idea of honor. The short-sighted fools keep making money on cotton and won't invest in manufacturing.

I read the old newspaper articles in The Cincinnati Gazette and the New York Evening Post from '56 about the Brooks-Sumner affair. Senator Charles Sumner was sitting at his desk in the Senate Chambers when Congressman Preston Brooks beat him over the head with his thick gutta-percha cane and knocked him to the floor, blinded with his blood on his face. He continued to beat him, wanting to kill him, until his cane broke. This was all about Sumner's abolitionist speech, 'Bleeding-Kansas', his denouncement of the Kansas-Nebraska Act and personal insults toward Brooks' family. When senators rushed to help him, Laurence Keitt blocked them, pointed his pistol at them, and demanded they let them be. After that, the southern senators passed out canes to commemorate their glorious act in defense of southern honor and wore side-arms to insure peaceful conduct of their astute deliberations."

Morgan continued, "They have tried everything to keep their way of life going. Senator Calhoun's gambit for South Carolina's nullification of tariff disadvantages, the positive good of their peculiar institution, Douglas's ploy for popular sovereignty in the west. Even moderates like Senator Crittenden made a last ditch effort to compromise and bend over backwards to appease the southerners one last time. None of it worked. Colonel Robert E. Lee had hoped Christianity would resolve the slave issue, but it hasn't.

Look at this old newspaper clipping I saved back when President Buchanan took office in '57. The abolitionists were livid about the Dred Scott Supreme Court decision. This is an editorial from the *New York Tribune*. You know I agree with them in their spirit, but think about the trouble it caused."

David read it and replied, "So do I most for certain. But that's very discouraging. It appears hopeless. President Lincoln wants to preserve the Union above all else. He wants to end slavery too, and has offered ideas to compensate the southerners for their economic loss. Nobody is listening to him. The radical southerners and northerners hate him and don't care."

Morgan looked crestfallen and said, "David, listen to the words of Harriet Beecher Stowe." He read them to him:

> *A day of grace is held out to us. Both North and South have been guilty before God; and the Christian church has a heavy account to answer. Not by combining together to protect injustice and cruelty, and making a common capital of sin, is this Union to be saved, but by repentance, justice and mercy; for, not surer is the eternal law by which the millstone sinks in the ocean, than the stronger law, by which injustice and cruelty shall bring on nations the wrath of Almighty God!*

"Throughout history man has always practiced slavery, the powerful subjugating the weak. But in America we have institutionalized it, become dependent upon it to fulfill our agrarian vision for our society and economy. It has become a greater thing than man has ever known before. Now we are justifying it. I don't know whether we will suffer God's wrath or reap what we have sown without Him, but the time to pay for it has come. The price will be horrific.

It's too late David. Hatred is imbued in both our societies. After decades of sectionalism and political wrangling and partisanship and compromises to delay it, now it comes to war."

The people in Baltimore heard about South Carolina seceding from the Union, followed by six other states, after Lincoln's election. The Civil War had begun with P.G.T. Beauregard's bombardment on Ft. Sumter, defended under the command of Major Anderson, in Charleston harbor in 1861.

David was 29 years old. He held the view that the southern aristocratic planters and slaveholders were descendents of the royal English noblemen his people despised. They were the nobles with their fiefdoms, fed by the enslaved peasants. The specter of hating and rebelling against upper-class nobility and cruel authority raised its pugnacious Scots-Irish head again. He would be in for the fight of his life.

Maryland was a border state and divided on slavery. Here, like in the other border states, brothers often signed up to fight against brothers. The choice was not a simple matter of good versus evil. David joined with those who would fight for the Union Army of the Potomac. Geoff and David signed up with Baltimore's Light Guard Infantry. Their outfit joined with others and would fight under the command of Ambrose Burnside from Rhode Island.

They met Patrick Allister with the Massachusetts 17th Regiment Infantry. Patrick was a serious-minded patriot coming from that long tradition in New England. They were issued their new 1861 Springfield, percussion cap, rifle-muskets and trained together in Baltimore for three months and learned how to drill, follow orders and use their weapons. Many men were in poor shape and needed to develop physical conditioning, but for the three of them, that was not a challenge. Patrick was an experienced hunter and taught David and Geoff what he had learned growing up with firearms and hunting and tracking large game in the woods.

The three of them spent their spare time together drinking and laughing in the taverns, awaiting their deployment. Patrick and David's friendship grew from their shared common knowledge of seafarers - Patrick's New England heritage and David's experience as a merchant sailor. Together they often entertained the men, arm in arm and under the weather, singing a duet of their favorite sea chantey - *The Sailor Likes the Bottle - O*. The men spent many happy nights - drinking and singing - in male bonding and companionship.

Always together, they were hail fellows well met at the end of their callow youth, celebrating gaily and excitedly before a war starts, unaware of the horror they were about to face before the killing and sadness begins, not knowing the difference between victory and despair, or when youth, with its innocence, is gone and forgiveness is sought for the remainder of their lives.

But the time came soon when they went off to war. It looked like their regiments would go to Virginia to whip the Rebels on their home ground. It was an exciting time for adventuresome young men. They left with Burnside's Expeditionary Corps in the late summer of '62. They would follow the campaigns of George McClellan and George Meade.

When he left Baltimore, David's father had bade him farewell, "Take care my son. I pray that you get through it and come back in one piece. Fair thee well."

"Thank you father. I love you. Be well."

For all he had learned and understood, not enough of love, he could not know the true source of his nature or where it would lead him. At its deepest root, from the long distant centuries past, and an ocean away, it was the spirit of Wallace - the warrior poet. It was the brilliant and beautiful sadness, so rarely understood. It was a view of injustice and the courage and conviction to fight against cruel authority. Awareness is not knowing. David was aware but would never know that was who he was.

Six - The Battles in the East

For its final campaigns, and more clearly defined than the earlier years in the east and the west, there were two major forces of will guiding the actions of the Civil War.

Lee was guided by his personal belief in God's will. He felt God's presence always and accepted his losses and victories in this way. Most days he sought solace from God for the tragic loss of his best friend and ally, Tom Jackson. This gave him his confidence and his peace, borne by humility, to persist. Lee had hoped that the South would remain united. But the men in the Carolinas and Georgia drifted away from the fight and went home. All Lee had left were the loyal men of Virginia.

Grant was guided by the will of Abraham Lincoln. Ultimately, Lincoln chose him and gave him a free hand to run the war. He was pragmatic and believed in the superiority of the numbers and the equipment. He staked his fortunes on attrition. He knew the Union had the strength. The Union would prevail some day.

For both Lee and Grant there was a dignity and a character that defined what a man would do. It was the total of their honor, their pride, their integrity, their word. If they said it to their men, they could not let themselves fail. This was true leadership. It would survive their deaths and be the way they could both triumph.

But for Lee and Grant, and everyone, there was a weariness that prevailed over the mood of the country. David Wexley fought in several campaigns - in Maryland and Virginia - for the Union Army of the Potomac and soon fell into that feeling.

Antietam - September 17, 1862

Ambrose Burnside was a large, physically imposing figure of a man. His distinctive style of facial hair became known as sideburns as a derivation of his last name. He was born in Liberty, Indiana of Scottish ancestry. His father had been a native of South Carolina and a slave owner.

His interest in military affairs and his father's influence led to his appointment to West Point where he graduated 18th in the class of 1847 as a brevet second lieutenant. He participated in the end of the Mexican-American war and western campaigns. Eventually he served in Rhode Island where he met his wife.

He resigned his commission for a time and participated in firearm manufacturing, the railroad industry and politics. He became a friend of George McClellan, and later served under him when he rejoined the army at the outbreak of the Civil War.

He was a brigadier general in the Rhode Island militia. After commanding a brigade without distinction in the First Battle of Bull Run, he became a brigade trainer for the new Army of the Potomac. In the battle of Antietam, he was assigned command of the right flank of the Army of the Potomac under command of McClellan.

While he was personally popular and well liked, his military reputation was less positive. Inexplicably, and even ironically given his own proclivity for delay, McClellan was upset that Burnside was hesitant to act when ordered to attack. His delaying tactic allowed time for A.P. Hill to arrive from Harpers Ferry and repulse the Union breakthrough. McClellan refused to supply Burnside with reinforcements and the battle ended in a tactical stalemate.

Grant found him unfit for the command of an army. Burnside understood himself that this was true. He had twice refused command of the Army of the Potomac and only accepted when told the alternative would be Joseph Hooker.

Early in the war, General George McClellan led the Union army as general-in-chief and organized the Army of the Potomac. In time, President Lincoln came to view him as too tentative and hesitant to seize advantage when opportunity for victory was presented. Eventually Lincoln replaced him.

Lee had taken full advantage of McClellan's hesitancy and it accounted for his early victories in Virginia. But with McClellan replaced, Lee lost the advantage and suffered poorly in the later battles.

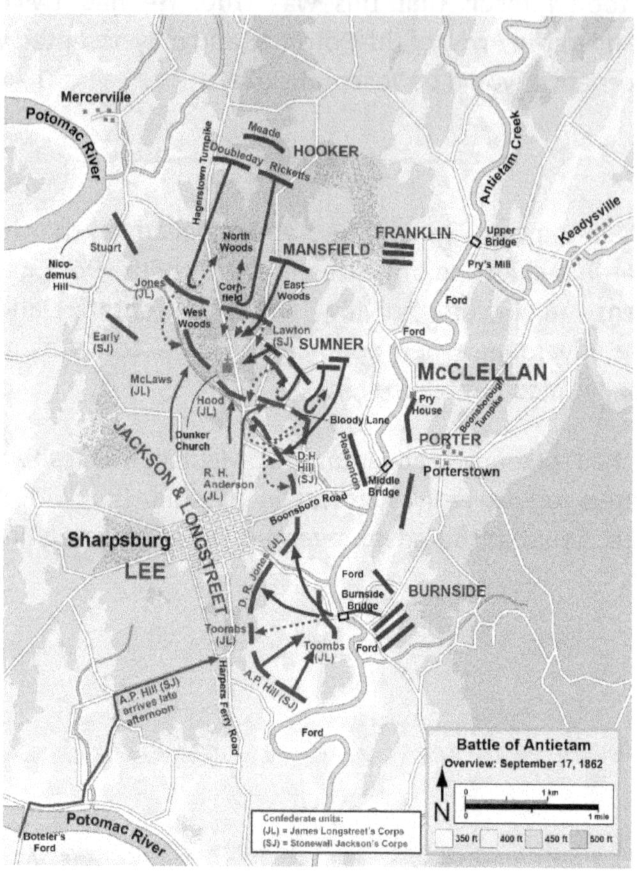

Union General Burnside played a key role in the battle of Antietam under the overall command of General McClellan. David had fought with Burnside's men.

Near Sharpsburg, Maryland, fighting had begun in a cornfield bordered by two stands of trees. At first Confederate General A.P. Hill used a sunken road as a defensive position and the Union was driven back. Then, because of confused orders, the Confederates lost advantage and fell back. Burnside followed orders to capture the arched stone bridge that spanned Antietam Creek. It would later be called the Burnside Bridge. It looked like the Union was going to prevail as they moved against both flanks of the Confederates and their center was broken at the sunken road.

As the Yankees pushed across Antietam Creek, they turned the Confederates' flank. Hill's forces arrived to stave off total defeat. Over several hours, he drove the Union back. David didn't see him, but Geoff Braxton was with the crowded blue wave crossing the Burnside Bridge. Halted and standing at the center of the bridge, Geoff saw the muzzle flash singled out from the enemy, felt the thud of the ball strike his chest, uttered an inaudible soft grunt, thought, didn't have time to feel, the excruciating pain in the core of his body, collapsed to the ground and his life was gone in that instant.

David eluded capture and fell back with the men as they retreated over the bridge. General Rodman was killed and the Union forces became demoralized. Stuart arrived, with Lee accompanying him on the Harpers Ferry road, to assist the Confederates.

General J.E.B. Stuart was most often called Jeb Stuart from the initials of his given names. He was Lee's secret weapon. Lee relied on his leadership of the cavalry to gather information from the front and lead gallant surprise skirmishes to disrupt the enemy. He moved his cavalry rapidly and appeared suddenly to the enemy's dismay.

Some called him Beauty from his time with his classmates at the United States Military Academy at West Point. His class rank was in the highest and he could have served in the elite Corps of Engineers. But he went with those of the second rank, to the cavalry, and excelled to the pinnacle of that throng. He was a born horseman in southern Virginia and of Scots-Irish descent.

Most everyone who stood out at the Point was given a nickname there, one that suited them in the view of their friends. William Tecumseh Sherman was nicknamed Cump because of his unusual middle name. Philip Sheridan was called Little Phil because of his small stature.

Northern and southern cadets were there together before the war. They had graduated as brevet second lieutenants and many had fought together as junior officers in the Mexican War, the frontier conflicts with Native Americans and the antebellum violence in Bleeding Kansas. They had enjoyed each other's camaraderie at the Point and would reminisce about those days of their youth, and the spirit of duty and the corps, for the rest of their lives.

Beauty was very plain looking but with a confident, flamboyant personality. His infectious spirit charmed his fellow officers and his men. The men would cheer, smile and say, "There goes Beauty" when he rode by - bold, gallant, chivalrous, tall and erect in the saddle, brandishing his saber in the air, his felt hat folded up on one side, his colorful bushy flowing ostrich plume flying above it, his bright yellow sash, often a red flower in his lapel, his red lined cape floating behind him.

The southern women loved him - his courtly bows, his chivalrous flourishes. He was an inspiration to the Confederates and Lee was deeply saddened when he was killed. He missed him almost as much as his closest friend, Tom Jackson. Lee loved them and sought God's solace for his loss of them both.

The Union regrouped on the other side of the creek. With less than an hour of daylight remaining, the engagement of the men and the artillery ceased until the morning. On the night of the 18th, the Confederates withdrew across the Potomac at Botelier's Ford back into Virginia.

The battle was considered a draw. Lee was not victorious. McClellan let him slip away and retreat back into Virginia. The Army of Northern Virginia gave up its ambitions to bring the war to northern territory for now. There would be one more attempt in Pennsylvania at Gettysburg.

Here, on this day at Antietam, 24,000 were dead, mortally wounded, captured or missing. The Union killed and wounded were nearly 12,000. The Confederate killed and wounded were over 9,000. The madness of Antietam was that the men didn't have a fighting chance. Too many died. Their officer's view was that they died with honor and were heroic. It was, in reality, tragic.

On September 22, 1862, after visiting the Antietam battlefield, President Lincoln issued a preliminary Emancipation Proclamation. Now the war was officially about abolishing slavery as well as preserving the Union.

Corporal David Wexley got through it without a scratch. He had lost sight of Geoff but learned later that he had fallen during the charge over the Burnside Bridge, had been shot in the chest and died instantly.

He wrote his father every chance that he could and reassured him that, "The fight is tougher than we could ever have imagined. Take heart and be reassured, I am alive and well. I can't have any certainty when it will be over."

He decided not to tell his father about Geoff.

He wrote in his journal on September 19th-

Father's vision was prophetic. Man has brought his own wrath upon himself. The price was horrific. We have not yet seen how much greater the price will be or how much more slaughter there will be to come. When it ends, I pray it will have been worth it.

Battle of the Wilderness - May 5-7, 1864

This would be David's final fight - Grant's overland campaign to capture Richmond, the capital of the Confederacy. After his successful campaign in the west, Lincoln met Grant in Washington to discuss the remainder of the war in Virginia. Lincoln chose Grant to lead the Union forces.

Grant made peace with his rival, George Meade and left him his command of the east. Meade had graduated from West Point in 1835; Grant in 1843. Both were brilliant military strategists.

Meade disagreed with Grant's philosophy of accepting heavy casualties to win the war by attrition. But, since Lincoln had chosen him, Meade did the honorable thing and offered his resignation. Grant refused to accept it and they agreed to form an alliance with Meade subservient.

They may have been rivals with battling egos, but they made accommodation for each other and honored each other's dedication to duty. Both agreed the true objective was Lee, not Richmond. However, at the Wilderness, Lee's Confederate Army of Northern Virginia successfully outmaneuvered and repulsed them and won a tactical victory.

Both armies' command structures were broken down in traditional hierarchy - corps, divisions, brigades. A majority of the commanders on both sides had been together and shared their military knowledge from West Point.

Union forces under Grant included Generals Hancock, Sigel, Meade, Butler, Warren, Sedgwick, and Burnside. McClellan had been de-commissioned by Lincoln earlier in the war. Confederate Generals under Lee included Ewell, Stuart, Anderson, A.P. Hill and eventually Longstreet. Jackson had been lost to friendly fire a year before.

Meade had previously attacked Lee's army north of Richmond. On the second day of the fight in the Wilderness, Burnside moved south from the Turnpike toward the Plank Road to confront A.P. Hill. Hancock joined Burnside and assaulted Hill there. Hill's troops became exhausted. Lee waited impatiently for Longstreet to arrive and relieve him. Longstreet arrived when it was over.

David fought under Burnside again. They attacked the Wilderness from the north along Germanna Ford on May 4th. At the time, the Orange Turnpike and the Plank Road joined and pointed east toward Fredericksburg, Virginia in the forested area known as the Wilderness. The unfinished railroad ran east-west and south of there.

Picket lines were positioned on both sides of the Turnpike and spread out on the edge of a wide field.

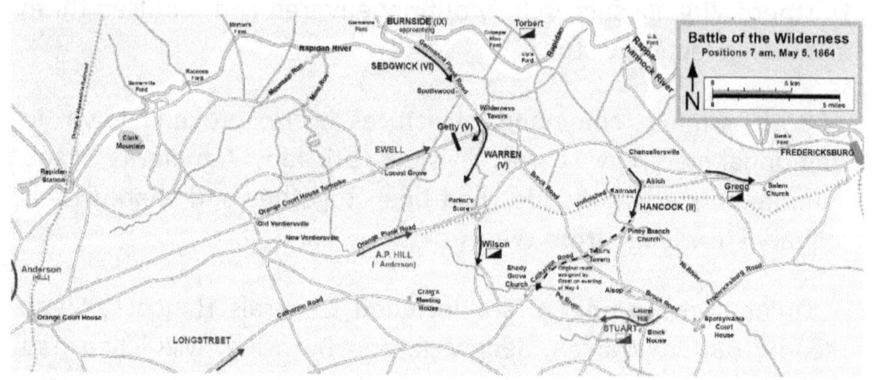

Movement inside the tangled forest was confused as the infantry on both sides had no clear view. Artillery and cavalry were ineffective. The commanders had poor field intelligence and could not form up and lead their forces effectively. Given the number of them, coordination was complex. Lee and Grant persisted.

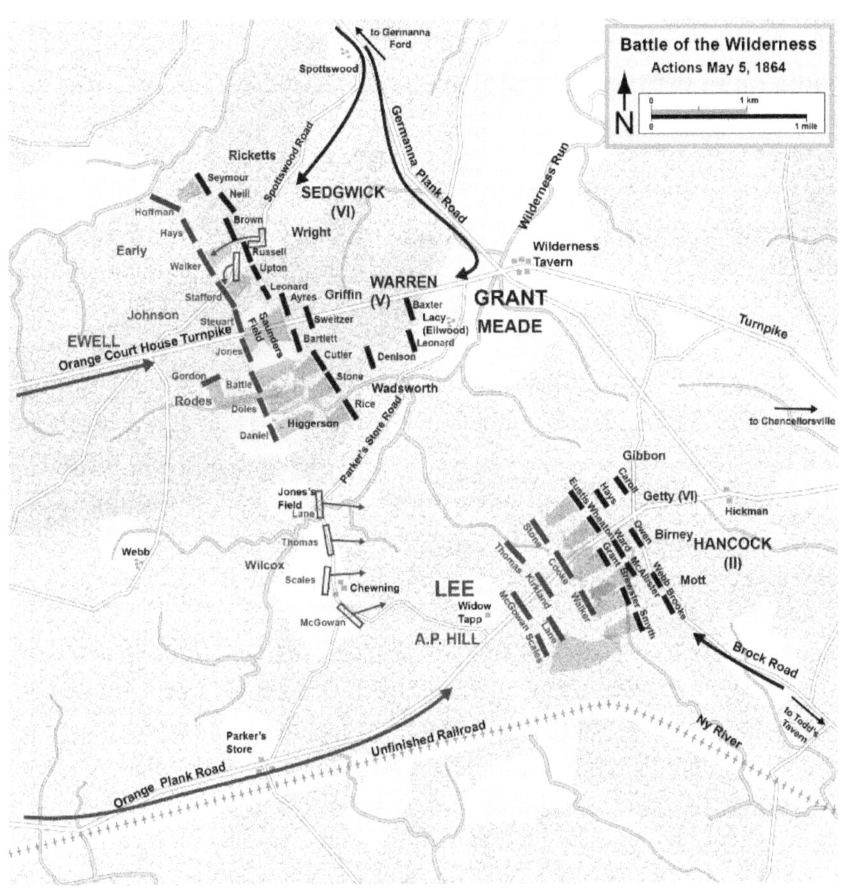

David struggled through the tangled briars and brambles in the woods. He was finding, like everyone in his company, that these were much more than a nuisance. His progress was not only slowed down, but he was cut up and bleeding from deep scratch wounds as he pushed closer to the Confederates. Just the effort to move ahead was exhausting.

The exchange of musket fire and occasional artillery was so intense at one point that it ignited the woods on fire. The men became terrified that they would be burned to death before they could meet the more honorable death from the enemy's bullet.

It was afternoon, but David could barely see his way through the haze from the wood smoke and clouds of black powder. The daylight looked to him like a thick morning haze. His comrades were invisible and if he hadn't heard their voices shouting, he would have felt he was fighting alone.

He chased surreal moving figures, with only parts of bodies visible like dismembered ghosts. He tripped and stumbled often on the uneven terrain. There were dropped logs and limbs in his path. He stepped on lumps that were the silent fresh corpses of the fallen from both sides. The unseen wounded shouted out in pain, desperate for help.

Suddenly the haze cleared and David saw three Rebels charging at him through the trees, closing the distance between them too rapidly. He was unable to reload his Springfield rifle-musket in time to fire at them. With bayonet fixed, he would have to take them on in hand-to-hand close fighting.

He swung his rifle as a club and knocked down the first to reach him. Just in time, he wheeled around and ran the second Rebel through the chest with his bayonet. He ducked just as the third one swung his musket butt at his head, tripped and fell on the ground. The Rebel stood over him, poised to drive his bayonet into David's chest. A Union comrade appeared from behind the trees and fired his musket at the remaining Rebel. The minie' ball blew the back of his head off and he was dead before his body landed on the ground.

David got up and ran out of the woods with the reformed blue wave. With fear and panic on their faces, they met the enemy on the open field. There, unlike the concealment and chaos in the woods, men were mowed down with brutal and greater efficiency. Now the artillery could participate to increase the carnage. The Union killed and wounded were over 14,000. Confederate total casualties were about 8,000.

David was in the thick of it and caught a minie' ball in the left leg from a rebel sniper 150 yards from his position. The bullet entered his thigh, grazed and cracked his femur bone and ripped through his hamstring muscle with profuse bleeding at the exit wound.

He screamed with excruciating pain as he fell to the ground, was unable to retreat, and became part of the carnage. He was one of 12,000 Union wounded and over 3,000 captured or missing. For David, it was done. He would not see the perfect slaughter of Cold Harbor and the others to follow.

As darkness fell, he lay on the field with the thousands of the dead and wounded. It was quiet after the cannon and muskets had ceased firing. The ghosts kept company with the wounded and suffering. It was so still. There was only the sound of the moans and cries for help from the living and those still to die.

The bullet had missed his femoral artery or he would have bled out in minutes. He went into shock and fainted. The Confederate medical and burial squads sorted through the blood and the bodies. They found David unconscious but alive and breathing.

For those charged with the aftermath, the scene was chaotic and the triage was overwhelming.

One of the squad shouted, "Over here. There's one alive. This one's a Yankee."

A medic came over and said, "Hold the lantern so I can see. His pant leg is soaked with blood."

He took the scissors out of his medical bag and cut off the soaked cloth.

"Put a tourniquet above the wound up here. Twist it tight. Bring over a stretcher."

They carried him to one of the horse-drawn ambulances and took him, along with many, to one of the hospitals in Richmond southeast of there. Many died on the 65-mile journey before they could get there.

During the aftermath of the devastating battles of the Civil War, a spiritual concentration occurred, of a magnitude rarely before at one time and one place since man's time on earth, as hosts of angels descended to American soil. As Enoch had described, the truth of the heavens was revealed as they intervened.

The four highest leaders of the seven Archangels - the second phylum with Michael from the south of fire, Raphael from the east of air, Uriel from the north of earth, and Gabriel from the west of water - worked together this once as allying generals and mustered and directed a great third army to descend to the earthy battlefields.

Hundreds of pale clouds of white light filled the black night. A dense feeling of electricity filled the cool night air and changed it profoundly. Sounds of the Cherubim and Seraphim - the third and fourth level of angels and most joyous phylum - fell upon the human spirits departing and joined their voices together to sing beautiful music for comfort and reassurance and assistance to the many dying and just-dead human beings, at the moment of the end of their earthly lives, for their last march - their last journey.

The Powers - fifth phylum - joined the others and with their energy, brought healing from the electrical force of their beings and healed the bodies on the ground cell by cell.

The Carrions - sixth phylum - escorted away the dark entities. The Virtues - seventh phylum - made the necessary changes, unknown to the living, to the charts of records of their lives. The ninth and tenth last phylums - the Thrones and Principalities - came as the Mother and Father Gods to warn and protect and guard against danger.

A funnel, like an inverted tornado, held fast to the ground, pierced a bright hole in the sky and lifted thousands of the fallen blue and the gray souls to their final resting place. All were redeemed - their fear and pain and suffering were ended for eternity.

Lincoln, Grant and Lee knew nothing of this. No living soul knew anything of this. It was only for the assent of the concentration of so many departing souls. God had commanded the competing Archangels to work together on this mission.

David had been unconscious, lying on the ground, bleeding out and close to death before the medics had found him. In a dream he had a vision of what had occurred that night as he began to ascend and look down at his own body lying there on the ground with the thousands. He took in the whole of the event of the intervention by the holy third army - all the images, the lights in the black night - all at once and completely as a vivid reality.

He would not remember it later. Memory knows but knowing can't remember. For the rest of his life, he was troubled knowing there was evil, but wondering, not knowing, if there was goodness. Was it madness to know one and not the other? It was unresolved and he was unredeemed.

Seven - Andersonville

David woke up in the hospital and was recuperated briefly. He was taken to the overcrowded prison for Union captured in Richmond later that May. He was fortunate that gangrene had not set in and amputation of his leg was not necessary in his case. This was all too common in Civil War field medical practice.

But most often it was at the hospitals that the great piles of the limbs were amassed - the countless arms and legs. With the constant sounds of the wounded screaming, they were tossed into buckets to make it easier to cart them away and dump them into large holes in the ground.

As Grant continued his campaign, and the noose was tightening around Richmond, the security of the capital of the Confederacy was threatened. Because the prisoner exchange program had broken down, large numbers of Union prisoners were held there. The Confederacy hastily built a new prison in southwest Georgia at Andersonville.

It was intended to hold 10,000 Union prisoners. It was not as one would imagine a prison. There were no blockhouses around the perimeter. It was a stockade with 20 foot high log walls around an open field with a creek running through the middle of it. It grew to 26 acres. It operated from February 1864 until the end of the war in April 1865. Over 30,000 men were crowded onto the grounds and lived unsheltered in the open.

David was brought by railroad to the depot in the small village of Andersonville in July of 1864 with a group transported from Richmond. They were marched the quarter mile to the prison camp officially called Ft. Sumter. When he entered the compound, he thought it looked like a biblical Old Testament living nightmare. There was a noise in the air from the hum of mosquitoes and flies.

He immediately understood the danger, as well as the destitution, in this microcosm of a cruel society.

He found the prison camp a disarray of men held in the enclosure and living in the midst of slow dying and death. The men were ravaged by dysentery, scurvy and gangrene. There was insufficient food and the creek became an open sewer. Starvation, illness and disease brought death at a rate up to 100 per day.

The men were emaciated and their clothing was in tatters. The air was hot and fowl with human excrement. The ground was a slimy field of red clay muck with an odor of indescribable filth. It was covered with morsels of food and human feces and alive with maggots falling off festering wounds and grubs from rotting cornmeal.

There were some makeshift shelters made from blankets and remnants of uniforms hanging on wooden posts. The stream entering the camp under the stockade brought in human waste, cooking waste, and filthy water from the guards camp upstream. The scurvy became prevalent, and so painfully evident, when men sneezed out their teeth.

Groups of men had formed alliances to prey on weaker men and take from them anything they valued. They called themselves raiders, but they were predators. They were the worst threat to their own kind in the prison. And they were part of their own army.

Another group of men called themselves regulators and tried to protect the weak and bring a vigilante form of justice to this lawless, cruel society. Without care or concern from the guards, the regulators executed the worst of the raiders.

David soon joined the regulators and patrolled the compound the best he could with his slowly healing wounded leg. His strength and health were better than the many sick so close to death. His sense of justice compelled him to help the helpless.

He listened compassionately to his fallen comrades, sick and dying and fearful of attack from their own men. They told him about their families, so far away back home, and how long the war had lasted, far more than they had expected from the Confederates.

On one of his walks, he saw two men falling upon a one-armed man on the ground. They were pulling off his boots and snatching his blanket out from under him. The man's eyes were rimmed with red and sunken into deep sockets in his skull. His skin had the white pallor of death and his body was emaciated like a skeleton with the skin still on it.

David lunged at the man with the boots in his hands and smashed his fist into his jaw. As the man collapsed prone on the ground, David whirled around at the other man standing next to them.

He said, "How dare you? Have you no shred of human decency or compassion for your fellow man - your own comrade? God damn your empty soul and curse you for eternity."

Fleeting fear flashed through the man's eyes at David's ferocity, as he slowly backed away, turned and ran off.

David looked down at the ground in shock, and tears of anguish came to his eyes when he recognized the man was Patrick Allister. He sat by him for three days and talked to him about their times and great days in Baltimore. Patty didn't speak but answered with his eyes and expression that he had understood. They sat by the bank of the polluted stream with Pat's nearly lifeless body propped up against David's chest.

With silent tears streaming down his face, David said, "Oh Patty, what has become of you?" Patrick looked up into his eyes and smiled as his chest rose and heaved his last breath. As the air left his body with the last soft gasp of his last exhale, David saw the instant change to a stillness, different and more complete than any stillness at rest he had ever seen in a living person. Staring up at the incongruous beautiful blue sky, Patty was frozen in stillness forever more. This was just an empty shell of a body; his soul had departed.

David was conflicted with mixed feelings of sadness and anger. He couldn't fathom the anger. The rush of sadness overtook him, surprised him with its suddenness and its intensity. His heart leaped in his chest with a fullness of instant grief, like a fear or a shock.

After the throes of death had completed its course for both of them, David looked at Patrick's calm face and thought, 'What a price you have paid Patty. What a price we have all paid for this cause.'

There was a "dead line" understood to be several yards away from the stockade poles. Any prisoner who crossed it approaching the stockade walls was shot dead. There had been escape attempts - men digging tunnels under the log stockade. Many got out of Ft. Sumter but always were caught by the dogs and human trackers in a day or two.

Union officers imprisoned in the camp could not comprehend why Grant wouldn't exchange prisoners. Andersonville became a symbol of the whole country losing its humanity. The North held Confederates in a similar prison in urban Chicago - Ft. Douglas. However, that prison had barracks and the resources to provide better care for the prisoners. Ft. Douglas posed a dangerous threat to the citizens of Chicago however, and its presence was most unwelcome.

The whole South was starving and couldn't care for its northern prisoners. Yet Grant wouldn't agree to release his southern prisoners held in the North. He feared rehabilitating them would resupply the southern dwindling forces. Truly, many thought Grant's view of using his superior numbers to wear down the Confederate forces a cruel approach. But Lincoln agreed with him and it proved successful, while the losses were horrific for the Union.

Ultimately, Henry Wirz, the commandant of Andersonville, was brought to trial for his actions during his command of the camp. He was convicted of conspiracy and murder and hanged in Washington, DC on November 10, 1865.

David questioned Grant's sense of humanity and authority. He felt the abandonment and loneliness of his boyhood and questioned God's mercy. He could not understand why God gave men free will, while the Lord required giving themselves over to Him for the promise of salvation. He would search for understanding of God's grace and His plan for him and mankind for many years and write about these questions in his journal.

From his arrival in July to his release the following April, David was famished and became so malnourished, he lost 40 pounds from his 6 foot, 185 pound frame. He suffered from dysentery and grew so weak he nearly died. But he lived.

Shortly after Lee's surrender, the prisoners were released and exchanged. The war was over. More than 650,000 Americans had given their lives and slavery was no more. The logic that drove the country to this solution was inexplicable, but in reality, the extent of it could not be expected or known beforehand. All the same, the nation had slipped into insanity. Slavery was barbaric but killing tens of thousands of men in a day was an awful price to pay to end it. Piles of humanity lay on the killing fields of Antietam and Shiloh. It was madness.

Many came to hope that future disputes could be solved with less passion and more patience. The country hoped for a return to normalcy and despaired for a time when men still believed they were creatures of God. Some had worn blue to preserve the Union and rid the country of slavery's evils. Other wore gray to preserve the homeland and defend against the tyranny of Federalism.

America's second revolution was lost; its Union preserved. The fight for independence from an oppressive government was finished. The fight for social justice had just begun. Perhaps even worse than the purgatory of the war itself was the real hell of the forced reconciliation. It took a lot longer. Foreign observers had believed we would never recover from its wounds.

President Lincoln's voice was stilled before his plans for forgiveness, and to heal the nation's wounds, could begin. Near the end of the war and his life, he had declared in his 2nd Inaugural Address that:

> *With malice toward none, with charity for all, with firmness in the right as God gives us to see the right, let us strive on to finish the work we are in, to bind up the nation's wounds, to care for him who shall have borne the battle and for his widow and his orphan, to do all which may achieve and cherish a just and lasting peace among ourselves and with all nations.*

His vision was never to come to pass. The devastated South and its people would be in chaos and live with civil conflict and inhumanity for a century to come.

After his release from Andersonville, David decided to head west because he believed there he would find things new - places, opportunities, life. It was a rural and desolate two day walk from Andersonville to Columbus and the border with Alabama.

He was so weak and tired; he rested there and wrote his father:

Dearest Father;

I pray and trust that you are well. My deepest regret is that I have not been able to keep you informed of my war's journey and so much that has happened. I was wounded in Virginia near Richmond but survived my life's most horrible experience. I fail to find the sufficient words to express to you what I have experienced and seen. The killing I saw and partook in will sicken my soul for the rest of my life. In the heat of it, there is no past, no future, only the moment. The mind crystallizes to a single pure focus as fear turns to hate and blood lust.

I was imprisoned in Georgia and lived through what this world would be like with no God to watch over it.

I saw Geoff Braxton's body carried away the day after the battle at Antietam. I held Patty Allister's wasted shell of a body and watched him heave his last breath at Andersonville prison. I know now man's original sin was not Adam and Eve; it was Cain and Abel.

At present, with the war over, I am traveling about the Deep South in Georgia and will take a look at Alabama. I need to find some meaning in all this and won't be home for the foreseeable future.

Forgive me for that and know that I have always loved you for the greatest father that you are. I hope you will understand that I must do this. Whatever lessons I have been given, I must learn their meanings myself this time.

Your unconditional love for me, faith in me, and unfailing support for me has provided me strength to survive this trial.

Yr obt svt and devoted son,

David

He posted the letter in Columbus and began his search for himself and his life's meaning. His wounded leg and his crippled soul might never heal.

After crossing the Chattahoochee River, he walked Alabama's bright red clay roads and passed through its eastern forested areas. It rained often in the spring. Some days there were brief showers with bright sunshine to follow, others a black sky with downpours for hours. The rain poured off the brim of his felt slouch hat. His sleeves were rolled up and his baggy pants were held up by suspenders over his thin frame. It soaked his shirt, his pants and his worn out shoes nearly through at the soles. The dry road turned to muck and the clay stuck to his shoes. His weak legs felt heavy.

He remembered the ground at Andersonville. It was miserable, but he had experienced it before in battle and in prison. It was bearable.

Along the way, he met some down-on-their-luck farmers who were kind enough to give him shelter and share what little they had to eat. He was grateful and paid for their kindness with his labor. Often they were badly in need of his carpentry skills. He was often invited to stay for a time and the respite helped him heal and gain strength.

He noted the simple lives of the plain folk and began writing about them in his journal. When he thought about it, David observed that it wasn't so much about what the South was, it was about what the North wasn't.

He thought, 'They speak of God and go to church more. They love their country. They love it more because they think about it as the land and their autonomy. It reminds me of Jefferson. He was a southerner, lifelong, from Virginia. I can see him back in those old times, playing his violin in his home - sweet southern sad melancholy American music from the earliest Colonial folk country tunes and Celtic heritage of those former days. It had the emotional tone of the old European classical folk music he loved too.'

He was repairing the broken porch steps on a farm house in Alabama when the farmer said to him, "Ya don't seem like a bad fella for a Yankee. Please come to service with us tomorra. We'd love to have ya."

The plain white folk had little to eat. But they had the land and they had the Lord. The church was full and the service was in the Baptist denomination - so prevalent in the South. He was raised a Presbyterian in Baltimore and attended services often with his father. But this was a different Christian worship. His had been warm and friendly, but dispassionate - with reassuring messages of salvation for believers.

This was full of passion and emotion. The people deeply felt the Holy Spirit. It pulled on their heartstrings; it made them smile; it made their eyes moist. It brought happiness to their hard-scrabble lives.

David watched them as they responded to the minister's powerful appeals. He sang with them the familiar hymns from his childhood. But he was surprised to see that in their tradition, with inadequate literacy, they did not use hymn books. They sang their familiar hymns from memory, learned from their oral tradition. They responded viscerally to the words of *What a Friend We Have in Jesus*.

As one, they swayed and looked heavenward to the soaring words and melody of *How Great Thou Art*:

Oh Lord my God, when I in awesome wonder

Consider all the worlds Thy hands have made,

I see the stars, I hear the rolling thunder,

Thy pow'r thro'out the universe displayed.

Then sings my soul, My Savior God, to Thee;

How great Thou art, how great Thou art!

Then sings my soul, My Savior God, to Thee;

How great Thou art, how great Thou art!

David would remember this. The power within those walls filled all its space and all the senses of the souls within. He had never witnessed or known of anything like this before. Perhaps the presence of God had actually been summoned forth.

He was deeply touched for them and the power of their faith. He felt it too, but couldn't cross over and make the commitment. He knew there was a Divine Providence - God's plan not revealed to him. He believed God intended for him to live by his free will and not to submit to authority, whether kind or cruel, whether Heavenly or of this earth.

He wrote in his journal on April 17th-

Their faith brings so much to their lives. It is their light and their anchor. I wish I could see it and feel it as they do.

David spent the rest of April and most of May in Alabama but didn't find anything there to keep him from going further west. Others were wandering in this way too. He met many groups of Negroes looking for farm work, or some lost family members, or the chance to put down roots on land of their own.

This was the Deep South in the aftermath of slavery and war - searching for something better while surviving the best it could.

Eight - Meeting in Natchez

After wandering west across the South for many weeks, David came to the port of Natchez in Mississippi. He walked along the wharves and docks and looked out at the wide river. He remembered his days in the merchant marines and his voyages departing from Baltimore.

For him, there was something appealing about the South. He had fought in battles in Maryland and all over Virginia and watched so many of his countrymen die. He had been imprisoned in an outdoor sewer in Georgia. He hated the plantation aristocracy and slaveholders for the men that they were. He felt a kinship for the plain folk. So many of them were Scots-Irish.

But he had a feeling about the South that was difficult for him to understand. There was a prevailing sadness, yet he was attracted to it. Perhaps it had to do with his feeling of abandonment from the loss of his mother when she had died. He had grown up with aloneness and restless loneliness. It had been something he was used to.

This sadness might have been his warm companion he drew comfort from. And here in the South, it was something like a peaceful, bittersweet nostalgia as though he had lived here in a former life, in its rural country, before the war. It was melancholy and inexplicable.

David noticed a man staring out at the river. He was very still, deep in concentration. Well past mid-day, the man was cloaked in the shadow of the waterfront buildings. He stood at a distance watching him and sensed a sadness and loneliness - an aloneness -

about him that he could understand well. There were several people in the area but no one nearby but he and this man.

He felt compelled to walk over to greet him and speak to him. He now saw that the man was a Negro. He noticed a strong resolve and sense of purpose in the man's eyes and wasn't certain how he would be received. He was curious and decided to speak to him.

David approached the man in a casual, friendly and cheerful manner and said, "Hello, my name is David, who are you?"

Josiah was startled by this stranger and his question. He was not sure if this man was a threat. Most white men he had known in his life had treated him harshly. For the most part, they could not be trusted. With hesitancy, he thought it best to reply and avoid trouble.

So he answered, "My name is Josiah, suh."

David immediately realized that the man was wary, possibly afraid, and continued, "I mean you no harm. I just wondered what you were doing here, looking at the river I mean."

Josiah looked at him closely and thought he sensed a sadness and loneliness in this friendly white man.

He hesitated for a moment and said, "I am a freed man from a plantation near here. I came here hoping to find what to do next and mostly to look for my lost wife."

"Well I guess we have more in common than we would expect meeting here like this", David said. "I have just been freed from a prison in Georgia and have walked across Alabama to come to Mississippi searching for what I will do next."

Josiah nodded and the two men continued to assess each other for a few minutes. Josiah was surprised to be approached like this by a white man. David had fought to end the inhumanity and injustice of slavery, had always known it was a sinful abomination, but had never met a former slave to talk to before this.

The two men sensed, and began to understand, some shared commonness and both thought there might be a possibility for friendship even though their skin color was not the same and there was no true trust yet established. Despite their initial wariness as strangers, they spent the afternoon talking to each other about their life's fortunes and hopes for the future.

The afternoon turned to dusk and with nightfall approaching, David asked, "Have you eaten today?"

Josiah replied, "I have been here two days and met some people on the dock. I helped them unload a ship's cargo. They gave me some food, a blanket and a place to sleep in that warehouse over there. It felt a little strange but good to work for myself, earn my keep and keep what I earn for my own benefit as a free man."

David said, "Well, I have met many strangers on my travels here too. Most of them were poor farmers who suffered damage and destruction during the war. I helped them repair some farm buildings and equipment and I baled some cotton. Like you, as payment for my labor, they fed me and gave me a place to sleep in their barns."

As darkness set in on the river's edge, the men talked more about their situation and future hopes.

Josiah wondered if this could be the start of a friendship with this white man from the North, but was uncertain how to act on an equal basis and careful not to offend him.

Hesitantly he said, "David, you can sleep at the warehouse tonight it you want. It is not very comfortable like a house."

David laughed and replied, "No, no don't worry about it. It will be fine. After my imprisonment in Georgia, I am not particular about where I sleep."

Together they left the waterfront for the night. As they walked toward the warehouse, Josiah noticed that his new companion was very thin and walked with a limp from his left leg.

The next morning they talked more comfortably about their concerns, hopes and plans. As they shared their past, Josiah described some of his life as a slave. He discovered that David was a very educated and knowledgeable man. Josiah thought that maybe David would be able to give him some answers to questions that had troubled him for years. David would learn that Josiah was a serious minded, purposeful man.

With his expression formed with resolve, Josiah asked, "David, how did you think we became slaves? I mean I know we were brought from Africa, but how and why did it start?"

David thoughtfully replied, "It's a long story Josiah. My grandfather used to tell me how our country began when the early English settlers came to Virginia. They believed they were noblemen like back in England. Slavery began then over 250 years ago when African slaves were brought to Virginia from the Caribbean. There was a trade going on between England, West Africa, the Caribbean and our colonies. Slaves were traded for tobacco, rum, sugar and molasses. Everybody was making a lot of money on the human traffic."

Josiah remarked, "The old slaves on the plantations told me that we used to be up in Virginia and Carolina. We planted tobacco. Life was not as hard then as it is now here in the Deep South. Massa Taylor never talked about it. He just said we are just cotton pickin' niggers and we have to work hard or we will be lashed."

David said, "Yes I know. That word, and the word Negroes, came from ancient Latin and was a word from back in Africa meaning people of black skin color. The plantation owners are ignorant southerners and were just trying to control you."

His fists were balled up when he said, "I hate the godless, evil, aristocratic bastards."

They were both quiet and reflective for a few minutes after that emotional outburst. Josiah was startled by David's feelings of rage. He didn't yet know David's nature when confronted with matters of injustice and cruel authority. He tried to take in everything David had told him and the sense it was given.

With calm restored, their talk moved on to their very different past lives and their skills. They began to speak to each other about their ideas for the future.

Josiah remarked, "David I understand I am free now and I own myself for the first time. I don't know what to do next to find work or how to begin to look for Josie."

David answered, "I understand what you mean. I started out in Baltimore. For a few years, I sailed ships as a Merchant Marine. What stories I could tell you about those experiences. I am a Yankee and I fought for the Union and Lincoln in Virginia. I was shot in the leg, captured and taken prisoner over to Georgia to the prison in Andersonville. When the war ended, I was released and I traveled around the South looking for a place for myself. I ended up here in Natchez just as you have."

Josiah listened and then asked, "What will you do now?"

David thought and replied slowly, "I'm not sure Josiah but I need to find a place where I can be free to work and live, just like you. Even though Baltimore is my home, I didn't feel happy living in the city. I could never have worked in a factory for wages or any other job for long where I was under the authority of others. When I left the Merchant Marines, I began to hire myself out to do carpentry. I built houses and other things, learning and using my skills as I went along."

Josiah agreed, "Yes I am similar. I learned how to build furniture. Woodworking is different than carpentry. It takes a long time to build a chair or a table. I learned carpentry from an older craftsman on the plantation. Slowly I found that I had skills and understood the figures and grains of good woods. You need to know how to shape and smooth the wood and finish the pieces with stains and linseed oil. It takes patience but the finished work makes me proud. It is slow but I really enjoy it."

David told him, "I can appreciate the beautiful things that you can make. But, for myself, I work much faster and work with rough wood and don't worry about the beautiful finishes. But I can throw up a strong house frame in two to three days. Maybe we can go together to find work and look for your Josie."

Josiah was touched and pleased that a man he had just met would throw in with him and be his companion and ally, "Yes, that would be a great comfort to have us travel together. In these dangerous times, two are stronger than one. I'm sure there will be times when trouble will come. By the way, my last name is Ashford, the name of my first owner in Missouri."

"Well it's a pleasure Mr. Ashford. Mine is Wexley from Baltimore. If you don't mind me asking, I couldn't help noticing how well spoken and serious minded you are. Have you read or studied? I thought slaves were not allowed to read or write."

"It's funny you asked that. You are right. Most slaves are forbidden to learn to read. My Josie worked in the mansion and sneaked books to our cabin when she came at night. I taught myself to read. I read some of the good ones."

He laughed to himself and said, "Your experience as a sailor in the Merchant Marines made me remember *Moby Dick*."

"Ha ha. I read that one too. I never fought an epic battle with a whale, but did fire some cannon at British ships."

Josiah and David had begun to form a bond forged from a common experience. They had witnessed the face of inhumanity in its most horrible expression. They were both burdened with survivor's guilt. This shared life experience was similar enough that it transcended any differences they may have had. The strength of their bond would protect them in the many difficult days ahead.

David understood better his conflicted feelings about the South and its appeal. It wasn't just about the places. It was about some of its people. It brought him a measure of happiness - something he had always searched for.

Nine - Rise and Fall of Savannah Oaks

The early years, starting in late 1835, were filled with back breaking work and ceaseless activity as Marcus built the plantation on his swamp timber land. He had purchased six field hands, a carpenter, a blacksmith, and a house servant girl at the slave auction in Natchez to get started. One of those field hands was the female named Sarah.

After two years, most of the work was completed to start the plantation operation. The first planting was started on 95 acres of his land. The cottonseed was in and work had begun on the mansion. The network of dirt roads had been established for entrance to the main house and access to the slave cabins and work fields. Funds were depleting from Hendrick's investment in his son's new business.

Marcus had made remarkable progress. By 1838, he was ready for and had procured the 50 slaves he needed to support his cotton production on 525 of his 650 acres. The rest would remain unused open or forested land. The main house was completed and Marcus and Rebecca moved out of their crude temporary house.

Rebecca was pleased to move into her mansion and settle the fine household she had waited for. She learned how to manage and direct her staff of Negro attendants. Marcus left her to her role since he was completely immersed in his. He was determined to make a success of the plantation and keep his promises to Rebecca and his father.

Hendrick made the trip to visit them shortly after that.

He looked the plantation over and told Marcus, "You have done well son."

He thought to himself, 'Even with its refinements, I wouldn't want to live in a place like this. There's nothing can be done about its rural crudeness.'

Marcus thought his father looked much older and less enthusiastic about his life.

Between the planting and harvesting seasons, he and Rebecca made the trip to Savannah to visit him. They gathered the family together. Jane was not well, but still alive and living with Hendrick in their home. Marcy and Constance and their families came to join them.

The Taylors held a party so that all the Stanleys could come down from Charleston. Rebecca was so happy to see them all again. She had missed her family and her brothers in particular. She had been very close to them from all the time they spent traveling together. But things seemed different now. Everyone was older and had gone on with their lives.

She thought, 'I guess there is no going back.'

She decided to make the best of it at Savannah Oaks. She began an effort to build a social structure with the neighbors in two of the nearby plantations. She planned and carried out many successful parties as she had known in the past.

But the scale was not as grand and the people were more concerned about their cotton and the control of their slaves than the social graces. This rural life would never be the same as she knew in the earlier days in Charleston or Savannah. But there was no going back.

Marcus and Rebecca had surely changed - they were slaveholders now. The Negroes were a means to their end. Their human property was the same as their other non-human property and equipment. The immorality of this became suppressed until it was forgotten.

They were morally corrupt and inhumane but viewed themselves as paternal and maternal benefactors caring for their inferior children. Their children were well cared for, but when they misbehaved, punishment was meted out with harsh brutality.

By 1843, Savannah Oaks had prospered better then Marcus had ever hoped for. He had 160 slaves and had brought his cash crops to market in Natchez for many seasons. The household was splendid and alive under Rebecca's management. There were cooks, seamstresses, housekeepers and servants looking after all her needs at the mansion. Noticeably missing were nursemaids since Marcus and Rebecca had never had children.

In 1852, Marcus bought Josiah and brought him to the plantation as a prime, 23 year old field hand with potential as a fair hand at carpentry. Josena was 15 years old and working in the house as a servant. Josiah fell in love with Josena and married her in 1853.

Marcus had fought with Rebecca for years over Josena. Rebecca had been unable to conceive and remained childless. She knew Marcus was Josena's father. He had no choice but to acknowledge that fact and care for his daughter. As Josena grew up over the passing years, Rebecca's resentment grew. Even when Josena married Josiah, Rebecca would never let Marcus forget his disloyalty to her.

Finally the pressure convinced him to sell her. He found a way to do so, and in February 1856, he secretly sold her in Natchez. He brought her by wagon and she never came back.

Josiah was up at the saw mill away from the main house and road that day. When he returned and Josena didn't come home from the mansion, he was beside himself with worry and didn't know what to do. His first thought was to go to Marcus and ask where she was but he knew that was not wise. He frantically asked everyone he saw if anyone had seen her or knew her whereabouts. Two of the slaves told him they saw her go off with Massa Marcus early that morning in the back of his wagon. The Massa came back with an empty wagon. They all knew what that meant.

Josiah went to Ned's cabin. He was angry, distraught, desperate and frightened.

He thought, 'This can't be true. Where is she?'

Sobbing so hard his throat would barely let him croak, "Ned, what has happened to Josie?"

Ned confirmed what he had heard about Marcus selling Josie.

Josiah hung his head and sobbed, "How could he sell his daughter? What should I do, Ned? I don't know how to go on without her."

Ned tried to console him as best he could, said, "Yo can't face up ta Massa, Josiah. Yo mus 'cept dis and go on with yo life. We neva understan da cruelty of a man like dat Massa. Yo mus let yo faith in Jesus hep yo go on. Josie wouldn't want anythin' to happen to yo; yo knows dat."

Josiah told him, "I don't think I can go back to our cabin. Everywhere I look there is a reminder of her. What am I going to do?"

Ned offered, "Come stay with me, boy. Leas' fo tonight. In the mornin' we kin think 'bout what we do tomorra."

So Josiah stayed with Ned and, after a few days, moved his meager belongings and a few treasured books that he had kept when no one at the mansion missed them, into Ned's cabin. Life went on in the slave quarters, as it had before, without Josena, just as though she had never existed.

Josiah grieved for her absence and wondered if she was still alive. He poured himself into his work and bided his time. On some bright clear days, his hands slowed down and fell to his side as he stared at the wood he was fashioning. He looked out across the cotton fields at the sad live oaks, draped in moss, lining the road leading away and wondered.

By July 1863 Grant had won the siege of Vicksburg and the Mississippi River was under the control of the Union. Grant had left the west to participate in campaigns in Virginia, but some Union forces remained behind to maintain control of the Mississippi Valley area.

For Marcus Taylor, this meant he could no longer access Natchez for selling his cotton or for trading in slavery. His slaves were theoretically freed, but no federal forces had entered his plantation.

When Marcus learned about the occupation of the federal troops in Natchez and Lincoln's emancipation of the slaves, he became very concerned for his plantation and his way of life. He knew it was only a matter of time until they discovered his remote plantation. He feared that the Union forces would emancipate his slaves and possibly burn his plantation.

While he and Rebecca no longer felt any love between them, they still shared a bond as master and mistress of Savannah Oaks. They were still partners in their life's business and livelihood. Marcus talked to her about his worries.

He said, "Rebecca, the Yankees have now occupied Natchez. We are in deep trouble. We can't bring our crops to market or buy or sell any slaves with them there."

"Can't we bribe some officials and get around them if only to sell our cotton?"

Marcus looked resigned and said, "No, we will get caught and then they will come here and find us."

Rebecca had a thought and suggested, "Maybe we will have to put more work into our vegetable garden and have our coloreds do the same for theirs. The men will have to spend their time hunting for game. We will have to live off the land until we see how this ends."

It ended when the federal troops arrived at Savannah Oaks in July of 1865. By then, the plantation had seen its better days. After nearly two years without income from cotton production, Marcus had let many of his slaves wander away. He had no means to support them. And his attitude and treatment of them had changed under the new circumstances. He had come to realize that his control over them was weakening while perhaps he and Rebecca were more dependent on them than before.

Some had stayed for lack of a better alternative until the authorities arrived and forced the decision. Particularly the older slaves stayed since they were more dependent on their owners for their welfare. But they were not as useful as the younger ones who had left.

Marcus and Rebecca survived the best they could, subsisting on Savannah Oaks plantation.

Josiah quietly kept to himself and stayed because he had become a respected craftsman and was treated better than most. The slaves looked up to him, often came to him to seek advice and accepted him as a leader. They were respectful of his loss.

He continued to try to improve himself and find his faith. He reread the books he had kept. He practicing reading them aloud to hear the sound the words made with his voice. His favorite was Harriet Beecher Stowe's *Uncle Tom's cabin, or, Life among the lowly*. It was Rebecca's but she had not missed it and likely not read it.

Alone at the saw mill he spoke out with emotion and passion:

A day of grace is held out to us. Both North and South have been guilty before God; and the Christian church has a heavy account to answer. Not by combining together, to protect injustice and cruelty, and making a common capital of sin, is this Union to be saved, - but by repentance, justice and mercy; for, not surer is the eternal law by which the millstone sinks in the ocean, than the stronger law, by which injustice and cruelty shall bring on nations the wrath of Almighty God!

It had been nine years since Massa Taylor had sold Josena. He had been bitter and angry about losing her for a long time. He wondered again and again, 'How could a father sell his daughter?'

No one had come into his life to replace her, nor would he want that. He drifted along and found gratification in his work.

When word came about the emancipation of slaves in Confederate controlled territories, he was still conflicted about what to do about it. He didn't see any way to do anything at that time. So he waited until the officials came and declared him free. He never gave up hope that he would find Josena again someday.

The year was 1865. The bright sun in the southern sky had faded by late afternoon in the late spring - past its former glory, never forgotten, but gone forever.

At the end of the war, Savannah Oaks became a sharecropper farm, with freedmen as labor, under the new post-war reconstruction arrangements. Their slaves had all left and their land was sub-divided into small plots for the new farmers - Negro strangers - to manage. Marcus and Rebecca moved to a small plot near the place where the new town of McComb was being built.

With their human property gone, they had lost most of their wealth. They sold off their land for what little they could get and kept a small plot of 20 acres for themselves. Marcus worked the land as a small farmer and hired a couple Negroes to help him with the planting and harvesting. He had no place for them to live on his land. He paid them wages and they came in from their cabins on the other side of McComb.

They grew vegetables for themselves and some cotton to help pay for what they had to buy. He hunted small and large game in the woods and fields of Savannah Oaks on their former property.

He cut wood and they survived the winters as the years passed away.

Rebecca kept the house and read her books about genteel people living their elegant lives in grand cities. They lived together as working partners and companions. They subsisted in that way too, since there had been no love between them for many years.

Finally Marcus's heart gave out at harvest time and she buried him in the cemetery in McComb in the fall of 1881. They had no rights for the use of the cemetery on the former Savannah Oaks plantation. After that, she lived by herself, never left the house, and retreated from the world more and more as time passed. She was a widow who had no grief for her husband but grieved for her own life throughout most of its remainder. That was, until she lost her mind.

The town folk passed by her house and saw her delicate frail hand holding back the lace curtain as she stared out of the window of her dark room. Each time they saw her, she never looked at them or knew they were there; her trace-like eyes were gazing at some other thing, some other place.

A Negress in town had been helping several white families keep house. She had come to Mississippi from Mobile, Alabama by herself to look for work. She did their laundries and was a nanny to their children. This black Christian woman gave their children love or a sharp tongue in just the best way it was needed. The white folk took exception to her color and loved her as the fine Christian woman she was.

She took mercy on the demented widow who lived by herself and began going to her house one day a week to help out in any way she could as an act of Christian charity. The Christian woman looked after the woman's needs and kept her company as her only companion. She patiently listened to the fantasies living in the old woman's mind.

Rebecca recounted her stories as she remembered them, not as they were in truth or knowing, "We had the finest plantation and the grandest mansion, just as Marcus had promised. We fed the brave Confederate soldiers that came through in our grand dining room with our best silver and services. The starving and famished men were served our most lavish diners and our musicians played them the glorious music of our south in our grand ballroom.

But after a while the niggers began taking our fine things little by little. I never could catch them but you can never trust niggers. Soon everything was gone and soon Marcus was gone. I look out the window for him."

The Negress companion listened patiently week after week to the old woman, sitting with her in the small dark living room with only the afternoon light coming through the lace curtains of the windows. She watched this woman in her dirty frayed dress, the same she wore each week. She saw that her mind had slipped its moorings - she was hopelessly insane.

She comforted her, "Now, now ol girl, yo kin always rely on de Lord. He make it right."

When Rebecca died in 1888, the Christian colored woman arranged Rebecca's pauper's funeral and the burial service in the McComb town cemetery. A few town folks came, more for curiosity than care. The woman had been the last person to speak to Rebecca and now was the last one to speak about her.

She prayed, "Oh Jesus, sweet Jesus, take dis wumun in yo eva luvin arms. Keep her soul in hevin with yo for all eternity. Amen."

She had come by herself from Mobile, Alabama to work for the white folk. She had never known her daddy but had heard her mamma's name was Josena.

Ten - Looking for Josie

Josiah and David were thinking about how to begin looking for Josena. Josiah suggested, "We should start here in Natchez. Let's talk to people who know about the slave auction and see what we can find out."

It didn't take long for them to find the market known as *The Forks of the Road*, the largest former slave auction, at the intersection of Liberty Road and Washington Road. The market was no longer in operation but a man there told them that all records of slave transactions had been confiscated by the federal government. They would need to go to the Freedmen's Bureau.

Josiah looked at David and said "We will have to go to the plantation and get Marcus Taylor to show us his records."

David was more than ready to confront Taylor and get the records of sale, even if he had to beat it out of him. And so they decided to begin their trek by first going back to Savannah Oaks.

They found Marcus there as a disheveled, beaten and defeated man. He had no fighting spirit left in him.

Josiah told him, "We need to see your records of sales for slaves you sold. We are looking for my wife, Josena that you sold away from me."

Marcus looked crestfallen - she was his daughter - and said, "I remember."

It was one of the most shameful acts he had ever committed, and one of the most regrettable.

He looked through his papers in his office of the plantation main house and produced a bill of sale. It was dated February 13, 1856 and stated that a John Manford from Alabama had purchased one Josena Taylor as an 18 year old house servant for $850. There was no location or plantation name for the buyer.

David said, "C'mon let's go. There's nothing more for us here."

Marcus said, "Before you go, stay for a good meal. You're welcome to stay here tonight and get a fresh start in the morning."

Josiah said, "We will take you up on your offer for a meal."

Marcus led them through the grand foyer to the servants' big kitchen at the back of the house. He instructed his cook to serve them a meal. They ate a good portion of crawfish, jambalaya, and fresh cornbread. As they got up to leave the kitchen, Josiah remembered building the large table there. He had made it several years ago from Southern pecan hardwood, milled on the plantation property. He was pleased to see how durable it had been.

Marcus joined them again as they walked out the grand front door of the plantation main house onto the veranda. Rebecca was sitting in her rocker on the porch but didn't look over at them.

She was staring off towards the fields, fallow now for these last few years. All the memories had come flooding back to her. She remembered the heady days of her youth in Charleston - the parties, the attention, the refinement- and the energy and excitement of Savannah. She remembered the broken promises for a life like that here. She remembered the years that Josena had been raised in the main house and had served there. Most of all, she remembered the supreme act of disloyalty by her husband. With no children of her own and living in this remote place, she had wasted all her best years. She despaired for what a disappointment her life had been.

When she heard the voices and the shuffling feet on the porch, she awoke from her bitter reverie, looked up and said to Josiah, "So you are looking for that young Negro woman are you? Good riddance to her and her kind."

Josiah was startled by her venom but responded, "I'm not looking for your opinions and won't concern myself with how I address you. I won't refer to you as my Owner, my Mistress, or my Massa's wife. I am a free man now. Goodnight Rebecca."

David and Josiah filled their canteens with fresh water from the pump in the front yard. Josiah looked back at the main house and across the side yard at the slave cabins. He remembered his 13 years here in human bondage. There were some pleasant memories. He had made friends and allies and was respected for his artisanship.

Most of all, he remembered Josena, the love they had between them, and their brief two-year marriage before she was taken away. He knew that much had changed in just a few weeks since he had left the plantation.

He envisioned much more change to come. His people would never again be treated like farm animals and beasts of burden and inferior human beings. There would be many good and bad white people and black people involved in the change that would occur over many, many years. He knew also that there would be special relationships, formed from some common bonds, between black people and white people - like he and David.

But he knew that, in the end, his people would have the opportunity for an equal share in American citizenship. People of

African descent would always consider themselves as unique and different because of their history as victims of the "peculiar institution". They had been slaves and had become freedmen. Because of their history of slavery, they would come to view themselves as African-Americans apart from white Americans. They would develop a pride that white people would not understand.

David broke into Josiah's reverie and said, "Let's get started. We have a couple more hours of daylight. I don't want to stay here tonight."

They started out together walking down the old road away from the plantation. It was another hot and humid July night in Mississippi. They would sleep in the fields and start out on their journey again tomorrow.

The next morning David suggested, "Since our answers might be found in Alabama, I think we should go to Mobile. I passed through there on my way to Natchez a couple months ago. It is a growing city and port to the Gulf. Maybe we can meet someone who will give us useful information to look for Josie."

The trip to Mobile was nearly 300 miles and took them the rest of July and most of August. They met many small groups of freedmen wandering from town to town. Planters, small farmers, and town's people viewed them with suspicion and there was always the threat of violence. They stopped in several places and traded their carpentry skills for food, shelter and provisions. They carried blanket rolls and gunnysacks necessary for travel on the road. Recognizing the potential for personal danger, David bought two old army .44-cal. Model 1860 Colt revolvers, holsters and ammunition. He taught Josiah to handle and shoot his if the need for self-defense arose.

Life was changing dramatically and rapidly in the Deep South. In 1865, Mississippi and Alabama had not rejoined the Union. Radical Republicans in the federal government had many ideas to experiment with the transformation of the post-war southern society and economy. Federal troops were stationed in regions of the South to impose martial law and maintain order. Whites were struggling to find ways to recoup their way of life. Blacks were struggling to find new ways to live as free men. The tension between them was palpable.

When they arrived at the port of Mobile, they found it occupied by federal troops and under martial law. In August 1864, the naval siege of Mobile had concluded with the fall of Fort Morgan. The Union army had also participated in the defeat of the Confederates there. The port was closed and blockaded.

David spoke to a federal officer at the town office center. He asked him if anyone kept any records with information about the whereabouts of an Alabama man named John Manford. He explained they were trying to locate him and it was believed he was a slave owner and likely had a plantation.

The officer said, "I don't know anyone here who would have kept records to help you locate him. I suggest you go to Demopolis about 150 miles north of here. Negroes had been excluded from that town as slaves before the war, but now the Freedmen's Bureau has a regional office there to assist them with relocation and finding family members."

David thanked him and looked over at Josiah and said, "Well Joe, that sounds like our next stop."

Josiah smiled and in a rare lighthearted moment, said, "Let's go Dave."

They found Demopolis to be a very small town crowded with freedmen milling about and looking hopeful that there would be assistance. They waited in line at the Freedmen's Bureau office for their turn.

Joe told the agent that they needed to find a slave named Josena Taylor. She was his wife and had been sold to a John Manford at the slave auction in Natchez on February 13, 1856. They believed he had a plantation in Alabama.

The agent said, "I'm closing in a half hour but if you will come back tomorrow morning, I'll let you know what I found out."

That evening they talked to several freedmen in the town and learned that they were all on a similar quest and were hanging onto hope. The next morning, they met the agent again.

He smiled and said "I have some good news for you. There is a John Manford who works as an overseer and agent for the Drish Plantation in Tuscaloosa. They are a major cotton producer in this region. Just now, many of their slaves have left and they are making the transition to sharecropping. Manford conducted a lot of business for John Drish and did buy a slave named Josena for him at the Natchez auction in 1856. They are located about 60 miles north of here."

Joe was excited and said to David "That's it. We will go to the Drish Plantation and get Josena."

Joe and David traveled north toward Tennessee and found Tuscaloosa and the Drish Plantation in west central Alabama a week after leaving Demopolis. They had followed along the Black Warrior River which flowed south to the Gulf at Mobile.

The area was located on the boundary between the Appalachian Highland and the Gulf Coastal Plain. The geography was diverse with heavily forested hills and low-lying marshy plains. The climate in summer was warm and the air was moist. Severe seasonal thunderstorms and tornadoes were common this time of year.

The new city nearby lie on the fall line upriver from the confluence with the Tombigbee River at Demopolis. During the last weeks of the war, Union troops had raided the area and burned the town and new college there.

John Drish was a physician from Virginia who settled near Tuscaloosa in 1822. He built his plantation in 1835 on a 450 acre plot of land. He ran a large cotton mill operation there with his slaves and, as an amateur architect, cultivated them as skilled artisans in carpentry, masonry and plasterwork.

Drish had completed his stuccoed brick mansion in 1837 and had it built in the Greek and Italianade styles unique to the area. It had full width Doric porticoes to the front and rear with two-story pilasters dividing the bays on four sides. He helped design the mansion himself and had it built by his slave artisans.

A three-story brick tower was added before the war. There was an oak tree lined entrance road leading up to the mansion from where there was a view of the Black Warrior River.

John Manford was the overseer for the Drish Plantation operations. He was standing in front of the mansion portico and watching the two men walking up the road approaching him. He briefly glanced over at his shotgun and hollered toward them, "What brings you fellas round here on foot this hot afternoon?"

They met him in the yard at the end of the entrance road. His shirt sleeves were rolled up and he wore suspenders to hold up his work pants. His wide brimmed straw hat shaded his round face and mutton chop sideburns.

They could tell he had been hard muscled once but was drifting toward sloppy fat in his late middle age. He was a short man who appeared affable and wore a sardonic smile. His friendly appearance was deceptive when Joe and David considered Manford's position.

They explained their purpose to Manford and Joe asked him if Josena was still here. The smile faded from Manford's face and he said, "Yes, she is here."

Eleven - After Bondage and War

On April 9th, with General Lee's meager forces surrounded in the Village of Appomattox Court House by the overwhelming forces of Grant's generals, and with all escape routes blocked, he decided to end the fight. When Sheridan saw Lee's defenseless forces huddled together, he asked Grant to permit him to ignore the fragile cease fire and for the order to annihilate them. He said it would only take five minutes.

Grant angrily told him, "No, that would place our names in infamy forever."

Lee waited in the home of Wilmer McLean for Grant's arrival. They met to discuss the terms of surrender as gentlemen and with dignity. They drafted brief documents and, through their attendants, exchanged them. Lee's final letter addressed Grant as commander of all the armies of the United States, including his own, and awaited his orders.

Grant would have nothing of Lee surrendering his sword. That would have brought no honor to the ceremony and would have only served the newspapers and politicians.

He remembered the words in the Old Testament of the Holy Book, and thought, 'The prophet Micah reminds us: *He has showed you, O man, what is Good. And what does the Lord require of you? To act justly and to love mercy and walk humbly with your God.'*

He paroled the men and permitted them to leave and go back to their homes. He required they surrender and stack up their arms and ammunition. Officers were permitted to keep their side arms.

All cavalry soldiers could take their personal horses and mules back to their farms. The terms were as generous as Lee could have hoped for.

Grant ordered Sheridan, "Provide food rations to the beaten Confederates. They have been starved for many months. Take care of them. That is my order. See to it." Sheridan obeyed.

Across the fields, a spontaneous celebration of cannon and musket fire broke out from the Union forces. Grant ordered it to cease immediately.

He expressed his belief, "There is no dignity or honor in humiliation. The enemy knows full well they are beaten. The Confederates are now our countrymen."

Both Lee and Grant knew that there was no glory in war, but there was dignity and respect between its combatants. For war's leaders, the purpose was to inspire men to march and face the enemy across the killing field - to fight for their country. They were trained to believe that and had lived their whole lives with that code. They had learned the meaning of duty and that guided all their actions and conduct. They understood the meaning of honor better than others ever would.

After Lee's farewell address to his army on April 10th, Union Brigadier General Joshua L. Chamberlain was charged with leading the ceremony for the formal surrender on April 12th. Chamberlain reflected on what he had observed and wrote a moving tribute containing these words:

Before us in proud humiliation stood the embodiment of manhood: men whom neither toils and sufferings, nor the fact of death, nor disaster, nor hopelessness could bend from their resolve; standing before us now, thin, worn, and famished, but erect, and with eyes looking level into ours, waking memories that bound us together as no other bond;—was not such manhood to be welcomed back into a Union so tested and assured? Instructions had been given; and when the head of each division column comes opposite our group, our bugle sounds the signal and instantly our whole line from right to left, regiment by regiment in succession, gives the soldier's salutation, from the "order arms" to the old "carry"—the marching salute. Gordon at the head of the column, riding with heavy spirit and downcast face, catches the sound of shifting arms, looks up, and, taking the meaning, wheels superbly, making with himself and his horse one uplifted figure, with profound salutation as he drops the point of his sword to the boot toe; then facing to his own command, gives word for his successive brigades to pass us with the same position of the manual,—honor answering honor.

No expression could have captured the common bond of esprit de corps for the soldiers of the North and South better than this.

After the war, the economic order of the old South was destroyed. For its people, like their many deserted battlefields, the economic playing field was leveled. In an ironic way, there was more economic equality. The many white poor remained desperately poor as before. The many freedmen became poor by virtue of their independence. The few and powerful rich whites became more poor with their system, based on enslaved labor, removed. All their human property had been taken from them. New alternatives would be required to rebuild their system. Without a significant industrial economy, the South would first need to invent a new agricultural system. Industrialization and the new South would come much later.

The social order was also destroyed. With their way of life gone forever and their cause lost, the defeated white southerners were consumed with bitterness toward the North and its victorious government. For the first time in their lives, the freedmen would need to find their rightful place in society.

Hatred, resentment, and even jealousy would be turned in their direction by the embittered whites. As a new reality, the freedmen would need to be dealt with by all of society. A century of racism and violence would follow before these matters were settled in law.

For Josiah and David, their journey was over. They had found the Drish Plantation in Tuscaloosa, Alabama and met John Manford. He had told them Josena was there.

Joe said to Manford, "Please, please take me to her."

He led them to an area in the field behind the plantation main house. It was surrounded by a wrought iron fence. He led them through the gate to a simple stone marker that was inscribed "Josena- Beloved House Girl - Died September 1864". Josiah stood before the grave and fell to his knees.

He wailed in anguish, "God, how could you do this? I can't believe this has happened."

Josiah sobbed bitterly and couldn't quell the tears running down his face. David stood beside him speechless with his hand on Josiah's shoulder.

David asked John Manford what had happened. He learned that there had been a slave uprising as word came that Union forces had seized Mobile and were occupying Alabama. The plantation slaves had charged the overseers with shovels, pitchforks, and clubs. There were shots fired and the rebellion intensified. The confrontation got out of control and several slaves were killed. Josena had been in the yard on an errand for the main house and was accidentally shot in the abdomen. She could not be saved and died two hours later.

When Josena had been bought and brought to Drish Plantation, she was three-months pregnant with Josiah's child. John Drish was a kindly man and always treated her well as part of his household servant staff. When he saw that she was going to have a baby, he was gentle and supportive. His wife took a special interest in her and, for the first time in her life, the mistress of the plantation had shown her mercy and human kindness.

Manford paid no attention to the household relationships or matters within the mansion. His work running the operations of the plantation filled his time and interest.

But Josena never stopped grieving for her separation from Josiah and remained despondent for the rest of her life.

Like the mythic, long-wandering journey to come home and find her, Odysseus, embodied in two men - the seeker and the wanderer - had found Penelope. But she hadn't been waiting faithfully, surrounded by duplicity; she had been killed too soon. This war, and its human stories, had ended in tragedy and heartbreak, not joy.

Manford said, "It was a tragedy. We all loved Josena. It broke the hearts of all of us - the Negroes and us alike."

David pulled Manford aside and left Joe alone at the gravesite.

Manford said, "Three days after the incident, the Yankee troops arrived and said our Negroes was freed. It was such a waste; four Negroes and Josena dead. There was Freedmen's Bureau government people who explained we could make contracts with our Negroes so they could work as sharecroppers. Many of them left anyway. We have been trying to convert the plantation since then. The Negroes didn't know how good they had it when we took care of them."

David looked at him steely eyed and said, "They didn't know how good they had it? You mean they were better off when they were whipped for looking at you the wrong way or speaking the wrong word. They were better off when they couldn't leave the plantation without your permission, or when you sold off their husbands, wives or children. They were better off when you raped their women. They were better off working for you from dawn to dusk in a gang until they died young before their time."

Manford said, "Well, what's done is done. You boys can stay for a couple days if Joe needs some time. I'll ask John Drish to have the servants prepare some rooms for you."

David responded, "If it's all the same to you, we'll stay in the barn with the horses tonight. I prefer the company."

Manford snuffed, "As you wish."

As he began to walk away, he looked back at David and said, "I forgot to tell ya. When Josena come here, she was light with child. We didn't know it 'til a few months later when she had a little picaninny girl. After Josena was kilt, John Drish sold the child off to a gentleman in Mobile as a house servant."

David decided that this would be too much to tell Joe right then, so he kept it to himself.

That night David had a chance to talk to Joe. As a loner, he had never felt adequate or comfortable in conversations like the one he needed to have with him. It was especially difficult seeing Joe so totally overcome with emotions of disbelief, anguish, grief, bitterness, anger and even loneliness.

He tried to begin by saying, "Joe, I am so sorry about Josena. It was a complete shock. I know there is a burning hole in your heart right now. I know it will never heal and go away completely, but I think in time it will get better."

Joe didn't look up or respond.

David had seen so many he loved die.

His thoughts formed more clearly and, full of rare passionate emotion, he continued, "Joe, hear me now. The feeling of love lives, but maybe it's like the ocean, full of conflict, full of pain. Sometimes it's for holding on and sometimes you must let go. Your love will never be lost. Your memories of love will always be of her. Let go now Joe. You must live."

Inexplicably, David's poetic soul had emerged to help his friend, but rarely, if ever, was it a help to himself.

Joe looked up at him, his face so full of pain, and said, "Thank you David. I will let go but never forget. I just hate men like Taylor and Manford for the power they have over us and what they can get away with."

David agreed and said, "I understand. I have always hated men like that too, and for the same reason."

But David had dealt with trouble before. The next morning Josiah and David rode out of the barn on two horses.

Manford saw them and shouted, "Hey, where are you going?" David shouted back "North."

Seeing them getting away with the horses, Manford picked up his shotgun he always kept nearby. He fired both barrels over their heads. David drew his Colt revolver and shot Manford. The 44 caliber bullet struck him in the abdomen.

Joe shouted, "That gut shot should take about two hours to kill you."

Penelope's betrayal had been avenged, but her life could not be restored. It was an unchangeable finality.

They rode north toward Tennessee. Neither of them would see the Deep South again.

Twelve - Heading North

They rode their horses hard like two men in a hurry and on a mission. But they had nowhere to go and their purpose was to put the Deep South farther behind them. As fatigue set in, they stood up on their stirrups, holding onto the pommels, to ease their saddle soreness. They rested their horses in small towns where they could get them feed, water and livery. Up along the Tennessee River, they came to Shiloh.

Tennessee was a slave state but was pro-Union before the war. It was the last state to join the Confederacy. During the early part of the war, Grant had moved into southwestern Tennessee along the Tennessee River and fought at the battle of Shiloh, or the battle of Pittsburg Landing, on April 6-7, 1862. It was the beginning of his western campaign to gain control of the Mississippi River and valleys to the south. In the end, the Confederates were forced to retreat and Grant was victorious. But like many of his victories, casualties were very high.

The cities and capital in the east had no idea of the magnitude of the battle to come or the loss to follow. They were concentrating on the eastern theater in Virginia nearer by. The newspapers didn't report the scope of it beforehand or the extremity of it thereafter. There were virtually no photographers on hand to take pictures of the aftermath. But it was going to be a monumental confrontation with over 110,000 men engaged. The infantry was enhanced by an assembly of the greatest artillery heretofore.

With Grant's plan to gain control of the all-important Mississippi, cut the Confederacy in half and prohibit its use of the river to supply the South, he started north on the Tennessee. Two great armies formed there just north of the Tennessee - Kentucky border. The Confederates had two forts to protect the strategic area at the point where the Tennessee and the Cumberland pass close to each other flowing northward out of Tennessee. With the aid of Andrew Foote's Federal ironclad gunboats, Grant and his forces bombarded Fort Henry, won an easy victory and Confederate commander Lloyd Tilghman surrendered. Fort Donaldson was more difficult but was also defeated. Confederate General Albert Johnston had reinforced it; but Grant defeated him.

The next objective was Nashville. Johnston decided to abandon Nashville, retrench southward and hold the Confederate defense at Murfreesboro. Grant confronted him there and was successful.

With these Confederate defeats as precursors, the Federal and Confederate forces met together for the monumental battle at Pittsburg Landing near Shiloh Church. There the two armies resolved to face each other in full force.

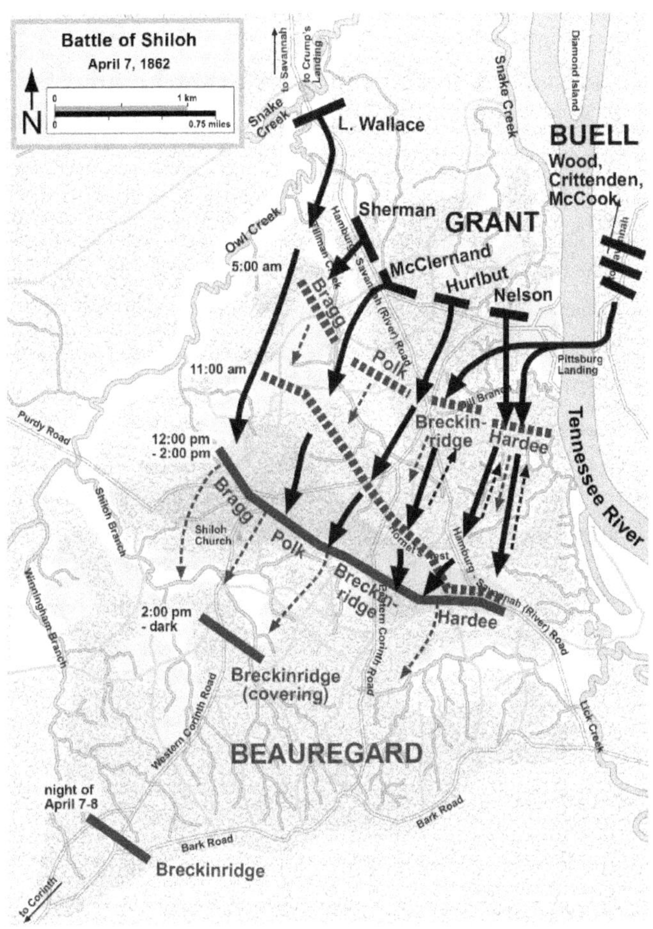

Grant's Army of the Tennessee was supported by Don Carlos Buell's Army of the Ohio, William T. Sherman and other generals.

William Tecumseh Sherman was born in 1820 in Ohio and was appointed to the West Point Military Academy as a 16-year-old in order to graduate in 1840. Ulysses S. Grant graduated from the Point just later in 1843. Sherman and Grant became friends and Cump served under him in the Civil War. Together they brought the war to its conclusion with Grant's final efforts in Virginia and Sherman's in Tennessee, Georgia and South Carolina.

The Battle of Shiloh was Sherman's first major test under Grant. He was reckless and unprepared but managed to rally his division and conduct an orderly, fighting retreat that helped avert a disastrous Union rout.

Finding Grant at the end of the day sitting under an oak tree in the darkness and smoking a cigar, Sherman felt some wise and sudden instinct not to mention retreat.

In what would become one of the most notable conversations of the war, Sherman said simply: "Well, Grant, we've had the devil's own day, haven't we?"

After a puff of his cigar, Grant replied calmly: "Yes. Lick 'em tomorrow, though."

His performance was praised by Grant and Halleck and, after the battle, he was promoted to major general of volunteers, effective May 1, 1862.

They shared a common persecution from the newspaper reporters who referred to Grant as a drunk and Sherman as a lunatic. Sherman and Grant both had a longstanding addiction to cigar smoking. It is not known who smoked the most in a day but it is believed that they each smoked twenty of them. Grant maintained a trunk full of cigars in the tent of his many field command headquarters throughout the war.

Grant and Sherman shared a field headquarters at one point in the war and Grant saved Sherman embarrassment by meeting him out in the woods on horseback for informal military strategy meetings. Grant would sit on his horse and observe field movements from the high ground with Sherman's company. On those occasions they sat in the rain, Grant would become irritable when the cigars he kept in his pocket became soaked and couldn't be lit. Cump would have the presence of mind to remain silent.

At Shiloh, Grant met Johnston's Army of the Mississippi, who was replaced after his death by P.G.T. Beauregard. The Confederates were under-manned, ill-equipped but resolute. The confrontation was devastating. The carnage after two days was nearly 24,000 dead, wounded or missing. The Union killed and wounded were over 10,000. The Confederate killed or wounded were a little less. The captured or missing on both sides were nearly 4,000.

As for the accolades and blame and shame among the Union leaders, the debate raged. Who were the winners and who were the losers? Who could claim victory and who made critical errors? This would be a problem that would eventually be resolved later in the war. Grant would prevail and emerge as the leader and winner despite his antagonists.

But as the battle of Pittsburgh Landing approached, Grant was plagued with the idea that his superior, General Henry Halleck, was always scrutinizing him, hated him, and would find a way to destroy his career. He hoped there would come a time when Halleck would stretch the belief in his own magnificence too far. Maybe Lincoln would see that Halleck led armies from behind his desk in his headquarters and decide to demote him.

This was the last war where men would line up in wide columns, face each other across an open field, and mow each other down in volleys. They would fall in alternating waves as each side reloaded their muzzle loaded rifles after expending them with a single shot at the other side. This was the old Napoleonic traditional way taught at the Point. But with modern repeating weapons, this was foolhardy and certain death with no honor. Their rifled barrels were more accurate than the smooth bore muskets no longer used since the Mexican War. Lee would listen to Longstreet and be the first to begin to use fortification and trench defensive warfare.

Joe and David met some local people in town while stabling their horses. A man told them that the battle had been the bloodiest of any up to its time. For Joe, the sight of the abandoned fields and graves was surreal. It was foreign to his experience since he had been isolated at Savannah Oaks during the war.

For David, all the memories of his battles came flooding back - Antietam in Maryland, Battle of the Wilderness in Virginia and others.

He thought, 'So many young men had risen, dressed and eaten that morning. They had run bravely into battle and then they were gone. Every moment of their lives was reduced to that single misfortune. Only the dead have seen the end of war.' His mind was overwhelmed, his heart sickened.

As silent unnoticed tears streamed down David's face, Joe began to gain a deeper understanding for what the horrors of the war had meant to his friend. David was quiet and withdrawn.

David looked up at Joe and said, "My God, this was happening three years ago here in April of the same year I was fighting back east at Antietam in September. We were killing each other everywhere."

Joe wanted to help but wasn't sure how. David kept everything inside. He wondered whether, just as David had helped him deal with the knowledge of Josie's death, he would be able to help David deal with his pain and suffering. But it wasn't in his nature to share his feelings. David had always relied on his journal as an outlet for his deep and sometimes dark troubled thoughts.

Just as he had done for him, Josiah reached out a hand to his friend's shoulder to offer comfort. Suddenly for David, it was as if the dam inside him broke. He found himself sharing with Josiah all the memories that were flooding his mind as he stood there.

He remembered Antietam in '62 and the long lines of the blue and the gray. He watched as so many fell and so many died. He saw the men thrown into the air and their bodies blown apart by the artillery. There was so much blood and so many bodies. At first they fell by the dozens. Finally they lay by the hundreds and the thousands. There was nothing noble or romantic about war for the men there.

He remembered hearing some of Lincoln's words spoken at Gettysburg, ".... that from these honored dead we take increased devotion to that cause for which they gave the last full measure of devotion - that we here resolve that these dead shall not have died in vain - that this nation, under God, shall have a new birth of freedom .... ."

When he finished talking, he wept silently for several minutes and then stared without expression across the field. He would never forget. The war was over, but the memories were fresh and raw. For the country, those memories were bitter and would last for generations.

While he had always understood to a degree the losses of those who had fought for his freedom, Joe now saw it closer and more personal. He understood that David and they had fought for his freedom. He would always respect and love him and them for that.

David understood that, at its deepest core, what it means to be human is the will to survive. A man's true character is his willingness to live. Without that, he will lay down and die.

He looked over at Joe, and thought about him. He thought about what Joe had been through, what he had suffered, and what he had lost. He thought about Joe's life in bondage and his loss of Josie. Yet Joe wanted to go on. He wanted to survive. He wanted to live.

"Do you want to stay here for a while David?"

"Just for this afternoon and tonight. Tomorrow we can head out."

With no plan in mind, they followed the Tennessee River north to Kentucky. They had been traveling since early morning. Yesterday had been a gut-wrenching, emotional trial for both of them.

In the lush farmland up along the Tennessee, they came to a secluded meadow grown up with alfalfa. Joe looked over at David and saw that his friend looked more worn and haggard than usual.

He called out, "Let's stop for a while and rest the horses."

"Sounds like a good idea Joe. They can graze for a while."

They dismounted and walked their horses by the reins toward the field.

"Let's take the saddles off so they can relax", David suggested.

There was a stand of willow trees along a stream back away from the road toward the field. They let the horses loose and filled their canteens with the cool water. They sat down, leaned against a willow and watched the horses drinking and splashing in the water - David's old dun mare, Joe's young bay roan cavorting in this peaceful place. As they sat there resting, with the sound of the stream gurgling in the background, a measure of peace settled on both of them from the respite and this place.

Joe said, "They got the right idea and that alfalfa will be good feed for them. They have earned it."

The horses came out of the stream and romped in the field while they ate their fill. The two friends rested quietly under the trees, lost in their own thoughts. After a while Joe took some hardtack out of his gunnysack and gave David a stick to gnaw on.

David noticed that Joe seemed to be a little sadder than usual. He asked him softly, "How are you feeling Joe?"

"I don't know for sure. Feels like it was me that was gut shot, not Manford."

"If you are feelin' guilty about him, you don't need to. He had it comin' when he shot at us with his shotgun", David replied.

"I guess so, but we can't blame him for all the troubles."

"You forgive too easy Joe."

Joe thought about it for a minute and explained, "I got to if I want to live with myself. The Lord gives me the strength and shows me what's best to do."

"Wish I had your faith. I cannot accept the authority or injustice of another. That gets in the way. That is just how I am. But life just keeps disappointing."

"How are you feeling about the war now, David?"

"I can't get all the pictures out of my head, especially after we saw the aftermath at Shiloh. It keeps comin' back, especially when I try to sleep. I try to write about it in my journal. That helps a little. Mostly I feel guilty since I survived and they didn't."

There didn't seem to be much more of anything to say, so both men just sat there with their private thoughts.

David wondered, 'Is faith in myself enough? Can I manage my burden alone? There are things beyond my understanding.'

Josiah thought, 'He can't see God as a help, only another authority he has to fight.'

"David, God loves us. If we can feel, we can love. If we can love, we can believe. He gets us started. Puts the Spirit there. At the end, He will bring us home."

David looked at him and smiled, remained silent.

Thirteen - Journey's End

They moved on and followed the Ohio River east. They traveled for a few days and both of them chose not to bring up talk of the war again. It was too painful for them and the wounds were still raw. They rode along and took a lighter road of conversation as David told Joe the exciting tales of his adventures at sea as a young man. He hoped that this would bring a smile to Joe's face and keep both their minds off all the painful memories.

They arrived in Covington late one afternoon. Joe spotted a boardinghouse and suggested they check in to bed down for the night. As they rode into town, the people in town looked at them askance. This wasn't the first time they had encountered this reaction. Two different looking men traveling together was not a usual sight, even in this area. But no one caused any trouble.

Joe and David were pleased to slow down and rest for a while. They stayed for two days to reconnoiter and regroup. The people became more friendly once they got to talk to them and know them a bit.

Joe and David were relaxing on the porch and looking at the lights of the big city across the Ohio. The reflections on the water were peaceful and somehow reassuring.

David said, "That's Cincinnati Joe."

"It looks exciting", he responded.

"Tomorrow we can go over and look around. It will be your first big city in the north. This will be as new an experience for you as my first visit to big cities in the South. I sure hope you like it."

Joe smiled, said "I think I will like it and look forward to it."

They sat quietly for a long time on the porch, with their feet on the railing, and watched the peaceful scene across the river. David was thinking about Joe's life and his own.

He looked at Joe's contented expression and said, "You know, a free man has to learn what it means to be himself. I'm still trying to figure that out myself."

Joe smiled at him and said, "It's all new to me, but I know what you mean. It's a great blessing to be able to do that and find out what it means for each of us as individuals. We will figure it out. What's best for each of us."

Troubled with guilt for holding back so long, David decided it was time to reveal the secret he had been keeping.

With a serious expression he said, "Joe, there's something I have to tell you. I couldn't do it until now because I didn't think you could bear any more. Back at Drish plantation, Manford told me that Josie had had a girl child a while after she arrived there."

Joe looked at him in shocked disbelief, cried out and sobbed, "Why didn't you tell me? That was my daughter. Where is she? We must find her."

David carefully replied, "He said they sold her off to a man in Mobile. I'm afraid she is long gone by now. We'll never find her Joe."

He waited quietly by his side. He knew there were no more words could be said to bring comfort. All he could do was be there as Josiah had been for him when friendship was most needed.

With a clarity of understanding and resignation Joe said, "Yeah, it's too late now for me to find her. But how can I forget her? I can never forget her. As much as my heart aches, I must find comfort in knowing that I have a daughter who was the result of my love for Josie. I can only pray that she will have the kind giving heart of her mother, and that God blesses her life."

"She will Joe, God knows she will."

The next morning they rode over the brand new suspension bridge and saw the cityscape of the city called the "Paris of America". The population was over 160,000 at the time, making it one of the largest cities in the country. The two men hitched their horses and took in the sights of the bustling city on foot. They saw the Music Hall, the Cincinnatian Hotel and the Shillito Department Store. They saw the Miami and Erie Canal completed in 1841 that originated from the Great Miami River.

Cincinnati had been the headquarters for the Department of the Ohio and a major source of supplies and troops for the Union during the war. However, it did participate in commerce with slave states and did have many southern sympathizers.

While they enjoyed their stay there, the city life had no lasting appeal for either of them. They made their way 50 miles north to the small hamlet of Hamilton. This place looked right to them - lots of space, beautiful land, and some friendly people.

After they arrived in Hamilton, they sought their opportunities and laid the groundwork to develop their own individual, separate lives. Together they sold their labor once again and pooled their savings. With this stake, Joe bought a small farm outside town.

David kept his horse in the barn there with Joe's. His dun mare died later that summer. They buried her on the back of Joe's property.

David got a place in town where he could keep a small apartment over his carpentry shop. They remained close friends and shared Sunday dinners every week at Joe's farm.

The general hardware store in Hamilton tried to carry everything the community needed. The owner would special order anything not on hand to better serve them. Joe frequented there often to purchase all his basic woodworking tools. He accumulated saws, block planes, chisels, wood scrapers, awls and drills. In a brief time, he outfitted a partition of his barn and established the Ashford Furniture Company.

After he opened his furniture business, his reputation quickly grew and his shop was always busy. His furniture was in great demand by the more affluent whites, freeborn blacks and newly prosperous freedman. He became known throughout the region for the unique artisanship, quality and durability of his products. His graceful chairs, tables and break-fronts became sought after. The unique carvings and finishes of Ashford pieces became his signature and hallmark.

His personal reputation grew with both black and white people in the area. He was held in high regard by everyone for his intelligence and optimistic forward-looking view. With his name and reputation for integrity so well known throughout his region, he was elected as the honorable congressman Josiah Ashford representing his local district for the Ohio state government. As a male property owner, he had legal qualification to vote and hold office. His life was busy and full with his growing business and his many newfound friendships.

He lovingly remembered Josena but was happy with his emergence from bondage and the direction of his life's trajectory. David remained his steadfast supporter and brother in the cause for justice.

Joe continued his lifelong learning process. He read less literature now, but read extensively in law, philosophy, economics and political science. He read Adam Smith, Lincoln, Frederick Douglass, de Tocqueville, Milton, Shakespeare and the Bible. He expressed his intellect externally - became a gifted orator crowds gathered to hear. His friend David expressed his intellect differently - internally with his private writing of poetry and observations of the human condition.

Joe attended the Baptist Church in Hamilton and became a member and an elder. He was a role model and leader for the freedmen. The congregation was mostly black freedmen, but included some freeborn Negroes and a few whites who felt no discomfort with the people and their worship. David often attended and enjoyed the working class people he had always gravitated toward.

By 1877, most of the post-war Reconstruction efforts had ceased in the South and state governments there had swept away most of the progress made by the 13th, 14th, and 15th amendments to the Constitution. In the North, steady progress was being made for social justice. The Republican party of Abraham Lincoln had continued to hold the Presidency throughout the post-war years of Reconstruction. Andrew Johnson, Ulysses Grant and Rutherford Hayes from Ohio each brought their personality to a moderate reform movement that met with some success in the North.

In his region, Joe was greatly admired by freeborn Negroes as a former slave and first generation freedman who displayed exceptional grit, achievement and character. In his case, they were able to set aside their view of superiority as freeborn Negroes. His fellow freedmen looked up to him as their leader and kinsman. Many whites put aside bigotry and saw him for the exceptional man that he was. He was well liked throughout southwestern Ohio and well accepted as their reliable man of dependable character to represent them in the Ohio state government.

Time passed. His bay roan had died and he buried him alongside David's. He bought a new, high-spirited young filly more suitable for a carriage than a saddle. Joe traveled to Columbus whenever the legislature was in session. On one return trip, he stopped in the hardware store to check the shelves to see if the dowel stock he had asked for had come in. He was still wearing his tweed suit, vest and tie from his trip.

His friend Roy was running the store and greeted him, "Hi Joe. How did the session go?"

Joe smiled and replied, "We're still talking about land sub-division requirements. I hope we get it settled soon."

Roy nodded and said, "Me too. A lotta newcomers are moving in and want to start small farms."

It was true. More Germans and Scots-Irish were coming from the east. Freedmen were coming from the South. They were all looking for their portion of the old, agrarian Jeffersonian American dream. The large landholders were selling off their vast holdings to new people trying to settle their lives and raise their families.

While they were discussing politics and conducting their business, an elegant young black woman came into the store looking for some cloth material to make new curtains. She was well dressed, prim and proper, and a refined lady.

She asked, "Roy, any new material come in this week?"

Roy said, "No, not yet. Mary, let me introduce you to Congressman Ashford. Joe, this is Mary Custis."

"Pleasure meeting you ma'am. Roy didn't mention my real job. I make custom furniture for the folks in the area."

"Do you mean Ashford furniture? Everybody has heard of that. Forgive me if I sound forward, but you must come visit my family. My father and mother would be honored to meet you as our congressman and good neighbor."

"Always a pleasure to meet the constituents, Mary. Sometimes new furniture customers too. Ha ha."

Mary Custis was the 3rd generation of freeborn Negroes descending from Martha Custis Washington's dowry slaves from Mount Vernon, Virginia. Unlike the freeman or freedman, their generations had never worn a slave collar. Her family had lived in Hamilton for years and was prominent and respected in the community.

This auspicious meeting in May 1868 between her and Josiah would change the direction of their lives.

Fourteen - Home

Mary and Josiah began a friendship which developed into a deep relationship. For Josiah, it was not the youthful passionate love he had felt for Josena during their bondage, but a free deeper lasting, mature love. She found Josiah to be a dear companion. They both shared fine minds with common interests in literature and philosophy. Mary had almost given up hope of finding a man like him.

In Mary, Josiah found a warm loving woman, not a young girl, but someone who was worldly, intelligent, with a humorous and witty nature that made life a joy for him. She was everything he could have wanted if he had written out a description.

In a short time, they were viewed in the eyes of the community as the couple to watch. Their marriage was a community affair attended by Josiah's friends from the state legislature, the freeborn Negroes from Mary's circles, and black and white farmers and merchants and professionals from the area. With Mary's best girlhood white friend as Maid-of-Honor and David as Best Man, the bridal party made a striking group.

They were family coming together for devotion and community. For all they had been through together, David and Josiah felt a love as brothers who had come home.

By August, southwestern Ohio usually had oppressive heat and humidity like the Deep South. But on their late spring June wedding day, the weather was a blessing. The sun shone brightly, the air was dry and comfortable, and soft billowy clouds drifted slowly across the blue sky. Gentle breezes ruffled the fresh leaves, while the sweet smell of wisteria entered and permeated the church.

The church was filled to capacity with friends and community. As the wedding march sounded on the organ, Mary came down the aisle on her father's arm. She wore a stylish white satin gown with a flowing train. Joe wore his finest white linen suit with black suspenders and black cravat, topped off by his best Sunday straw hat.

With David at his side, Josiah watched her come down the aisle. For a fleeting moment, he remembered that day long past when he and Josena had jumped over the broom and had their humble African marriage ceremony. But when he saw the smile on Mary's face, the memory quickly faded and he smiled back with moist eyes as he returned to the complete happiness of the present. As they joined hands to take their vows, he felt that he was the luckiest man in the world to have been blessed, to have found love again, with such a wonderful woman.

The reception at the town square lasted all afternoon with dining, dancing and joyful wishes from everyone in attendance. Mary's parents were thrilled that she had found a good, sound, truly Christian man to share her life with.

They renovated Joe's old farmhouse and converted it into a beautiful large country home just outside the town. Their home became something like an annex for the Ohio state capital in Columbus for the citizens of the Hamilton region. There were many political meetings and rallies there with Joe officiating and Mary entertaining. David would share his historical perspectives and experiences to contribute to the deliberations.

With their marriage settled in and their love deepened and grown, they pleasantly surprised their friends and community, when a year after their wedding, Mary gave birth to twins, a boy they named David and a girl they named Josena.

With his factory located on the farm property, Josiah's home-based business and success afforded him the opportunity to spend time with his children and actively participate in rearing them. Later, in his old age when they had moved on in the world, he would count this among his greatest blessings.

As time passed and the children grew, they listened to conversations at the dinner table and watched the adult meetings in the parlor from the staircase across the foyer. The household was always alive with guests and animated discussions.

Mary explained to them what it meant to be freeborn, just as she was and they were. She told them about the Revolutionary War and George Washington, the first President, and how his wife Martha Custis Washington owned her own slaves as part of her dowry. When they were freed upon her death, some of the Custis line of former slaves had moved west out into the Northwest Territory and ended up here in Ohio.

When Uncle David came to dinner, he told them about President Lincoln, the Civil War - the long four-year tragedy - required to preserve the Union and end slavery. They discussed the political events leading up to it and the southern argument of social Darwinism asserting the fundamental inferiority of Negroes to justify slavery.

David explained to them the distinction between slavery and racism, now that racism had increased with the parting of the slaveholders and the enslaved. Joe told his children what slavery had been like for him as a young man in Missouri under the task system, and later in Mississippi under the harsher gang system employed to grow short staple cotton. They both gave them the perspective of the clash of cultures and economics.

The children were eager and attentive students. They understood the sadness, loss and sacrifice that had been made to rid America of the sin and shame of slavery. They understood the bitterness that remained, and would remain for many years to come.

The Ashford home was awash with the ideas of the human spirit and the ideals of the American experience. Their father explained to them the distinction between the balanced concepts of social justice and civil rights versus individual responsibility, community service and societal obligation. The children would grow up grounded in the important values. They understood that their extended family had directly participated in - been directly a part of - so much American history.

Joe's business grew and the old barn would not do. He needed to build a larger building dedicated to just the Ashford Furniture Company. David helped him and, together as before, they accomplished their job. This time they built a magnificent factory. They outfitted the building with large work tables and wood clamps and fixtures to hold glued joints. They built racks for organizing wood storage. David brought innovation to the manufacturing process. He invented, designed and built machinery to plane wood surfaces and remove the unnecessary manual work that didn't affect the craftsmanship of the finished product.

Joe formed alliances with his suppliers - the saw mills in the region. He visited them personally to select the best woods for his furniture. He eventually hired a staff of twelve workers to look after the many manual labor and management tasks to keep up with the growth. Appreciating how fortunate he had been to have learned a skill as a slave, he felt a responsibility to help freedmen who came to the area seeking a new life. He hired and trained as many as he could as his furniture business grew. He discovered that he enjoyed teaching others much in the same way Ben had worked with him. He delegated a lot of the work but kept a vigilant eye on the quality to assure that his artistry did not get lost.

Joe had found a lasting satisfaction and a complete happiness grounded in love and family. His family prospered. The area where they lived did too. He was home.

With Joe's influence, young David and Josena were permitted to attend classes at Miami University of Ohio in 1889. They were not permitted to graduate, and it wasn't until 1906 that Nellie Craig graduated there as the first African-American.

Joe asked his daughter, "How are your studies at college coming along?"

Josie looked worried and wasn't sure how to say it but said, "Papa, Dave and I are doin' fine in our studies, but those white folks are only gonna let us take a few courses because you are the big congressman. They ain't gonna let us finish and graduate."

Joe, looking upset said, "Is that right honey? First of all, you need to learn how to speak properly if you expect to get ahead in this world. You meant to say 'Dave and I are doing fine' and 'the college administration won't let us finish and graduate.' Second, you should have come to me with this sooner. We'll look for another way to do this. There are other colleges. Go find Dave. We need to talk about this."

"OK Papa, I'll go get him. We talked to uncle David about this and he got angry at the university. He said we must come and tell you about it."

They held a family meeting to discuss college plans for the twins. Joe and Mary tried to give the young ones a fair ear, but made sure that they provided parental guidance to their young, immature, and sometimes impetuous, dear children. Uncle David was invited to give his perspective. They knew he cared deeply for the welfare of their children.

Joe offered his best idea for them. He told them about the new Oberlin College - founded in 1833 - up near Cleveland. It was a school with strong programs in music and theology, and with emphasis on all the humanities - English literature, the Roman and Greek classics, philosophy, sociology, anthropology, religion, history, government and political science. There, blacks and whites studied together, grounded in the classics and humanities, with unique opportunities available to study the ideas and writings of great leaders like Frederick Douglass and Abraham Lincoln, and to learn about social justice and new directions for civil rights.

Young Josie and Dave became encouraged and grew excited about this solution. It seemed to be the very best for them and their parents' wishes. They decided to transfer to Oberlin and set a course for a brighter new direction for their young lives.

From the earliest colonial days, even while the Revolutionary War was being fought, and long before mercantilism would be usurped by industrialization, the early American pioneers and settlers were pushing westward to establish their lives for themselves and their families. Thomas Jefferson recognized this and had a vision for an agrarian society of small independent farmers and landowners as property owners - the Jeffersonian yeoman freeholders - as the basis for the American dream.

In those days, Ohio was the western frontier and the earliest remote inland region to establish farms and a rural American society. The founders and framers of the Constitution wrote the Northwest Ordinance of 1787 as a model to define how all new territories would be established. As one of the founding documents, it defined the conditions under which territories would be sub-divided to become future states.

It was about the land - how it should be allocated, divided and owned - and how society should be governed. It determined that slavery would be prohibited in this and all future territories. It allotted land for educational use so that schools would be built. It required freedom of religious practice for its citizens. For the future of America's development, it was an all-important document.

In Josiah's time, the Ohio legislature would convene in early summer - between planting and harvesting - to deliberate matters of governance and law for the citizens of Ohio. Land use, and related matters, was still a political issue to be deliberated and resolved for them, their futures and their livelihood.

He drove to Columbus in his carriage for the main session each June. On some occasions he brought Mary and the children with him as a family trip and for the education of his son and daughter. His family was permitted to view the floor of the session from the visitors' gallery.

The speaker rapped his gavel and announced, "Order, order. Gentlemen, this session is hereby convened. We are called here today in our assembly to deliberate, decide and vote on Ohio senate bill SR403 passed by our esteemed colleagues in the Ohio senate. I call before you our esteemed colleague from the southwestern region, the Honorable Josiah Ashford, to present its matters before you."

The leader looked to his right at Josiah and raised his hand upward in his direction, "Congressman Ashford."

Josiah rose from his seat, walked to the podium and shook the speaker's hand. He looked out at the assembly, paused to look across the room and smiled. He stood bolt upright and with his left thumb in his suspenders and right hand raised in the air, spoke to his colleagues.

His face turned to its characteristic resolve as he spoke eloquently and clearly:

> "Speaker, esteemed colleagues, we find ourselves at a crucial moment. What we decide today will affect our constituents - our people, our citizens, our families - for the remainder of their lives and for the lives of their descendents to follow.
>
> The great Ordinance of 1787 gave us a plan and guidance to follow. It provided land for schools. The schools were built. But education has been left to us - the great state of Ohio to resolve for ourselves. Much has changed since then; much has run afoul. I will speak to you about that today. We have the opportunity, the authority and the responsibility to change that, correct that and rectify that."

The room was silent in rapt attention. He continued:

"The intent of our founders was clear. We would establish a great nation to the extent of its boundaries, not even known at that time, where free men would live their lives and prosper under the grace of God, as no nation had ever done before."

Loud cheers and applause broke out and drowned Josiah's words. The speaker rapped his gavel for several moments and spoke out, "Attention! Attention! Call to order!"

The room returned to silence and Josiah continued to speak:

"Many of our aspirations have come to pass to fulfill our original ideals. We have turned around the subversions of our southern fellow citizens with the sacrifice of the blood and treasure of our people. Abraham Lincoln brought us to that eventuality and shall ever be remembered for the salvation and redemption of our nation."

The room remained silent in anticipation. He continued:

"Today we have many laws establishing the rights of property owners and for our citizens to vote and hold public office. Our schools are flourishing, our children are benefitting from this, and our country is improving."

They waited for his next words:

"But there is more to be done. There is always more to be done. We will never achieve perfection, but we must strive for it, reach up for it, as Americans and God loving human beings.

We have before us SR403. It will guarantee equal access to higher education for all our children without regard to the color of their skin. It will be based on the content of their character and our character. Surely, honor and integrity will compel us to pass this as the right thing to do. I urge you to vote for it in the affirmative."

Applause broke out one last time as Josiah returned to his seat. Assembly bill SR403 was passed by a narrow margin. It ratified and finalized the senate bill that preceded it. Citizens of all races would attend Ohio's educational institutions. Mary and the children understood that Josiah had played an important part in this change. They were proud of him.

David benefited from the expansion of small farms in the Hamilton area also. The agriculture in Ohio was primarily based on wheat. This area, and the Midwest in general, was the "Old Wheat Belt". Other cash and subsistence crops were grown also - corn, rye, buckwheat, oats, barley, potatoes, meadow (feed grasses for animals), clover, sorghum, tobacco. The Miami Valley area especially grew tobacco as a precious cash crop.

The balance of subsistence and cash crops farming on small plots proved smarter than the agriculture in the South for its time. Huge agri-business corporations would come later and farther in the west.

David renovated the older farm buildings, built new houses and barns, and soon became the man to go to for the newcomers to the area. He studied architectural and mechanical engineering books and learned more about structures. He became a designer and self-educated architect. When the time was appropriate, he hired two workers to take over the heavy lifting and mundane tasks. He prospered too.

One gray Monday morning, David was in town to go to the hardware store for some supplies. He had stayed over at the farm after Sunday dinner with Joe, Mary and the young ones. He came into the store and saw Roy at the counter.

"Good mornin' Roy. Looks like some rain comin' later today."

"I expect so David. What brings you in today?"

"I need a keg of ten-penny nails if you got them."

"Yep. I do. Just a minute. I'll bring them in from out back."

David noticed two men outside on the street talking. He hadn't seen them before.

"Here you go David. That'll be $1.50."

"Thanks. Oh, I'll need a small, flat bastard file to sharpen my saw teeth too."

"That's another 50 cents."

David put the file in his pocket and hoisted up the heavy keg, hugging it to his chest. Roy said his goodbye and watched David go out the front door, still with his slight limp. David lifted the keg of nails into the back of his wagon. He looked over at the two men, thought they were farmers.

He walked over and said, "Good morning. Haven't seen you fellows before. I'm David Wexley."

The bigger man with the beard said, "Hello. I'm Jeremiah Johnston and this is Bill Wallis."

"Are you settling here and starting a farm?"

The smaller man said, "Oh no. We are from Buffalo, New York and just passing through, heading west."

David saw they were drifters like he had been much of his life.

He learned they were Union veterans and had fought in Virginia and the Carolinas. They sat down on the sidewalk bench and told each other their war stories. They learned that the three of them had fought at Antietam that day.

Bill told him, "Jeremiah and I fought with the 4th New York Volunteers, 3rd Brigade, 3rd Division, 2nd Corps under Lieutenant Colonel John McGregor. We lost a lot of our boys that day at the Sunken Road when A. P. Hill drove us back."

David said, "We did too. I lost a good friend, Geoff Braxton when we charged over the Burnside Bridge. I had worked with him as a carpenter apprentice in Baltimore before the war. We signed up together and fought under General Burnside's command. I knew him a long time and we saw a lot together. It was brutal how fast we took casualties."

He surprised himself that he could talk about it so dispassionately now.

He was curious about what they intended to do now and asked, "What's your plan for out west, Bill?"

"We don't know for sure, but there is a lot going on out there and lots of opportunities since they finished the railroad in '69."

Jeremiah said, "They started the Pacific railroad in '63 while we were all still fighting the war. Now you can link up to it in Iowa and go all the way to California."

It was true. The new transcontinental railroad was built to connect the end of the eastern railroad in Council Bluffs, Iowa and Omaha, Nebraska on the Missouri River to Sacramento, California. The project began at each end by two working crews and met at Promontory Summit in Utah to drive in the last spike, uniting the two halves, the Union Pacific Railroad and the Central Pacific Railroad, together. A railroad bridge was completed across the Missouri to finalize the connection in 1873.

David asked Jeremiah again, "Where are you planning to go and what will you do out there?"

He answered, "We might go to Colorado and work construction or mining. If that doesn't pan out, we'll head farther west and see what opportunities there are on the Pacific coast in California or Oregon."

David said, "Well it was good to meet you fellas and I wish you best of luck with your adventure."

This encounter with Jeremiah and Bill was intriguing to David. He missed the days when he had wandered and explored the country. He enjoyed meeting regular people and hearing about their experiences. But he was settled in Ohio and his life was peaceful. There was a freedom in this life too. Even with this newfound peace and freedom, his thoughts often drifted back to the troubled past.

Journal entry, October 12, 1879-

We were told, and we all believed, the war was just a rebellion and we would lick them and end it in a month or two. None of us knew how long it would last or the price we would pay. My view of slaveholders has not changed, nor will it ever do so. It is a good thing that the sin of slavery has been wiped away from our country forever. But I have learned, as I have always believed, that the poor whites in the South fought us as an invading force intent on burning down their farms and killing them. I can never blame them for fighting for their survival. It is a shame that they are forgotten in all the passions and death of those horrible times.

But finally, at last I have learned something of love - what it means to know and understand another human being and a tolerance for many, to care and put the other above you, beyond you, in place of you. This is God's grace and his plan.

He gained the respect of the community and formed many friendships with working-class people - black and white - with whom he had always felt a kinship. But he never had the good fortune to have a family.

Fifteen - Love Lost

During the late 19th century in Hamilton, Ohio, race relations were tentative but tolerable. There were no laws explicitly requiring segregation, but the community of small family farms formed a natural separation of the races. They kept to themselves and the area was generally peaceful. The races didn't mix and miscegenation was considered a deeper sin than incest. As a carryover from the abuses of slaveholders toward their black female property in the past, black people didn't take kindly to interracial marriage or sexual relations. Whites looked down on it as well based on their prejudices. It happened occasionally, but rarely, and was severely discouraged as a taboo by both races.

In town, blacks and whites traded in the same stores and ate at the same taverns, but worshipped in their separate churches. With some exceptions, parents naturally aligned their children in racially divided schools.

David worked and moved freely throughout both communities. He and his small crew built barns, farm houses and out-buildings for black families and white families. His foundation and framing carpenter John was white. His finish carpenter Sam was black. He was well liked and accepted by all his customers. They understood his views of tolerance and deep friendship with Josiah.

He and his men - John and Sam - were often invited to share a meal with the families he served on their farms. It was traditional for farm people to take their mid-day meal as the main meal for the day and as a long break from their work.

David met Estelle. The Culpeppers were a kindly and outgoing family and enjoyed the company and friendship of David when they contracted him repeatedly to help them expand their prosperous farm. Jim and Lucy Culpepper had three grown children - a daughter and two sons. Estelle was the oldest and well along toward spinsterhood. She was a beautiful and serene black woman with a quiet grace that attracted all that knew her.

Estelle and David felt a mutual attraction. She often watched him directing and working with his men as they erected new buildings. She saw the goodness in David and his strong spirit of justice in the treatment of people. She knew about his reputation and how much he was respected in the area.

She brought David and his men a pail of cool water on hot afternoons. It was a good reason to see him and they both looked forward to spending a few moments together. After their refreshment, she often stayed a while longer, hoping he might glance over her way and give her a smile.

David and Estelle talked about the crops and the weather and eventually the deeper things. They talked about the human things - kindness, forgiveness, acceptance and love. And they spoke of the spiritual things like God's grace and forbearance. They shared an intellectual view of life with the human heart as its source. They had not found this in the others in their lives. They fell in love.

He told her about his childhood in Baltimore and his time as a sailor. He told her about the horrors of the war and the friends he had lost. He told her about meeting Josiah, their long journey together and their long friendship.

She told him about her family and how grateful she was to be freeborn and raised in the North. Life had been good for her growing up in Hamilton. Sometimes though, it was lonely on the farm. They both had been lonely.

He took time from work and they walked across the fields into the meadows and to the forest at the end of the Culpepper property. Sometimes they met in their secret meadow away from all people, alone together in their enchanted place and time. Their lovemaking was gentle and giving with care for the other. Estelle caressed David's disfigured leg and looked through his eyes into his heart.

But this happiness was not to last. When Jim Culpepper learned of their relationship, he was upset. He ordered David to leave his property; to just gather his tools and his men and to go away immediately and never come back. This time David chose to not fight, but to comply. He believed it was best for Estelle and everyone else to obey her father's wishes.

With resignation, he stood in the pouring rain outside the barn and watched Estelle standing across the barnyard. The downpour soaked them both and it was difficult to see each other's faces. The rain made invisible the tears on David's face.

He stared at her across the yard with a pained smile and said, "I love you."

From that distance she could not hear his voice but understood the words and the expression on his face.

She answered back, "I love you", and David understood.

The love affair had caused no commotion in the community and David continued his work as before. He knew Estelle was a once-in-a-lifetime woman and would always be the irreplaceable love of his life. His bright hope had been dashed and he grew despondent.

Whenever Josiah was not around to look after him, David spent his free time in the tavern. Whiskey became his solace and helped him to sleep at night. He drank too much. Too many nights he staggered back to his bed from the tavern. His men tried to talk to him and change his new destructive behavior.

Josiah knew what had happened and tried to bring David around. He was troubled that his best friend was falling in a downward spiral and might not survive it. He brought David to church with his family and hoped David would re-connect with them and take interest in young Josie and David as he had in the past.

David spent his evenings in the tavern and spent time with Jeremiah Johnston and Bill Wallis he had met on the street some weeks before. They had both come from Buffalo and continued to stay in Hamilton for a time. It reminded David of his nights in Baltimore before the war - before the age of innocence had ended. But like a firefly escaping his grasp, innocence had long ago escaped and could never be caught again.

Jeremiah and Bill told David they still planned to head west and would be leaving soon. They had decided by now they would split up, go in different directions and pursue different opportunities. Jeremiah told him he would head for Texas. Bill would go to Colorado. They promised to write David and keep him informed of their experiences and fortunes.

Jeremiah found east Texas an extension of the old Deep South but with promising differences. Cotton production was booming under large agriculture corporations with free labor. Galveston was growing as a new port to the Gulf of Mexico. The state was expansive and optimistic. A feeling of freedom was prevalent in this post-war economic boom. Opportunities were bountiful, with unanticipated new ones to come, for adventurous men of all ages and skills moving into the area.

Bill found the silver mining in Colorado to be a frantic rush, almost a panic, to find riches. Men were pouring into the area at a phenomenal rate as land was staked out and new mines were beginning every week. Towns were sprouting up from nowhere and people were moving in to service the boom. Bars, brothels, banks, assayers, livery and heavy machine equipment suppliers all benefitted from the insanity. Often they were the best winners. Law and order would come later. For now, it was a dangerous and wide-open place. Men had to have the skills to handle trouble on their own as it surely would come.

The Comstock Lode was discovered in 1859 and news of its discovery had set off the whole mad rush fueled by the insane thirst for quick riches. San Francisco had accumulated great wealth from the enterprise and California was growing faster than any area in America. Later in 1879, silver had been discovered in Colorado. It was exciting to work there in any capacity.

David heard from Jeremiah and Bill and thought, 'I wonder about Colorado. Maybe it's time for a fresh start.' He considered it for several weeks and became obsessed thinking about it and weighing it against his settled life in Ohio. He had so many friends here and knew what to expect for the future. But his life was static and maybe at a dead end. It would be painful to live here near Estelle and not be with her.

Finally he decided to talk to Josiah.

Joe told him, "David, it's not practical or a wise move for you, especially at your age. You have a good life here with many friends and people who care about you."

David thought and said, "I know it Joe. But I'm living on the sidelines here. You have fulfilled all your dreams and, with your life's work, you now are enjoying it's fruits. I cannot live my life as just a spectator watching you and Mary and young Josie and David from the sidelines. It isn't enough."

He sold off his tools and equipment to John and Sam, said his goodbyes to everyone who mattered and, with his savings, took the railroad to Colorado. He went to work in mine safety construction. After a year, he had established himself as an engineer and architect with a crew working for him.

Mining for silver required blasting and digging to the fault line where the rich vein of the valuable mineral resided. The underground mines needed heavy support structure to maintain the access and safety of the tunnels to the working face deep within them. David and his crew built these heavy wooden beam supports. The work was lucrative and kept them busy.

There was no danger of fire in silver mining from explosive gases like the methane deposits so lethal in coal mining. But in 1900, there was a crisis at the mine David was servicing. A charge had been set off at the working face and the fault line shifted. The workers waiting outside heard the deep rumble after the planned explosion. The ground shook and a thick plume of gray stone dust poured out of the entrance.

After the movement had settled, David and his crew ran into the mine to check the shoring structure and make certain the roof had not collapsed. There was an aftershock at the face and the ceiling fell in behind them, trapping them inside. For three days crews dug through the rubble deeper into the mine until they found the crew. It was for naught. David and his crew had been killed instantly from the falling rock during the aftershock. Life is difficult and sometimes ends abruptly and unexpectedly.

As a matter of policy, all workers on the site had filed a Last Will and Testament with the mining company headquarters. Since he had no family, his had been very simple. It instructed that all his money and possessions would go to Josiah Ashford or his heirs in Hamilton, Ohio and that Josiah Ashford was to be executor to the will. He further requested that upon his death, subsequent to any local memorial service that might be given, his body was to be sent by railroad to Hamilton, Ohio and buried near the plots allocated for the Ashford family. Finally, he wished to have identified on his grave marker or tombstone that he was a veteran of the Civil War and served with Baltimore's Light Guard Infantry.

The Wexley male line ended, and left no heirs, with the passing of Morgan and David. The Ashton male line continued from Josiah to David and to his children.

Two ordinary men had borne great hardship and suffered extraordinary tragedy. Life was difficult, but both had survived. One had risen above it and managed to find home and happiness. One had not. Both had achieved a greatness; their lives mattered and made a difference to others.

Ultimately, they had lived their lives, and did what they did, as free men. And free men they were.

Epilogue

The one constant in life is that it brings changes. America was changing. After more than 20 years in one place, David had again grown restless and felt the pull of wanderlust. In 1887, when he was 55 years old, he needed to find things new - places, opportunities, life - once again. He had heard that men were mining silver in Colorado and that there were great opportunities in a place called Aspen. He needed to go West to see it for himself. This time he would go alone.

He had packed his old blanket roll and gunnysack. Joe went with him as far as Cincinnati. David took the railroad west to Colorado. He would remain in the West for the rest of his days.

On the day they parted, they clasped forearms in the old Roman way as men do that have great respect, admiration and affection for one another.

With his expression so typically formed with resolve, Joe had said, "I will never forget you. We have shared together so much of our lives. I will think of you always. God speed and be well my brother."

David smiled and with moist eyes, had said his last words to him, "You know me better than anyone in my life. You know I have to go. I will think about you and wish you were with me for all the new things I will discover and do. You are the best friend I have ever known and I will miss you the rest of my days."

David would remember the lessons of humanity he had learned from Josiah. He knew that for the human spirit to be human, it must be free. He died near Aspen the summer of 1900. His body was brought back to Hamilton and the Civil War Society placed a fresh

American flag next to his grave marker every year to honor his service.

Josiah knew that because of David, there was hope for free men to live in harmony. David had fought for his people but even more important, he had fought for him. He had kept the last poem David had written and sent him before his death. He read it at David's graveside memorial service.

Josiah died later in 1906 and was buried next to him in the Hamilton cemetery. At his funeral, David Ashford gave the eulogy and spoke of his father's life and the road he had helped pave for a better America - one that would someday realize its ideals. He told them how Josiah Ashford had chosen his given name - from a lifelong friend who supported him, defended him, loved him and helped him pave that road for justice. It was forty years ago.

The times of their lives were powerful and taught them life's most important lesson. David and Josiah learned that man is a sentient being above the beasts and below the angels. They learned from their individual lives and from each other that there are, and always will be, good men and bad men on the earth, but there is great value in good men finding each other and being together "by the better angels of our nature".

After Bondage and War

From David- For Josiah and others I have loved; I have made my peace-

I've known enough days now; I fear if I know more,

I'll become disenchanted with the ones I've known before.

So now in summertime, In summer time, I'd like to go;

While there's still sun enough,

I want to go in summertime, in summertime, in summertime.

To die in silence, without a single sound,

To touch the earth as gently as a dead leaf, when it hits the ground.

To leave behind a mem'ry soft as summertime,
For those one loves and has to leave behind.

To fold as softly as the grass blades fold,

When wild things trample them on mornings damp and cold.

To leave behind a fragrance, carried on the wind
for those one loves and will never see again.

To die in summertime, or not die at all,

While I'm still running,

While I'm still running forward,

While I still own my own mind,

I want to go in summertime.

To Die in Summertime - Rod McKuen

end

Acknowledgments

All of us are the product of our times and experiences. We see the history we live in and that our lives have phases. We learn and grow under the watchful eyes of our parents and learn the facts and ideas of the world from our teachers. We learn the skills to make a living and provide for ourselves on our own. We marry, raise our children and watch them grow, and learn, and go out, and forward the same as we.

I am grateful to my parents, teachers, and my loving wives. I am proud of my children and the lives they have made for themselves. After seven decades of life, I thought it was time to put down the mantle, relish my remaining time, and enjoy the fruits and blessings life has brought me.

Sometimes life can take unexpected turns, open unexpected doors, and bring new self-discovery. It can happen at any time and surprise us. I have always gravitated toward younger people as my friends and co-workers, especially more so as the decades have rolled on. There are two who have inspired and have come along at this twilight juncture. There are two more who have cared and helped, one who stands close by and one appearing from the distant past.

Thank you Abraham, my African son, for teaching me what it means to be human. Thank you for your lessons of courage, resilience of the human spirit, perseverance and faith.

Thank you Jim, my passionate teacher. You are my professor, but I call you teacher for its higher meaning. I have known a lot of the facts for many years, but you have opened my eyes to the meanings. You taught me to feel history. Thank you for awakening my passion for learning and igniting my love for history and writing.

The ideas are planted now and need to grow, mature, and be harvested.

Thank you Nick, my literary and insightful son. You have been with me every step of the way; patiently reading it all, discussing it all, analyzing it all, and the sounding board for the important ideas.

Thank you Joan. As my old friend, so long far way, you have appeared back in my life when I needed you most. As a teacher of teachers, I couldn't have hoped for a better mentor, editor and partner. You believed. Your generous words were your gifts to me. I understand you now. Your words - words of writing, words of ideas, words of encouragement - were gifts of love and friendship. Your gifts made a poor book a good one. You brought me the last mile.

Author's Comments

Writing narrative is easy. It flows along like a river. Writing dialogue is more challenging. It requires knowing your characters intimately, how they think, and what they care about. The visuals of the settings and the story action attract the mind, but in the end, the characters capture the heart. It is more accurate to say that my characters revealed themselves to me, rather than that I created them. They often surprised me and I learned important things from them. For its writer, a book can be a catharsis, with teaching moments that test the truths and falsehoods of his beliefs. Hopefully, this will inform the reader in this same manner.

The storyline is centered around 1865. Some historical events were described with detail to build drama. Others were merely alluded to in passing since they would be familiar to readers. The story portrays the power of friendship in deeply troubled times. It is a blend of political, military and social histories and uses fictional characters to tell the story, with historical figures to provide the backdrop.

I visited Andersonville in 1987 and never forgot the sadness I felt there. The village and prison camp are an historic site. At present, the long rows of graves are arranged neatly and marked with aged alabaster stones spread across a beautiful green field for visitors to reflect upon. Many have names with dates of birth. The dates of their deaths were all within a year of each other.

The village and site are near Oglethorpe, Americus and Plains - the home of former President Jimmy Carter. His home is a modest ranch house and the old railroad station is a museum for his early campaigning. The area is rural, very poor and desolate. It leaves a northerner with a feeling of what the old South must have been like after the Civil War.

There were three groups of people affected by the Civil War and reconstruction in the South. Like my character, David Wexley, I too have inexplicable feelings about the South; an inexplicable attraction that is appealing, melancholy and conflictive. Part of it is my Scots-Irish heritage and its manifestations in the poor whites of the South. Part of it is my bond with, and love for, my friend Abraham and his strength of character and great heart. Most of it is the lessons of humanity and inhumanity so vividly taught there.

I wanted to write about the old verities. I chose the context I understand best to illustrate them. This historical fictional work has depicted our American tragedy, during the most powerful period of our history, surmounting our greatest challenge, with triumph over horrific circumstances affecting the lives of all our American people. In the end, the book is about hope. All of life comes to that conclusion and finality.

Influential References

Webb, James, *Born Fighting - How the Scots-Irish Shaped America*, New York: Broadway Books, 2004 - eISBN: 978-0-7679-2295-1, v3.0

Foner, Eric, *Reconstruction America's Unfinished Revolution, 1863-1877*, New York: Harper & Row, 1988 - ISBN: 978-0-06-093716-4

Stowe, Harriet Beecher, *Uncle Tom's Cabin or Life Among the Lowly*, University of Oxford Text Archive, 1852

Jakes, John, *North and South, Part I*, New York: Penguin Putnam, 1982 - ISBN: 0-451-20081-0

Cornwell, Bernard, *The Bloody Ground, The Nathaniel Starbuck Chronicles, Book Four, Battle of Antietam, 1862*, New York: Harper Collins, 1996 - ISBN: 0-06-093719-X

Shaara, Jeff, *The Last Full Measure*, New York: Ballantine Publishing, 1998 - ISBN: 0-345-40491-2

Shaara, Jeff, *A Blaze of Glory, A Novel of the Battle of Shiloh*, New York: Random House, 2012 - ISBN: 978-0-345-52735-6

Reasoner, James, *Shenandoah, Book 8, The Civil War Battle Series*, Nashville: Cumberland House, 2002 - ISBN: 1-58182-294-4

Hackman, Gene and Daniel Lenihan, *Escape From Andersonville, A Novel of the Civil War*, New York: St. Martin's Press, 2008 - ISBN-13: 978-0-312-36373-4, ISBN-10: 0-312-36373-7

MacDonald, John, *Great Battles of the Civil War*, New York: Chartwell Books, Inc., 2014 - ISBN: 10:0-7858-3095-2, ISBN: 13:978-0-7858-3095-5

Knauer, Kelly (editor/writer), *The Civil War - The Final Year*, New York: Time Books, 2014 forward by Jeff Shaara

Grahame-Smith, Seth, *Abraham Lincoln: Vampire Killer*, New York: Grand Central Publishing, 2010 - ISBN: 978-14555-1018-4

Faulkner, William, *Absalom, Absalom!*, New York: Random House, 1936 - ISBN 978-0-679-73218-1

The poetry and tender heart of Rod McKuen, the courage and fortitude of Nelson Mandela, the grit and forceful character of Theodore Roosevelt

Fictional Characters

The Protagonists-

Josiah Ashford - slave and freedman, Savannah Oaks plantation

David Wexley - northern Union soldier from Baltimore

The Antagonists-

Marcus Taylor - Savannah Oaks plantation owner and slaveholder

John Manford - Drish plantation overseer

Supporting Cast in order of appearance-

Hendrick Taylor - Marcus's father

Jane Taylor - Marcus's mother

Marcy and Constance Taylor - Marcus's sisters

Benjamin - Plantation overseer, Savannah Oaks

Ned - Slave carpenter, Savannah Oaks plantation

Rebecca Stanley Taylor - Marcus's wife, Charleston southern belle

William and Francis Stanley - Rebecca's brothers

Josena Taylor Ashford - Josiah's wife and a slave, Savannah Oaks and Drish plantations

Morgan Wexley - David's father

Geoff Braxton - Master carpenter, Union soldier from Baltimore

Patrick Allister - Union soldier from Massachusetts

Mary Custis Ashford - Josiah's 2nd wife

David Custis Ashford, Josena Custis Ashford - Josiah's children

Jeremiah Johnston - Drifter, Union soldier from Buffalo

Bill Wallis - Drifter, Union soldier from Buffalo

Jim and Lucy Culpepper - Freeborn Ohio farmers

Estelle Culpepper - Daughter

Historical Characters

The Union-

U.S. Grant - Union Lieutenant General

George McClellan, Union Major General

Henry Halleck, Union Major General

Ambrose Burnside, Union Major General

William T. Sherman - Union Major General

Philip H. (Little Phil) Sheridan - Union General

George Meade, Union Major General

The Confederacy-

Robert E. Lee - Confederate Brigadier General

Thomas J. (Stonewall) Jackson - Confederate Lieutenant General

A.P. Hill - Confederate Major, Brigadier and Lieutenant General

James Longstreet - Confederate Lieutenant General

P.G.T. Beauregard - Confederate General

J.E.B. (Beauty) Stuart - Confederate Major General

Albert Johnston - Confederate General

The Politicians-

Abraham Lincoln - U.S. President

John C. Calhoun - South Carolina U.S. House of Representatives and U.S. Senator, U.S. Secretary of War, U.S. Secretary of State, U.S. Vice President

John Crittenden - Kentucky Governor, U.S. House of Representatives and U.S. Senator, U.S. Attorney General

Stephen Douglas - Illinois U.S. House of Representatives and U.S. Senator

Henry Clay - Kentucky U.S. House of Representatives, Speaker, U. S. Secretary of State

The Slaveholders-

John Drish - Owner Drish plantation near Tuscaloosa, Alabama

Locations

Savannah, Georgia - place of Marcus Taylor's birth

Charleston, South Carolina - place of Rebecca Stanley's birth

Atlanta, Georgia - Confederate city destroyed by Sherman

Natchez, Mississippi - port near Savannah Oaks Plantation

Mobile, Alabama - Gulf port site of Union occupancy

Demopolis, Alabama - Freedmen's Bureau assistance center

Tuscaloosa, Alabama - John Drish Plantation

McComb, Mississippi - town developed near Savannah Oaks

Baltimore, Maryland - place of David Wexley's birth

Sharpsburg, Maryland - Battle of Antietam

The Wilderness, Virginia - Battle near Richmond

Richmond, Virginia - Capital of the Confederacy

Andersonville, Georgia - Prison camp for Union soldiers

Shiloh, Tennessee - Battle of Pittsburg Landing

Covington, Kentucky - city across Ohio River from Cincinnati

Cincinnati, Ohio - large city north of Ohio River

Hamilton, Ohio - small farm community near Cincinnati

Aspen, Colorado - silver mining town out west

Part Two – Hanna's Promise

A Story of Grace and Hope

Contents

Prologue

Long after the cruel war had ended, the Deep South was reeling from its devastation. Its white people were struggling to find a way out of their loss. Its black people were struggling to make a different and better life of their own. The land and infrastructure were destroyed. In their agricultural based economy, cotton continued as their mainstay cash crop. But the world market was declining as other foreign competitors reduced America's share.

Slavery was abolished. African Americans would never wear a slave collar and chains on their ankles and wrists again. They would never be lashed with a whip for saying the wrong word or for trying to learn to read or for leaving the plantation without permission. Their families would not be broken apart and their wives and daughters would not be raped by the slaveholders ever again.

The Republican reformers – the carpetbaggers from the North and scalawags from within the South – were two of the same kind of thing. Both groups were trying to force change in the Southern politics of the Democrats there who were trying to recoup their glorious way of life and undo the defeat of their beloved lost cause. The Southern redeemers there were looking for state and local legislation to circumvent the new 13th, 14th, and 15th Constitutional changes - the so-called Civil War Amendments – while trying to be re-admitted to the government of the Yankees in the Union Federal government up in Washington DC.

Often their adventures were motivated for both good purpose and self-gain. Often for the carpetbaggers, their tools were mendacity and duplicity. Many of them sought graft and enrichment through government control. For the scalawags, especially the vocal ones, like even former Confederate General James Longstreet, their fellow white southerners viewed them as sellouts to their southernness and their great cause for their advocating the new Radical Republican ideas and changes for their country. The Civil War continued with words and politics. Some of the combatants had changed sides. While some lasting positive improvements in education resulted, it was mostly the result of rapid expansion of government services.

In the end, by 1877, they were threatened by the redeemers' violence and repulsed by the stronger southern Democrats. Reform was abandoned. The country once again looked toward the West. By the 1880's, the South fell into quiet desperation.

Share cropping and tenant farming provided something for the freedmen to survive. But they would be economically enslaved and join the poor whites in the meager, but best, agricultural system the South could devise. Bitterness, hatred and poverty would characterize the Deep South for generations to come. Racism would abound after the slaveholders and enslaved parted their ways. Laws would be passed to keep them separate and limit their freedom. But there were glimmers of hope for the races to live together in harmony.

The black Christian woman had come from Mobile, Alabama to McComb, Mississippi to care for the people and their children, keep their houses, and heal their ailing bodies and spirits. She was their Negress but she brought her faith and her love and it spread to those around her.

She was born in Tuscaloosa on a plantation in the sweltering heat of Alabama – born of a young slave woman brought there from another crueler plantation in Mississippi and conceived back there from a slave father lost to her when her mother had been sold.

She had been treated special there in Alabama, maybe out of pity or maybe because the owner was a more kindly man. But it was in the middle of America's time of greatest cruelty and human injustice, nearer the end of it before the great war. It was a hard time in the country.

She grew up as a fatherless child with a loving mother until her mother had been killed. Now, as a complete orphan in the depth of a human tragedy, it seemed as though God had not noticed her, wasn't paying attention or didn't care in that time of America's deepest sinful shame when His people had turned their backs to His intentions. That was true of them, but not Him.

With the help of some kind older people, she was able to survive her childhood and overcome the horrific events of those early years.

God kept His promise when her mother had been killed so long ago; for He was keenly interested in those troubled times and this young life.

Her impact on the people in her life would seem disproportionate to her humble status. Perhaps it was just because of that that her life was so profound.

The South soldiered on long after its men had surrendered. Ignored and on its own, it rebuilt itself and its people endured on its American land.

Illustrations

Hanna Drish in McComb, Mississippi in 1895

John R. Drish House in Tuscaloosa, Alabama

Historical Oberlin College, Cleveland, Ohio

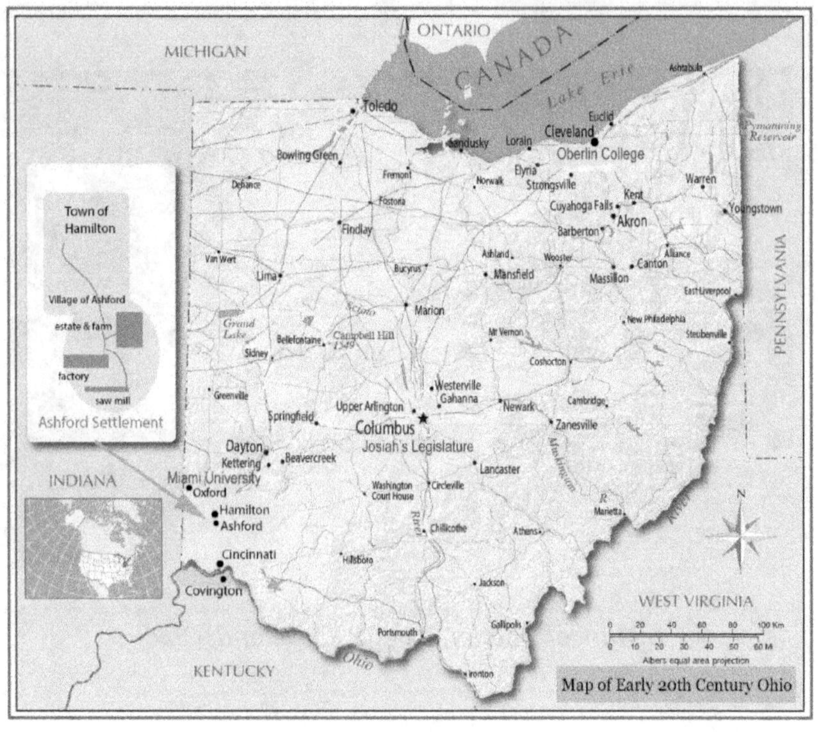

The Ashford Family Ohio Homestead in the 1920's

One – The Twins

Josiah rose from his seat, walked to the podium and shook the speaker's hand. He looked out at the assembly, paused to look across the room and smiled. He stood bolt upright and with his left thumb in his suspenders and right hand raised in the air, spoke to his colleagues.

His face turned to its characteristic resolve as he spoke eloquently and clearly:

"Speaker, esteemed colleagues, we find ourselves at a crucial moment. What we decide today will affect our constituents - our people, our citizens, our families - for the remainder of their lives and for the lives of their descendants to follow.

The great Ordinance of 1787 gave us a plan and guidance to follow. It provided land for schools. The schools were built. But education has been left to us - the great state of Ohio to resolve for ourselves. Much has changed since then; much has run afoul. I will speak to you about that today. We have the opportunity, the authority and the responsibility to change that, correct that and rectify that."

The room was silent in rapt attention. He continued:

"The intent of our founders was clear. We would establish a great nation to the extent of its boundaries, not even known at that time, where free men would live their lives and prosper under the grace of God, as no nation had ever done before."

Loud cheers and applause broke out and drowned Josiah's words. The speaker rapped his gavel for several moments and spoke out, "Attention! Attention! Call to order!"

The room returned to silence and Josiah continued to speak:

"Many of our aspirations have come to pass to fulfill our original ideals. We have turned around the subversions of our southern fellow citizens with the sacrifice of the blood and treasure of our people. Abraham Lincoln brought us to that eventuality and shall ever be remembered for the salvation and redemption of our nation."

The room remained silent in anticipation. He continued:

"Today we have many laws establishing the rights of property owners and for our citizens to vote and hold public office. Our schools are flourishing, our children are benefitting from this, and our country is improving."

They waited for his next words:

"But there is more to be done. There is always more to be done. We will never achieve perfection, but we must strive for it, reach up for it, as Americans and God loving human beings.

We have before us SR403. It will guarantee equal access to higher education for all our children without regard to the color of their skin. It will be based on the content of their character and our character. Surely, honor and integrity will compel us to pass this as the right thing to do. I urge you to vote for it in the affirmative."

Applause broke out one last time as Josiah returned to his seat. Assembly bill SR403 was passed by a narrow margin. It ratified and finalized the senate bill that preceded it. Citizens of all races would attend Ohio's educational institutions. Mary and the children understood that Josiah had played an important part in this change. They were proud of him.

After Bondage and War, Josiah Ashford

David and Josena Ashford were born on May 17th in 1870 as the twins of Josiah and Mary Custis Ashford. David was five minutes older than Josena. They were raised in Hamilton, Ohio and for years they had heard the stories from their father, his white friend David and their mother about the past – slavery, the Civil War and failed Reconstruction. They had heard that there was an older half-sister from their father's tragic first marriage in Mississippi.

The twins' names were chosen with care and purpose when they were born. Josiah had wanted to preserve important memories from the past. His wife Mary understood this, and because she loved him so, she lovingly agreed to his wishes for her children. It was not her history, but it was his.

For David Ashford, it was Josiah's abiding friendship with David Wexley, the Union soldier from Baltimore. He had first met him in Natchez at the edge of the Big Muddy when David strolled over to him and asked him who he was.

Josiah had walked over there, just emancipated from the plantation Savannah Oaks nearby to the east. David had walked much farther from the east, just released from the Confederate prison camp called Andersonville in southwest Georgia. By either pure happenstance, or divine providence, they arrived there together the same afternoon within a couple hours of the same time. This chance meeting had profoundly altered their lives. It had set their whole lives on a trajectory of redemption and fulfillment. David would never forget their history or the history of his country.

For Josena Ashford, it was her father's loving sad memory of his first wife, Josena Taylor Ashford and his lost daughter whose life and name he did know. Her father had had a brief marriage when he was a slave in Mississippi. She had been taken away and killed on another plantation in Alabama. It was a poignancy Josena would never forget, as though she had lived the life of her namesake – as though it had been her own life.

As fraternal twins, they had a similar general look about them. They were close comrades of thought throughout their whole lives. But from there they departed.

David grew to be tall and lanky. He was taller than his father but not so big and robust – more wiry. He had a sharp mind and a thirst for learning. After he had done that – learned – he became professorial. He was contemplative and reflective, but once his mind was clear, he would launch into long lectures to teach you what he knew and wanted you to know. He was always careful and skillful to avoid unnecessary confrontation if he thought it served no purpose. He was generally affable and gregarious.

Sometimes he would miss the mark, but was gracious when someone he respected pointed him in the right direction. That would be his sister.

Josena grew to be short and heavy – some would say dumpy. But she was not frowsy. She may have had to look up at you, but was always put together and immaculate, maybe elegant in spite of herself. She had a fat elegance once you got to know her if that makes any sense. It was about her mind too.

She was smart as a whip and self-assured. She never suffered fools gladly and would rip into you if she thought you were misguided or ignorant. David had to hold her back on many occasions for her own good and the good of the circumstance.

Together they reminded you of Abraham and Mary Todd Lincoln, had they not been a brother and sister of color from a more modern time.

They grew up together on a parallel path and supported each other as the alter egos that they were.

The twins began their college attendance in 1887 at Miami of Ohio University in nearby Oxford. The college had been built on land provided by the Northwest Ordinance. George Washington signed for the land purchase from the Miami Indian tribe and the village of Oxford was laid out in the college township. The original purpose of the school was to train teachers, so it was referred to as a normal school.

They took introductory level courses there permitted under a new pilot program for Negroes that showed promise. It was a program urged by their father, Ohio State Congressman Josiah Ashford. But the university had no intention of conferring degrees on Negroes. It was too soon for that precedent and they weren't going to be the first. It wouldn't be until 1905 before Nellie Craig would graduate there as a teacher and the first African American.

When Josie and David learned that they would never be permitted to graduate, they brought their concern to their father. Josie told him the program was a sham. She was more emotional about injustices than David and became more easily outraged.

Josiah was upset, but ever the pragmatist, he counseled them to apply to Oberlin College up near Cleveland. This prestigious college founded by Presbyterian abolitionists would provide them opportunity for any degrees they wished to pursue. Miami of Ohio's time for equal treatment of the races had not arrived in time for his children. Oberlin was more established than Miami and offered the twins a broader selection of courses and degrees. It had worked out for the best.

Josie would never forget the slight she felt from the treatment she and David had received at Miami of Ohio, but would someday become a prominent professor there. She became more pragmatic as she matured.

At Oberlin, providence was kind to the Ashfords. Despite its abolitionist foundation, Oberlin was prominent as a Protestant conservatory of music with a white majority and few blacks.

David and Josena were a curiosity. They were different in the eyes of most of the student body. But as a curiosity, their classmates were drawn to them, not viewed as people to be avoided.

They were recognized as progeny of a prominent family with a father a powerful politician in the Ohio government. And they were Ohioans like Grant from Point Pleasant, the former general and president who had just passed away five years ago. No one viewed them as ignorant Negro farmers from Mississippi or Alabama.

David had a good sense of this and used his affable nature to form many friendships with his white classmates. Josena learned too that her father's advice would be fruitful in forming relationships. They were colored for certain, but in this environment, that could be advantageous. They became that best of all things in college – popular.

When they stood beside each other, it was humorous – two such uneven fence posts. "How could they be twins?" their classmates wondered.

Their campus life grew to a point where they could discuss race openly, and they did so through many a long night of the brutal harsh winters near Cleveland along the southern edge of Lake Erie.

When David spoke of history, they wondered why it was not he, rather than the professor, standing at the front of the classroom.

Josena organized and led an all-woman string quartet to feature the beloved works of Mozart. Her second violin, cello and viola players from Illinois, New York and Maryland were young passionate white girls. And how they loved Mozart. Their music sparkled and filled their artistic souls. When Josena put her bow to the strings of her violin, she fairly took their breaths away. She held them speechless in rapture. Their throats tightened and their eyes shone.

Their college life was gratifying and it was painfully sad when they graduated and had to leave.

After they had graduated college and remained in their home area for a few years, they decided they wanted to travel into the Deep South to see what it had become now. They had learned in college the murmurings of an emergent movement for social justice and civil rights still denied to so many Americans.

And just maybe they might find their lost older half-sister who had been spoken about in such mysterious, almost mystical and even mythical, ways. Their sister's existence was an enigma. No one knew about her with any certainty.

David Ashford was smart. And he was thoughtful and wise beyond his years. He learned early how to observe those around him and how to gain understanding. He learned from his father and mother and from his father's friend, Uncle David. He absorbed all the knowledge available to him.

At Oberlin College he learned about history. He knew that those that didn't know history could not think historically. Without that training, if would be difficult to understand the world and its meanings.

David learned that history study is a discipline that approached understanding like viewing the layers of an onion as they are peeled away. He learned about all the important facts – the events in the Classic, Old World and American histories. With this comes the understanding of the causes and outcomes, as event leads to event in succession. And with those events are the people positioned in power to drive the events – the game-changers. These are the facts, the outer layer of the onion. There is not much in doubt or dispute here. When assembled together, they form the first layer – the information.

With thought, discussion and reflection, David gained insights into the ideas of history as the next layer becomes revealed. Certainly personal perspective and bias begins to creep in with this step, but information becomes knowledge. He is a black man – an African American son of a former slave – and nothing would change that.

Finally, the ideas he considered are merged together to reveal the meanings. Individuals depart to different conclusions here as more perspective is invariably applied. But here, in this inner layer, knowledge ends with wisdom. His college education was more profound for him than some of his classmates because of his experiences in his formative years.

He came to understand that for many, truth is the facts that they choose to love. He knew that it is a mistake to look back at a period in the past and base truth on ideas and values of the present. Only by placing yourself in that past period can true understanding of those past motives, beliefs, events, causes and outcomes be gained. The truth is for those past people, their truth, not the truth of the observer many years after. David understood this as the purpose of history study. It helped him understand the present.

Josena had attended Oberlin College with David and graduated with her brother. She had studied the arts and the humanities. This brought a different perspective to her intelligence. Hers was based on sociology and understanding the nature of human kind.

She studied violin and became an accomplished musician. From the classics of Beethoven, she gravitated to the old sweet American tunes as Jefferson had played them at home in Monticello.

She was a black woman and understood she was different when white people looked at her with the prejudice of Social Darwinism, convinced she was inherently inferior. But she knew better and never suffered fools gladly. She used a sharp tongue when circumstance went beyond her limits.

David and his twin sister Josena had grown up on the Ashford estate in a life of comfort, but not one of ease. There on their land, the successful Ashford Furniture Company assured the family's wealth. But they were black and never at ease.

The region surrounding the town of Hamilton had seen progress in its rural economy and in its societal improvement just in the two decades from 1870 to 1890 as the twins grew to adulthood. It would take many decades more before full civil rights and social justice would be realized. But it would come sooner than in the South.

Racial harmony was an entirely different matter. It couldn't be legislated or forced. It had to come with the change of hearts. Old attitudes had to be unlearned. After the chains of slavery had been broken, the chains of hate remained. The twins knew this and were attuned to it more than their parents.

Racial prejudice was to be found everywhere. It troubled Josena more than David. He listened to her impassioned arguments with their father. Her emotional outbursts to the great man were common in their family life.

"White men are ignorant father. They have no basis for their stupidity", she said.

Josiah, with his wisdom, tried to convince her that her attitude would never resolve it or change it.

He told her, "Never bow or scrape. You are entitled to your pride. You must maintain your integrity. But if you want to change their hearts, you have to kill them with kindness – but by using your intelligence. It takes time. I have seen it work in my life. You know I have made progress in the legislature with the white men I have worked with there. It wasn't just about convincing them to pass legislation. It was also about winning their respect."

And also, "My sweet, beautiful brilliant girl, remember always with pride, our relationship is special because your name is the same as the brave slave woman that was once my wife."

She nodded in tacit agreement. It was something more she would have to learn.

Right from the start, David was reflective and thoughtful; Josena was reactive, impulsive and passionate. Both were resolute.

Two - Hanna

With a clarity of understanding and resignation Joe said, "Yeah, it's too late now for me to find her. But how can I forget her? I can never forget her. As much as my heart aches, I must find comfort in knowing that I have a daughter who was the result of my love for Josie. I can only pray that she will have the kind giving heart of her mother, and that God blesses her life."

"She will Joe, God knows she will."

After Bondage and War – Josiah Ashford and David Wexley

She was born on the Drish Plantation in Tuscaloosa, Alabama in 1856, six months after her mother was brought there and eight years before Josena would be accidentally killed there during the slave revolt. John Drish and his wife had treated her kindly, as they had her mother when she had been bought and brought there.

John Drish gave her her name, Hanna Drish, even though her mother had been Josena Ashford. Hanna's father, Josiah Ashford, knew that his lost wife had had a baby girl before Josena was killed. He lived in the North and was never able to find her. He knew about her but never knew her.

Little Hanna was raised as a house servant like her mother had been. She was a happy baby, not as light in color and without the pristine beauty of her mother. But her little heart and pure soul was all Josena. Her smiling face brought happiness to the Drish household. Without any children of their own, they loved her as their own.

She grew up with the other slave children in the household and on the plantation. There was something bright and spiritual about her – like the glow from the Alabama sunset. It touched the heart of those that knew her. She reached out to others in her special childish way.

Following her mother's lead, Hanna went to work and learned how to help out in the big house and minister to the slaves in their cabins. Together they tended the sick.

As she grew older, she began to ask a lot of questions as children do. She wanted to know who her daddy was, and where he was. Didn't she have a daddy like everyone else?

Josena would hold her close and smother her against her breast. She sang lullabies to her softly, clearly, sweetly:

Them that's got shall have
Them that's not shall lose
So the Bible said and it still is news
Mama may have, Papa may have
But God bless the child that's got his own
That's got his own

and:

Swing low, sweet chariot,
Coming for to carry me home.
Swing low, sweet chariot,
Coming for to carry me home.

I looked over Jordan, and what did I see

Coming for to carry me home?
A band of angels coming after me,
Coming for to carry me home.

Sometimes I'm up, and sometimes I'm down,
Coming for to carry me home.
But still my soul feels heavenly bound,
Coming for to carry me home.

The brightest day that I can say,
Coming for to carry me home.
When Jesus washed my sins away,
Coming for to carry me home.

If you get there before I do,
Coming for to carry me home.
Tell all my friends I'm coming there too,
Coming for to carry me home.

Hanna learned very young that there is so much beauty, solace, forgiveness and truth in faith.

Josena whispered through Hanna's tears that she had a wonderful daddy but he wasn't there with them.

When Hanna grew older, she stopped asking about her father because she saw it made her mother very sad. Hanna had an instinct about people and their feelings. She was like an old soul that had seen so much of life. She tried hard and learned how to make people happy. But for her, it came naturally. She didn't understand yet that God was inside her and working through her.

Hanna noticed the times her mother seemed to be off in another world, one of memories of her life past. During those moments her mother would seem to be silently praying or quietly crying. She intuited that there had been great pain and loss in her mother's life.

Not wanting to see her mother so sad, she would often do something silly to try to make her laugh and forget. Most times she was successful and lifted her mother's spirits. Hanna was learning how to love and make people happy. She possessed a calm and quiet maturity and a wisdom associated with someone much older.

When she was seven years old, on one evening when the day's work was done and Hanna and Josena were alone, her mother drew her into her arms and holding her tight said, "Hanna, time I'se tole you somethin' about your fathah 'n' wheres we's lived. But when I'se done, we's nevah talk 'bout it agin. You understan' chile?"

Hanna was surprised and a little scared. Her mother had never spoken to her like this before. She could see the sadness in her mother's eyes, but at last maybe some of her questions would be answered.

"Yass, Momma" she replied and waited for her mother to speak.

Josena opened her heart as she spoke, "Your fathah was a wunnerful man. I'se love him from de minut' I'se sees him. He's handsum 'n' very smarts – like's you he's question everthin'."

"We jump de broom 'n' be marry by de Savannah Oaks Massa. We's live ina small cabin. I'se work in de house 'n' ya fathah, Josiah, he be a carpenter on de plantation. My lands, you's shoulda seen sum de beautiful furn'ture he make fo' the big house!"

She paused a moment as if deciding how much to tell her young daughter. She had never talked about her life at Savannah Oaks, preferring to enjoy the love and affection she received from the

Drishs than to remember the hatred of Rebecca and the betrayal of Marcus who sold her away from Josiah.

But Hanna was getting restless, so she continued her story.

"You's look mo' likes him than me. He's a big heart 'n' a lotta faith in de Lord. I'se done tole you, he's very smart; he's even teached hisself to read", she said smiling quietly to herself. "'N' he done it wid books I'se smuggle out uv de Massa's house."

Like every good mother, she didn't want to burden her child with some of the painful and grownup truths about her own life. So she didn't tell Hanna that Marcus Taylor, the Massa, was her father who had raped her mother, and how hurt and betrayed she felt by her father selling her. She only wanted Hanna to feel loved and protected.

Hanna listened closely and, as an intelligent child, she had another question.

"But momma, where my daddy? Why ain't he be heah wid us?"

The tears flowed quietly down Josena's cheeks as she answered, "He don't knows I'se havin' a baby when I'se sole 'way from Savannah Oaks. Iffen he's knows 'bout you, he's very proud uv you, justs Is'e am. You such kindheart' 'n' lovin' girl. I'se knows you always makes me proud, 'n' him too iffen he's knows 'bout you."

Josena and Hanna sat holding each other quietly for a while. Josena didn't know why she had chosen this time to tell Hanna about Josiah, but she just had a feeling that it was the right time. Maybe God had chosen this time to move His plan along with these human beings.

"Now 'member Hanna, we's ain't nevah goin' to talk 'bout this agin, but you's ole enuf to knows about your wunnerful fathah 'n' whys I sumtime get sad when I'se think's 'bout him 'n' how much we loves each othah."

In another year Hanna's mother would be gone and hell would be on its way to the Drish plantation.

As the war drew to a close in 1864, Hanna was eight years old. Dr. John Drish, and his wife Sarah, brought her to live with a friend in Mobile, Alabama for her upbringing, safekeeping and wellbeing. She was raised there in their mansion where she helped them keep their house and was a companion to their children. She was a member of their white family.

Hanna helped out around the household working with the servants. But she was more like an adopted daughter growing up in her parents' home. She had her own room on the second floor family suite with Ken, Abigail and their two daughters. As was the custom, the live-in household servants had their quarters on the third floor apart from the family.

One night when she was 13 in 1869, she was sleeping in her quiet room. She was having a dream of vivid proportions. She suddenly awakened to the sound of soft beautiful music. In the room, dimly lit with the sputtering light of the oil lamp on the table, a heavenly visage appeared. He was imposing, very tall and magnificent in his warrior raiment.

"Hanna, do not fear. I am Michael from the South of Fire. God has sent me to meet you."

The Archangel of God's second phylum smiled at her and his strikingly handsome African features reassured her. His beautiful coffee colored skin was aglow and lit the room. It was so bright, it was like looking at the sun as it sets on the horizon in the southern sky.

Hanna was calm and at peace. She waited to hear his message.

Michael spoke clearly without equivocation as he began, "God has watched you every day since you were born on the plantation. He was with you the day your mother Josena died. He guided the Drish family and compelled them to single you out and love you."

She sat on the edge of her bed speechless in rapture and awe.

"God knows your pure spirit and has chosen you for a special life to serve Him by ministering to the black and white people of the South. He knows that they are hurting, disheartened, bitter and hateful. He wants you to work through Him and dedicate your life to heal them."

She nodded her head but couldn't believe what was happening.

"This is God's covenant with you Hanna. He will keep you safe from harm from all humans for the rest of your life. You will never marry or have children or a family of your own. Your promise to Him will be to serve Him always by spreading His spirit of true love to all white people and black people you come to know."

He waited for her understanding and response.

"I will", she said simply.

Michael smiled at her and she felt God's warmth through His powerful messenger. He came over to her and held her in his arms.

"God loves you child", he said and disappeared from the room.

Hanna grew up to become a strong woman of purpose who was courageous and resilient. She had no fear of people because she believed God's promise as Michael had spoken it.

Her appearance was plain. Her face had none of the soft smooth beauty of her mother's. It was creased with the lines of care and concern. She had the stern serious expression of resolve like her father. It wasn't angry or unfriendly, but rather formed from the passion of her mind. It was an unfamiliar look for kindness. She lived the words of Micah – act justly, love mercy, walk humbly with your God.

Three - The Drishs and the Blanchards

John Drish came from Virginia. He was born there in Loudoun County near Arlington and the Potomac River in 1795. The county was established from Fairfax County in 1757. George Washington was still President then and it would be two more years before his Vice President, John Adams would assume the Presidency. The District of Columbia was not established and it wasn't until 1800 that Adams became the first President to live there in the President's House. His rival and Vice President, Thomas Jefferson would take over later that year.

He studied medicine at Harvard University in Massachusetts and met Kenneth Blanchard there. Kenneth had studied business. He had come there from his home in Charleston, South Carolina.

John and Ken had much in common and struck up a close friendship from the moment they met. They were both southerners, chums in college and graduated the same year. They were southern gentlemen in the truest and best sense.

Certainly they behaved with refined gentility and courtly manners. They spoke slowly at the same melodious pace, taking their time as though the words really mattered as they flowed from their lips like sweet molasses. The lilt from the rise and fall of their intonation was seductive to the ear with a lightness like the scented breeze through the pines in Virginia and the ebb and flow of the tidewaters in Carolina. That is how it sounded in America. But its roots came long before from their forbearers back in the British Isles.

John and Ken were kind, as well as charming, but never gave a thought about the immorality of keeping human property. Long before them their society had ceased caring about that in the South, and few cared about it in the North either. The incongruity with their Christianity was not apparent.

It was understood that the southern system really began when the English Anglicans came to Jamestown in 1607 and established the first enduring settlement. They were the Royal Cavaliers and thought of themselves more like noble soldiers than farmers.

They had no desire to make a society out of moral piety and build a shining city on the hill for the glory of God as John Winthrop had just sermonized to his Pilgrims as they alighted from the Arabella onto the soil of the New World. The Virginians were ill equipped to suffer hardship in service to their God.

Like the Spanish Conquistadores before them, they came in search of gold and riches in the new land. Many perished when none was to be found and they were threatened with the necessity of having to work with their own hands.

But they did discover something as good as gold. The Indians took pity on their sad helpless situation and befriended them. They taught them to grow tobacco. All they lacked was the labor to do the hard work. The slave triangle system developed with the trading companies and in short order the Virginians profited mightily from their tobacco crops and their dreams of wealth were fulfilled. Tobacco money bought more slaves and more slaves produced more tobacco in an escalating spiral until the soil wore out.

As much as they might have wished to be viewed as conquering knights, they settled for agricultural nobility with their own fiefdoms and peasants. As tobacco profits began to wane in Virginia, rice and indigo wealth arose in the Carolinas. The plantation dynasties had established a firm foothold.

But John and Ken grew up in cities and had no ambitions for vast land holdings and grand plantations to grow cash crops and profit from the sweat of their human property. They stayed up nights at Harvard and talked about their plans for their lives.

"I'll be practicing medicine because it will be my vocation and I want to care for people. But my selfish love will always be architecture", John would say.

Ken would answer, "I know you John and know that's true to your nature and good heart. For me, I'll probably not settle in Charleston. My roots are in the Gulf South. If not New Orleans, I'll be making my life along there somewhere."

John thought about their lives and suggested, "It'll be interesting to talk to each other twenty years hence to see what we did and how the world changed."

Ken sighed, "One thing I'd bet on is that slavery will be abolished. It won't last much longer. Then our beloved South will be changed forever – for the good I believe."

John had a wide range of diverse interests and was restless to get started. He loved artisanship, architecture and machinery. Ken favored the commercial business model of New England mercantilism even though his ancestors had come to Carolina from the Gulf Coast.

After they left college, they didn't see each other for years until they found each other again in Alabama.

When John came to Tuscaloosa in 1822, he built a most unusual mansion on his 450 acre property and operated a most unusual plantation business. He was a widower and came to Tuscaloosa as a man of sorrows. He eventually married Sarah Owen McKinney, a wealthy widow herself in 1835.

He was a slaveholder for certain, but followed the old Upper South tradition of the task system and treated his slaves much better than the hasher treatment they typically received there in the Deep South.

He was a medical doctor, a successful physician, a building contractor, and a plantation businessman, but his passion and avocation was architecture. He designed a unique Greek Revival and Italianade styled mansion with full width monumental Doric porticoes and invested in training his slaves as mechanics, masons, plasterers, blacksmiths, artisans and craftsmen so that their labor would construct his dreams. It was completed in 1837. The University of Alabama was established in Tuscaloosa just before that in 1831. It was mostly destroyed during the Civil War.

An extensive addition was put onto the mansion prior to the Civil War. In 1860, his slave William began construction of a three-story brick tower. The front columns were changed to Ionic and cast iron side porches were added.

His workers ran machinery and he provided a cotton ginning service to the planters in the region who didn't want to gin their own cotton. It was much like farmers bringing their grain to a gristmill facility, but an unusual service for the cotton agricultural industry.

He treated his household slaves as family as long as they conducted themselves as obedient children. His Negroes were never whipped and, with the task system, they were given more free time for their families and their gardens. He never broke up families and sold family members away. There was almost a loyalty in this more benign relationship of human bondage. John was kind and there was mutual affection between the master and his charges. But he was understandably a paternalistic and controlling parent.

When his overseer, John Manford purchased Josena at the auction in Natchez, her background from Savannah Oaks was not known. The slave brokers did not make a practice of bothering to learn or pass on the life stories of the commodity they were selling. John Drish was unaware that Josena had been taken away from her husband, or that she was the daughter of the former slaveholder, or that she had grown up mistreated and abused by the mistress of the mansion where she served, or that she was light with child when she arrived. It would be much later, too late, when he would find these things out.

The Blanchards were Catholics. Their people had come to Charleston from the Gulf Coast French. When they settled there, it was an immutable fact that they were an inferior breed of

Christians in the eyes of the Anglo Saxons. The Carolina people paid more mind to what kind of a Christian you were, not how good of one you were.

After college in Massachusetts, Ken moved back home for a brief while. Then he moved to the Gulf shores to seek his fortune in business. He settled in Mobile nestled in its bay up river from the Gulf.

Ken met Abigail before the war up in Virginia. She had been John's first wife's best friend and was introduced to him through that relationship. When they moved to Mobile, the Blanchards maintained a long distance friendship with the Drishs up in Tuscaloosa.

Ken became a wealthy merchant who made his fortune in the import – export business from the port of Mobile in Alabama. There had been plenty of opportunity before and after the war. Despite the upheaval the war caused, the change in the status of the Negroes, and all the changes in the agricultural system of the Deep South, the cotton business had been steady enough for his purposes.

He owned slaves as domestics and stevedores but 1865 brought them their freedom. Many stayed with him after that and were paid wages for their services. Without further cost for their direct care, it worked out about the same for him. And of course they were free to leave if better opportunity came along. The relationships changed mostly as a matter of perception.

With their emancipation, many of the Negroes were still working where they worked before as slaves, but now they had a way about them as free people – celebrating in gatherings off to the side and out of the scrutiny of the white folks. Cooking food, laughing, singing, playing banjo music and developing their own free culture, poor but glad to be alive and happy for themselves. They were themselves for the first time in America and were nothing but happy for that.

But their war had just begun at the conclusion of the white man's Civil War. They strived to better their lives with education and active participation in suffrage and political office. Their progress was breathtaking at first. But invariably the southern governments took much of it away with the support of the hateful and violent redeemers. The African Americans persevered and endured with steadfast courage. Their rock was their church and their colleges were the promise of their future.

As all men are, they were a product of their time. But their fundamental goodness would be their oar to steer them through the currents and eddies of an uncertain future.

The Drishs and the Blanchards had adjusted to the new realities. They were not selfish and hateful people. Their kindnesses and generosities made life better for the extended families that were part of them. People like them would be the hope for the South as the changes came in the future generations.

John died in 1867 at age 72. He had weathered the storm of war, and its ruin, and managed to help with the rebuilding. He was still solvent from the financial ravages and managed to leave Sarah a life of comfort and ease in his absence. He had fallen down a staircase and was accidentally killed. Sarah lived until 1884. The folklore about them and their home spoke of ghosts and hauntings that would persist for decades.

Ken missed him and their frequent visits between Tuscaloosa and Mobile.

Four- The Slave Revolt

John Manford was upset with his employer, John Drish. Manford was the overseer, but Drish wouldn't permit him to whip the slaves in his charge to keep them in line.

With all John Drish wished to accomplish on his land, with his people, and through his many interests, all did not go perfectly with the approach he had taken. Many of his slaves had risen to great accomplishment from the skills they had obtained.

Some were not suited or inclined to join him in his dreams. They were jealous of their fellows who had. Particularly, two of his slaves were bitter, sought attention and fomented trouble. They were ignorant, wild and reckless.

Daniel and Isaac had taken every advantage of Drish's demeanor and understood Manford's authority was limited. When they were sent unaccompanied to town to pick up supplies, they often listened to the white folks visiting there from the North. The abolitionists incited them with stories about the war and their imminent freedom.

On one visit they heard one who said, "Listen brothers. The Union soldiers are on their way to liberate you from your slaveholder oppressors. Soon you will be free to claim what is yours. There are plans in the government to pay you back for all the labor they have stolen from you. Rise up brothers. The time to defeat them is now."

Isaac looked wild eyed at Daniel and said, "We's needs ta ovathrows them white Mastas now."

Without thinking or realizing that if they would wait just a few days or weeks more, the soldiers would come and resolve it, Isaac too replied, "Let's git that Manford 'n' kill'im."

When Daniel and Isaac got back to Drish plantation, they sought out several of the slaves at the compound of cabins during their personal time after the work day. Daniel didn't know how to plan a revolt, or even how to think it through. He just knew they must overthrow the Massas. There was no plan. They were just angry. They didn't think about their circumstance every day but they did that day.

When Isaac told them, "Them Yankee soldiers is winnin' de war. Purdy soon's they's gonna beat de white devils 'n' we's be free. We's kin fights 'em heah whiles they's weak", one of the group replied, "I heahs 'bout how is on othah plantations. But Drish ain't whips us or takes our families 'way. He ain't paid us fo' ours work, but he's treat us purdy good."

Daniel got angry at this and replied, "Buts we's not free! We's cain't goes 'way whens we wants. We's gots ta kill'em now so's we's be free. That's what's they sayin' in town."

A few in the group went along with them and they staged the revolt.

The revolt they fomented involved nineteen of Drish's slaves, including Daniel and Isaac. They were incensed and fired up to take action and do something. They followed the ill-conceived advice they were given and charged at Manford and his men one morning at the beginning of the work day.

Manford had his three men with him when the slaves came at them. They had shotguns and revolvers like the cavalry had always used for close quarters fighting on horseback. Percussion cap rifled muskets were more suitable for long range use which was deer and wild boar hunting for them.

Their strategy was to keep as much distance as they could against the pitchforks, shovels and wooden axe handles the Negroes were wielding. Those would only work for direct hand-to-hand fighting. The overseers were outnumbered nineteen to four. But they had the advantage of fire power. It would be no contest. All they had to do was not let them get close. The shotguns served as cover fire.

The slaves took whatever cover they could find behind a hay bale or a wagon, even the side of the barn. They did not know how to fight for keeps – for mortality. They acted on instinct only and avoided the shotgun shells this way. The way they figured it, they had only four overseers to kill. But the revolvers got them when they charged senselessly forward.

At this point the yard was clouded with shotgun smoke and pandemonium had broken out. Without thinking, the overseers shot as fast as they could in a panic at anything with black skin.

In the middle of the bloody fracas, Josena was crossing the yard on an errand from the big house. The violence erupted so quickly, she didn't see the danger and couldn't get out of the way in time. She was accidentally shot and killed by one of Manford's men.

When it was over, the ground was pooled with slave's blood. Six of the slaves were killed and eight wounded before they gave up. Two of Manford's men were beaten bloody unconscious but survived. The bodies were scattered over the yard. Josena's body lay there on the ground amongst them in the middle of the yard. It was ghostly quiet when it ended.

When John heard about it moments later, he didn't know what to think. He was stunned and numb – his mind blank at first.

Drish was a physician. He had spent much of his life caring for people. It was rare that he felt or displayed anger toward them.

He had a close relationship with his overseer, John Manford. They did not see eye-to-eye on many things, but there was mutual respect developed over years of working together. Manford was not hesitant to call his boss by his surname and confront him with his opinions. The one thing Manford had to swallow was that he was not allowed to discipline his charges.

After it was over, he said to Manford, "The fools. The bloody fools. I can't feel responsible for the outcome of this stupidity. Now my Josena is gone and Hanna is only eight years old."

Manford looked at him disgusted and replied, "This was bound to happen John. I expected it. I told ya we should have been tougher on them. It's the only thing those animals understand."

It was a shame and an unnecessary tragedy.

In the aftermath, when it was quiet, the bodies were taken away and buried in the cemetery behind the Drish plantation. Sarah was heartbroken when she heard what had happened. She looked at Josena's fresh grave and sadly reflected.

She wondered, 'What will become of Hanna?'

She spoke to John and expressed her concerns, "What are we going to do now?"

"I don't know what to do dear. I thought we were doing a good job of running our lives and theirs."

She said, "I think you should write Ken and Abigail and see if we can bring Hanna to safety."

"That's probably for the best. I'll send him a telegram."

He posted the telegram:

Ken. Coming to meet you on an important matter. Two days. Stop.

Hanna helped Sarah pack up a trunk with all her clothes, dolls and personal keepsakes. Sarah added some personal items of her own so that Hanna would remember her when she got older. She braided Hanna's hair in pigtails with red ribbons, dressed her in the flowered print shift she had made for her, and her white canvas shoes.

The Drishs drove off in their carriage with little Hanna sitting between them. It was a sad and bittersweet trip for them as they headed south to Mobile that sunny morning.

The Union army did come. And they came in force.

In 1865, Lee surrendered to Grant at Appomattox on April 9th.

The cities of Montgomery and Mobile, Alabama surrendered to Union forces on April 12th.

President Lincoln was assassinated in Ford's theater on April 14th.

Confederate General Joe Johnston surrendered to Sherman at Durham Station, NC on April 26th. Like Lee's surrender, Joe Johnston's was cordial and done with honor and mutual respect in keeping with the code they learned at West Point. Both men, and most military leaders on both sides, had more respect and trust in each other than they did for the politicians. The politicians were more suited as their common and natural enemy.

Ironically, so many military leaders followed their war careers in peace time with political office – Grant became President and McClellan tried to run for that office also. All Sherman ever wanted to be was a soldier. The rest of them wanted to go back home and be teachers, farmers, or merchants – whatever they were before – and put it behind them.

Johnston had been fearful his men would be punished for the assassination of Lincoln which had just occurred. He spoke to Sherman of him and said that Lincoln was a man of compassion and forbearance. He felt that if the war ended badly for the Confederacy, Lincoln would have meted out terms that were just and charitable. But now with Lincoln gone, killed by a Confederate sympathizer, he was worried.

Taken with the spirit of their meetings, Sherman offered Johnston terms even more favorable than Grant had done with Lee. He didn't even require that the Rebs abide by Emancipation. Washington - Edwin Stanton - responded angrily to rescind his generosity and General Grant visited Durham Station to retract Sherman's overly generous terms and replace them with a simple agreement as he had done with Lee.

Sherman reflected upon the war after the terms were settled and waxed philosophical about its meaning. He had earlier sent a letter to Confederate General Hardee commiserating about the loss each of them had suffered with the death of their sons. He wrote that now they had both lost their sons at the same time, how unnatural this age is when God's stratagem is violated and the young are unbodied of their souls before the old.

He tried to roughly paraphrase Ecclesiastes when he offered, "As some leaves fall and others grow in their place, so too with the generations of flesh and blood, one dies and another is born."

Grant was solemn also after the cease fires and surrenders because he knew 'Our civil war, the devastating manufacture of the bones of our sons, was but a war after a war, a war before a war'.

Sherman reviewed in his mind the horrific campaign he had waged in the Deep South.

By Christmas of '64, he had destroyed Georgia and occupied Savannah. He had prepared to turn north and continue into the Carolinas. By then he had accumulated a large entourage of freed blacks and displaced whites. Secretary of War Stanton was harshly critical of him for not taking better care of his unwelcome charges. Sherman was livid – ten thousand had been fed and clothed under his orders.

Sherman was deeply resentful of Stanton's visit to Savannah to review his progress and assert his criticisms. He responded with Special Field Order No. 15 just to relieve the political and tactical pressures with the civilian mob that had attached itself to his army. He allocated all the abandoned plantation acreage along the rivers for thirty miles inland in South Carolina, the Sea Islands from Charleston south, parts of Georgia and the country bordering on the St. John's River in Florida for black resettlement. Every free Negro head of a family was given title to forty acres of tillable land, and the seed and equipment to farm their properties.

Sherman was no abolitionist but, in his view, this would shut up Edwin Stanton and disengage the niggers who would stay on their land and plant their forty acres. In those days nearly everyone used that word to describe Africans. For whatever their reasons, that was just how it was.

In Alabama they attacked with infantry and cavalry from the north and naval forces at the port of Mobile in the south. The goal was to capture Montgomery, the first capital of the Confederacy.

Tuscaloosa and surrounding areas in Jefferson and Bibb counties were overrun as Union forces made their final sweeps to destroy any potential military support for the Deep South. The iron furnaces that had forged the metal for John Drish's home had been destroyed as well as the Selma industrial complex.

The abolitionists in town had been correct in their assessment of the situation before the slave revolt. The war had been effectively over for quite some time.

Five- The Old Road South

David decided the answers he was seeking lie in the South. His father and Uncle David had told him all the stories of what happened almost forty years ago. But he needed to see it for himself and see what he could do.

He said to his sister, "Josie, I need to go back there and retrace Father and Uncle David's personal history."

Josena could see the troubled look about his face and conviction in his eyes and replied, "I have felt the same way these last few years. I have come to realize the troubles in our country must be solved first in the South."

"I see it that way too."

"Let's go together Dave. We've always put our minds together since we were little babies."

"Ha ha. That is the truth little sister", he replied with his face shifting to a bright smile.

She pouted and answered, "Listen mister, you are only five minutes older than me."

Still smiling broadly, David said, "Let's go tell Father and Mother what we want to do. But we must show them that we have thought it through and have a good plan."

Josiah and Mary thought that their idea for this trip was a good one. They offered their best horse and carriage for the long journey. They warned them that they would face discrimination in the South with a greater intensity than they had ever experienced in their lives before. They believed that the young ones would likely face danger as well.

Mary told them, "Children, don't think that your clothing, fine carriage and refined speech and appearance will protect you from all white people. There will be some who are ignorant and will look past all that and only see the color of your skin. You will need to know how to handle that."

This consideration led Josena to a greater concern that became a contentious matter for the Ashford family before David and Josena left. She had been thinking about the sociology and the psychology of the people they might encounter and spoke more about it with her mother.

"I agree that our appearance won't protect us, but worse than that, I fear that our refinement of dress and appearance will get us into trouble, Mother."

Mary answered, "It's true you will be traveling through many rural areas like some parts around here, but what do you think you can do about it?"

"I don't know but I don't want to provoke an attack or get robbed. It would be awful if someone stole Father's horse and carriage."

Mary thought it best they have a family meeting to discuss it. The four of them gathered in the dining room to hear Josena's concerns and ideas.

Mary suggested, "I think they would be safer if they don't wear their finest clothing traveling through the South."

Josiah mistook her meaning and angrily replied, "No children of mine are going to pretend they are field niggers to fit in with the locals. What are you suggesting? Do you want them to go in a buckboard work wagon with a plow horse?"

David had been listening to everyone and understood where the conversation was going when he spoke up, "I think Josena is concerned that some of the poor whites might think we are uppity and become provoked. But listen, whether we dress as rich dandies or poor black folk, it won't make any difference. Either way, if there are jealous blacks or mean-spirited whites, we will have to deal with it."

Josena came up with the reasoned compromise, "Let's take your old carriage and leave you your best one here. We will dress properly but modestly, not ostentatiously."

David was considering the ideas and added, "We can take along our work clothes from the furniture factory in case we need them. The wood stain and ground in wood dust might help our look and come in handy in some circumstances."

Mary and Josiah worried about their children and feared for them as all parents do. They knew they had to let them go despite the risks. Josie and Dave were grown up, educated, smart and sensible. And, in the end, they knew that this was very important for them. The understanding of the realities of American life could only come from this exploration. They had to have confidence in their children.

Josiah reminded them again the lessons he and David had learned back in those days. They had seen many good and bad people of both races throughout the country. It would be best if they avoided the bad people and the troubles they might bring.

Josiah told them, "Look for the goodness in the people you meet. Form friendship and alliance with them. That will serve you the best and keep you out of danger."

They smiled at the old man's wisdom. They loved him for his care and concern.

Josena responded to his advice, "Thank you Papa. We know you are right. We will follow your advice. You needn't worry. You raised us well."

When Josiah and David Wexley had traveled through the south, they didn't have any maps. They relied on dead reckoning from landmarks and hearsay. But now, when David and Josena were preparing for the trip, Josiah found a map from the 1870's he kept as a memento. So on the day David and Josena Ashford announced they were leaving, with intent to travel south and retrace the route, Josiah offered it to them to bring along.

"Thanks papa, this is a treasure", David said respectfully as he took the old document the day they left.

He and his sister knew it was already badly outdated. But it was interesting to look at it as a piece of history. Much was still the same.

Josiah had marked the route from recollection. Mainly, they had followed the valleys, avoiding the mountain ridges, along the great rivers - the Mississippi, the Tennessee and the Ohio - heading north and then east. The roads were known and well-traveled by pioneers and soldiers before. David and Josie would travel them in reverse.

They left in the spring of 1900 and stayed a couple days in Cincinnati. They had been there before for sightseeing and shopping, but this time they looked up some old college friends who they knew from Oberlin College in Cleveland. They found them there settling their lives in southwestern Ohio, a northern state but with influence of southern climate, culture and values. How different they seemed after years had passed since the youthful college days up in Cleveland.

They were all getting older and the memories of their campus life together were just that - a sweet remembrance. Their classmates were excited to see them. They asked Josie if she was still playing her violin and asked David what he was doing now that he was no longer an academic.

"You two look the same, you down there and him up there", her old girlfriend said. They all laughed.

"What have you been doing Josie? Have you kept up your music?" her friend asked.

She smiled at her friend and said, "I have. We live in Hamilton where you remember we came from. For a few years now I have been running a small music school to teach children violin. Oddly, most of my students are girls. I've learned I enjoy teaching. Soon I plan to go back to college to graduate school and pursue sociology, anthropology, and archeology. That has always been my passion. I haven't married. I have been too busy working at my life.

And David over here, he works at Ashford Furniture Company helping out our father. I expect he will take over one of these days. Our father is getting old."

"That's true Josie", he said. "I also continue my study of history on my own. I have begun writing in my spare time. No wife for me either yet."

They noted together that racial relations were much harsher out in the real world where life happens. That was a shared sadness for them after their youthful idealism had faded.

With their brief reunion over, they crossed the Ohio River and recalled the story of the night Josiah and David had stayed there in Covington, Kentucky – how they had talked through the night looking at the bright lights in Cincinnati. By some inexplicable fortune, they found the same boardinghouse where their father and David had stayed.

The place was over twenty years older and a bit run down and the management wasn't the same. They sat on the same porch one night, more worn than it had been when Josiah and David had sat there.

Josie reflected on the river scene, looked over at Dave and said, "Imagine they were sitting here before they had discovered Hamilton. Before Father had met Mother. Before he had built Ashford Furniture with Uncle David's support. They didn't know then what the future would bring."

David smiled and said, "Just like you and me little sister."

She wrote her father about the place they had found:

7 May, 1900

Dear Papa,

We crossed the Ohio the day before yesterday and stayed in Covington last night. Amazingly, we found the boarding house you told us about. It looks like you described it, maybe a little older.

We looked across the river from the porch and watched the night lights in Cincinnati just as you did.

It was wonderful.

All our Love,
Josie and David

Josie and David followed the old route Josiah and David had followed coming north to Ohio. They rode in their carriage westward in Kentucky along the Ohio River to the Tennessee River and then headed south. There in southwestern Tennessee, they came upon the little hamlet of Shiloh Church.

They knew from the stories they had been told that this was the place where the bloody battle of Pittsburg Landing had been fought.

Josie looked around at the lush landscape, the beautiful manicured fields, the huge weeping willow trees along the river, the quiet pretty hamlet of Shiloh Church and said, "This place is so beautiful. It's nothing like Papa and David described it."

David looked at the long rows and columns of alabaster gravestones, sadly reflected and answered, "Things, places and people change. Without experiencing the history here, we cannot know what it was like then. Imagine that day – the thousands that died so brutally, so fast, the land torn apart from the artillery, the bloody dismembered bodies piled up, the dead quiet when it was over. I can almost see it. But I can never feel it like they did."

"Josie, I've finished reading U.S. Grant's personal memoirs. It was published in 1885 just before he died. He wrote in two volumes about his whole life as a boy, a soldier and a president. He said in the preface that 'Man proposes and God disposes'. At the end of the first volume he wrote about this place and the battle of Pittsburg Landing.

He commanded the Army of the Ohio here and was reinforced by Buell nearby in Corinth. They fought against the collected army of Johnston. Sherman supported with his Army of the Tennessee. On Friday, April 4th, he was injured by his horse falling with him while trying to get to the front.

But he had deep sympathy and understanding for everyone who fought here and died or survived. He dedicated his book to the commanders and soldiers of both the National and Confederate governments."

Josie wondered, 'What must it have been like then for Uncle David coming to see it'?

She looked at the vast flat green space populated so full of the white death stones in an almost endless, perfect geometric grid.

"David, when they were here it was the aftermath of the carnage. The ground was still torn up and scorched from that day. But the bodies had been collected and buried. There were so many at once they couldn't do it with care. They just wrapped them in white cloth, piled them into large pits and poured lime on the ground before they covered them up. I don't know how they could sort it out later to identify anyone to rebury them proper."

David replied, "They didn't. The markers are just ceremonial. The names were known from the records of the soldiers that had been killed or missing. Their bodies are still under there with their comrades-in-arms piled together. They never had time or inclination to place grave markers. I read that whenever they knew the man's name, they wrote it on a scrap of paper, put it in a bottle and tucked it under the blouse of his tunic."

"They were so young, our age or most of them even younger", Josie reflected.

"I know it. This was the place where they gave the last full measure of devotion, like President Lincoln had said. That's why these places are hallowed ground", David answered.

"Papa understood this. He was here with Uncle."

David smiled at her knowingly and said, "Papa knew that both sides had given their last full measure of devotion for their cause. He learned that here. That's why he came to care about all the American people when he began his political career."

"But how could he forgive them for slavery?"

"I don't know for certain. But his faith brought him to forgive so he could live his life in peace without hate consuming him. Our father is a very special and great man."

Josie looked seriously at David and said, "I know he is. We are blessed to have him."

She wrote her father:

14 May, 1900

Dearest Papa,

We stopped today at Pittsburg Landing to visit the site of the battle of Shiloh as you and David Wexley had done so many years ago. It is a national monument now for its important role in our history.

I'm sure it looks different than when you were here. It is green and lush and pretty, but of course somber as well. The grass is manicured and the lime from the mass graves must have leached out of the soil and diluted by now.

David said this battle had been misunderstood at the time. Grant was here and commanded his forces from a gunboat on the Tennessee, stepping off to the landing to get a closer look at his forces. Lee was back east and not involved.

This battle was more monumental than Manassas or Wilson's Creek, but the public didn't know the scope of it or the size of the forces aligned there or the number of losses that occurred. So many men died there for their own two causes.

We could see in our mind's eye Grant looking up the bluff from the landing, the men assembled on the field above – Grant's General Sherman facing the Confederate attack from Johnston's Army of the Mississippi led by Beauregard's Generals Bragg, Polk, Breckinridge and Hardee.

Twenty four thousand men died here in two days. It is heartbreaking to remember that. Thank God the Union was preserved and our people emancipated. But what an immense price to pay. No one expected that.

Be well. We will keep in contact as we go along.

Love and Respect Always,
Josie and David

They left Pittsburgh Landing and headed down the Tennessee to Alabama, next to the border of Mississippi. The plan was to find the Drish Plantation in Tuscaloosa.

David said, "We'll have to head south and stay in Alabama. Tuscaloosa is almost due south of here. It's almost half way down the western side of the state going toward Mobile at the Gulf of Mexico."

"Yessir big brother. No more big rivers for a while. The Mississippi River is way west of here on her western border."

Josie was thinking about the Mississippi River as an important part of the South and said to David, "You know Dave there is a literary South. That is, there is a lot that has been written about it. Harriet Beecher Stowe made a powerful case for ending slavery in *Uncle Tom's Cabin*, Samuel Clemens from Missouri has been writing about the Mississippi for years now. He worked as a riverboat pilot there and chose his pen name, Mark Twain, because of the term the men used to call out the river depth of two fathoms, twelve feet, which was a safe depth for steamboat navigation.

Those literary Souths tell us some more about the history you have studied. They are intellectual and poetic and describe the landscape as well as the people. The land has always been important to the southerners. The writers describe the landscape, including the seascape, and the sky with the eye of the artist. So often it is about the light – the sunrises, sunsets and vast panorama of stars in the night.

They write about the southern angst of guilt and inferiority – apology for lack of refinement and the deep sins past. They write about glory, chivalry, gentility and courtliness, maybe sewn from an older European past. They write about the human condition and the old verities of good and evil, love and hate, cruelty, kindness and faith."

David agreed, "I know that's true. You're the humanities woman."

He launched into a big lecture on the South, "But there are at least five geographical Souths – maybe more.

There is the South along the Atlantic coast, maybe starting from Annapolis, Maryland near where Uncle David came from, and going all the way to the Spanish South in Florida. All along this coast there are diverse geographies. In the Upper South, it is the Chesapeake Bay, the Potomac River and the Shenandoah Valley. Along the coast there are the ocean ports of Norfolk, Virginia and Charleston, South Carolina and the river access ports at Savannah, Georgia and Saint Augustine, Florida. Along South Carolina and Georgia there is the low country with its sentimental tidewaters and its mysterious sea islands.

There is the Creole South and the Gulf South of Louisiana and the southern shores of Alabama and Mississippi, the panhandle of Florida and even the Gulf coast of Texas. It's so different there – French and Catholic. The Africans there were freed before the Civil War. There is a strong Caribbean flavor, so different than what we know about.

There is the Mississippi River South, the line where the river waterway bisects the continent from north to south and extends from the heartland to join with the Missouri in St. Louis, continues through Tennessee, passes along the border of Arkansas, to its delta in Louisiana where it terminates in the Gulf of Mexico.

There is the Appalachian Mountain South, with the Blue Ridge, the Ozark and the Allegheny in North Carolina, West Virginia and Arkansas.

There is the rural South in the remote and desolate inland backroads of southwest Georgia, Alabama and Mississippi.

All of these are bound together with a similar, if regionally unique, culture spread over a vast region of America.

We northerners can't ignore how big and important it is."

Josie looked at him and said, "I guess so. There's more there than I realized. Thanks for that geography lesson. I know it's a big and diverse region of our country. I think about it as just three vast regions – the northern South, the southern South and the western South."

"I see what you mean. That does encapsulate it quite simply."

As they continued south from Tennessee into Alabama, they realized the great river meandered to the east. They broke away and turned south toward the Muscle Shoals area where Andrew Jackson had fought the Cherokee peoples. Their Chickamauga faction had moved south from there and settled along the Chickamauga River. David and Josie followed their old trail. It was rural and they didn't encounter any cities or any sign of modern civilization.

They got lost on a dirt back road in a remote wooded area. David spotted an old cabin next to a small farm and they headed up the entrance road. Before they got too close, an old man came out of the cabin with his shotgun pointed at them. It wasn't pointed at them exactly. Both barrels were loaded with fresh shells and it was broken open laying over the crook of his left arm – friendly but cautious.

"Where do ya' think your goin' niggers?" he asked.

Josie was annoyed and started to rebuff him, "Who the hell do you ..."

David cut her off quick, "Hush up your mouth woman. I'll speak to this gentleman".

He calmly answered, "Don't mean no trouble mister. We got lost back up the road".

"You looks like uppity northern niggers to me. What you doin' in these parts?"

David continued, "We're just tryin' to find the main road to Tuscaloosa. If you would be kind enough to tell us, we'll be on our way".

"It's back up the road ya jus' come two miles. Ya missed the turn."

Josie finally smartened up and said, "Thank you kindly sir. We be right otta your way."

"Good then, stay offa my property and good riddance to ya."

South of Lake Tuscaloosa, they found the city. There they found the imprint and remnants of John Drish that had dominated Tuscaloosa's early development and recovery after the war. The college had been rebuilt and revived. But John and Sarah were long gone and buried thirty one and fourteen years before.

They found his house but Josie said, "I think we need to talk to the people at the University of Alabama and find out what happened here."

David smiled and offered, "Thinking like the academic you are little sister."

"Of course, and you can stop that little sister nonsense any time you like. We're both thirty one years old", she snapped.

"Sorry Josie. You are right. Let's go talk to the local historians at the university."

"We're tired from a long day of travel. Let's get something to eat and a good night's sleep before we do that."

Six – Redeeming Hanna

After breakfast the next morning, they found the history department at the university.

Professor McPherson told them, "I remember John and Sarah well. They were good people."

"But they were slaveholders, Professor", Josie offered.

"Yes they were. But they were different than most around here. They treated their people very well - like family. You sound like northern coloreds. You don't know how it was for everyone here in the South."

David could see that Josena was about to enter into another argument. He knew it was more important to find out what they could about their father's daughter than win the debate.

Annoyed, he changed the tone of the conversation, "The Drishs had a female slave named Josena there before the war. We heard she had a daughter on the Drish Plantation before she died. We are trying to find the daughter."

"What for?" he asked.

Josie answered, "Because she is our sister. Our father, Josiah Ashford, was married to the slave girl, Josena".

The Professor offered, "All I can tell you is that it was very confusing at that time. The Union was at our door ready to demolish our city. The Drishs left and I guess they took the girl with them. When they came back after we were overrun, she wasn't with them."

David looked crestfallen and said, "That's it then? No one knows where she disappeared to?"

"I have an idea though. It's just a guess", the Professor offered. "They had some good friends, the Blanchards who live in Mobile. Maybe they took her there. Do you know how to find Mobile?"

Josie smirked, "Thanks. I think we can manage."

"Thanks for the help, Professor. We'll be on our way there", David concurred.

The areas south of Tuscaloosa became more populated as they headed toward the great port of Mobile on the Mobile Bay. They knew they were getting close to the Gulf of Mexico when they began to smell the salty air.

The Blanchards were easy to find. They were a prominent family with a prosperous well-known business. Their beautiful city estate was a wonder to see. David and Josena felt more comfortable in this more "civilized" location.

As they walked up the sidewalk to the Blanchards' beautiful red brick mansion on the morning they came to call, Josie said, "I wonder what they will be like, David."

"I wonder if she is here."

A servant answered their knock at the front door.

"We are here to see the Blanchards", David announced.

The butler was guarded and suspicious of the colored strangers appearing at the front door. He had his rules to follow.

"I'se sorry folks, niggers has ta go to the back do'", the butler told them.

Josie thought, 'I don't have to bow or scape. I am entitled to my dignity. I must maintain my integrity. I am supposed to kill them with kindness, but I am not my father. And this is not the white man, but his person.'

She paused a long moment staring at him, trying to think what to do and at last said, "Go back in that house and tell your master the Ashfords from Ohio are here on an important family matter and need to speak to him. We will wait for you here."

The butler stood there looking at them, their refined appearance, their educated manner, their comportment, and wasn't sure what to do. He was colored like them, but they were different. These folks weren't holding their hats in their hands figuratively or literally.

They tried to explain their purpose. The butler was still uncertain what to do. But he became more relaxed and decided to go speak to his master. He smiled at them and asked them to wait while he conferred with Ken Blanchard.

When he came back to the door, he invited them in to wait in the grand foyer. It was spacious, cool and dark and adorned with Italian marble floors and columns.

He said, "Please wait here. I'll git Mista Blanchard to come speak to ya."

Ken came along to the foyer in his dressing gown and leather slippers. But he looked dressed up with his white silk shirt and scarf under his formal morning wear. Abigail trailed along right behind him to see who had come to visit. She was dressed for the day and looked like she might have an important engagement planned for later.

David started the conversation, "Mister Blanchard, thank you for receiving us so early in the day. We are on an important mission and need to speak to you if you are agreeable."

Ken saw that they were a fine young well dressed and well-spoken colored couple and was curious what they were about.

"It's all my pleasure son. I'm interested in what your mission might be. We don't get to talk to many young folks anymore. This is my Missus, Abigail and you can call me Ken.

We have finished our breakfast, but would love to have our coffee and have you join us. If you haven't eaten, our cook will want you to have your most important meal of the day."

Josie smiled, said, "Most kind of you Mister Blanchard. I am Josena Ashford and this is David Ashford."

"You're a handsome couple and it's good to meet you", Abigail chimed in.

David laughed, "We are brother and sister. She is my twin."

Wondering where they were from, Abigail asked, "Have you traveled far to come to Mobile, Josena?"

Josie nodded and said, "Yes. We live in Hamilton, Ohio. That's just a bit north of Cincinnati. It has been a long trip."

It suddenly occurred to Abigail that the young woman's name was familiar and maybe a coincidence.

"Oh my. We raised a little colored girl here years ago. Her mother was killed and her mother's name was Josena. It's an unusual name", she said.

Josie gasped, "My Lord in Heaven. Wait until we tell you our story. That little girl you raised may be our older sister."

"Pray tell Josena. I need to hear this story", Abigail said.

They joined the Blanchards for breakfast and spent all of the morning telling each other their stories.

Finally Ken told them, "The little girl we raised here was named Hanna – Hanna Drish. John and Sarah had named her when she was born on their plantation. They truly loved her as a daughter. They had no children of their own. It was heartbreaking for them to bring her here and give her up.

Of course that was years ago when Hanna was eight and the war was ending. She's a grown woman now, older than you. She left in '82 and let me see – she must be about forty four now."

David anxiously asked, "Why did she leave and where did she go?"

"Hanna is a very unusual woman with a spiritual mission. She received a calling to go west and seek her solutions. We have not seen or heard from her in many years. We just know she was heading west, probably into Mississippi", Abigail replied.

They exchanged departing pleasantries and thanked the Blanchards for their kind help.

As they walked down the street to their carriage, Josie opined, "Well now we have lost the trail, David. What are we going to do?"

"I think we should just head west and look for Father's old plantation – Savannah Oaks."

They wrote home again:

28 May, 1900

Dearest Mother and Father,

Josie and I are leaving Mobile, Alabama heading for Mississippi. We met the Blanchards, a white couple, who raised our sister here in their home. Ken Blanchard told us her name is Hanna Drish.

She was named after the Drish family at the plantation you and David Wexley found. When we were there in Tuscaloosa, we learned the Drishs were dead. A professor at the college thought she might have been taken to their friends, the Blanchards at the end of the war.

But for now we have lost the trail for her whereabouts - we just know she went west. We will head that way too and look for your old plantation over near Natchez.

Be well. We will write you again soon.

Love Always,
David and Josena

They didn't want to get their father's hopes too high or theirs either. And so they continued, not sure what they would find or learn next.

Traveling west by horse and carriage, they traversed the little bit of Alabama quickly and soon came to the border of Mississippi. Near Biloxi, they regrouped and had a talk.

"You know Mobile was once part of Mississippi, David?"

"Yes, I knew that it was captured and added to the Mississippi Territory in 1813. Then it became part of the Alabama Territory in 1817."

"Well anyway, since we are headed toward Natchez, I know we have to swing north at some point. I was thinkin' we might stay along the Gulf Coast for a ways. We'll come to New Orleans. What do you think, Dave?'

"It might be fun and interesting, but I really want to get to our destination and find Savannah Oaks plantation."

"Well then we can cut across a corner of Louisiana as we head northwest toward Natchez. I am really interested in the Louisiana people from a sociology standpoint. We studied the Creole culture, the French influences and the African Voodoo pseudo-religious beliefs in my old classes."

"That's interesting Josie. I remember too that many of the slaves there were freedmen long before the war. Let's do that."

"Sadly, some of them had businesses and held slaves themselves. What a cruel sellout to our own people, David."

After a brief stay in New Orleans, they passed through some remote areas in northeast Louisiana and did meet some of the people there – all poor black and white farmers. The topography and the people didn't change much as they crossed the border again back into Mississippi.

David and Josena remembered their father telling them that Savannah Oaks was about sixty miles west of Natchez on the Mississippi.

"We'll need to aim for Natchez", he told her.

They rode across Mississippi from its southeast to its central west. It was all much the same – a country with no big cities, small towns, rural areas, simple mostly friendly white and black folks, a few living together, most living, working and worshipping apart, the same country culture with white folks and black folks going into and out of their churches on the Sabbath, worshipping their same God, together in large extended family outdoor gatherings to share food and fellowship, playing music on banjos, washboards and fiddles, singing and dancing, loving their families, tilling the same soil, loving and respecting their freedom and independence – in the South.

After many days, they came to the small town of McComb, Mississippi. David knew they were close to the old plantation, Savannah Oaks. The locals explained to them that the town was formerly part of the plantation and directed them out the old road to the mansion nearby – still standing.

As they approached the old plantation on the entrance road, the long unattended branches from the live oaks hung down so low that the gray Spanish moss brushed their faces as their carriage pushed through.

When they arrived at the circle in front of the majestic mansion, Josie said, "Let's look inside."

David pushed the overgrowth away from the entrance and they entered into the cavernous, dark, cool and musty foyer. Nature had reclaimed her grounds and the mold, mildew, weather, insects and pests had wreaked their havoc on her insides. Forty years of abandonment had surely taken its toll.

From years of neglect, the paint on the ceilings had mostly peeled away and hung down in stained strips revealing the tarnished sheet metal underneath. The tapestries on the walls were black with mold from the years of shaded dampness.

Damage to the roof had let years of rain pour into the grand rooms on the second floor. All throughout the house, the floors were covered with debris and small creatures scurried away as they approached. Most of the furniture was gone, had been stolen by the Yankees and the remaining after by the locals.

David looked at Josie and said, "This must have been a great place of grandeur for the white folks here once."

"Yes, and their colored slaves must have served their every need in their grand way of life", she sarcastically added.

As they continued to explore through the wreckage, they came to the huge kitchen in the back. The large pecan table, covered with dirt, still stood solidly in its place.

"I remember Father telling us he built this when he worked here as a carpenter and woodworker. He was proud of it", Josie recalled.

David thought and said, "This was maybe the first great piece of Ashford furniture ever made."

After a while, their reconnoitering became too painful and they decided to leave. In the bright sunshine in the yard they passed by the whipping post, not knowing what it was or what had happened there. But God knew and He remembered.

"I must see the slave cabins", Josie told him.

The cabins in the long row were dilapidated – their roofs mostly caved in and their walls leaning over, long out of square and plumb. They entered one of the small rough buildings and saw the years of feces pellets and urine stains from the mice and the squirrels that had infested the torn covers of the cotton stuffed mattress on the small bed. There was broken glass scattered on the small table from the smashed oil lantern still sitting there.

"This is where Father lived as a young slave", David imagined.

They followed the narrow dirt path to the top of the hill and found an open-sided building with a collapsed roof covered with dirt and leaves.

David noticed the rusty machinery underneath and remarked to Josie, "This must have been the saw mill where Papa milled the wood for the plantation".

With heavy hearts, they looked back as they left the plantation and drove their carriage back to town. They were worn out and needed rest.

"I am so despondent David", she told him.

"Me as well Josie", he said.

"I'm going to write father and at least tell him we saw Savannah Oaks", she said.

"That's probably a good idea until we figure out what to do now. Don't sadden him though. Try to keep it kind to his heart."

"I will", she said and wrote him:

12 June, 1990

Dear Father,

We found Savannah Oaks today and saw where you lived and worked. The place is abandoned and run down now which probably doesn't surprise you. We even saw the cabins you lived in and your old sawmill.

Raised in the north long after emancipation as freeborn people, it was quite an experience for us. You were so strong and brave and suffered so much to get where you are today.

All our love and enduring respect,
Josie and David

They stayed in town with a colored family who took them in as boarders. The way that came about was circuitous and disconcerting. There they put aside their conflicted melancholy feelings about the plantation and thought about their sister. They found an old colored woman walking on the street and stopped to speak to her.

Josie asked her, "Have you heard about a black woman that might have come here from Mississippi years ago?"

The colored woman thought and spoke, "They's a wuman like dat. We don't gets many stangahs comin' heah so I'se 'membahs ha comin'."

"Who was she?" David asked.

"She a healah in these heah parts. She live wid dat ole witch, Nora Travers down suth ovs town in da swamp forest."

"What is her name? Do you know?" asked Josie.

"Course I does. Evrabody know ha. She Hanna Drish".

They were astounded. They had found their sister.

Seven – The Klu Klux Klan

Shortly after the conclusion of the war, retired Confederate General Nathan Bedford Forrest participated in the emerging KKK. He was embittered about the loss of the war. His motive was to preserve the American traditional way of life as he viewed it as a southerner. Later, his son William's son, Nathan Bedford Forest II, from Oxford Mississippi became the Grand Dragon of the KKK.

They knew the southern way of life was changing and the lost cause could not be won back. Some southerners thought the next best thing they could do was to take the law into their own hands, for their own purpose. Many white men in the South saw it that way.

It would be a great mission of intimidation, of dominance, of retribution and punishment. It would be a lesson to all of white superiority over Negroes, Jews and Catholics – all the peoples that didn't belong, or shouldn't belong, and had no rightful place in the purity of American society.

Their means was to organize a group of like-thinking men. They would disguise themselves in white robes and hoods and ride on horseback into the night as an army of reformers to terrorize the black freedmen and their white sympathizers.

They would hold ceremonies and secretly celebrate their cause on the hillsides. They would shoot and kill Negroes who they viewed as a threat. They would burn them out of their houses and hang them with rope nooses from trees until they were dead. They would burn crosses on their front lawns to terrorize them and strike fear into their hearts. This scourge of society would be a lesson and a way to strike back for the injustice suffered by the Confederacy.

Why wouldn't God intervene and stop this cruelty and inhumanity by some white men against their fellow man that they viewed as inferior? Now that He was old, He didn't seem to care and strike them down. But surely He had been young once and had brought His wrath upon man when He knew they had gone too far.

Maybe, because He was old now, He had seen too much of His children's hate for one another and decided they must resolve it for themselves. He still had the power to solve it, but was tired and disappointed in His creation. He had given them free will and He knew the price of that.

He watched and He waited and He hoped. He knew that His Angels had enlisted humans like Hanna to work as His instrument.

In a simply amazing turnabout and change of heart, the old General met with black southerners in 1875 at a meeting of their organization, the Independent Order of the Pole-Bearers Association, when he declared to them in his speech the following:

> *Ladies and Gentlemen I accept the flowers as a memento of reconciliation between the white and colored races of the southern states. I accept it more particularly as it comes from a colored lady, for if there is any one on God's earth who loves the ladies I believe it is myself.*

This day is a day that is proud to me, having occupied the position that I did for the past twelve years, and been misunderstood by your race. This is the first opportunity I have had during that time to say that I am your friend. I am here a representative of the southern people, one more slandered and maligned than any man in the nation.

I will say to you and to the colored race that men who bore arms and followed the flag of the Confederacy are, with very few exceptions, your friends. I have an opportunity of saying what I have always felt – that I am your friend, for my interests are your interests, and your interests are my interests. We were born on the same soil, breathe the same air, and live in the same land. Why, then, can we not live as brothers? I will say that when the war broke out I felt it my duty to stand by my people. When the time came I did the best I could, and I don't believe I flickered. I came here with the jeers of some white people, who think that I am doing wrong. I believe that I can exert some influence, and do much to assist the people in strengthening fraternal relations, and shall do all in my power to bring about peace. It has always been my motto to elevate every man- to depress none. I want to elevate you to take positions in law offices, in stores, on farms, and wherever you are capable of going.

I have not said anything about politics today. I don't propose to say anything about politics. You have a right to elect whom you please; vote for the man you think best, and I think, when that is done, that you and I are freemen. Do as you consider right and honest in electing men for office. I did not come here to make you a long speech, although invited to do so by you. I am not much of a speaker, and my business prevented me from preparing myself. I came to meet you as friends, and welcome you to the white people. I want you to come nearer to us. When I can serve you I will do so. We have but one flag, one country;

let us stand together. We may differ in color, but not in sentiment. Use your best judgement in selecting men for office and vote as you think right.

Many things have been said about me which are wrong, and which white and black persons here, who stood by me through the war, can contradict. I have been in the heat of battle when colored men, asked me to protect them. I have placed myself between them and the bullets of my men, and told them they should be kept unharmed. Go to work, be industrious, live honestly and act truly, and when you are oppressed I'll come to your relief. I thank you, ladies and gentlemen, for this opportunity you have afforded me to be with you, and to assure you that I am with you in heart and in hand.

His kind words and ovations to the colored people were well received.

But when God heard this, He was more skeptical. He remembered that just seventy years ago Thomas Jefferson had made the same kind, friendly offerings to the Native American nation in 1806. He spoke to them in person, just as Forrest had done here to the colored people. Behind their backs, President Jefferson had told William H. Harrison, his governor of Indian Territory that we must live in perpetual peace with the Indians, but if they did not incorporate as cooperative American citizens with the many white settlers moving into their areas, they must be pushed out of the way and removed beyond the Mississippi.

Forrest's farewell address to his troops at Gainesville, Alabama on May 9, 1865 is also revealing of his heart and character:

Civil war, such as you have just passed through naturally engenders feelings of animosity, hatred, and revenge. It is our duty to divest ourselves of all such feelings; and as far as it is in our power to do so, to cultivate friendly feelings towards those with whom we have so long contended, and heretofore so widely, but honestly, differed. Neighborhood feuds, personal animosities, and private differences should be blotted out; and, when you return home, a manly, straightforward course of conduct will secure the respect of your enemies. Whatever your responsibilities may be to Government, to society, or to individuals meet them like men.

The attempt made to establish a separate and independent Confederation has failed; but the consciousness of having done your duty faithfully, and to the end, will, in some measure, repay for the hardships you have undergone. In bidding you farewell, rest assured that you carry with you my best wishes for your future welfare and happiness. Without, in any way, referring to the merits of the Cause in which we have been engaged, your courage and determination, as exhibited on many hard-fought fields, has elicited the respect and admiration of friend and foe. And I now cheerfully and gratefully acknowledge my indebtedness to the officers and men of my command whose zeal, fidelity and unflinching bravery have been the great source of my past success in arms.

I have never, on the field of battle, sent you where I was unwilling to go myself; nor would I now advise you to a course which I felt myself unwilling to pursue. You have been good soldiers, you can be good citizens. Obey the laws, preserve your honor, and the Government to which you have surrendered can afford to be, and will be, magnanimous.

Nathan Bedford Forrest was revered by his men for his spirit, his boldness and his leadership. Like his fellow flamboyant

Confederate cavalry general, Jeb Stuart, they loved him and held him with deep affection.

Confederate General Bragg had sent him north over the Tennessee River, deep into enemy territory, where he was surrounded on all sides and placed himself in a tight spot.

General Forrest led his cavalry on surprise raids and ruined the Union's strategic railroads, captured hundreds of their soldiers and their supplies desperately needed by the Confederacy. He escaped their traps brilliantly and with some good fortune. His efforts delayed General Grant's eventual victory at Vicksburg and the ultimate Union control of the Mississippi.

He was admired also by the other Confederate leaders and feared by those of the Union. It was a shame after the war for himself, and about himself, that he turned his passion for his country to such a bitterness toward its newly freed African citizens.

Nathan Bedford Forrest, like much of the southern country, had turned his sorrow for the lost cause to a dark place of hatred – racism. But that is what he did, the man he became, and he shall forever be remembered in infamy.

He had lent his good name to the cause of the KKK and that solidified his reputation in history. A man has to be considered for all his life's deeds and hypocrisies. Only God can judge him.

Hanna knew of the KKK's presence. Their actions were known to all people of the South. They all had seen them or, at the least, heard the stories about them. She couldn't just ignore them or, even as a Christian woman, forgive them. But God had warned her of evil.

She chose to follow her own path. She knew her best way to serve her God was to subvert them by her example, as she had learned in the bible, by mustering the forces of good white people and good black people working together. This would allow her to keep her promise and offset the evil hatred of the KKK.

She would leave the vengeance to Him. She knew from Ezekiel 25:17, God had said:

> *And I will execute great vengeance upon them with wrathful rebukes; and they shall know that I am Jehovah, when I shall lay my vengeance upon them.*

Hanna had nothing to fear. She had felt the spirit and had read the book, knew the Revelation, and how it would end for mankind. She has seen the Alpha and the Omega and understood the meaning of the beginning and the end. The Lord had told her there will be a day of reckoning when He would return and we will all pay for our sins.

All her life He had told her what that will mean for us here – here in our time and our country. But she knew the time was drawing near when we would pay for our sins. Our chance for salvation as a nation under God was slipping away.

Someday the old God of Abraham would return with a vengeance because man had failed to follow His Lamb Jesus. Those that did not repent would be smote to ashes by His might.

The KKK was not her worry. All she had to do was act justly, love mercy, and walk humbly with her God.

But she remembered something Ken Blanchard had told her back in Mobile when she was younger. He had helped her understand the important difference between two words – empathy and sympathy.

He had explained that empathy was a feeling we could have for people who are different. It meant we could not understand them very well because they are different, but we could walk a mile in their shoes to understand them better.

Sympathy is a feeling, he explained, we can only have for people who are the same as we are. But if we practice empathy long enough and far enough, we can become more the same. When that happens, we can begin to have the rarer feeling of sympathy.

Hanna realized this understanding and practice would help her keep her promise. She followed it more and more as she became older and wiser.

Eight - Tuscaloosa

Shortly after the slave revolt, and with Josena fresh in her grave, the Yankees came to Tuscaloosa. Within sight of the Union forces at their gates, John and Sarah were horrified and fled for their lives. Their concern was more for Hanna than themselves.

They knew that Mobile was occupied by the Yankees – had been for some time. From regular communication, they knew that Ken and Abigail were safe there. They were hemmed in but safe, the conditions more quiet and stable. The Yankees did not destroy their infrastructure since they needed the port for their purposes.

John hated to leave. He was panicked and feared they would burn his house down in his absence. If that was to be their intent, they would burn it down in his presence anyway. So they decided to leave for Hanna's sake, and left their property in the hands of fate and their people.

Their house was spared. But the University of Alabama wasn't. Almost all of the buildings on the new campus were burned and nearly destroyed.

It wasn't a siege like in Vicksburg or Atlanta. With little defense, Tuscaloosa was merely overrun in short order. There were fires spread all over the small city. John was gone by then and didn't see it. His beautiful home was mostly masonry and iron, so it wasn't worth the extra trouble to put it to the torch. Most of its contents were looted. Whether they deserved it or not would be up to God to decide.

Union Brigadier General James H. Wilson was under orders from and served under Grant in the Western Theater. Wilson came from Illinois and died in Delaware long after the war.

He had defeated Nathan Bedford Forrest in the Battle of Franklin and again during his raid through Alabama in what was called Wilson's Raid. He sent 1500 men under John T. Croxton to burn the Roupes Valley Ironworks and Bibb Naval Furnace at Brierfield and the University of Alabama at Tuscaloosa where a prominent military school was attached. Cadets from there graduated to serve as officers in the Confederate army.

When the college was burned on April 4, 1865, it was only five days before Lee's surrender at Appomattox. Only four buildings survived the fires. In retrospect, the destruction appeared unnecessary.

John changed after the war. That is, he made changes to accommodate the new reality. He was forced to by the circumstances, but it was for the better. He was the same man but became more so. He never liked the system of slavery anyway. The changes made him happier.

He remembered his overseer, John Manford and thought, 'He managed things for me well enough but when he was gut shot and killed by that freed slave and Yankee soldier after the revolt and Josena's death, I knew it was time for things to be done different. They had had an altercation with Manford and stole two of my best horses when they shot him and fled that day. I'd had enough of the plantation way of the South by the end of the war anyway. Emancipation of the slaves was long overdue.'

His interest in growing cotton had always been secondary, so he parceled off most of his land. The new schemes of share cropping and tenant farming held no appeal for him because he could see that these solutions kept the farmers in another form of economic bondage.

Most plantation owners, after releasing their slaves, had kept their land as the last asset of value that remained for them. John had a better vision, so he sold off his land to small independent farmers - freedmen and whites – who bought it outright. John helped them finance it and held their mortgages.

The Drishs concentrated on their strongest enterprises – the cotton ginning services and mechanical repair services and sales of equipment in support of the independent cotton producers.

The growing city of Tuscaloosa bought 100 acres of his land to facilitate their recovery and expansion. John and Sarah invested in rebuilding the University of Alabama that was destroyed there during the war. With the urbanization of Tuscaloosa, Drish plantation became Drish estate and blended into the city. His beautiful home was now located on 2300 17th Street.

But Sarah and John were lonely. It was too quiet on their estate now. They missed Hanna but knew she was doing well with Ken and Abigail in Mobile.

Alabama's history was closely related to and derived from Mississippi's. John was there in Tuscaloosa for many of Alabama's transitions throughout its evolution. He witnessed and lived through it but with his gentler Virginia sensibilities. He most often followed his own path apart from the regional culture.

He told Sarah on many occasions, "My dear, I don't see the benefit of slavery to anybody in our country, our state or our city. I know it will end because it must."

She loved him for that and agreed, "Ultimately God will punish us and the South for our sins and transgressions. We have gone against nature and Him and will be punished for it in the end."

Prior to the admission of Mississippi as a state in 1817, the sparsely populated eastern half of the territory was named the Alabama Territory. It had been created by the U.S. Congress later that year.

The former town of St. Stephens was the territorial capital until 1819. Then Congress selected Huntsville as the site for the first Constitutional Convention of Alabama after it was approved to become the 22nd state. Delegates met to prepare the new state's constitution. Huntsville served as the temporary capital of Alabama until 1820.

Alabama fever was well underway when the state was admitted to the Union. Settlers and speculators poured into the area to take advantage of fertile land for cotton cultivation. It was part of the frontier in the 1820s and 1830s with a constitution providing white men suffrage.

Like John Drish, southeastern planters and traders from the upper South brought slaves with them as the cotton plantations expanded. The economy of this central Black Belt, named for its dark soil, was built around the large plantations. The owners grew wealthy from their slave labor.

Alabama also drew many poor white people who became the disenfranchised subsistence farmers. By 1810, the population was still under 10,000 but increased to more than 300,000 by 1830 after John came in 1822. Native American tribes were removed from there shortly after the Congress passed the Indian Removal Act in 1830.

From 1826 to 1846, Tuscaloosa was Alabama's capital, until Montgomery became the capital after that. Its former capital building, built in 1827-1829, was designed by a man named William Nichols, a friend of John Drish, who shared his passion for architecture.

In 1846, the Alabama legislature voted to move the capital city from Tuscaloosa to Montgomery. A new capital building was erected there under the direction of Stephen Decatur Button of Philadelphia. Barachias Holt of Exeter, Maine designed it. It was burned down in 1849 and rebuilt in 1851.

By 1860, Alabama's population had increased to nearly one million people. Nearly half were enslaved African Americans. A small number of free people of color lived there along with them. When Alabama seceded from the Union, it joined the Confederacy just a few days after being an independent republic. Montgomery was the capital of the Confederacy at that time.

Nathan Bedford Forrest's battalion from Kentucky were joined by cavalry solders from Huntsville, Alabama. Their company wore yellow trim on the sleeves, collar and coat tails of their uniform to distinguish themselves. Hence they were greeted as Yellowhammer which later became the nickname for all of Alabama's Confederate troops.

Officially Alabama's slaves were freed by the 13th Amendment in 1865. The state was under military rule from the end of the war in May 1865 until its official restoration to the Union in 1868.

From 1867 to 1874, most white citizens were temporarily barred from voting, while freedmen were enfranchised. Thus, many African Americans emerged as political leaders in the state and were represented in Congress.

Following the war, the state remained chiefly agricultural, with an economy tied to cotton. As part of their share of, and requirement of, reconstruction, the state legislators ratified a new state constitution in 1868, creating the first public schools and expansion of women's rights. Public projects for roads and railroads were hampered by allegations of fraud and misappropriations.

Organized insurgent groups arose to win back the lost cause of the Confederacy and the southern way of life. These resistance groups called themselves redeemers, but were predatory raiders who fomented violence in an already deeply devastated part of America. The original Klu Klux Klan was short lived but other groups like the Knights of the White Camellia, Red Shirts and the White League carried the banner of southern honor.

Reconstruction in Alabama ended in 1874, when the Democrats regained control of the legislature and governor's office through an election dominated by fraud and violence. They wrote another constitution in 1875, and the legislature passed the Blaine Amendment, prohibiting public money from being used to finance religious-affiliated schools.

That same year, legislation was approved that called for racially segregated schools. Railroad passenger cars were segregated in 1891. After disfranchising most African Americans and many poor whites in the 1901 constitution, the Alabama legislature passed more Jim Crow laws at the beginning of the 20th century to impose segregation in everyday life.

John lived through the war and its immediate aftermath until his accidental death in 1867. Sarah lived through the brunt of all that and the many changes that followed. She remained there in Tuscaloosa for almost all of it until her death in 1884. She lived alone as a widow grieving for her husband nearly twenty years after his tragic premature death.

The Drishs were largely responsible for the growth and development of the city. Their family name remained prominent throughout most of its history and was memorialized after their passing. They left no heirs and memory of them eventually faded away into the veiled cobwebs of myth and legend as the new age emerged.

During her years alone, Sarah was supported by a wide circle of friends throughout the community. But it was her friendship with the Blanchards in Mobile that kept her life centered on an even keel. She made the trip to Mobile as often as her failing health allowed and saw Hanna grow up under the kind care of Ken and Abigail.

Abigail had been faithful to their friendship. She knew how much John and Sarah had loved Hanna. She wrote Sarah often after John had died. She would tell her what wonderful things Hanna was doing and the extraordinary woman she was becoming.

She told her that John, as a physician, would have been so proud of the work Hanna was doing in Mobile's hospitals accompanying her as a nurse. She remembered that Hanna had accompanied John on his rounds when she was so little.

She told her that they wished they could make the trip more often to see her. She offered hope that Hanna, as a grown woman, would come up on her own.

Nine - Mobile

The Blanchards had settled their lives in Mobile long before the Civil War. Ken was a business man with a thriving import and export business even before the war had begun. They took Hanna Drish into their care near the end of the war.

Mobile had been part of Mississippi but joined prominently Protestant Alabama and became a diocese of the Roman Catholic Church, likely due to its French and Spanish origins and orientation as an upriver port to the Gulf of Mexico, and second only to New Orleans. In 1847, the Jesuit Order took over the Spring Hill College established earlier in 1830.

Early in the Civil War, Admiral Farragut had blockaded Mobile's port, which had been heavily fortified by the Confederates, and cut off commerce from the outside. Food, raw materials, cloth and other sundries were in short supply. Women gathered on Spring Hill Road and stormed up Dauphin Street with brooms and axes and banners demanding bread or blood.

In August of '64 his warships fought their way past Fort Gaines and Fort Morgan and defeated Confederate gunboats. Mobile was not defeated but was isolated. The end came in April of '65 when the city of Mobile was overrun by Federal forces, couldn't hold out any longer, and surrendered.

During the last quarter of the 19th century, Mobile was in turmoil. The Reconstructionist Republicans held control of her in 1867. In 1874, Democrats used violence and extreme measures to wrest control of the city back and keep African Americans and non-

Democrats from voting. By 1875, the Democrats had put the city into decline.

Ken Blanchard was a Catholic and a slave owner, but operated under a different situation than those on the cotton plantations. He and Abigail lived in a large mansion in the city with household slaves who were charged with all the household operations and had a degree of autonomy. The slaves outside the homestead worked as dock hands, stevedores and warehouse workers for the Blanchard Import-Export Company.

While appearing similar to the living patterns on the rural plantations, the two groups were adapted to a closer, more intimate urban setting. Their surroundings in the city – those inside and those outside the household - were more crowded and there was less land to spread out spacious areas for slave cabins. Well before emancipation, living together closer as they did, there was more democracy, as well as intimacy between the slaves and their white owners.

Ken had discussed these subtle differences in relationships with John Drish on several occasions.

When John and Sarah came to visit, he often said, "We have to live with them closer than you do, so we necessarily form closer relationships. It seems to work out for the best."

Eventually though, as Mobile developed, there was a section provided by the group of business owners that was entirely allocated for housing the slaves. As they became more like dayworkers, the intimacy diminished. They had their own neighborhood for their own kind.

The women of the black families still worked as domestics in the owner's households, while the men worked away and outside on the docks and in the warehouses. A few black families still lived right behind the city mansion lots and were more closely available to the white owners as virtually live-in servants.

When the slaves were freed, the sections of town that were entirely inhabited by them became the black side of town. In reality, the only difference for them was that they were paid to work and required to pay for their housing. They became the city version of the small tenant farmers established after the end of the war.

The Blanchards had slaves in their household and maintained a small compound of cabins at the back of their property for the slaves that worked for them as stevedores and warehouse workers at the waterfront docks.

Eventually Ken joined too with the other businessmen to pool their resources and help build the neighborhood of brick buildings for the aggregated slave family housing. After the war and emancipation, African Americans went out to work for wages and had their own place where they were on their own. They belonged to themselves.

When John and Sarah Drish arrived at the Blanchards' with Hanna, Ken and Abigail were surprised to see a shy, nicely dressed Negro child, hiding behind Sarah's skirts. Their telegram had been cryptic but implied a serious matter. As old friends, they trusted each other implicitly so they welcomed the threesome into their home.

The Blanchards couldn't help but notice how quiet and sad Hanna was. She did not seem like most 8 year old children they had met or known. Abigail suggested that perhaps Hanna could go into the kitchen with the cook and have something to eat while they talked in the parlor.

John and Sarah told Ken and Abigail about the slave revolt and Josena's unfortunate death. John was visibly upset that his slaves whom he had always treated kindly could do something like that – more so when their beloved Josena had been senselessly killed.

"I couldn't have imagined that would happen, Ken. We loved Josena and were devastated when she was needlessly killed in an instant. She was a member of our family. And now poor Hanna who never knew her father, has lost her mother. She was born to us and has spent her whole life with us.

But then, in a matter of days, our tattered Confederate defenders were rushing to the outside of town to meet the Yankees. Their artillery pressed closer and their forces overwhelmed us so fast, so furiously and so deadly. We didn't know how they would treat us, or our property, so we had to hasten and escape to safety."

Ken was saddened by John's words, thought for a moment and said, "I can see how close you have become to Hanna and why. I have always known you to care for people and care about them."

"She has come with me to visit and tend to my patients. She's very special, Ken. There's something odd about her too. There is a spiritual aura about her I can't understand. It's almost eerie. She seems to know things a little child couldn't possibly know or understand. I just know she has captured my heart."

"What are you going to do?" Ken asked.

"Sometimes when you love someone so much, you have to let them go. It's for the best. I don't feel she would be safe with us now after all that has happened. I want you and Abigail to take her and raise her. I trust you completely. She needs your protection and your safety."

Abigail offered, "The Union forces have occupied our port and city for over a year now. They control everything and Ken has had to work with them to keep our business going. They are our customer now. But it is peaceful here and we have no fear of being burned out or killed."

Ken asked her, "What do you think Abby? I'd like to take Hanna if you would undertake it."

She saw the tears running down Sarah's face, looked back at Ken and said, "Of course I would. She will be one of our own."

John held Sarah's hand, looked at her and smiled. The Blanchards could almost hear their sigh of relief.

Ken said, "Don't worry dear friends. This will be her safe harbor."

Sarah said, "We are relieved and in your debt. Now we need to prepare Hanna for this big change in her life. She just lost her mother a few days ago and she is very distraught. That's why she appears so quiet and shy here today.

She is very smart and loves her bible. You will come to love the real Hanna once she becomes adjusted."

Now it was time to talk to Hanna. She was so mature in many ways, it was sometimes hard to remember that she was just a little girl. These last days she had been so quiet it was hard to know what she was thinking or how she was doing with her loss.

Abigail went into the kitchen and brought her into the parlor. Hanna sensed that the adults seemed very serious and that frightened her. She clung tightly onto Abigail's hand, not sure what was about to happen.

She vaguely remembered seeing the Blanchards years ago when they visited the Drish plantation, but they were still strangers to her. Her heart was beating rapidly and she was fighting to keep back the tears that threatened to flow.

She missed her mama. As she remembered her though, a sudden calm entered her consciousness. It was as if she could feel her mother's arms around her telling her that everything would be alright and that she would always be there in her heart for as long as she lived.

Hanna entered the parlor and went to sit by John Drish, looking with wide eyes at everyone in the room.

John took her hand and gently said, "Look at me child. You know that Sarah and I love you just as we loved your mother. We are so sorry that we couldn't keep her safe, but now we want to make sure that you are safe and have a good home.

You remember the Blanchards, they came and visited us a few years ago. They have this beautiful home in the city and two children who are just a little older than you. They would like you to come and live here with them here in this house and help out just as you did at our house. We promise to come visit you from time to time. We just want you to be happy and safe. What do you think?"

No one had ever asked Hanna what she wanted to do. She didn't know what to think or say. But somewhere inside her a little voice was telling her to do what the Drishs wanted. So she just shyly nodded her head yes and waited for one of the grownups to say something more.

Abigail Blanchard came over, sat beside her, took her hand and said, "Hanna, we really want you to come and live with us. We know you will be happy here. So welcome home child."

The Drishs needed to get back to the plantation. They had left hurriedly and with the situation the way it was, they didn't want to be gone long. So they gave Hanna a big hug and left to go home. Hanna watched from the porch as their carriage went down the street. She felt so alone, but like her mother, she squared her shoulders and went to face her new life with a smile on her face.

Just two years later, when Hanna was ten years old, John Drish died suddenly in a tragic accident. Grief-stricken, Sarah sent word by telegram to Ken and Abigail. They hurriedly packed up some things and, with Hanna accompanying them, drove their carriage to Tuscaloosa to be at Sarah's side and comfort her.

As they approached the Drish house, Hanna remembered it from just two years ago when she had left. From her earliest recollections, she remembered the extensive addition John's slave William had put on it just before the war had come to Tuscaloosa. The columns in the front were magnificent and the place looked like a great castle to her young eyes. The iron work on the new porches was unique. There was nothing like it she had ever seen. It was certainly different from the city mansions where she lived now.

They found Sarah so lost to reality that they took over John's final arrangements. They asked what her wishes were for memorializing him.

"Contact Prince Murrell", was all she could say.

Reverend Murrell was the pastor of the new First African Baptist Church on Stillman Boulevard and a friend of the Drish's for most of their lives. The new church had humble origins moving from Hood's Mill and Barr's store to its own permanent building on Stillman. There would be a long history of Christian scholarship to follow Murrell's footsteps with a succession of prominent pastors, including one graduate of Tuskegee Institute and another of McGill University in Canada.

The friendships reached across racial barriers all the way back to when the Murrels had first attended the old First Baptist Church with blacks and whites attending in equal numbers – all of Tuscaloosa's Christian people.

Sarah knew that Reverend Murrell was a kind man who would give solace to the community of Tuscaloosa. Everyone held him in high esteem. Hannah had fresh memories of the Reverend teaching Sunday school to her and the other children.

The community came out in full numbers for the service to give John a reverent sendoff. The Reverend gave the eulogy and many got up to share his memory. Sarah was pleased and, through her tears, felt their love.

Before they left for home, the Blanchards visited Sarah one last time to say their goodbyes. Remembering the sad past history, they led Hanna out to the yard behind the Drish house and the small gated cemetery there. She knelt down at her mother's gravesite looking at the headstone. They read the words on the stone, "Josena- Beloved House Girl – Died September 1864".

The Blanchards stood there in a moment of reverent silence while Hanna knelt at the gravesite and prayed, "Oh Mama, I miss ya so. Give ha peace at last Lord. She was a good Cristchen wuman. Doan worry 'bout me. I'se doin' fine Mama. People tekin' care of me good. I love you Mama."

Ken rested his hand lightly on her shoulder and smiled lovingly into her face. He and Abigail, one on each hand, led Hanna away.

Sarah Drish was alone and lonely in the big house on 17th Street after John was gone. Her grief consumed her and her sadness never subsided. The neighbors and the community did what they could – what she would accept and tolerate. She kept her spirits up the best she could.

She told her servant to harness up the carriage and she set out for Mobile to see the Blanchards. He drove her there in the good weather and felt better he could do something for her. They stayed in the mansion on Dauphin Street – he in the servants' quarters.

Ken and Abigail enjoyed her visits and reminisced about the old days when they were young and coming up.

"That was just a moment ago", Sarah said.

Hanna was so happy to see Sarah again and they renewed their care and concern for each other. Sarah was old now but Hanna remembered the days with her in Tuscaloosa and the love they shared.

"Wonderful to see ya mama Sarah", she said. "I missed you and the good days in your house. Its bin so long."

"How grown up you have become", she said.

It warmed Sarah's heart to see Hanna growing up and becoming the young woman she was. But she remembered. She thought how it was when she was so little - her tragic loss and how brave she was.

Hanna thought about Sarah often after John died. She talked about it with Abigail.

"Maybe I shud go up thereah and be wid ha'", she said.

Abigail told her, "There is a limit to how much you can do – for her and yourself. She comes down here when she can and seems fine for a grieving widow. She's doing all right and you have much to do here."

"Maybe you right Abigail. Wid your daughters grown 'n' gone, maybe I stay hereah wid you."

"We want you here and we have work to do together at the hospitals", Abigail reassured her.

Abigail didn't have a sense about Sarah's failing health. Hanna stayed.

During their troubled times, like everyone else, the Blanchards made do. They participated in trade with the blockade runners when they could or traded with the Federals when there was that opportunity. It was tenuous either way.

Abigail believed in the southern cause and way of life. She was active in charity for the many new poor and wounded spawned from the "War of Northern Aggression". As an affluent and patriotic citizen, she helped out where she could. She rolled bandages and cared for the wounded. She went weekly to the sewing circle of her church and helped make clothing and blankets to be given to those in need.

She volunteered at Mobile City Hospital to care for civilians with yellow fever, cholera and other diseases. She volunteered at the Marine Hospital for Confederate soldiers who were wounded or ill. She learned something about herself – that she got fulfillment from caring for others in need. She enjoyed nursing.

With her two daughters cared for in her home or away at school, she spent whole days at the hospitals – arriving after breakfast and staying until just before dinner. She believed she was helping the war effort and it was a great satisfaction.

She learned about the medicines administered in her day. Since aspirin would not be synthesized until 1897, there was just willow bark tea for the treatment of headache and mild pain. Paracetamol became available in 1887 for treatment of mild pain also. Laudanum – opium dissolved in alcohol – was used since 1800 for cough and pain.

For severe pain, morphine, made from poppy plants, had been in wide use since 1827 and through the Civil War. Many young soldiers had become addicted from its overuse. General Grant wrote his memoirs while using Vin Mariani, a cocaine infused wine, to keep awake and for pain from his throat cancer.

Morphine became available, as a form of opium disguised in various tonics, from the Sears catalog. Doctors and nurses however, administered it by hypodermic syringe when that was invented in 1853.

For the Yellow Fever, not much could be done except for treatment of its symptoms. Without saline IV, rehydration was accomplished by administering drinking water. Without anti-viral drugs, aspirin was administered when it became available.

Abigail learned about these medicines and treatments as she became a recognized nurse. While practicing her skills, she was sensitive to the trauma Hanna must have endured from her mother's death and uprooting from the Drish house to the Blanchards here in Mobile.

She often brought little Hanna with her. It became apparent very quickly that for Hanna it was a calling, more than a satisfactory cause. John Drish sensed this from the earliest when he brought her with him on his doctor visits. Hanna had a gentle light and a sensitive touch that soothed the suffering of the patients. It was a reassurance to them when she touched their face or their hands. A peace and a calm came over them when they looked at her face.

Long after the war, as Hanna grew older, she learned the practicalities of nursing from Abigail, just as Abigail had learned them before. Together they continued to heal the sick and infirm.

For her religious upbringing, Hanna had learned the rituals and formality of Christianity in the Catholic Church with the Blanchards. When she became a teenager and had accepted her covenant with God, she began attending the African Methodist Episcopal Church with other African Americans. The AME worship was more personal, more emotional, and more soulful. It fit better with her nature. There she learned God's love and His purpose. She better understood her purpose and how to fulfill her promise.

As she grew to adulthood, Hanna had read her bible in its entirety so many times that she had nearly committed its words to memory. She was often called upon to give brief sermons at the AME Church. The African American community knew her as a spiritually gifted woman of God and often called upon her to visit when a member was ailing in body or spirit.

With their growing concerns for social justice and racial equality, the African Americans in Mobile often sought violence in retaliation for violence in their frustration for equal treatment. Hanna told them that the path to freedom was faith. She suggested to the angry leaders that the churches should became the epicenters for the leadership fighting for civil rights. To be successful, it would be done peacefully and with passive resistance.

She reassured them of her certainty that God would guide them with His providence to find the goodness in people of both races. It could be done only that way – with the hearts of good people coming together. God had shown her this truth. She continued to follow her mission well into her twenties.

Eventually, with the early experience she had gained as a child with John Drish and the mature experience and practice at the Mobile hospitals, Hanna was paid a stipend for her healing work. She was able to save some money of her own. It was purely a practical matter. Hanna had never paid much attention to or cared about money.

Ten – God's Reflection

I thought about the order of things as I have made them,

'The angels are My most sentient beings. They watch the humans and are aware of their actions and thoughts. But they do not act without My direction. The thousand thousand of them are but a few compared to the numbers of the humans.

They follow the commands of their leaders, the archangels, I have placed before them. I have given my archangels some freedom to act on their own just as I have given the humans. But unlike the humans, my archangels understand My wishes completely. I can trust in their spirits.

Only once did I cast one of them out of the heavens. He rebuked My authority and so I banished him to the netherworld. He resides in the dark places of the earth and in the hearts of some of the humans.

I have permitted him to continue to exist and serve as the source of evil in the world. Rather than destroy him, I have kept him to suit Me. He is needed in the balance of things.

He has tempted the lowly humans as a test for their devotion to Me. When they do rebuke him, they prove their worthiness to Me. For I have created them with free will knowing that they would struggle with the evil within them and strive to find the goodness.

And so it will always be that the humans will carry good and evil in their hearts. Each will become what they choose to become. Only those that overcome their evil, and are good, will I reward.'

When I spoke to Michael, he told Me about the birth of the slave girl, Hanna born on Earth. He had come to Me out of fear for her – how she would spend the span of terrestrial life given to her.

He said to me, "Yahweh, this little one must be salvaged. I see in her spirit the promise of goodness. I wish to visit her when she is older and command her to bring her spirit to the humans in her war-torn country. I seek your permission to use her for our purposes."

I thought for a moment,

'Michael - he of the terrible swift sword - most often seeks violent methods to solve problems with the humans. His nature since I created him has been to do battle against evil. He rarely has interest in the cultivation of goodness. Usually he is impatient and chooses to fight. He has always done so over the eons.

Gabriel has the lighter touch. Even Raphael and Uriel take the gentler approach to My missions. Usually I use Michael in times of a great war when My might is most needed. But Michael has come to Me. He has found this little one. Perhaps it will be different this time. Perhaps it will be good for Michael to act for peace – for him to learn patience and avoid the temptation to fight. This Hanna must be special to have attracted his interest.

Michael has always been my greatest warrior in our continuing war that the humans know nothing of – the war between good and evil. The battleground has been the Earth with the humans as the unwitting participants. The forces from the heavens have met those of the underworld there and Michael has led My angels into the struggles unseen by My humans. But now he is inspired by this insignificant human child.'

I have made my decision Michael. When she reaches the age of budding womanhood, before she becomes bound to a man for the remainder of her life, go to her. Use the wisdom I have bestowed on you and give her the mission to act for our goodness and mercy. Bind her with her vow to spend her lifespan working for my plan. Go when it is time and watch her life closely. I want you to tell Me where she prevails and where she fails.

I thought once again,
'I saw right from the beginning when Eve bore her sons Cain and Abel that the humans were given to jealousy and anger. Cain was the first to be born of human and Abel the first to die under human hands.

I made my covenant with Abraham and he founded the great nation of Israel. Then he sired his sons, Ismael and later Isaac when he was one hundred of the years they use to measure time. They founded the two great religions from their tribes. But they fought over their differences in faith and so acted falsely to Me.

I remember the conflict between the brothers Jacob and Esau over the birthright from their father Isaac. Born together from their mother Rebekah, all their descendent nations were at war and separated over the selfishness, deception and greed of her sons. They made war and wasted human life.

But these are my greatest species that dwell on the Earth. I require they care for each other, shepherd the animals and tend to the land. I knew that my creatures would try to bring themselves to ruin - that there would always be tribal strife. For many days of their time they would try to bring cataclysm upon themselves.

I often intervened in small ways caring for them so much as I do. But I leave their destiny on My Earth in their hands. That was what I decided.

I have seen many men who are unaware that they are filled with the spirit of evil. Very few have professed it openly and consciously.

Many others have invoked My name and have believed their actions brought glory to it. Some might be forgiven for their transgressions for their hearts were pure. Robert E. Lee, Thomas Jackson, Ulysses Grant and William Sherman were such men – good men, honorable men, moral, pious, with righteousness and rectitude, dutiful to their cause as they believed their cause to be, loyal to their men, consistent in their belief in Me until their deaths. When they had done all they could do to prepare for their great battles, they professed that then it was in My hands.

But they have broken My 6th commandment – they have killed, committed murder. This is a grievous sin no matter what their cause had been. In other times it was I who commanded tribes of peoples to rise up and smite their enemies without mercy. My chosen people of the twelve tribes of Israel were told to do this when they were forming their great nation. This case with the Americans is like that.

It depends on My judgment and I am Yahweh, the One true God.

As long as they know that it is wrong to kill My children and ask for forgiveness, I can forgive them.

I created all and only I can judge all and forgive.

I must forgive them.

I see that Hanna must be girded for confrontation, for she will face the evil of men like Nathan Bedford Forrest. She must deter them with her spirit as her only weapon. I know that when that happens I will be at her side and she will prevail. It is the meek that I love the most and they must survive.'

Michael said to me, "It shall be done Lord. I will watch over her and protect her. She will be one of us and use your power of Love to wage her battles."

I saw that it was done.

I watched with disinterest as the hurricane began to form up in the Caribbean. I spun it up and pushed it west and then northwest as it passed Florida. It struck land across the Gulf at Baton Rouge. I was angry at the South and felt like punishing it for its transgressions. But I thought better of myself and wound it down after it made landfall.

I just gave them a week of black sky and miserable rain. It suited My mood. They were too pitiful to bring down My wrath. Let Michael and the others see what they can do.

I'm not angry really. I don't feel any fire or passion. I'm just in a bad mood – kind of disappointed, despondent and feeling some despair. It's fatigue. I'm just tired. It's happening more and more now that I am getting so old.

I don't require blood sacrifice anymore. That was mostly their idea to prove their worthiness anyway. All I have ever required is that they love me and each other.

Micah told them all that I require when he said, "He hath shewed thee, O man, what is good; and what doth the Lord require of thee, but to do justly, and to love mercy, and walk humbly with thy God."

It's been a tiresome day for Me – this history of America. It started out with such promise when I sent the people across the land bridge to populate the new continent.

When the Europeans first came, they brought such cruelty to My children. They claimed to do it in My name. Then the others came with so much moral piety and devotion to Me. Their intentions and plans were filled with such goodness. But then they turned to cruelty again. I can't help but think it was better for them before they tasted the tree of knowledge. It was simpler. Now the moments of peace are so short lived.

I have relied on My messengers to advise the humans to choose the true path. But, as I reflect on the humans and what that has done, I think about their past and the old ways then. I looked into their souls, into the darkest places of despondence and hopelessness. There I struck with light – so bright I blinded them with the truth. There was nothing visible to them but a universe of pure white light. It was the goodness they were needing. I reached them that way then, all of them, even the darkest, even the ones farthest away, and they knew.

I will rest. Tomorrow will be a better day.

The rain has stopped. There, there is a rainbow.

Eleven - Michael

Red clay dust from the road covered her legs and the hem of her white dress. Perspiration ran down her face and its salt burned her eyes. The cotton fields were empty. She had been walking for days and hadn't seen a living soul by the time she crossed the border from Alabama into Mississippi yesterday.

"Oh Lord, I is so thirsty", she muttered as her field of vision grew narrower and darker in the bright afternoon sun.

Hanna stumbled off the road and lay down on the edge of the field. Her heartbeat slowed down as she fell into a deep sleep.

The recurring dream came back again as it had for more than a year. The big man in the white linen caftan looked sternly, seriously and with resolve, but his eyes were loving as he stood over her once again.

"I'm your father, girl. We have never met but I have been with you always."

His deeply lined face looked like hers as he smiled, backed away and waved goodbye.

She had felt compelled to travel west in the direction of the sunset. There was something there she would find. It would be important, she felt.

Her eyes opened and the farmer was standing there over her with concern on his face. He wore a wide brimmed felt hat and dusty coveralls over his rolled up cotton shirt. The straps and the bib from his coveralls hung down his legs and in front of his waist and his shirt was opened wide down the front of his chest. He took off his hat and his curly dark hair glistened with sweat on his head and his chest.

"Are you alright wuman?" he asked.

"I couldn't tell if you was alive 'cept for yo' faint breathin."

Hanna said, "Kin I get a drink a watah?"

He smiled with relief and said, "Let me hep you up and tek you to my house. It's coolah."

A day earlier out of Mobile she had heard a feint thunder of hoofs ahead up the road. As a cloud of dust arose, she saw a group of men riding toward her. There were about five of them wearing old gray Confederate tunics. They had a rough look about them. She thought right away they were a group of KKK raiders on the prowl and she was in danger.

In a moment they had surrounded her carriage and forced her to pull up on the reins and stop.

She was quiet and calm and showed no fear.

With distain on his curled lips, one of the men said, "Well looky here at this fine nigger woman. Where are you goin' in yo pretty dress?"

She calmly held him in a steady gaze.

"You look like you ready fo' a fight", he continued.

She finally answered, "Goin' west."

The man asked again, "Where to?

Hanna just said, "Mississippi, I 'spose."

Another man, young with a red beard, agreed she looked feisty, "Let's have us sum fun. I ain't had no juicy dark meat in a while. I luvta watch the disagreeable ones squirm."

She ignored him and looked at the older one with the long dark beard and the cold black eyes. He hadn't said anything but she could tell he was the one in charge.

He saw something in her steady stare that made him pause and have doubt.

"No, leave her be. We have somewherah to go and don't have the time."

Red beard said, "Nathan, it won't tek us long. We been ridin' hard. We needs some receashun."

His horse became agitated and whinnied. It pawed the ground with its front hooves, bounced up and down on them and reared up on its hind legs. Red beard struggled with the reins until his horse stood still once again.

Forrest watched curiously, with disinterest, almost indifferently, and repeated again, "I said leave her be. Take her horse and wagon and leave her heah."

N.B. Forrest had never backed down in war. In fact he charged forward in battle, often ahead of his cavalry, at full gallop, slashing his sword at the enemy, without regard for his own safety, and with all odds stacked heavily against him. He never backed down. He was either one of the bravest or the most deluded the South had ever produced.

He had believed that Grant and Sherman were wrong – that he was on the side of right – the side of the Constitution. So the superior numbers didn't dissuade him, nor the superior armaments either. And neither fatigue nor hunger dissuaded his men from following him.

The Union underestimated the depth of this belief as they faced opponents like Forrest, James Longstreet, Pierre Beauregard and Albert Johnston and Tom Jackson before they were killed. The Confederates were fighting for something, not against something. They were imbued with old romantic notions of chivalry and glory which, as nonsensical as they were, empowered them to victory in many battles they rightfully should not have won.

But that was during the war. And that had all come to ruin. It wasn't for God and country anymore.

Now he was leading a small ragtag band of malcontents and losers. There was no winning the lost cause. He had changed from the flamboyant cavalry soldier to this embittered and hateful man.

In this encounter today, with this pitiful ex-slave woman, there was no honor – no victory to gain – nothing to win. Red beard's horse had acted curiously. That didn't make any sense.

"Let her go", he had said. He rode away ahead of his men with indifference – alone in his thoughts.

They grabbed her arm, flung her to the ground and dumped her carpetbag beside her on the road. They went off on their way with one of them driving her carriage and another holding the reins of his rider-less horse.

Hanna, got up and watched them ride out of sight. Her shoulder and backside were sore but she knew she still had her bible in her bag. "Thank you Lord", she said.

She sat down on the side of the road and watched down its distance as the riders disappeared and the dust dissipated. She was alone and in silence except for the steady buzz of the cicadas in the fields. The sky far off toward the horizon just above the roadbed shimmered as the midday heat rose from the surface.

She stared at them as they vanished and thought, 'I had believed in showing mercy to others. God had taught me to do that. But when it was my turn to be shown mercy, I surrendered all belief in mercy. Then mercy was granted to me.'

In her thoughts she wondered, 'He has seen so much of human livin', now that He is old. He has watched and witnessed so much lustful sinnin', greed, cruelty and despair. So much unnecessary killin' and death. So much immorality, selfishness, arrogance and indifference. Only God could love us after all that. Only God could still smile upon us and make a rainbow, now that He is old.'

She got up after a long while and continued down the road on foot. The blazing sun and oppressive heat sapped her energy as she walked along tugging her carpet bag beside her in the dust. She came to a greener area, collapsed under a shade tree and immediately fell into a deep sleep. In a dream Michael came to her once again.

He stood towering over her and smiled without uttering a word. There was just his brilliant white visage looking down upon her, comforting her.

She cried out to him in a language of thought clearer than she could ever speak out loud, "Why does the Lord allow humans to act so cruelly to one another? Why has He given us that free will?"

He squatted down and balanced on his heels so that he could be closer to her as she lay on the ground. He smiled at her conveying his love.

"Why doesn't He just make us obey His will?" she asked.

After a long silence Michael spoke, "God made that choice long ago when you tasted of the tree of knowledge. He gave you free will because you have a soul Hanna. Your soul is His gift and it means human beings have free will."

"But some humans use their free will in defiance of the Word", she thought.

She felt his love and had no fear of him. She just wanted to understand.

Michael understood her need and spoke again, "The Word is God. He has given it to you. Hanna, your faith is a choice. And if faith is a choice, it can be lost – for a man, an angel or the devil himself."

He waited while she thought.

"You have been faithful and God is pleased with the direction you have taken to keep your covenant with Him. There is more for you to understand. God has sent me to you again because it is time for you to learn more."

"Tell me angel. I want to know what I must do."

Michael was pleased she was ready and said, "My kind understand His purpose more completely and follow the Word without free will. Faith is not needed for us. He has made us this way."

"We are given certain powers not of the Earth, but not free will. You see that we have no need for it. We have knowledge of Him and so do not need faith either."

"Your kind will never understand God's plan completely. But understanding part of it as you do, your part, is what it means to have a soul. In the end that is what being a human being is about. With your soul you can love. That is His gift to you" he continued.

"When your life of this Earth is completed – when He decides it is time - you will share our immortality."

Hanna smiled full into his face.

"But while you live in this mortal coil, He has commanded me to give you a power only a few humans possess."

He reached out his hand and said, "Take my hand".

She was not fearful exactly, more like timid and awestruck, as she tentatively took his hand.

When she did, he asked, "Do you feel that?"

She felt a slight electrical tingle and nodded to him in affirmation.

"You are given the power to heal with your touch. God has said that this will strengthen your mission with those you will encounter. In many cases, your touch will heal their illness. In every case, they will feel His love through your instrument."

Michael reached into his robe and held out an orange in his hand.

"I was helping the humans in Florida after the hurricane and picked this up for you. Take this and eat it", he said. "I have no use for food and you are in need of nourishment."

She held it in her hand and it was cool. She peeled and ate it. It soothed her dry throat.

"One thing before I go. I heard that you were concerned that God is old, maybe he is too tired to care anymore. I have it on good authority that is not true. He is timeless and ageless. Time as you know it has no meaning for Him. The world had a beginning and will have an end. But He had no beginning and will have no end."

At last Saint Michael told her what she needed to know and said,

"Hanna, the time has come to tell you the pure truth and its essence – God's truth. It is more than your God-given mission and the covenant you made with Him when you were a young girl – for harmony among people. It is beyond that and more deeply rooted in understanding what is man and what is God.

You are old enough, strong enough and wise enough now to know it. So here is the truth of it, all of it.

God has forever watched man, His creation. He has seen all things. He knows man's frailties in every way and beyond what you can imagine – man is mendacious, selfish, thieving, murderous, warmongering, power-seeking, lustful, fornicating, sinful, immoral, narcissistic, self-centered, self-motivated, arrogant, cruel, tribal, petty, unilluminated, untranscendent, unfeeling, uncaring, heartless, mindless, ignorant and blind - and knows the essence of the meaning of human life.

How could God let man be these things? It is because He has given him free will and man is not God. He has expected him to listen. He has expected him to understand. Many have done this. Many have not.

I give you this now on His authority. You know what it is. When I tell you, you will already know that you know it. It is love."

Michael stood and began to move away. His brilliance rose and blended into the light from the sun until he was no longer visible. She awakened under the cool shade of the tree.

Hanna had known that to love is good and that it pleased the Lord. But now she knew three more things. She knew that God wanted us to love each other for certain, and that God is love and when that is known for certain, that is grace – God's grace. Now she was illuminated, risen up, transcended, and forever imbued with His Spirit.

Twelve - McComb

All across Mississippi she saw the devastation of the land and the gaunt lost look in the eyes of its people – the scattered few she encountered. Both black and white, they were starving and had no hope.

As Hanna began her traverse of Mississippi, about a week or two out of Mobile, she met a couple heading in the other direction. They were an elderly white couple in a fine carriage and dressed more refined than anyone she had seen in the region.

She hailed them with a smile and upraised hand and said, "'Scuse me folks. I sees ya goin' east. Wheah ya headed?"

They told her they were going to Alabama – to Mobile.

"Tha's a blessin", she told them. "Would ya does me a favah ifs ya cans?"

They were decent people and were willing to help.

"Please wudya look up de Blanchards on Dauphin Street whens ya theah? Tell 'em they Hanna fine 'n' doin' well comin' 'cros Mississippi."

They smiled and promised they would. So Ken and Abigail, still mystified about Hanna's departure, knew she was well.

When she eventually arrived in McComb, Mississippi, she found a small quiet town without much activity. The local people didn't move around very much, or very quickly. There was little to do and the steamy humidity of the nearby swamp forested area discouraged strenuous effort. There was no relief and no breezes coming in from cooler bodies of water either.

For Hanna, this was much different than Mobile for certain, but harkened back to her childhood long ago in Tuscaloosa. The people were friendly enough to a stranger. Their curiosity about her broke the tedium.

She talked to a man at the general store. In country towns, this was the place to get information and even the place to send and receive mail. The man was at the small counter serving as the local post office when she approached him.

"Good aftanoon", she said. "Knows any place Ah cud stays whiles Ah's heah?"

He told her there was one boardinghouse but not for coloreds like her.

"Theys a colored famly wud put ya up 'n' feed ya ifs ya wants."

"Thank ya kindly mista", she said.

He gave her their name and she went on her way.

Hanna met a local, a white man, on the street and declared, "Ah come heah ta look fo' work."

The white man she met was of middle age and was clean of appearance. She didn't mention she had some money saved up with her.

"Does ya knows any folks who needs someun ta care fo' they youngins, or keep they house, or needs sum healin' fo' they ailmens?"

She didn't want to tell a stranger a greater mission had driven her to this place, or at least in this direction, or how it had come to be.

He suggested, "Theys sum folks cud use that. Reckon Ah cain't think 'bout any names jus now."

"Thank ya sah. You kind to a strangah. De otha thang is Ah thinks my mama she come from heah long 'go, back bafor' tha war. Ah thinks shes on a plantation round heah."

He looked at this pleasant black woman, nearing middle age herself, and remembered, "Yas. Theys a plantation heah onct. Called it Savannah Oaks."

"Oh my stars, how does Ah find it?"

He pointed in two directions.

"Ya see dat road ova theah? Dat's tha ole road bafor' they be puttin' tha new un ova heah."

She looked at the overgrown narrow path leading away from town.

"It go jus 'bout haf mile ta tha ole place. Ya can 'most see hit from heah. Not much ta see theah tho'. Jus a ole broke down buildin' 'n' some wreak cabins. Use' ta be, 'afor tha town built, right heah was part ov tha plantation."

She thanked him kindly and trudged double time out the old road. The man watched her go, amazed at her speed in this damnable heat. When she came up to the mansion, she saw it wasn't as bad as the man had described it. It was shaded dark with the huge live oaks.

The house was still beautiful and majestic, but overgrown so much with vines and green vegetation. Nature has taken its toll in just a few decades, but not completely.

The slave cabins were mostly rotten and fallen apart from the incessant onslaught of the humidity and moisture.

She stopped there and soberly reflected, 'This must be where my father lived with my mother so long ago.'

She became saddened and she cried. She prayed for their immortal souls.

Hanna stayed in McComb. It felt right to be close to the memory of Savannah Oaks. Before long, she began to meet the people there and began to find ways to help them. She began to settle in. The people of both races liked her; became drawn to her.

She did begin to keep their houses, and look after their children, and take care of their sick, and give spiritual solace to their dying. They came to see her gentle light and she made them happier and more at peace with their lives.

Before very long, she turned to the African Methodist Episcopal church there for her solace and spiritual sustenance. It gave her a community of sympathetic souls.

Hanna met an old woman named Nora Travers who lived on the edge of town just south off the main road. Some folks in town thought the wrinkled, stooped over old white woman was a witch. It was because Nora spent her time foraging for roots and herbs and brewing healing potions.

When Hanna found her, they struck up a friendship. Hanna knew there was much she could learn from her new friend. Nora could see the kind goodness in Hanna and that Hanna accepted her for what she was.

They became dearest friends with the common mission of healing. Nora had a bountiful knowledge of how to cure the body's ailments. Hanna had a gift for healing the tortured and hateful soul.

They foraged together in the fields and the forest and tended the herbal garden around Nora's old ramshackle cabin.

"Now lookit dis deah", Nora told her in her creaky, almost inaudible voice.

"Hit's call fevahfew 'n' hits good fo' headaches, fevah, so' bones, sick stumick 'n' wumen's time ov month."

Hanna remembered and told her, "Ah knows 'bout willow bark 'n' how hits hepful fo' tha aches 'n' tha fevah too.

"Ah gets dat from tha willa trees in da swamp. Ah shaves tha bark 'n' boils hit up ina tea", she said.

"Us learns 'bout dis from da animals", she continued.

Hanna asked her what she was growing in the garden.

Nora said, "Ah gots mint 'n' chamomile good fo' tha digestin. Sumtime mix wid tha sage 'n' tha thyme ta mek hit taste bettah.

Gots ta be careful 'bout sum thins like poison hemlock n' nightshade. Cud kill ya if'n ya donts know wat ya doin'."

Nora gave her a small leather satchel with a string she had made so that Hanna could keep her herbs and roots around her neck when she visited the people. Hanna wore it next to her necklace with the cross. Both of these vestiges meant healing to Hanna.

They spent so much time there together at Nora's place that she invited Hanna to come live with her. Hanna was happy to have a place to live and a friend for companionship. The two of them became inseparable there.

But Nora, as a recluse, preferred to stay at her home tending her garden, while Hanna spent most of her time with the people in McComb – looking after them and taking care of them. The little money she took more than provided for her and Nora's modest needs. They lived simply and purely.

Hanna never missed Sunday worship unless she was tending the sick. The Lord would understand that. It fulfilled her, and was her joy, to hear the word, to read from the book, to sing and to pray, and to laugh and to cry.

When she ministered to the sick and applied her herbal remedies, Hanna laid her hands on her patients and said a prayer. They came to recognize that she had a spirit – a special way about her – that was not to be feared but to be cherished. It was goodness and based on love.

Hanna was not above doing the hard work of cleaning the folks' houses, or doing their laundry, or the smart work of caring for their children. She got to know everybody that way.

Word spread about her among people of the region and she was sought after. Many wanted to just be with her, in her presence. God was grateful for Michael's initiative and He was smiling.

By 1888, she had been living and working in McComb for many years. She had heard about the crazy old woman who lived by herself and spooked the town folk. She went to visit her and took pity on her.

She smiled calmly at her while the old woman kept talking about thievin' niggers right to her face - as though she was not even there or that she didn't even look just like the people the woman was babbling about. It was a test of her faith. She acted mercifully as she had been taught, as she practiced, as she believed.

Hanna had no way of knowing that this was the woman who had been so cruel to her mother Josena when she had been a child under the woman's control. The old woman had no way of knowing that this kind woman was the daughter of the same Josena she had abused.

Now that God was older, He enjoyed His irony. He must have. He couldn't help it. It was like the playwright who enjoys the private story note he has written especially knowing his audience cannot.

The old woman waited for her husband to come back from the war. He was a gallant, chivalrous Colonel leading his brave Confederate men to defend their way of life. He had been gone too long. In fact, they had hidden out together in their remote plantation awaiting the end of the war. They had lost the plantation and her husband had died. Her remembrances were the pure fabrication of her mind lost to its denial. Abuses and disappointments of the past had been long forgiven, or at least forgotten as though they had never happened.

Wordlessly, Hanna listened to the woman's fantasy remembrances. She couldn't know her past or the truth of it, but she knew the woman had been powerful once before she had lost all her material things. She had fallen from power but had not known grace. Without that, she had no hope and so lost her mind as well.

Her shining eyes stared away at the distance, at nothing. She spoke without remembering, knowing nothing about Charleston or Savannah or the backland of the Mississippi delta, couldn't know what she didn't know, dreaming every day, some romantic notion, her reality, what she would have wished her life to be, her own selfish picture made up in her own head as her own self-preservation, protecting from the harsh truth of what her life had been, the mind preserving her dignity without her even knowing that either. She didn't know who she was or who Hanna was or what she represented. She had denied herself the salvation of grace and the sanity of hope.

Hanna understood these things and listened. When at last the old woman paused, she took the woman's hands. With her palms turned down and the woman's turned up, Hanna bowed her head and closed her eyes. She rubbed her thumbs in gentle circles in the woman's palms and the woman became calm and quiet and at peace.

Hanna came back often and looked after the woman until the woman passed away. If nothing else, Hanna helped the town folks understand. The woman had shut the world out, except for Hanna.

And they shut the woman out too. She had been a monument to things past, painfully reminding them of lost glory, the way life used to be for them, for everyone who believed in the cause. But she was a burden, a heavy load they could not carry. Best to look the other way and forget.

With their curiosity satisfied, they had no need to come to her funeral. Hanna took care of that too.

Thirteen – Ashford Reunion

They drove their carriage the short half mile south of McComb to Nora Travers's place. David and Josie were not surprised to see how run down the old gray weathered shack appeared.

When they pulled up in the yard, the old woman came out to see who was coming. She looked very old, wrinkled, stooped over, maybe a little crazy, and wary of strangers coming to her place. She was holding a long stick, like a walking staff or a spear with no tip.

"Who yo' folks 'n' wha' does yo' wants heah?"

Josie stepping down from the carriage, said, "Good morning. We heard good things about you in town."

Nora became more relaxed and said, "Good ta heah dat."

"We learned you make potions to make sick folks better", Josie continued.

"Dat's right. Ah does".

David felt Nora was comfortable enough with them and decided to tell her their purpose.

"We are here looking for our sister, Hanna Drish. We heard she lives with you."

"My stars, she do", Nora exclaimed.

"We have been traveling all over Alabama and Mississippi to find her. We've never met her but she is our older sister. We have the same father", David explained.

The old woman beamed and broke out into a broad smile.

She looked like a different woman and said, "Come in da house den. She in tha kichin. We's havin' sum tea."

They looked at each other in wonder and followed old Nora into the house. There, sitting at the kitchen table with her saucer of tea was their sister, a middle aged black woman of large stature, her lined face full of an expression of resolve. In front of her was her bible, opened to Corinthians.

Josie gasped and blurted out, "You look just like our father."

Hanna looked at them puzzled and bemused. She wasn't wary or suspicious, just puzzled.

"You folks sound like Yankees. Hits been a long time since Ah heah da refine' talk ov da educated rich whites or da Yankees."

Josie offered, "We can imagine that. You left the Blanchards in Mobile years ago, didn't you?"

Hanna was confused and wondered how these strangers could know that.

David said, "Hanna, we are your brother and sister. Josiah is our father and yours as well."

She stiffened and looked at them dumbstruck. It had been a long time since she heard her father's name. Suddenly she remembered Mobile and the Blanchards and shifted her manner of speech.

"What are your names? Where do you live? Tell me about my father."

Josie smiled warmly and offered, "Well Hanna Drish, we are from Ohio. Our father lives there and has a furniture factory. Our mother's name is Mary. We were born there thirteen years after you. I am named Josena, after Father's first wife, your mother."

Tears poured down Hanna's cheeks. Her eyes shined. She had so many questions. Nora watched and listened. God was pleased. It was time Hanna found some happiness for herself.

Hanna's head was swimming. She had never given up on finding her father, but now it had come to her so fast and all at once. She struggled to grasp all she was learning.

They spent the whole of the day there together, talking and getting to know each other. The Ashfords agreed to stay in McComb for a while and be with their sister. Eventually they convinced Hanna to leave her settled life, and her mission, and come north for an extended visit, or maybe more.

When they had first arrived in town, they located the one boardinghouse with rooms available for visitors. They found it easily and saw the sign on the front door as they approached to go in. They went in anyway and inquired with the matron at the makeshift front desk in the living room.

"Sorry this is for whites only – no coloreds", she informed them.

"Ya'll can check at tha general storeah. See if they kin hep ya", she offered.

Exasperated, they followed her kind advice and learned there that there was a colored family that took in visitors to town.

With the money the colored family took in from its boarders, they were able to put on a better meal than they would have had on their own. These were hard times in the country, especially for folks like them.

David and Josie got all they could eat of barbeque pork, collard greens, rice with black beans and cornbread. Chicory was the best they could do for coffee. It was a feast and nobody left the table hungry.

The patron had the duty of the supper prayer and told them after, "Hopes ta sees ya'all in church Sunday."

David and Josie said they'd be pleased to come.

"Yankees are Christians too", they told him.

The matron said, "We's all American Christians in ouh country, sum mo' faithful than othas. We's all sinners too, buts we trys ta respec' tha Lord's commandments."

They stayed in McComb several days – visiting Hanna and Nora, sleeping in town in the colored family's home.

Hanna said, "Come wid me ta town wheah Ah works 'n' see ma friens."

She introduced them to the plain folk that were her community.

"Dis heah ma brothah 'n' sistah. They's Yankees from tha North buts still good people."

One Saturday she said, "Now ya come ta church wid me tomorra."

Josie and David smiling said, "Course we will big sister."

Hanna got up and spoke to the congregation that Sunday at her AME church as she did most Sundays during sharing time.

"Ah blessed ta have found ma brothah and sistah", she told them.

"They's wid me taday. Gives dem a warm southurn greetin'."

David and Josie were touched by the welcoming smiles from the congregants. They were with their own people.

"They's fixin' ta stay a while", she added.

"They's be ovah ta Bessie Johnson's place til she decides ta throw dem out. So if'n ya'all sees dem roun', give dem ya best southurn comfort – yo spirit not da whiskey."

The congregation laughed out loud all at once as one.

Josie leaned over and whispered to David, "And their best southern humor."

He looked at her and burst out loud laughing.

"Let's raise ouh hans togethah 'n' sing *What a Friend We Have in Jesus*. Calpurnia please lead us in praise."

'Hanna is happy here', David thought. 'Will she want to come back with us?', he wondered soberly. 'Ours is a different world.'

'We must be together. Hope she sees it that way too', he concluded.

After the long service was over, they held an informal, plain folks, reception for the Ashfords in the church yard. Mostly it was just lemonade and animated conversation for the whole of the afternoon. The congregation was curious about the northerners and had many questions.

Southerners have to know more about new people whether they be stranger or kin. They are curious and want to spend time asking questions to get acquainted.

Regardless of class or race, they need to know where you are from and who your people are. The reason and root of this is uncertain. Maybe it is a sense of family or interest in the land and places. Maybe it is a protective paranoia from fear of invasion – a closed view of protecting their own – from outsiders or a sense of guilt or inferiority or shame. Maybe it is just a view of country people everywhere – something city people don't know, care about or have time for – a difference in the pace of life. But it is always there and strangers must respond to it when the cultures clash.

So the church members had good conversation with Josena and David. The twins didn't think of it as being nosy. But they wanted to tell them about Hanna too – how much they loved her, how much she meant, how much she had done for their families, their wives and their husbands, children and old folks. She was a Christian inspiration to McComb the eight years she had lived there with them. She was a Christian who walked the walk and had the kindest and most generous heart. She was a Christian pillar and institution.

After she agreed, when she finally decided, to go north with her siblings, David made some preparations. He appeared before the three women at Nora's place one day in his old work clothes he had brought along on the trip.

Hanna asked him, "Wha' ya doin' Yankee brotha'? Are ya tryin' be like us?"

"No", he laughed. "I've got some things to do."

He bought an old buckboard with a broken axle and wheel. He sold the carriage and set about to repair the buckboard and make some modifications. He fixed it up in good running order and built an extended bed with new planks he had fashioned. He added some storage shelves secured for travel and a third seat so that each would have a comfortable place to sit for the long ride.

When they saw what he had done they understood what he had been up to and appreciated his ingenuity.

Just before the day they were to depart, David announced he had one more thing to do. It was a surprise.

"I'll be back later this afternoon", he told them as he shook the reins on the old horse and charged out of Nora's property in a cloud of dust in his new wagon.

While they were waiting for him, the three women sat in Nora's kitchen talking and enjoying cups of chamomile tea. Josie noticed an old fiddle in the corner of the room.

"Nora, do you play that old fiddle?" she asked.

"Ah does onct in a while", Nora answered.

"Mind if I try to play a tune?" Josie asked.

"Course not. Go 'head."

Josie picked up the old relic, held it close to her ear and plucked the strings. She turned the thumbscrews to tighten them into perfect pitch.

"Got a bow?" she asked.

Nora looked in her bedroom and brought her out the bow.

Josie smiled at Nora and said, "See if you know this one".

She warmed up with a slow soft rendition of *Brahm's Lullaby*.

Hanna and Nora's mouths fell open.

She played a lively version of *My Old Kentucky Home* and a deeply heartfelt *Amazing Grace*. Hanna asked how she had ever learned to play like that.

"I have been playing since I was little and I studied violin at university. My college started out as a music school for colored students."

The women smiled at each other, impressed with Josie's hidden talent.

David came back later with a pile of wood in the bed of the wagon. The three women watched him arriving in another cloud of dust.

"Wha' ya got?" asked Hanna.

David smiled at them and proudly declared, "It's dissembled to lay flat for the trip and I know you can't recognize it. It's Father's old pecan kitchen table from Savannah Oaks. We're taking it home to him."

Hanna hadn't seen it in the old plantation when she was there and didn't know what it was. The day she was there, she hadn't gone inside.

David told her, "It will be a surprise for our father. You will see."

They hadn't wanted to tell their father about bringing her home to Ohio until they were sure she would come. They hadn't wanted to tell him they had found her but she wouldn't be coming north either. That would have compelled him to come to Mississippi to see her and he was too old for that. It had worked out for the best as it often does – God's providence solving life's dilemmas.

Fourteen – Going Home

They left on a beautiful summer morning late in June of 1900. Hanna said goodbye to Nora and admonished her to continue their work.

"Now ya look afta' our patiens ole girl. Ya git out mo' 'n' go sees 'em. They's depen' on us ta take care of dem. Our people need ya mo' wid me away. I be gone a long time."

That was the last Nora and Hanna ever saw each other. But they would remember each other fondly.

David told Hanna, "You'll be seeing parts of America you never saw before. We'll be traveling north, following along most of the route Papa traveled with his old friend David, who I'm named after, back in the fall of 1865. I think you'll like it."

Hanna asked if they could visit the Drish plantation. David apologized for it to her – saying it was hundreds of miles out of the way. He explained to her that the trip home would not swing east, but go directly north up the Mississippi to Tennessee, Kentucky and Ohio. While they had covered Josiah and David's trip in reverse, this leg with Hanna was direct and differed somewhat from the old route.

But Hanna saw the regions and land traveled in the past by Josiah Ashford and David Wexley - from Natchez north along the Mississippi River to Tennessee, continuing north to Kentucky, east along the Ohio River to Covington, Kentucky, and finally across the river through Cincinnati to Hamilton, Ohio. For her, of course, the North had a different flavor.

David telegraphed ahead: *Papa, arriving home Monday with our sister Hanna. Stop.*

Josiah and Mary watched for them and were out in the front yard when they heard the carriage arriving.

"Here is your daughter Papa", David told him.

"Hanna, this is our father."

"Hanna, it has been half a lifetime waiting for you my dear girl. Come here and hold me."

"Papa, I never gave up waiting for this day. I never forgot you. All the years I prayed for you."

"God has blessed us both", he said.

The family stood there in the yard for this extraordinary moment, as tears were shed all the way around. It was a monumental reunion, half a lifetime in the making.

Mary's heart melted as she watched them there together.

"Come with me Hanna. I want to show you the room we have begun to prepare for you. It's on the second floor", she said.

"Joe and I moved our bedroom to the main floor a couple years ago, now that we are getting older."

Hanna said, "Thank you for your kindness. What shall I call you?"

"Whatever suits you. Think of me as your old mother. Mama Mary if you like."

Hanna smiled and followed her up the stairs. In the big room they had placed a new Ashford Furniture bed and dresser.

"We can work together on the rest of it after you settle your things. Josie's room is the one next to yours. She is gone a lot but still lives with us."

There seemed to be an understanding that this was not going to be a prolonged visit. The expectation was that she would live here from now on. That evening they had their first family meal together in the formal dining room seated around the majestic mahogany table.

After dinner, Josie brought her violin to the dining room. She explained to Hanna that it was an American-made Guarneri model made by George Gemunder in Astoria New York. It was only a few years old and was beautiful to the eye.

"I'd like to play this to welcome you to the family", she said as she raised it to her shoulder and tilted her neck to its base.

With her arm held perfectly parallel and the bow poised over the strings, she attacked Mozart's Concerto No. 5 in A major, the second movement. It was breathtaking.

"My word", Hanna said. "I'se nevah heard anythin' like dat."

"Thank you Hanna. I wanted you to hear some real fiddle playing."

Not certain of the family protocol in their home and trying to be respectful and mannerly, Hanna asked, "What should I call 'ya Josena".

Josie laughed and said, "You can call me little sister if you want. You have earned the right. I don't permit David to do that anymore."

"But you's twins, da same age."

"I know, but he has this strange notion that since he was born five minutes earlier than me, he is my big brother."

Hanna laughed, "Don't ya worry little sister. Us girls, we stick togetha."

David said, "Well if you are both through, I'd like to show you around the rest of the house Hanna."

She smiled and said, "That be fine little brotha."

David rolled his eyes and led her out of the dining room along the foyer to Josiah's study. He took her into the room and showed her his big mahogany desk and all the bookcases filled with his books around the room.

"Hanna, Papa accumulated a lot of books in his life. Most of them are his law books from his career in Ohio government.

David Wexley was Papa's best friend. He wasn't a master furniture maker and cabinetmaker like our father. He was a master carpenter. But they always worked together and he helped Papa build all these bookcases. I'll tell you more about our Uncle David after a while. Wait 'til you see all the machines he invented in the factory for Father's furniture business. He was an extraordinary white man and part of our family."

Among other things, he explained to her, it was the curiosity about the Union soldier, David Wexley that led David Ashford to study history. He needed to gain a better understanding of how it was – make it live again in his mind.

After Hanna had been with the family a few days, Josiah asked her to come with him for the day.

"Hanna, let's take a carriage ride. I'd like to spend the day with you, show you around and talk to you. Most of all, I want us to get to know each other."

"That would be so fine, Papa. Me too", she said.

They rode out toward the factory and Josiah told her, "You should have seen this when we first came here. David Wexley and I raised a few dollars doing carpentry for the folks in the area and I bought the old farm here. We started Ashford Furniture in an old barn."

Hanna looked at his face – into his eyes - and said, "I heard so much about Mister Wexley. He meant so much to you didn't he?"

"He did. With his help we built a new life here. More than that, he saved me from drowning in despair when we found your mother had died."

"It must have been a very sad time for you Papa. But I see that God brought you through your trials along with your friend David."

"He did and still does my girl."

He showed her around the bustling factory and she looked in wonder at the activity and size of its operation.

“This is amazin’ Papa. All this is yours?”

“Yes, it belongs to our family. That includes you now Hanna.”

He drove up the hill to the saw mill and stopped the carriage there. No one was around that time of day.

He turned to her and looking into her eyes said, “No one has said this yet, but I’d like you to live with us from now on. I lost your mother, but I never want to lose you now that you are found.”

“I have been thinkin’ ‘bout my life in Mississippi and the people I tended to there. It will be hard to leave them behind and I will miss them dearly. But I want to be with you and my family now. I have longed for you for so many years of my life. I can’t leave you now.”

He reassured her, “You can find people here to care for in this community. Your mission can continue. You’ll get to know them from our church. There are good people that go to the other church too – some good white people.”

She smiled and said, “I have loved the good white people I have found – just as I do our own - just as the Lord taught me to.”

Smiling back he said, “I wanted us to have this private day together so that I could tell you about your mother and our life together.”

“I have heard ‘bout some of it from her when I was a little girl.”

”Yes. It was so long ago.” He paused, stared away toward the distance thoughtfully, and then added, “But just yesterday”.

"We only had two years together. The master – Marcus Taylor married us and she lived with me in my cabin nights and worked in the main house as a servant during the day. One day he took her away and sold her."

"Why did he do it?" she asked as tears began to form in her eyes.

Josiah's eyes began to well up too when he asked, "Are you sure you want to hear the whole story? It is painful?"

"Yes, I need the answers I have waited to hear."

"All right then, I'm going to give you the plain cruel truth. The master, Marcus Taylor bought a slave named Sarah at the Natchez auction when he first built the plantation. He raped her and she gave birth to your mother, Josena. They are your grandparents.

Josena was raised in the planation mansion and the mistress, Rebecca Taylor hated her because of her husband's vile repeated acts with Sarah and because he showed love and affection for Josena and cared for her in the house."

"Wait stop, Papa", Hanna gasped. "I know that Rebecca. I cared for her as a crazy old woman in McComb. I didn't know who she was and she didn't know me either. She made a lot of nonsense talk I couldn't figure out. But she did say her name was Rebecca Taylor."

"That was many years later of course – after the war ended and the plantation fell to ruin", he concluded. "She was always cruel to your mother. She took out all her hate for her husband on his daughter. And Josena was my wife."

"But what you should know is that he sold your mother away when she was grown up and married to me as a young woman. He decided to rid her from his life. It was so that his wife might stop fighting him about it. Her presence every day, and the things he had done, were ruining their marriage".

Hanna began to cry and sobbed, "But how could a father do that?"

Josiah was crying too and said, "My wife was taken away from me at the Savannah Oaks plantation. I didn't know where she went until later, when I found out she had a baby girl soon after coming to the Drish plantation. We both know she was killed there later."

Hanna's eyes were red and brimming with tears.

She said, "I know the rest Papa. Mister Drish cared for her until she died. He brought me to Mister Blanchard for my safety when the war came too close to him. But now Papa – now at last – at long last – God had delivered me to you and we are together."

He was silent for a long moment and throwing his arms around her said, "Now we are together forever."

After their emotions subsided, Josiah drove the carriage back to their house and they joined the rest of the family.

Two days later David Wexley's casket arrived on the train in Cincinnati from Aspen, Colorado. Josiah had explained to his children what had happened with the mining accident out west. David and Josena remembered him fondly as their Uncle David during their childhood years. Hanna was so heartened to see the love between these two great men of different races so long ago after the great Civil War.

Josiah wisely explained to his family again, this time for Hanna's benefit, the way it was this way, "After the war, David Wexley was never content – never satisfied, never happy. He liked people well enough and had a passion for justice. The problem was himself – inside himself.

David had seen too many men exploded by cannon, torn apart by muskets. Those that survived it could never be the same – never right again. Those that didn't experience it, could never know what it was like.

So he kept wandering and searching. He was working as a structural engineer at a silver mine out west in Colorado. There was a planned explosion that went badly and trapped workers inside. He rushed into the tunnel and got killed by a second cave-in from the aftershock."

As an afterthought Josiah reflected that David had written him several times the eight years he was out there. His words presented a brave front, but were dark and sad between the lines.

David hid the table from his father. He worked on it in an abandoned room in the factory, once used for hand finishing of furniture. In this quiet remote corner of the original building, he assembled the old pecan wooden table and cleaned off the decades of grime with turpentine. He hand sanded it with fine grit and rubbed in linseed oil until it shined like gold.

When he brought old Josiah in to see it, he told him, "This was the table you made for the kitchen in Savannah Oaks, Papa. Do you remember?"

Josiah looked at its gleaming finish, the rich pecan with its subtle beautiful straight grain, and the deep beauty marks of character from a generation of slaves preparing food to serve the Massa and the Mistress. He remembered that they gathered around it to eat their own meals together there – all the household women servants, laundresses and attendants, and the male butler and livery man too.

He stood silently looking at its rich gleaming surfaces and sturdy legs- running his hands over it and touching the marks of character stored in its memory and he remembered. He remembered Josena and when he was a young buck full of fire and promise of emancipation and a life better for him and his own.

He smiled through tears of remembrance and said, "Thank you for this gift son. You can never know what it means to me."

David choked up too, said, "We'll put it in the showroom of Ashford Furniture as your first fine piece. It is history, Papa."

They embraced silently for a moment.

Hanna had a few years to spend with her father. Of all her family - her kin now - he was the one she could share a spiritual connection with.

He told her, "I know God has a plan for all of us. He has blessed me."

She knew he had lived all his long life believing that – and what a life it had been, rising above slavery, persevering, enduring and making a difference with it. She adored him for that and understood him better than the others did.

"Father", she said, "we have lived very similar lives. We have been blessed".

But she had more to tell him. It was about her life-long secret.

"Papa, I has sumthin ta tell ya. I nevah told nobody 'bout this bafor", she said.

He looked at her with the mystery of curiosity and lack of understanding in his warm eyes and told her, "You can tell me. If it is something bad, I will keep your secret."

"No it wasn't that. When I was a young girl, livin' with Ken and Abigail, somthin' amazin' happened one night. I was in my room sleepin' and thought I was dreamin'. God sent his angel Michael to me. I swear He did. He was so big and powerful, at first I was scared. But I felt his love right away and knew it was all right. He told me God had picked me out and His plan for my life."

His mouth fell open. He looked into her eyes and saw the sincerity.

"What happened? What was it?" he asked.

"He said I would nevah marry or have a family of my own. He wanted me to carry out a special mission fo' Him all the days of my life. It was more than worshipin' and believin' in Him."

"What was it?"

The tears flowed from her eyes when she said it at last, "He wanted me to bring together the white people and black people I meet in this world. Harmony between them was what God was longin' fo. I think His heart was brokin' seein' all the hate and killin' goin' on in the world."

He realized she had spent her life doing that.

"I believe you my girl. And I see it in you. It is real and I love you."

"He didn't tell me how to do it. I jus' undastood I have ta learn it myself as I go along."

"And you have Hanna. You figured it out better than most of us. Sometimes, rarely, it happens naturally. Remember the improbable friendship I had so long with David Wexley – a white man from Baltimore, a Union soldier I met after the war. We were brothers Hanna. He taught me what was possible."

She knew that it was.

"He came to me agin' papa. It was on the road when I was walkin's 'cross Mississippi. He lifted me up when I was down. He gave me the power of touch fo' healin'", she said.

When at last she was finished, they sat together looking across the fields from their porch. It was warm but the air was dry. The Ohio sun made the brown grasses glisten like gold. He held her hand and wondered.

Years later, when he was older and sick, she touched him and he felt it. He understood and believed then for certain.

He had a very special love for her.

She took it real hard when he passed away.

Fifteen – To Everything There Is a Season

And a time to every purpose under heaven

A time to be born, a time to die
A time to plant, a time to reap
A time to kill, a time to heal
A time to laugh, a time to weep

A time to build up, a time to break down
A time to dance, a time to mourn
A time to cast away stones, a time to gather stones together

A time of love, a time of hate
A time of war, a time of peace
A time you embrace, a time to refrain from embraces

A time to gain, a time to lose
A time to rend, a time to sew

The legislature up in Columbus was not in session, so Josiah had been around home. He had been slowing down anyway.

He got up one morning and had breakfast with Mary. As old folks do, they reminisced about the children growing up and how much life was changing in the modern age.

He was restless and told her, "Mary, I'm gonna go over to the factory and poke around a bit. I'll be back before noon."

"Don't stick your nose in where it's not needed dear."

He smiled and went upstairs to dress for the day. He put on his favorite white linen shirt without a collar, and open in the front, and his baggy comfortable slacks and left for the short walk to the end of his property. He looked up at how big the factory had become. It had certainly taken on a life of its own in recent years. He felt more apart from it.

He located his superintendent and asked him how business was going.

Frank, uncomfortable with the boss's question, had to admit, "Production has slowed down and inventory is up because sales have been fallin' off the past two months."

"I want to have a meeting with the department heads and talk about this. Would you gather them together in the conference room right now?"

"Sure Josiah. Give us about fifteen minutes."

He nodded and walked around the production floor to observe the workers and their output. He looked at the raw stock inventory, the finishing rooms and the finished goods staged for delivery.

When the meeting was convened, Josiah looked around at them from the head of the big table with his stern expression of resolve, this time maybe more sinister, and asked, "What's going on? What's happened to sales?"

David and Josena were not present.

There was a silent pause until the head of sales spoke up, "As you know the economy is not good and we've about saturated the market in our region."

Josiah put his hand to his chin and postulated, "By now I would have expected we would have increased our reach beyond Ohio to New York, Michigan, Indiana and Kentucky."

"You know we have been selling into Kentucky for years boss."

"Well I want something done about it. This is not acceptable", he said as he got up and left the room.

He was concerned and couldn't stop thinking about it. That evening he found David, met him in the study and told him about the meeting. David listened attentively and respectfully. He had heard about this himself.

"Papa, maybe it's time you stepped down and let me take over. You've got enough to do around here."

Josiah glared at him and said, "What enough? You think I'm too old to run my own company?"

"No of course not. I'm just suggesting maybe Josie and I have more energy to carry on the fight."

Josiah remained silent for so long David began to wonder what the old man was thinking or whether he was thinking at all.

Finally, Josiah got up abruptly from his comfortable leather chair in the study and said, "Well all right then. I will step down and the next generation can take over."

"We will always come to you for advice Father."

He smiled and said, "You'd better boy, if you know what's good for you."

The end of an age had come.

Shortly before he died, while his intelligence was still at its full capacity, Josiah Ashford gave his last speech. It was a private one for his family.

They were gathered in the big kitchen of the estate for the family reunion when he said:

"History is a tragedy, not a morality tale. It is a record of what happened because of what some men did.

God knows this is true. Because He is eternal, His clock runs on a different scale than mans'. What for us is scores of years, is seconds to Him. He knows what I have always said to you, and you have now learned for yourselves to be true. That is, that man is a combination of goodness and evil.

Man is most often motivated by his self- interest. It is rare that he is self-sacrificing. All we can do is seek out the goodness in ourselves and in others to strive to make life better for as many as we can. You have all seen and done this as well. For that, you know I am proud of all of you. Hanna's life is a sterling example of that motive. Her life proves there is divine intervention.

But it is rare that God intervenes anymore, like he did in monumental ways at the beginning of His creation. He had decided to give us free will and knows the consequences of that better than any of us ever can.

Only now He has decided to act in more gentle and softer ways. He has made some of man His instruments and placed them among us. Some have seen His signs and others have no knowledge of the purpose He has placed within them.

All that we can do is what we have always known – act justly and show mercy."

Mary had been watching his eyes and smiling said, "Joe, you should have been called Peter. Like Simon called Peter, you have been the rock of this church."

Josena looked at her mother and said, "God knows that's true Mama."

Josiah laughed and looking at Mary said, "You have always been so smart and now you are wise. Only God knows how you can still be so beautiful at seventy four."

David reflected and thought out loud, "It's true what he said about the perspective of the span of time. He was born a slave in 1829 in Missouri. Now he is a respected, revered and successful old man here in Hamilton, Ohio in 1905."

He had been thinking, 'Just 30 miles north of here Orville and Wilbur Wright are inventing and building experimental flying machines in their bicycle shop. There are conducting tests flights there on Huffman Prairie and in North Carolina. Just in the span of one man's lifetime.'

Hanna looked at all of them and said, "God has blessed us all for our family."

Josiah woke up one morning in the spring of 1906 with a desire to look at his land. He went outside where the air was fresh and the temperature was beginning to rise from the early sun's warmth. He walked over to his barn but decided not to drive his new Ford motor car.

Instead he saddled up his prized white stallion, put his foot in the stirrup and swung onto his back. He galloped out of the barn and across the yard. Along the road, as he came to his sawmill, he slowed down and decided to stop.

He dismounted and walked over to a pile of fresh cut maple planks. As he bent down to pick one up and look down its edge to see how flat and straight it was, he smiled when he remembered he and Ned doing this all those years ago on Savannah Oaks plantation.

He winced as he felt a sharp pain in his arm. With a shortness of breath he sat down on the ground. The blue sky grew dark to his vision as he passed out, drawing his last breath.

It was quiet there that beautiful morning. His horse nickered, knowing something was terribly wrong. When his sawmill attendant heard this, he came over and found him dead.

What good fortune the family had been there all together to bury him in the family cemetery and memorialize his life.

For reassurance to the Ashfords, the minister had said, "May He support us all, till the shades lengthen, and the evening comes, and the busy world is hushed, and the fever of life is over, and our work is done. Then in His mercy may He give us a safe lodging, and a holy rest, and peace at last."

After the funeral, Mary was like a ship without a rudder. She spent long days daydreaming on the porch looking out over the fields. Her memories were more sweet than bittersweet.

Hanna became her companion and kept her connected to this world for the last years of Mary's life. During their long afternoons together at the Ashford house, Mary told Hanna about her long life and family history as though she was talking about a life that was finished.

"Hanna, my life was very different from yours and your father's. Martha Washington, George Washington's wife, kept her slaves until President Washington died.

They were called dowry slaves. That was because she was given them from her family when she married him and they belonged to her. Since they were her property, she decided to keep them until after old George died. We were all named Custis because that was Martha's family name.

She freed them shortly after his death in 1799. Many of us left to come west to Ohio here. It's been three generations we have been freeborn since then. I am the fourth.

Mary wanted Hanna to understand something about slavery that Hanna might never have known.

She said, "We all think about President Lincoln with love and gratitude because he freed the slaves. It's true he believed in abolition but he didn't believe we were equal. He wondered how we would get along in life on our own. He thought it might be better if we were sent back to Africa."

Hanna's mouth fell open in disbelief.

"There is much people in the north don't know about the South", she continued. "Before George Washington was President, he gave up his comfortable life and sacrificed everything for his country – he led us in the Revolutionary War."

"I knows that", Hanna said.

"He had a slave – a personal servant – who was with him through all the troubled times. The man was loyal and believed in him even though George owned him as property. He was a Custis like all my people. George talked to him more about things sometimes than he did white men. There was an abiding affection – an intimacy - between them based on their constant companionship. My ancestor loved him. When George died, he grieved for him like he would his own kin. People don't know about that, or if they do, don't understand it."

Hanna listened attentively, then said, "That may be true Mary, but I know how colored people were treated in the South. I have seen it and lived it. The cruelty of white people who call themselves Christians and the way they acted toward other human beings was a sin God will surely punish them for."

Mary shook her head in agreement and said, "I'm certain that is true too and I don't want to minimize your father's suffering. Believe me, I have seen the scars on his back."

Mary continued, "When I first met your father, he was a freedman. That's different than a freeborn person. It means he once was a slave, whereas my ancestors and I never were. We always felt somehow we were superior to the former slaves because of that.

But I saw great qualities in your father. His spirit and gift of looking to the future made him exceptional to all the notions we might have had."

Hanna had seen this herself and replied, "I know that's true Mama Mary. I thank the Lord I got to know him finally at the end of his life."

They sat quietly together and reflected on their conversation.

Later, after Mary died too, Hanna still yearned to know about the early life of her mother and father on the Mississippi plantation. She went to David to see what he could tell her. She told him she had heard about the tragedies and the hardships, but she wanted to know about the happiness.

David looked at her sympathetically and told her, "The stories from father and his friend David are full of their struggles. Unfortunately, that is what has been told the most."

"I knows it", she said. "Papa told me all that, but just said they were in love and married a short time. Mama Mary talks 'bout papa's success and hows he rose up here in Ohio in his new life."

He tried to help her understand and said, "Father didn't keep a diary or write letters. He wasn't much for looking back. With him and David and your mother gone, there's parts of the story we will never know. Sometimes it happens that way. All the things we long to know from the past, we can't get once the generation has left us."

"All I know is that they were deeply in love and helped each other all they could in their troubled times", he said. "Maybe that is enough for us now", he added with resignation.

"I 'spose it is. I know my mamma was a wonderful mother to me in Alabama befor' she was killed. I kin still remembah that."

"And father never gave up looking for her until he learned the horrible truth and lost you for so long", he added.

"But de Lord brought us together in the end David. Thass the mos' important thing."

When David Ashford finally came to the decision to take over management of Ashford Furniture in earnest, he began to find out a lot of things about its corporate rot that had led to its decline and could have led to its demise.

He asked his sister to help him and Josie did all she could with the time she had available. More importantly, she was his sounding board when he needed one. They were both very intelligent and had always sounded each other out since they were children. They were twins and nearly alter egos.

First he learned what he always thought to be true – that Frank, a large, beefy, affable white man that had been with Josiah since manufacturing had first taken on a true factory operation, was a good man. He was honest and loyal and always looked out for the best interests of the company. He had a steady hand running the everyday operation of all aspects of the production. David liked him and knew he could count on him.

When David closely examined the company ledgers, he found some discrepancies. Some money had gone missing. He traced it carefully and found out the bookkeeper, a sour, unpleasant black man Josiah had cultivated from the ranks, had been slowly absconding with small amounts of money for over a year.

He called him into his office and told him exactly to the penny how much he had taken. He reckoned his back pay and severance wouldn't cover it, so he kept it and sent the man packing that day. David kept the books himself for three months until he found a reliable man, a Yankee from Philadelphia, to take over.

He fired the sales manager who had been resting on the laurels of his former glory, taking kickbacks from the owners of the retail store outlets he had been selling to, and not getting out with the sales reps to find new channels of distribution. He hired a seasoned salesman who had been a graduate of Miami of Ohio business school, specializing in marketing. Within a year the company had begun to turn around.

He sat in his office, feet on the desk, looking out the window at their house across the field and thought, 'I'm glad Father never lived to see this. He would have been so disappointed after all he did to build the company. At least Frank has maintained the quality. That was always the source of Papa's pride.'

He was also thinking about the many homes and stores that had emerged for the families that were dependent on his furniture company. The hamlet of Ashford, Ohio was a part of it. It had become an integrated community where the races lived together in relative peace and harmony.

He had an inherited responsibility to all those people for their livelihood and sustenance. He had not let them down.

Josena had remembered the satisfaction she had experienced from teaching. She had taught children – mostly girls – how to play the violin. When one or two of them excelled, it was a joy and a fulfillment. Now she was a doctor of philosophy in sociology, anthropology and archeology.

She had spent all her youth mastering her knowledge and never married. She had studied, traveled, written a book. Now it was time to teach what she knew to the eager college students. She knew there would be a few that would embrace it and it would set their lives on a path.

So Josena began teaching at university. She befriended a younger associate professor of history, Elizabeth Jefferson – a white woman. Her friends called her Peggy.

Her family had moved to Hamilton from New York during the Depression of 1893 when her father, Sam Jefferson had sought work. He found it in the Ashford Furniture Company and rose from a laborer to a highly skilled craftsman.

As Josena and Peggy became more inseparable, Josie brought her home and introduced her to the family. They had a family dinner and David was quite taken with Peggy's looks and perky personality.

She was a surprise for him. He had known Sam from the factory for years but never learned much about his family. He didn't know Sam had such a fetching daughter. He became more interested when he learned she was a history professor.

When he called on her at her home, it was awkward for many reasons. Sam was surprised to find that David was interested in his daughter.

"This might not be a good idea, Mr. Ashford", was all he said.

David asked him why.

He was surprised when Sam told him, "You are so much older than my girl and I work for your family at the factory."

"Oh. Well look it Sam, my passion has always been history and I share that with Peggy. She is so smart and delightful. If you can abide it, I plan to continue seeing her."

"That would be entirely up to you and Peggy. I just think it's not a good idea is all", Sam said.

"Maybe it's because I'm black and there will be trouble", David offered.

Sam frowned and said, "That will be a big problem for some but not me. I'm thinkin' it will be the biggest problem for the two of you."

He knew Sam made sense and couldn't dislike him for his honesty. Still he couldn't help his irritation.

"I'll bear that in mind", he said.

Peggy and David did continue to keep company and they did discuss race. They were determined to face it clear-eyed, head-on and with no recriminations between them. They knew that if they couldn't resolve it conclusively between themselves, they would never be able to stand up to the prejudice that people would throw at them.

David appreciated Peggy's agile mind and soon came to fall in love with her. By that time in the North, miscegenation was not viewed as so sinful as in the South and in the recent past.

On one occasion he told Peggy, "I know racism and slavery are closely related – the former spawned by the latter."

"I think of it as cultural and, of course, societal", she offered. "It's so much about the notions of nobility and class."

David smiled in agreement and added, "When I think about our country, I recall the two groups of English who founded it – so different, the pious New Englanders in Massachusetts and the arrogant Royal Cavaliers in Virginia. They were all Anglicans or at least Protestants. But it is because of their different view about class, the North always tended toward equality and the South became so much like the Old World repeating itself."

"You're right", she said. "I see exactly what you mean. Christianity is all tied up in it for sure. Certainly, in the early history of the mercantile North, there was white indentured servitude and black slavery. But in the South, the planters built a true new England with nobles and their land, their fiefdoms and their peasants. They had no middle class, just the few nobles and the many peasants – black ones they owned and white ones struggling at the bottom."

"I agree with you that that is how it happened. But it is changing. Like the poet might say, 'There is a new day dawning'."

She smiled at him lovingly. David, this black man was 43 and Peggy, this white woman was an energetic 34.

It is a big decision when a couple decides to marry. For David and Peggy, it was momentous. They would be the first mixed union in Butler County, Ohio in 1912 and they knew it. But because it was with the Ashford name, the people there had little choice but to accept it, no matter how begrudgingly. Ashford Furniture Company employed many of them directly or else their independent businesses and farms were directly affected by the manufacturer, usually profoundly. The village of Ashford was a one-horse town.

David had few friends in his own life, mostly just many acquaintances that respected him. So he asked his production manager Frank to be his best man. They liked and respected each other and the bi-racial connection would be important. Frank accepted his role graciously. He has always been loyal to David and Josiah before him. Besides he knew what was in his best interest.

The white people would attend the AME church for the ceremony, and the reception at the Ashford estate afterwards, alongside the black people. Some stayed home and some blacks did too. There were many whites that viewed blacks as inferior. There were many blacks that couldn't abide by the mixing of the races of either gender from the stigma of bitterness going back to slavery.

While Sam Jefferson was for the Union – had fought with Grant's 131st Ohio Infantry in '64 – and for emancipation, it appeared he was not for this union. Like Lincoln, he wasn't convinced the races were equal.

It seemed he wouldn't come to the wedding to give Peggy away to her Negro groom and sit there with his wife. On the day of the ceremony, Sam appeared and carried out his fatherly duty.

If David had not been an Ashford, odds were he wouldn't have come. But he did and walked Peggy down the aisle in the AME church. He didn't have a change of heart. It was a pragmatic decision for his daughter, his wife and his employment.

In the middle of the hard winter of 1915, Peggy delivered a baby boy. They named him Josiah Ashford II. He was coffee colored with bright hazel inquisitive eyes. And he grew to be a handful – smart like his father, energetic like his mother and precocious himself.

Joe was the first mixed race boy in the minds and recollection of the people in the area. But there had been others in the family. Only the direct family – David, Josena, Hanna, Mary – knew that his grandmother Mary was a descendent of freeborn blacks that had come from Martha Custis and George Washington's slaves. They might have been inbred if George or his white people had raped their slaves like Tom Jefferson had. No one knew either way for sure. His father David and aunt Josena might have been of mixed race too because of that lineage. It got complicated in a hurry.

And his step aunt Hanna. She had been born from the slaves Josena and Josiah, Joe's grandfather. But that Josena, a slave girl down in Mississippi, had descended from her mother, the feisty slave girl Sarah and her father, Marcus Taylor who had raped his slave as an act of lustful loneliness, desperate dominance and vile vengeance.

African Americans in the future would make this investigation – this tracing of roots - their life's work. But so often it was only to find sympathy for the black members and pride in their hard brave heritage and to condemn the white members for their evil cruelty. This would be the emphasis that would be taught to them as they achieved their higher education in modern colleges. It was a true harsh reality that needed to be understood, but would do nothing to promote racial harmony. Quite the contrary, it would delay it for the foreseeable future.

God would wish them to remember. It would be an important lesson. But He wanted them to find harmony and peace, despite the hurt of the remembering, the knowing and the understanding. He longed for it. Hanna knew this.

This was the way it was in Ohio, in the early 20th century.

The winds of war began to blow again. This time it was in Europe. In 1914 the Archduke Ferdinand, heir to the throne of the

Austro-Hungarian Empire, was assassinated in Sarajevo, the capital of Bosnia. Germany and Russia joined into the dispute between the Empire and Serbia.

President Wilson was determined to remain neutral and keep America out of the fight. He was successful for a while.

Sixteen – War in France

When the Spanish American War broke out in 1898, David was 29 and traveling through the South with Josena to trace the route his father had traveled before. He had been following the national politics and viewed the attack on Cuba as an imperialist act by the United States to remove the last of Spanish influence from the Western Hemisphere. The flamboyant actions by young Teddy Roosevelt were viewed by some as heroic and patriotic.

By then David had seen much of the post- Civil War South and, with his background and passion for history, had decided to become a newspaper correspondent.

The United States joined its allies to participate in World War I in 1917. So in the spring of 1918 when he was 48, David Ashford responded by attaching himself to the U.S. army as a war correspondent. This was late in World War I. President Wilson and the will of the American people had delayed involvement in the European war of German aggression as long as possible. German atrocities at sea had forced the decision to enter the war.

The draft raised nearly three million men. Two million more volunteered. Four hundred thousand African Americans enlisted or were drafted. Fifty thousand went to France. There their units were segregated and they served under white commanders.

When the Selective Service Act was passed in 1917, African American males joined the war effort to prove their loyalty, patriotism and worthiness for equal treatment in American society. In World War I, there were four all-black black regiments – the 9th

and 10th cavalry and the 24th and 25th infantry. Only a few got the opportunity to serve in combat units. The 92nd and 93rd Divisions were created as primarily black combat units.

David had nothing to prove to his country about his worthiness as a patriot but joined up with General Jack Pershing's American Expeditionary Force and sailed to France to join the Allies and defend against the German invasion. This was the first time an African American Ashford had been to France or even Europe.

As a war correspondent, he had attended the black officer trainee's camp at Fort De Moines under command of LTC Charles Ballou. He trained along with the regular infantry, was in the top of his group, and was commissioned as a Captain. He observed and fought with the 93nd formed from National Guard units in Ohio and under direct command of BG Roy Hoffman. They fought bravely at the front lines in the Argonne forest.

He had full access to the front line action and reported the events for back home. Standing with the front line commanders, he observed officers as leaders who had to constantly motivate their men to engage in battle and face almost certain death.

He found out that the British and French Allies were worn out from the fighting there that had gone on for three years and had reached a stalemate in the trenches. The Russians had left the fight.

With the impetus of the American forces, the Allies repulsed the German offensive at Chateau-Thierry, just fifty miles from Paris. Shortly after, at Muese-Argonne in the Argonne Forrest, the Americans pushed the Germans back to their border. The Germans sought an armistice before their country was invaded.

For the Americans, the fighting was brief but with heavy casualties. David would spend only eight months there before the war would be over.

He had experienced those moments when he watched across from the trenches the surreal dark moving figures like ghosts in the smoke and the mist, and the moments when the men left the trenches, climbed out of them and formed a charge at the enemy line.

Blindly charging into the blazing machine guns, so many fell instantly and were gone. In that moment, that intense moment of terror and clarity, there was no past or no future, only that brilliant moment in the present. As the consciousness narrowed and focused, there was no fear either any longer. It was replaced with rage and blood lust until it was over.

It was like his father's friend David had said about the Civil War. Not much had changed about men killing men on the grandest scale. Lee had learned from Longstreet about fortification and trench warfare to slow down the rate of the killing.

Chemical warfare was used here on a large scale and the soldiers shrieked with pain as the mustard gas burned their faces and exposed parts of their bodies. Mostly though the casualties in the trenches were from heavy shelling. A "no-man's land" formed a space between the two lines of trenches. But ultimately one or both sides had to move at the enemy. But then once again in World War I, the killing had become even more efficient.

Again the young men who were there would wonder why God would permit it, why he would turn a blind eye to his human beings – his creations – destroying each other for land and resources or for differences in their ideologies.

In the thick of the fighting, from his observation point, David's mind often wandered. He pictured his father's dearest friend David and the stories he had heard about the Civil War.

He now understood what Uncle David had meant when he described it. Now he had learned about it for himself. It would change him for the rest of his life as it had so profoundly changed Uncle David and all soldiers who had served in mortal combat.

With his father and Uncle David gone, he wanted to share his thoughts and experiences with his mother and sisters when this nightmare was finished. His mind steered his memory to his father and he grieved once again.

He was lonely and homesick and grew despondent. He longed to re-unite with his family when this was over. He wanted to hold them all in his arms – his wife and little son, his sister and his mother. Pieces of his heart remained home with them. But the heart grows and is not diminished. It remains intact and lives beside the soul.

Mary passed away in 1917 while David was overseas in France and eleven years after her husband's passing. Hanna had brought her peace in her last years and she died fulfilled with no regrets.

Josena remembered to send word back to Virginia so that the funeral was delayed until the Rev. Bernard W. Custis arrived from there to participate in the ceremony. She met him at the train in Cincinnati and drove him up to Hamilton. The Reverend traced his Custis lineage from Martha's people, but he had known many of the later generation freeborn men and women on the other side of the family that had kept the name.

On the morning of the funeral service he was made welcome in the Ashford family's African Methodist Episcopal Church as kin. The huge chapel was filled to capacity by family, neighbors and the community of both races. Everyone knew Mary and loved her for her grace and soft-spoken kindness. Josena and Hanna sat in the front with Joe between them.

The chapel was warm and noisy with the crowd huddled together there that bright morning. A hush fell over them as the two men walked over to the pulpit.

Their AME pastor looked out at the crowded room, seeing as many white faces as black, and introduced the guest pastor Bernard Custis as a childhood friend of Mary's. He acknowledged the presence of her daughter, step-daughter and little grandson. He mentioned that it was a pity that her son David was overseas and could not be there with them. He opened the service with a prayer of reassurance and stepped aside as Rev. Custis stepped to the pulpit.

The reverend shared his childhood memories of Mary and said, "She always called me Bernie when we grew up together in Fairfax. It was long before the war and a time of peace for us.

Mary was the 3rd freeborn generation tracing back to Martha Custis Washington's slaves. She had let them go free when George died in 1799 in Mount Vernon.

So much has passed before God's eyes since that time. So many trials and tribulations. But today we are together, all God's children, to remember Mary and the gift her life has brought us.

Take a moment to look around at each other. Look into each other's faces and see the shining eyes. God's love is with us. He lives in our hearts. Bless you and may His peace be with you."

As he sat down, the AME pastor nodded to Josena and she rose from her place in the congregation and walked up to the pulpit. The pastors each gave her a brief embrace before she turned toward the people with a small piece of paper in her hand.

She smiled at them and spoke to the guest pastor, "I am so gratified you are here with us today Bernie. It is fitting that you were my mother's first white friend.

These were my father's last words he wrote to my mother before he died:

> *Grieve not for me nor speak of me with tears but laugh and talk of me as though I were beside you – I loved you so it was heaven here with you.*

My mother felt that way about all us here today. She loved us all and she loved our community. She will be dearly missed. But we will remember her with a smile for the time she graced us with her life. Time cannot steal the treasures that we carry in our hearts, nor dim the shining thoughts our cherished past imparts."

She slowly folded the paper and, with her head down, walked backed to her seat next to Joe.

After the congregation joined together in the hymn, *What a Friend We Have in Jesus*, the pastor raised his hands and closed the service with, "God has said, 'Never will I leave you; never will I forsake you.' God bless you and be with you as you face this time of sorrow. And may He give you hope and strength to meet each new tomorrow."

Josena and Hanna buried her in the family cemetery on the Ashford estate. She was placed to rest next to Josiah's plot on his right. David Wexley was buried on Josiah's left.

It was a time of joy – something Christians understand when they bury their dead. The body they put in the ground is just an empty shell of their loved one. They know that the spirit has departed and they rejoice with that promise and solace.

After the armistice was signed, the war was over and David returned from overseas to the States on a military ship. From the port of New York City, he took a train to Cincinnati. He had forwarded a message to the family and they all gathered at the train station to welcome him home. David was excited to see his sisters Josena and Hanna and his wife Peggy and little Joe, now three years old. He noticed right away his mother was missing.

"Where's Mother, Josie", he asked.

"I'm so sorry David. She passed away and we couldn't get word to you. You were in the heat of it and we weren't allowed to contact you", she replied.

"I knew her health was failing, but I'm devastated I missed her funeral."

Hanna said, "After we git you home, we will visit her grave and have a family prayer. She passed peacefully brother. We was with her when her soul was sent to heaven".

"Let's all go home", was all David could say.

Exhausted, he kissed Peggy, scooped up Joe on his shoulder, and Josie and Peggy carried his luggage to the car. They went home.

He did visit his mother's gravesite and grieved for her and his father and David Wexley. He began to feel his own mortality at age forty nine. He was thinking about his little son Joe – Josiah Ashford II.

"Joe never knew his grandfather or David Wexley and he won't remember his grandmother after he is grown up", he told Peggy.

Peggy looked at his crestfallen expression and reassured him, "It is the way of life David. Some leaves fall and others grow in their place. To everything, there is a season."

"I know it. But I've been thinking about writing a book. I need to capture our family history in the context of our American history", he had decided.

He began the book and Josie helped him as his editor. But more than that she helped him to remember – the story of Josiah brought to Savannah Oaks as a slave from Missouri, his wife the first Josena, the cruel Civil War, his devoted friend David, the struggle of the freedmen and poor whites after the killing was over, Ohio, their mother Mary, the discovery of their divinely inspired sister Hanna, The World War and the century of changes in America.

More than a family biography, it traced the origins and path of slavery from Egyptian and Arabic culture in northern Africa to Europe and the British colonies in North America. David wrote about the earliest slaves brought to New Amsterdam by the Dutch and to Virginia for the English tobacco planters.

He wrote about the little-known practice of indentured servitude of white children and white young adults imported to the northern Colonial cities. Poor families in England sold their children to America for a seven-year term contract to pay off their debt, or for money to survive, or for prisoners to fulfill their penalty for their crimes.

Peggy had told him there were also the many poor Irish enslaved in America. The "servants" were worked so hard and treated so harshly, they often died before their terms were completed. They had little opportunity for a better life here.

But David's message was predominately a positive one, as inspired by his family, from its heroes like his father and David Wexley, and heroines like his sisters and mother. He made sure Hanna's message of love and hope for humanity's harmony was not missed.

He spent eight years writing it and finished it in 1926. He entitled it *The Son of a Slave in America* and Random House in New York published it the same year as William Faulkner's darker view of humanity, *Absalom, Absalom*!, was released. David's biography was on the best sellers list.

He mailed a copy of his book's first printing to Professor McPherson at the history department at University of Alabama to give the man more perspective.

Before the war, David had been an infrequent contributing writer to the local newspaper. With his experience in France as a war correspondent, he returned home to the Hamilton-Oxford newspaper as a regular weekly contributing column reporter. He wrote editorial commentary on the news and events in the country from his unique historical and sociological perspective.

America was changing rapidly in the 20's. He enjoyed discussing these things with his sisters – the advancements in airplanes since the early days of the Wright brothers, the aftermath of the war in Europe, women's suffrage, the Scopes trial right up in Tennessee, the incredible appreciation in the stock market from speculative investment.

Sometimes he waxed philosophical – said that history took care of its own, that it was in the hand of fate, not men. Hanna disagreed with that and told him it was in God's hands like General Lee had thought – providence. He was impressed that she could think of that example for her perspective. His divinely inspired, older sister from the South and another mother was amazing really – the way she looked at things and considered them.

With her insight, Hanna told David how it was. She said, "David, you knows I grew up in the South wid two while families. I lived da history you talk 'bout. I lived wid dem long after I be freed. They believed in da Confederacy and der cause long after the war was ovah. Da Drishs and da Blanchards, they adjusted to da changes 'bout colored people, but nevah forgot der dreams 'bout der way of life. So I hear all dese stories all dose years 'bout der Generals who was heroes to dem.

They specially love Robert E. Lee and his faith in God. I heard 'bout General Thomas Jackson they call Stonewall too. He used to pray evra night frum de New Testament. Den every day he fight wid da fury of da Old – smiting his enemies mightily as God had commanded. Dat was just how they were and how hit was."

He wrote a newspaper article about Hanna's recollections for his Ohio readers to understand how it was.

Seventeen - Spotted Horse on the Hill

She comes down easy soon after the leaves fall
A spotted filly's hooves coming down the hill in the soft brown earth
Easy-like walking tender over the wet leaves
Cooler and quiet and gentle

The winds blow colder near the bottom of the hill
She struggles harder and the land turns dead
At the bottom dead sticks and gray sky
Clouds moving fast from the west bringing her harder

Snow falling silently all the dark days and nights
Sparkling ice in the bright cold sun
Blurry sad moon waiting long nights for her journey to end

She stumbles and goes on older up the hill
An old mare tired and worn

Her last steps bring her back to the top of the hill
She steps lighter in the warm sun
The land is soft and green again
She is young once more

The winter of 1924 was harsh in Buffalo, New York. Crista Hannon left in the spring with her husband and baby daughter. She was pregnant again and feeling worn but hopeful. Hans was out of work and they were looking for a better life.

They drove west in their old Ford motor car packed with all their belongings. They headed southwest after Cleveland and kept going almost to the Ohio River across from Kentucky. When Hans spotted the large factory, they stopped near the town of Hamilton - just south of it next to the village of Ashford. German migrants like the Hannons joined the African Americans coming from the South there in that rural, hopeful patch of earth.

This had always been the American story for whites and was becoming so for blacks. This was a big country with plenty of room for everybody.

After the war, and as a result, America would be changing again. There would be another "Great Migration" of blacks from the rural South to the northern industrial cities. Seventy thousand went to Chicago from Alabama and Mississippi. Once again, as after the Civil War, blacks sought opportunity in the North. Many came to the Industrial Belt in cities like Cleveland and Detroit for work in the factories. The industrial boom of the war had brought new hope for a better life.

Labor became available throughout rural areas as well. Migrants of both races came to the Hamilton area and some settled in the new town of Ashford. They brought a talent for working with their hands and mechanical skills.

Ashford Furniture Co. had grown under its management and Josena's oversight while David was overseas; but now with the new labor pool available, David brought it to a new level as a major manufacturer in southwest Ohio. He hired a middle management staff who developed programs for training. The raw talent of the labor pool was honed and shaped for the skills needed to make fine furniture.

Hanna took full advantage of the growing Ashford village community to spread her care to its bi-racial residents. As a result of Ashford Furniture's success and growth, the area was developing rapidly with new churches, bars, restaurants, shops, parks and municipal offices. The white migrants moving in from the east and African Americans from the south came to raise their families and for a better life. She cared for the working class people's homes, their children and their health. At last she had a bigger calling than the town of McComb back in Mississippi. And conditions were more modern, not as primitive as that poor southern town.

She met the new arrivals in town. Like a one-woman welcoming committee, she offered to help them settle and adjust, mind their children and heal their illnesses where she could. All this she did in the name of Christianity and friendship.

When she met Hans and Crista Hannon from New York, he was a machinist and a new hire starting work at the furniture company. Crista was six months pregnant with their second child and feeling poorly.

"We haven't known any coloreds in New York", Crista told her.

"But you are nice enough", she said.

"I'm Crista Hannon. What is your name?" she asked.

"I'm Hanna Drish. My brothah David Ashford runs the furniture factory and my sistah Josena teaches at Miami of Ohio."

"But you don't have the same name as your brother and sister", she said.

"I knows dat seem funny. We had the same fathah, Josiah Ashford. I kep the name my owner in Alabama give me."

"So you are part of the family this town is named after?"

"Yes I is. My family owns the factory and I lives with them on the family farm. Hit's a long story how I was found in Mississippi by my brothah an sistah and brought back here to live wid my fathah years ago. Lord sakes, listen to me chatterin' away like a squirrel treed by an ole hown dawg."

Crista laughed, "You are funny."

Hanna told her, "We git along jus' fine onct we git ta know each othah."

Crista smiled and said, "I can see that, and your help is much appreciated, a Godsend really."

Hanna sat with her some days while Hans started his new job.

She came to the Hannon's run-down rented house one early summer day and no one answered the door. She could hear the baby crying and let herself in. Crista was in bed moaning and uncomfortable.

Hanna asked, "How ya doin' today girl?"

"Oh, I'm feeling sick", she said. "The baby's kicking me day and night. I can't sleep and don't want to eat."

"I brought sum chamomile wid me. Let me fix you some tea. It'll hep wid yo stomick and yo digestin. I knows that baby pushin' hard on yer innards."

"Thank you Hanna. I'm feeling poorly and can't wait for this baby to get out."

"It'll be soon I reckon, from the look of you", Hanna reassured her.

"I want to do sumthin' to figure how yo doin' and hep ya'", Hanna offered.

"What is it?"

She laid her two large hands flat and gentle across Crista's swollen belly. She bowed her head and mumbled an inaudible prayer.

"Feel dat?" she asked.

Crista felt an electric tingle all across the middle of her body.

She smiled and said, "I feel better."

"Seems everythin' is right. Ya shud be deliverin', soon", Hanna reassured her.

She delivered their first son two weeks after that and named him Ashford Hannon.

With things more settled, Hanna kept up her friendly visits. Crista's recovery from this second baby was harder. Hanna would take the older child off her hands and out for walks in the village – to the corner store for penny candy. Townsfolk got used to seeing them together and looked forward to it.

She offered to get Crista out more too.

"If hit make ya feel bettah, yo be welcome ta come to church dis Sunday. Ya might like hit if ya wants", she said.

Hanna attended her own AME church most Sundays, but sometimes visited the Baptist and Presbyterian churches the white people attended. She wanted to make a point to bridge the gap between all Christian believers.

They all knew her from the community and they loved her dearly. It was always so spiritually gratifying when she was invited to get up and speak. Her simple language, her simple message of truth, her beautiful being, radiating God's truth from the inside. She had found her spiritual home at last.

Eighteen - Atlanta

Fear dominated the minds of the people as word spread that the Yankees were heading toward their city from the west. Atlanta was right in the path of General Sherman's march across Georgia. It was late in 1864 and the Civil War had entered its final chapter.

As a hub for southern railroads and as a manufacturing center, the city was an important strategic target for the Union. When Sherman captured it in September, he ordered its military resources, including munition factories, clothing mills and railway yards, burned to the ground. The fires got out of control and left Atlanta in ruins. Her people harbored a special intense hatred for the North for the century that followed.

After the war, Atlanta eventually rebuilt herself and became the flagship for the New South. She displaced the older cities like Savannah and Charleston and surpassed their prominence. But with failed Reconstruction and the rise of Jim Crow laws, she became a hotbed of racial discontent and civil strife.

Out of those turbulent decades, the modern era of the civil rights movement would be born. Its leaders would often be educated in theology and use the pulpit to preach the message of racial equality. Their hope would be that Christianity would solve the issue of racial prejudice as others in the past had hoped it would end slavery.

In 1948, a young man born in rural Georgia in 1929 earned his degree in sociology from the prestigious Morehouse College. He attended a prominent school of theology in Pennsylvania and graduated as the valedictorian in 1951. His doctorate came from Boston University in 1955 after completing his dissertation in 1954. He became impassioned with the civil rights cause and he too believed Christianity and peaceful protest would overcome the practice of segregation most prevalent in the South. His participation in the Southern Christian Leadership Conference with Ralph Abernathy would be a testament to his intended peaceful approach.

As a second generation freeborn man of mixed race raised in the North and in the Christian faith by his parents and his Aunt Hanna, Josiah Ashford II grew up with a special sense of self-awareness. His grandfather Josiah had been a slave and his mother was white.

He earned a dual degree in sociology and history from Miami of Ohio University and came to Atlanta in 1955 as a 38 year old man still in search of answers.

He met the young 26 year old newly ordained minister on the sidewalk outside a Baptist church. They spoke to each other as strangers who immediately felt like kindred spirits.

"Hello, my name is Josiah Ashford. My friends call me Joe", he said.

"It's a pleasure meeting you Joe. I'm Martin", the man replied.

They met often at a small restaurant down Jackson Street from Ebenezer Baptist Church. It was a run-down old place frequented by blacks in the segregated city. Martin loved the soul food – southern fried chicken and catfish, barbequed ribs, hocks, black eyed peas, buttered hominy grits and collard greens - the best of the south, especially the South Carolina low country food.

They talked about the problems of segregation and racial equality facing African Americans now, almost a hundred years after emancipation.

Joe told Martin he was mixed race. His mother was white.

Martin smiled to himself and told him, "Truth be told, most of us African Americans are mixed race. We just don't often know the whens and the whos and the whys so much."

Joe nodded his head.

"Seriously though Joe", he continued, "I pray every day. Some days more than once. Still I can't claim to know God's plan. Maybe he intends for the races to mix until we are all brown. Don't know."

"Don't know either", was all Joe could say.

"What I do know though, and I'm certain God would be right with it, is it's past the time when we should be kept separate and treated inferior by our white brothers", Martin offered.

"You should have known my grandfather Josiah and my aunt Hanna", Joe told him.

"Grampa was a slave and a freedman who built a furniture dynasty for our family up in southwest Ohio where I am from. I never knew him but heard he was a fierce man of God. He fought for our people but believed in friendship as the solution for the inhumanity of man."

Martin was pleased to hear stories like that. It fit with his passionate approach to life.

"Maybe the most important thing about his life Martin was his friend David, a white Civil War veteran. They supported each other every step of the way. David was troubled and Grampa tried to help him, tried to get him to know God. They were different in that way too. But they loved each other. David is buried right next to him."

Martin nodded his head with pleasure.

Finally Joe told him about Hanna. "You should have known my aunt Hanna. She was one of the last freed slaves when she passed a few years ago. Like you, she made her life a mission to serve God – maybe a mission to improve harmony between the races, more than equality. She did it well, peaceably and with love – down in Mississippi and up in Ohio. She helped raise me as a little boy and taught me all the bible stories."

"What about you?" Martin asked him.

"I am at a point in my life where I see the strife and cruelty in the country once again and I want to do something about it."

After they shared each other's life stories and got to know each other well, Joe came to a decision. He would follow the young Martin Luther King, Jr. to Montgomery, Alabama where King would become the pastor at the Dexter Avenue Baptist Church.

When Joe caught Martin's impassioned fire, he became enthusiastic and so excited he wrote his mother, Elizabeth Jefferson Ashford:

Dearest Mother,

I met the most magnificent man in Atlanta. His name is Martin Luther King, Jr. He is inspirational, and charismatic, almost messianic. You would love his mind and his spirit. He is of the purest heart and so smart.

He has a vision. He told me he has seen the mountain top. It is very steep and high though, Mother. Our people have so far to climb.

But Martin and I have so much in common, we are sympathetic souls. I plan to follow him on his mission and see where God's amazing grace will lead us.

Please take care to share this letter with father.

Warmest Love and Best Wishes,
Joe

Together they would spearhead the effort to de-segregate Montgomery's city bus system. They would be there to support the arrested protestor Claudette Colvin in March and later Rosa Parks in December in the citywide bus boycott.

Martin was, among many extraordinary things, a leader of men. He saw in Joe a valuable asset to his organization and movement. Joe had the right background and with his racial makeup, could help him bridge the racial gap.

While his old father continued to run the factory, Joe and his family's economic security had always been assured. Young Joe had joined with his mother Peggy and aunt Josena to further the cause. They continued the work begun by his grandfather before the turn of the century. Together they organized peaceful protests and petitioned the Ohio government to advance participation in suffrage, educational and job opportunity for people of color.

With renewed inspiration from Martin, Joe continued his work now on the national scene. His life's path was determined and he would remain Martin's loyal friend and by his side in Washington, DC for his historic speech and again on that tragic day in Memphis when Martin would be struck down by an assassin's bullet.

After Martin's passing, Joe remained active with the National Association for the Advancement of Colored People the rest of his life. He would return often to Ohio – to his home in Ashford and his campus in Oxford.

Joe carried on the work as his vocation – long into his mature years and made his mark as his grandfather had before him.

Years later, as an old man, he would become a frequent guest lecturer who would tell the young students there on the Miami of Ohio University campus about his grandfather Josiah and his aunt Hanna – about how they lived their lives and how they persevered and prevailed with grace over adversity.

Nineteen – Promise of the Future

When Josena Ashford went back to university in 1907 to get her Master's Degree in African studies – that is the study of the continent of Africa, its anthropology, its peoples and its sociology – she was confronted with a conflict between her faith and the new science of evolution. She resolved it easily and wrote about it in her book, *The Soul of Africa,* and taught it to her students at Miami of Ohio University, this way:

In the beginning, the Creator created the whole of the universe out of nothingness in an instant with a bang. As it is written, he created all of it in six days and then rested the seventh.

By the end of the fifth day, He had created the firmaments and the heavens, the stars and the planets and the Earth. Upon the Earth, the oceans and the land were in place. The seeds of the land had produced the lush green fields and the forests and the mountains. The beasts were bountiful in all of the Earth's places.

We think of those days as we are accustomed to thinking about time. We speak of them as the Creator's days. But the Creator's clock and time is not the same as ours. What for Him was one day, would have been hundreds of thousands of years to us had we been there as an observer.

He then turned His attention on the sixth day to the creation of man. In Africa, He created man in His image. Throughout the long day He made many adjustments.

The tall grass of the savannah required that man stand upright to see above it. His body shape and skeleton were adjusted so that he could rotate his shoulders, grasp with his opposable thumbs to hold tools that he fashioned, and throw a spear at his prey.

His skin was as dark as possible to block the strong sun but still allow its vitamin D to nourish him. After a while, some men courageously crossed the Red Sea and left Africa to explore the rest of the Earth. They spread throughout the Middle East, Europe and Asia and crossed the ice bridge over the Bering Strait from Siberia to North and South America.

They had learned to sew and fashion warm clothing from the furs of animals they had killed to keep them warm and insure their survival in the colder climate of the age. Later, after the ice age was over, the ice bridge went away and the native peoples of the Americas were isolated by the vast oceans until the future time when others would be able to cross them.

To survive in the ice age, the pigment of those that left had to be adjusted for their survival. They became lighter and paler to still get vitamin D from the weaker sun, but without as much need for protection from its rays. Other than that adjustment, and a couple other minor adjustments like that, man was exactly the same. There was no need for further adjustments.

The Creator continued His work until the whole of the Earth was populated with man by the end of that long day. And then, tired, He rested.

After His work was done, He gave man free will and autonomy on the Earth. Much remained the same in Africa. Life was simple and basic. Eventually man formed family units and then communities and then villages and then tribes. The trouble began.

Some of her students took the meaning of this, but some did not. There was an inexplicable recalcitrance, even an irony, in some minds. There were some ignorant poor whites who viewed educated successful blacks as inferior. It was almost like a jealously as well as a bigotry.

Josie had always felt that intellectually, beyond emotionality, there was a stupidity in their non-thinking way that went beyond reason; yet the stupidity was there all the same. She wondered and considered, 'God knows how Hanna could so gracefully work around it, push through it, and most often change peoples' hearts.'

He does. He knew that the meek like Hanna could melt their hardened heats and turn their hatred to love.

Yahweh, the Creator of the Universe, had used His mighty power in past millennia to punish the wicked. The people held Him in such awe, they dared not speak His name.

Jehovah, the keeper of the Heavens, had spoken directly to the Prophets to compel them to warn the people. God had sent His angels as messengers to inspire hope and provide reassurance. God, the Eternal Spirit of Love, had even sent a Son to teach by example and sacrifice.

Giving His creations free will had limited His power. He had seen what worked and what didn't. He was still adjusting. He developed better plans as He lived through His eighth day and began His second week.

Josena reconciled the apparent conflict between creationism and evolution in that way. It would be a few more years before the controversy on this subject would explode across American education. It was a contest between theology and modern science.

In 1925, a high school teacher named John Thomas Scopes would be brought to trial for teaching Darwin's theory of evolution in the classroom. He was in violation of Tennessee's Butler Act which made it illegal to teach that subject in state funded schools. William Jennings Bryan argued for the prosecution and Clarence Darrow for the defense. In the end, Scopes was found guilty and fined $100, but the verdict was overturned on a technicality.

But Josena was teaching about more than that in her classes at University of Miami. She was arguing, as she always would, against Social Darwinism as well. She rejected, and made it clear, that the notion of the inherent inferiority of people of color was nonsense. She based her assertions on the anthropological evidence of the origin of man – in Africa. The white man was a derivative of the black man and therefore could not be superior. She knew this even if others did not.

One day when Josena was off her duties at Miami of Ohio University, she and Hanna went over to Ashford Furniture to visit David in his office. Somehow the conversation with his sisters turned to Abraham Lincoln and his presidency.

Hanna offered, "Ya know Abe Lincoln, he free our people. God blessed us with his life."

"That is true Hanna, but the way it came about was not that simple. He was just a man after all.", Josena replied.

David thought about the conversation, sensed Josena's meaning and launched into one of his lectures. It was a long one but informative and insightful.

"When I was a young boy David Wexley told me after the war he had thought about it. Here in Ohio, he had many years to reflect on his experiences and their meanings for him. His father had discussed many things about slavery and our politics with him before the war, but this was after it and his own reflections. He studied it as a man who was there and needed to know more about the men he had never known like Lincoln and Grant and Lee.

He told me that in the middle of the war, some twenty months since it began at Fort Sumter, President Lincoln was in trouble. He was struggling to preserve the Union up to that point. Emancipation of the slaves would come later. The war had come to a halt and a stalemate. Both sides were entrenched holding their gains and not moving forward.

Lincoln was beset with so many problems just then; he was alternately standing still, moving forward and making mistakes, and constantly changing strategy trying to end it. His generals were pulling him in all directions. The American people of the Union were out of patience and despondent from the loss of blood and treasure and time. They blamed it all on him.

His own Republicans in Congress, the Radical ones, and the newspapers were constantly harassing him, calling him an ignorant and incompetent fool. Even some members of his own cabinet were against him. But he persevered and spent his time thinking and writing. He believed he could convince them if he could just craft the most compelling words.

He had written a preliminary Emancipation Proclamation but his Secretary of State, William Seward advised him to put it in a drawer until the time was right. He taught Lincoln that timing was everything.

When he released it, the time was right. You might not believe this, but freeing the slaves was not its purpose. He had learned the skill of politics and the Proclamation would benefit him and the federal government fourfold.

First, it would not offend the tenuous relationship he held with the Union border-states – Delaware, Kentucky, Maryland and Missouri - who held slaves. They would be allowed to keep their slaves.

Second, it would not free slaves in the north – in the Union. He wanted to appease certain members of Congress. It only freed slaves in Union controlled Confederate states.

Third, he needed replenishment of troops by then and black freedmen could serve in the Union army.

Fourth, and not much known, he was constantly competing with Jefferson Davis for foreign sympathy and support in England and France. They needed the South's cotton but hated its slavery. Lincoln hoped this would fool them and sway them to the Union side. It might not have been convincing to some overseas who saw through to its veiled purposes, but at least it kept them from swinging to Jefferson Davis's side. Lincoln was walking a tightrope.

About that time, Lincoln came into his own. He had begun master-crafting those compelling words he needed. In his December message to Congress, a long fifty thousand words delivered by a moderator in his absence, it began with a blessing followed by well- wishing, a grieving about the war, and launched into a long host of boring humdrum matters. It was a dry beginning.

After nearly losing them, it began to hit its stride at mid-point when the tone changed.

He wrote, "A nation may be said to consist of its territory, its people, and its laws. The territory is the only part which is of certain durability. 'One generation passeth away, and another generation cometh: but the earth abideth forever.' It is of the first importance to duly consider and estimate this ever-enduring part. That portion of the earth's surface which is owned and inhabited by the people of the United States is well adapted to be the home of one national family, and it is not well adapted for two or more.... There is no line, straight or crooked, suitable for a national boundary upon which to divide. Trace through, from east to west, upon the line between the free and slave country, and we shall find a little more than one-third of its length are rivers, easy to be crossed and populated, or soon to be populated, thickly upon both sides; while nearly all its remaining lengths are merely surveyors' lines, over which people may walk back and forth without any consciousness of their presence."

What he was getting at and talking about here was his own native, interior, land-locked, region needing access to seacoasts and ports for the good of the nation.

He added further that, "Our national strife springs not from our permanent part, not from the land we inhabit, not from our national homestead.... Our strife pertains to ourselves – to the passing generations of men; and it can without convulsion be hushed forever with the passing of one generation."

This brought him at last to the heart of the matter in his mind when he wrote, "Without slavery the rebellion could never have existed; without slavery it could not continue."

His last words to the Congressmen on this occasion were, "….. The fiery trial through which we pass will light us down, in honor or dishonor, to the latest generation. We say we are for the Union. The world will not forget that we say this. We know how to save the Union. The world knows we do know how to save it. We – even we here – hold the power and bear the responsibility. In giving freedom to the slave, we assure freedom to the free – honorable alike in what we give and what we preserve. We shall nobly save or meanly lose the last, best hope of earth. Other means may succeed; this could not fail. The way is plain, peaceful, generous, just – a way which, if followed, the world will forever applaud, and God must forever bless."

David told me that the cost for what Mr. Lincoln was requesting was immeasurably great. Of course "we here" would not be able to do anything to assure anything he said. It would have to be done by young men who are farmers or teachers or merchants and follow old generals into battle.

He questioned whether the incalculable price was worth it. After all he have seen on the ground, it pained him to consider it glory. He still believed it was right, but said there is no glory. No glory whatsoever.

He recalled that the commanding officers talked about glory. They were doing their job – what they were trained to do – getting us to march, to entrench, to stand up to withering fire from artillery and muskets, to charge with clashing bayonets, to staunch the bleeding, to bury the dead. There is no glory, just aggression meeting aggression.

Some called them killer angels. He never saw it that way. It may have been about honor. He did not know. It was not noble. Our father tried to help him understand it and bring him peace through his God. David was not a Godly man. From my experiences in World War I, I understand David Wexley better than either of you ever can."

David Ashford looked back at the war before he was born as an historian would. He learned and understood the politics of how Lincoln's and David Wexley's Civil War was going. The months following the Emancipation Proclamation, the number of visitors to the people's house increased. In those days, visitors had generally free access to an audience with the President and the Secret Service was not highly focused on security.

Abolitionists were generally pleased with Lincoln's performance and his popularity began to turn for the better. His political strategies for public support were working. The progress with the war however, had much to be improved.

Lincoln was pained to break the law – the Constitution – as he saw it while he suspended Writs of Habeas Corpus and invoked conscription. The poor Irish in the North were embittered about the new draft laws of military service and embittered further with being forced to fight for the Negro cause – not to mention the threat of free Negroes taking away their employment.

David Ashford, as well as David Wexley before then, understood that Lincoln had continued to be beleaguered. Josena Ashford had continued to follow it the years later when her brother had studied it, but Hanna had no idea. That was probably for the best because it wouldn't have helped her. It would have confused her and stood in the way of her divine mission.

Josena and Peggy were away at the university most days; so Hanna took care of baby Joe. Before she passed away, while David was overseas, Mary spent her last days with pleasure and satisfaction watching them from her rocking chair.

Over the years Hanna became the boy's companion and as he grew older, she read him the exciting stories in the bible. He loved the stories of Samson and Delilah, Daniel in the lion's den, Jonah in the belly of the whale, and old Noah saving the animals from the flood.

Hanna loved telling him, "Now Josiah, when Joshua fit the battle of Jericho, he free his people. 'N' old Moses led his people out of Egypt to be free in the Promised Land. Abraham Lincoln, he free our people."

He smiled at Aunt Hanna's face and remembered every word.

Some days, with little to do, Hanna accompanied Josena to Oxford in Josena's Ford motor car. While Josena taught her classes there at Miami of Ohio University, Hanna spent her day on campus watching and listening to the young students. She heard some strong emotional diatribes of racial injustice and some vitriolic language of racial prejudice. The arguments fell just short of physical violence.

When she could she engaged the students. "I'm an old wuman that has seen a lotta cruelty in my life in the South. I've seen kindness too from people you wouldn't expect. The best I can tells y'all is right in the good book. Love is patient, love is kind. It does not envy, it does not boast, it is not proud. It is not rude, it is not self-seeking, it is not easily angered, it keeps no record of wrongs. Love does not delight in evil, but rejoices with the truth. It always protects, always trusts, always hopes, always perseveres."

Eyes shining with passionate faith and glistening aglow with abiding love, arms raised outstretched with upturned palms, body bent beckoning toward them, she smiled at them and said, "Love is not just a feelin', it's a choice and an action and a blessing."

Most listened to her, many smiled, some wanted to believe, some decided and were profoundly affected and came to her and took her hands and knew love.

David too was trying to resolve issues in his mind from his life's experience and it was time for another brainstorming session with his sister, Josena. It began, as it often did, with him delivering her a lecture.

He told her, "History is transitory. And it is generally cyclical, but manifesting itself differently with each cycle. It is like a mutating organism."

Darwinism dominated the intellectual thinking at the time.

"Its truth", he continued, "is there but illusive and temporary. You can never wrap your arms around it and hold it still long enough to draw ultimate conclusions.

From its multitude of little ideas, you can draw only a misty vision of the biggest ideas. But it is the only teacher that we have."

Josena responded, "Hanna would tell you that there is a better teacher, one we can learn from with certainty after all our intellect is exhausted."

He knew what she meant by that; the conversation became silent while he pondered what she had said.

At this point in his mature life, David had grown to have doubt in his faith. As he most often did, he turned to his twin sister again.

"I don't believe I am a Christian in every sense. I mean I believe in God, His creation and Providence, but I'm not convinced of all the tenants of Jesus Christ. I haven't made the leap of faith or the final commitment.

Maybe it is because of what I have lived, learned and seen – all of man's inhumanity, father's early life and those before him. I can't believe in altruism for its own sake. Charity is goodness, but it must be voluntary not demanded. I will help people because I believe it is right, but never if it is somehow expected of me.

Hanna is surely different. She has the faith. She follows the command to love as her purpose in life. God bless her for that."

Josena tried to grasp her brother's belief and said, "But David that is not what we were raised to believe. I am surprised. I don't believe you have changed like that."

"I believe in the individual, in the pursuit of one's happiness, as the founders of our country believed", he said. "It looks as if their ideals are beginning to be realized for the rest of us at long last. Now we must look out for our own, our people, our family."

She reflected on that and replied, "And our country David. For the good of us all."

"I'm not so sure about that", he responded.

"War changes a man. Look at David Wexley."

"What do you mean by that?", she asked him.

"Before we went to war, we had such moral certainty. We were idealistic, everything was clear – simple. War changes all that. We hope to return not just to our families, but to the man we once were. I'm not certain how to answer you any better than that.

David Wexley tried to pursue his happiness, but somehow he failed to realize it. It is very complicated and confusing."

She offered, "Well a man's life is the best he can make it. David Wexley made a difference in the world. Hanna has too. I think you should talk to Hanna."

"Thanks Josie. I'm sure you are right", he answered.

One summer evening, he stood on the porch looking across the yard at Hanna. She was sitting on the old family bench under the oak tree. In the netherworld between day and night, Hanna was looking at the sky – dark blue with a pale moon and the North star visible at the same time as the daylight.

He walked over and stood next to her beside the bench, staring out at the broad sky with her.

"What is it David?", she asked him.

"I have been trying to think about God and the meaning of all this", he gestured to the panorama.

"Sit down brother."

Without conversation, or need for it, he sat down next to her and took her right hand in his left. They sat there together for a while, looking ahead, tears flowing down David's cheeks.

She turned toward him and smiling at him, placed her left hand on top of his.

They looked at each other lovingly and with a poignancy of understanding. He felt a gentle tingle – a pulsation – flowing up his arm and throughout his body, and he knew.

He knew for the first time what she knew. He had not learned of it in college, in the factory, from his father, overseas, on the road across America, or in Ohio - had only a glimpse of it when his son had been born. It was the ultimate and real truth.

It was how she had survived, endured, surmounted, prevailed, didn't need to be endlessly searching, found happiness. The face of God was inside him, before his mind, a part of him, for the first time a certainty, a permanent unshakable truth never to be taken away.

One Sunday David attended the AME Church. As a prominent member of the community and its chief employer, he was welcomed – welcomed out of respect and yes curiosity too.

There was an interesting dynamic in the churches in the town of Hamilton and the little village of Ashford. From all the years that Hanna had been there, with her influence on all the people of the community and the Ashford family as the primary employer for the area – essentially the founders of Ashford, Ohio - the churches were attended mostly evenly by both races. It was odd that so many whites attended the African Methodist Episcopal Church and so many blacks the Presbyterian Church, but that was how it was. The division was more along the lines of class. The poorer people who earned the lower wages tended toward the AME congregation, whereas the more affluent tended toward the Presbyterian one.

So is was a bit unusual for David to show up at the AME Church with his wife Peggy and son Joe; more so than Hanna. They sat all together as a family.

David asked the pastor if he would be allowed to speak a few words to the congregation. The pastor nodded to him with a smile in the affirmative. This once David's words were short and, on this occasion, a heartfelt prayer.

"Pray with me", he said. "Dear Lord, I want to give my thanks for all You have given me in my blessed life, my wife Peggy who with her love and devotion, has been my partner in breaking down the barriers of color here in our beloved community of Ashford and Hamilton, our son Joe who we know will be the hope for our future and last and most of all our dear sister Hanna – sister to our family, our community and yes even many parts of our country.

Her life and love and inspiration has been the greatest blessing I have seen God bring into our lives. And for me, she has shown me the right way to live and to be and made me free at last. For all these things and people, I thank you Lord."

"Once a great King David pleased the Lord. Here is David's confidence in God's grace. A Psalm of David. Pray with me the words of his 23rd Psalm in the good book where we are taught to give praise to His name –

The Lord is my shepherd, I shall not want.

He maketh me to lie down in green pastures: he leadeth me beside the still waters.

He restoreth my soul: he leadeth me in the path of righteousness for his name's sake.

Yea, though I walk through the valley of the shadow of death, I will fear no evil: for thou art with me; thy rod and thy staff they comfort me.

Thou preparest a table before me in the presence of mine enemies; thou annoitest my head with oil; my cup runneth over.

Surely goodness and mercy shall follow me all the days of my life: and I will dwell in the house of the Lord for ever."

The pastor embraced him before he returned to his place with his family.

After all the years living with her father and the Ashfords, Hanna Drish never changed her last name. It was given to her by her adoptive white parents, John and Sarah and she would forever honor their love for her.

When she passed away during the throes of World War II, the town commissioned a bronze statue of her and placed it in the center of the square there in Ashford, Ohio.

The plaque at the base of the statue was inscribed:

Hanna Drish (1856-1942) – slave, freedwoman, healer of hearts, beloved sister to our community.

David and Josena were there for the commemoration, along with David's wife Peggy and their son. The community remembered her as their historical heroine for generations and to this day. She was known as the woman credited for the extraordinary racial harmony enjoyed in that region. Miami of Ohio history school included her life story in their classes. She had kept her promise.

Epilogue

By November of 1942, America had been at war again for almost a year. The Japanese had attacked in the Pacific and captured the Philippines by then. While fighting them there, America was preparing to fight the Germans on a second front in Europe. Once again the world was coming apart. God was saddened and grew more tired still, now that he was older.

On the 25th of that month and year, Hanna Drish left this mortal coil. Josena sat next to her on her bed and held her in her arms. David was in her room watching from the rocking chair. They waited quietly. No one spoke.

Hanna's face was serene. The lines of care were gone and her skin seemed to glow with a lambency, inexplicably brighter than the ambient light that filled the room from the late afternoon sun coming through the lace curtains of the window.

Josena watched as soundless tears ran down her cheeks. She was remembering how Hanna had sung the words to her that Hanna's mother Josena had sung to her as a child – those sweet words from *God Bless the Child* and *Swing Low Sweet Chariot.* As she remembered, she hummed them softly and gently rocked Hanna.

Hanna's eyes opened and she looked at her sister one last time before they flickered and closed. Josena smiled as she watched Hanna's chest heave and exhale her last breath. David heard the last rush of air as his sister became motionless – more still than a living person could possibly be.

She was gone. Only her motionless body lie silently in the bed. Her work was done. She went home. For that moment, God was happy. He was pleased and He was smiling. His Hanna would be with Him very soon.

David looked out the window at the golden sun sparkling on the fresh snow just fallen on the ground in the fields of Hamilton. The air was crisp. It smelled new and seemed to offer promise and hope.

At that same moment, white billowy clouds, with golden fringes from the glorious late afternoon sun, were moving rapidly across the sky in Alabama over the patch of Earth where she was born. One of the smallest of them had a golden brilliance more than the others.

Michael's wings were spread wide and his arms were folded tightly around the embodiment of Hanna's immortal soul as he climbed higher and higher until he was just a pinpoint barely visible or discernible or comprehendible to any person on the ground.

And Grace had led her home.

end

Characters

Yahweh, Jehovah, God, the Creator of the Universe

Michael – Archangel from the South of Fire

Hanna Drish – freedwoman from Drish plantation, daughter of Josiah and Josena Ashford

Josiah Ashford - slave and freedman, Savannah Oaks plantation

Josena Taylor Ashford - Josiah's wife and a slave, Savannah Oaks and Drish plantations

Mary Custis Ashford - Josiah's 2nd wife

David Custis Ashford, Josena Custis Ashford - Josiah's children, Hanna Drish's half siblings

David Wexley – friend of the Ashfords

Dr. John and Sarah Drish – Owners of Drish plantation near Tuscaloosa, Alabama

Kenneth and Abigail Blanchard – Wealthy merchants in Mobile, Alabama

Nora Travers, Hanna's friend

Elizabeth Jefferson – David Ashford's wife

Sam Jefferson – Elizabeth's father

Crista and Hans Hannon – migrants to Ashford, Ohio

Locations

Hamilton, Ohio – Ashford family farm and estate

Tuscaloosa, Alabama - John Drish Plantation

Mobile, Alabama – Hanna Drish's adopted home

Montgomery, Alabama – First capital of the Confederacy

Atlanta, Georgia – Industrial center of the South

McComb, Mississippi - town where Hanna settled

Buffalo, New York – City where the Hannons were from

Character and Historical Timeline

1795 - John Drish is born in Virginia

1807- Marcus Taylor is born in Savannah

1809 - Rebecca Stanley is born in Charleston

1820 - Missouri Compromise

1822 - John Drish came to Tuscaloosa and bought 450 acre property

1829 - Josiah Ashford is born on a Missouri plantation

1832 - David Wexley is born in Baltimore

1837- Josena is born on Savannah Oaks plantation

1837 - Drish House completed

1852 - Marcus bought Josiah for his Savannah Oaks plantation

1853 - Josiah and Josena marry on Savannah Oaks

1854 - The Kansas-Nebraska Act

1856 - Josena is sold from Savannah Oaks to Drish plantation

1856 - Hanna, Josena's daughter, is born on Drish plantation

1860 - Lincoln elected President, South Carolina secedes

1861 - The Civil War breaks out

1864 - Josena is killed on Drish plantation

1864 - Hanna, age 8 is sent to the Blanchard family in Mobile, Alabama to raise her and care for her

1865 - Lee surrenders to Grant at Appomattox, April 9th

1865 - Lincoln assassinated in Ford's theater, April 14th

1865- Joe Johnston surrenders to Sherman at Durham Station NC, April 26th

1865 - 13th Amendment passed abolishing slavery

1865 - Josiah is freed and meets David Wexley in Natchez, Mississippi

1866 - KKK supported by Confederate General Nathan Bedford Forrest to terrorize the South

1867 - John Drish died in an accidental fall

1868 - Josiah meets Mary Custis in Hamilton, Ohio

1869 - Josiah and Mary give birth to twins – David Custis Ashford and Josena Custis Ashford

1869 - Hanna, age 13 meets the Archangel, Michael in her Mobile, Alabama home

1877- Post-war reconstruction abandoned

1881 - Marcus dies in McComb, Mississippi

1882 - Hanna, age 26 comes to McComb and cares for old crazy Rebecca

1884 - Sarah Drish died

1887 – Public schools in Ohio are integrated

1888 - Rebecca dies, Hanna buries her

1892 - The twins, David and Josena graduate from Oberlin College

1898 - Spanish American war (David is 29)

1900 - The twins, age 31 travel south, retrace some of Josiah and David's old route

1900 - The twins unite with Hanna, age 44 in McComb

1900 - Telephone transmission extends across and between major cities

1900 - David Wexley dies in Aspen, Colorado

1900 - The twins return to Hamilton with Hanna and for David Wexley's burial

1903-1909 - Wright brothers in Dayton, Ohio develop flying machine

1906 - Drish House converted to a school, Drish property sub-divided

1906 - Josiah dies in Hamilton, Ohio

1906 - Hanna gets close to Mary and cares for her

1907 – David runs Ashford Furniture, Josena (38) attends Miami of Ohio for her master's degree

1908 - Henry Ford introduces first viable gasoline powered automobile

1909 – NAACP founded by W.E.B. DuBois

1910 – Josena introduces Peggy Jefferson to David

1912 - Woodrow Wilson elected President, social Darwinist racist who liked Birth of a Nation

1912 – David (43) marries Peggy Jefferson (34)

1915 – David and Peggy have a son

1915 - The Birth of a Nation movie debuts

1917 - The United States enters World War I

1917 - David enlists in U.S. Army as a correspondent with 93rd division under BG Roy Hoffman

1917 - Mary dies while David is overseas, Josena, Peggy and Hanna bury Mary

1918 - David returns from the war and reunites with Peggy, his son (3) and sisters

1918 - David and Josena again revitalize and run Ashford Furniture Company

1918-1942 – Hanna (62-86) serves the community and becomes a legendary figure for unification and harmony

1920 - 19th Amendment ratified for woman's suffrage

1925 – The Scopes Monkey Trial in Dayton, Tennessee

1929 – Martin Luther King, Jr. born in Atlanta, Georgia

1942 - Hanna dies at 86, David and Josena are 73 with her in Hamilton, Ohio

1968 – Martin Luther King, Jr. assassinated in Memphis, Tennessee

1968 – Josiah Ashford II, David's son, frequents Miami of Ohio Campus

Ashford Family Tree

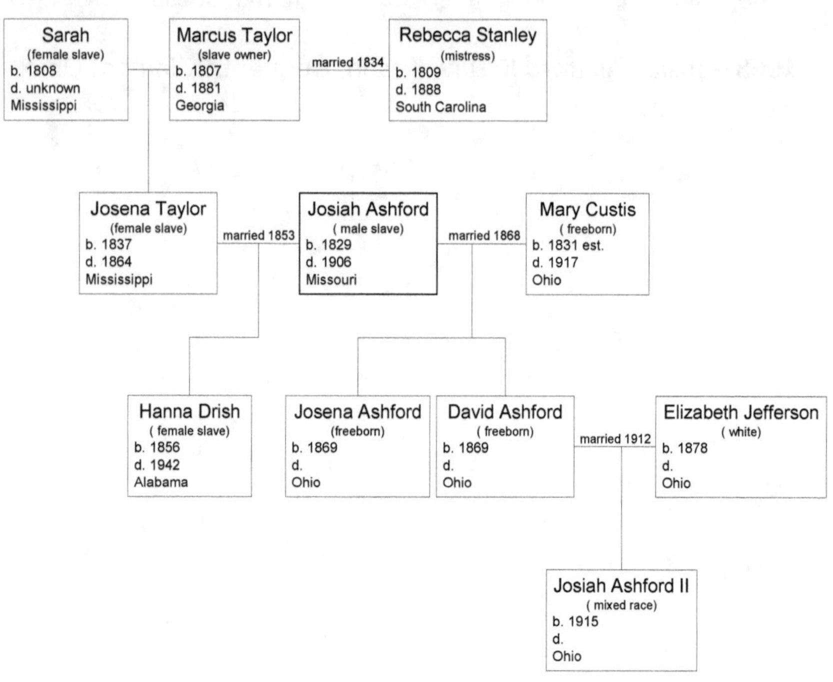

Part Three – The American

A Man's Life

Contents

Prologue

What happened to him the thirteen years after he disappeared to go west, before his casket brought him back to Cincinnati on the train?

He had not found a settled life, or even what he was looking for, not even by the time he was fifty five in 1887. He saw the worst of it and it affected the rest of his life.

Men had talked to him about glory. He had heard about it and dreamed about it when he had gone to be a soldier. Ever since man held a spear and fashioned a sharp-edged weapon, he longed for glory. Homer wrote of it epically and he read it. He believed in it but learned that glory is a false God in the end.

Those years he was a man in the Gilded Age but not of it. Others were making fortunes by nefarious means. He was still trying to sort out the troubled past – to make what meaning he could out of it and get by.

America had disappointed him and there was little source of solace. The great men he had known, or known of, had made his country as bad as they had good. For many it looked like America wasn't a country; it was a business.

There was the economic Panic of 1873 resulting from government patronage and abuses in the Union Pacific railroad development. There was carryover debt from the Civil War and troubles with bonds and paper currency. The efforts to tie all this economic lunacy to the soundness of gold had failed too.

He was a man of little import in the greater scheme of things – a man of great courage and heart who cared for his fellow beings and made what little difference he could. He was a man of his time who tells us his story in the first person voice. He saw, thought, felt, believed what he experienced as it affected him and his country.

He was an American.

Illustrations

David Wexley in 1862

Map of the western United States in the late 19th century

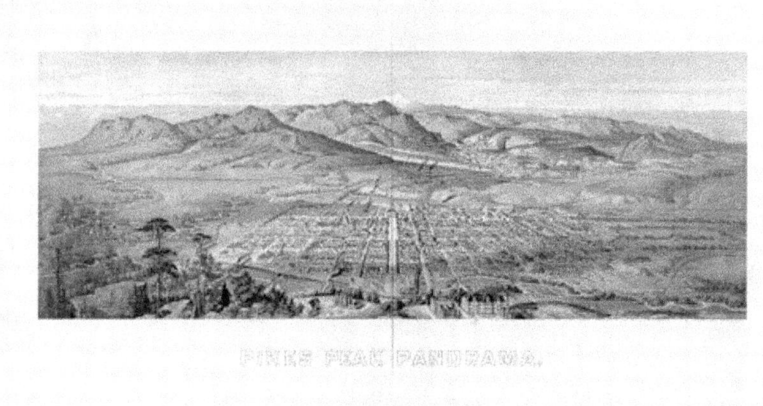

Pikes Peak in the Rocky Mountains

One – David

War is cruelty. There is no use trying to reform it. The crueler it is, the sooner it will be over.

- William T. Sherman.

War is hell. War is never glorious. It don't matter what the cause, the purpose, the intent, or the outcome of it is. Human beings are killed. I know that because when I was a young man I seen it and participated in it. I killed human beings.

When I was a young boy in Baltimore, my life was comfortable. My widowed father Morgan had raised me in a fine house not far from the harbor. I was his only child. He was a successful banker, while he filled my mind with the things about history and politics he believed I needed to know. I neglected to mention my name is David Wexley.

But my young spirit was filled with youthful things. I wanted adventure. With his blessings, I left Baltimore's harbor at sixteen and headed to sea with the Merchant Marines. It was 1848 and in those days we still sailed in topsail schooners.

Those times I kept a journal of my travels. It was what we did the long lonely weeks out at sea and a good way to record my memories. Besides, I could share my stories with my father someday back home.

After a few years, I had grown up some and seen the American Atlantic coast at ports-of-call in Boston, Norfolk, Charleston and Savannah. I had learned something about the American people and what they valued in their lives as that differed from the North to the South. The beautiful coastal southern cities were charming. I fell for the southern gentility and elegance of the high-tone people there. Their lives were full of their traditional history, comfort and ease.

I was still so young then. There was no capacity of experience to draw from for me to understand, or even recognize, what was behind the façade of refinement. I would learn later what it meant and would ultimately lead to.

But genuine, salt-of-the-earth, hard-working people were in all those places too. I knew that even back then as young as I was. In any event, the life on the sea was out of my system. That was before the war.

When I returned to my father's house in Baltimore, I was ready for change and maybe new adventure. Following in the footsteps of a banker was not the life I wanted for me.

I wanted to build things, so I entered the carpentry trade as an apprentice. It was gratifying building new homes for Baltimore's people as I watched the city's growth begin to really boom. I enjoyed the comradery with my tradesmen in the long after-hours in the taverns after the day's hard work and began to understand the working-class men as I became one of them.

That is when Morgan began to teach me the grownup things he said I needed to know about the direction our country was headed.

By then my travels and maturity had given me a sense of our history and my idealism was in full bloom.

We read the Maryland newspapers together and discussed the events as they were revealed and depicted by the conflicting viewpoints of the reporters and their editors. We talked about the abolitionists in the North and the slaveholders in the South and the troubles in the West. The rift in the country between North and South would surely soon tear it apart. Decades of compromise had only prolonged the inevitable.

It had started as early as Adams and Jefferson. Washington had warned us in his kindly, affectionate way when he left office and wrote us his parting Farewell Address letter. He wanted us to be one nation with love for each other and our brand new country. He gently reminded us with his passionate, patriotic love to work together – east to west and north to south – and avoid factions and parties that might destroy us before very long. He had a good sense of the future.

For Adams and Jefferson had had two different visions for our country, while both loved our land and its new Constitution. Later Lincoln would see it as Washington had and tell us once more what we needed to do as a country and as moral human beings.

War would come soon and it was time to take sides. In Maryland both factions were present. The split often occurred in one family. My sense of morality, instilled from Morgan, was strong. I signed up for the Union with my best friend, the man who I worked for and had taught me the carpentry trade. He was Geoff Braxton from Baltimore and we signed up together.

Geoff and I met a man from Boston, Massachusetts who had signed up at the same time and joined us for our military training. The three of us became comrades in arms. We were going to fight for Burnside. We became close friends, the three amigos, spending our times in the taverns at night.

This was all brand new. It was going to be a great adventure. Our heads were full of visions of glory. We were so certain we would lick the rebels in short order. Everybody said the war couldn't last more than three months. It turned out the southerners were a hell of a lot tougher than anybody knew. We were so innocent of the reality that was to come.

I fought in two major battles in the Civil War. The first was near Sharpsburg in Maryland by Antietam Creek in '62. We repulsed Bobby Lee's first attempt at advance into the North and he had to retreat across the Potomac back into Virginia. The price we paid in lost lives was horrific. I came through it with sound body but lost one of my two friends there on the Burnside Bridge.

Late in '64 I fought my second battle in what they called the Battle of the Wilderness. We got caught in the swamp forest on our way to take Jeff Davis' Confederate capital at Richmond. The battle was a draw and General Grant disengaged. They had stopped us short of our goal. I was shot in the leg and the enemy who captured me thought I was a goner. I had lost so much blood. I woke up a prisoner in the Confederate hospital in Richmond.

They transported me to the Confederate prison at Andersonville and I suffered in that hell hole most of the last year of the war. There I found my other friend. He died of starvation and disease in my arms. The war changed me in so many ways I cannot tell you. I left my youthful idealism there in southwest Georgia. I was no longer that man of moral certainty, that man of innocence who knew just what must be done.

My wartime experiences are engraved in my memory and have permanently scarred my soul. I had learned a new master trade and, through my apprenticeship in battle, had learned the skills of how to kill and not be killed. My time in prison camp had showed me what it all came to, the heart-wrenching loss of friendship, the vindictive cruelty of the victors over the vanquished, the predatory behavior of our own comrades toward each other, the worst of humanity and the futility of war.

When I was released, I didn't want to go home. I missed my father but just could not. I had kept up my journal through the war, although not as faithfully as during my maritime adventures. Then I stopped. My last entry was made when I was walking across Alabama and met some poor plain folk who shared their ideas of faith with me. It was only then that I could write my father a letter explaining all that had happened in the battles, at Andersonville and the deaths of Geoff and Pat.

Inexplicably I was drawn to these people and their lives in the South. They were common but there was a nobility in their resilience, grit and unconquerable spirit. Much later in my life I would learn where it came from and why it compelled me.

I wandered west for many weeks on foot until I came to the Mississippi in Natchez. Beside the Big Muddy that afternoon, I met a man who would become my lifelong friend – my brother. But that is getting ahead of myself.

After the war and on my own without my father, I made a study of the Civil War I had fought in, needing to understand it better. I studied the great men behind the scenes I had never known – men like Lincoln and Grant and Lee.

In the middle of the war, some twenty months since it began at Fort Sumter, President Lincoln was in trouble. He was struggling to preserve the Union up to that point. Emancipation of the slaves would come later. The war had come to a halt and a stalemate. Both sides were entrenched holding their gains and not moving forward.

Lincoln was beset with so many problems just then; he was alternately standing still, moving forward and making mistakes, and constantly changing strategy trying to end it. His generals were pulling him in all directions. The American people of the Union were out of patience and despondent from the loss of blood and treasure and time. Even his Secretary of War said to him about a military appointment, "Well, you have made your choice of idiots. Now you can await the news of terrible disaster." They blamed it all on him.

His own Republicans in Congress, the Radical ones, and the newspapers were constantly harassing him, calling him an ignorant and incompetent fool. Even some members of his own cabinet were against him. But he persevered and spent his time thinking and writing. He believed he could convince them if he could just craft the most compelling words.

He had written a preliminary Emancipation Proclamation but his Secretary of State, William Seward advised him to put it in a drawer until the time was right. He taught Lincoln that timing was everything.

When he released it, the time was right. You might not believe this, but freeing the slaves was not its purpose. He had learned the skill of politics and the Proclamation would benefit him and the federal government fourfold.

First, it would not offend the tenuous relationship he held with the Union border-states – Delaware, Kentucky, Maryland and Missouri - who held slaves. They would be allowed to keep their slaves.

Second, it would not free slaves in the north – in the Union. He wanted to appease certain members of Congress. It only freed slaves in Union controlled Confederate states.

Third, he needed replenishment of troops by then and black freedmen could serve in the Union army. Runaways from the South and Border States were encouraged by his action and joined the army. Newly freed blacks in Confederate areas joined the Federals right on the spot when they came through. Lincoln was planning for this and knew what would happen.

In all arms, two million men fought in the Civil War. This was near the end and eighty thousand Negroes joined and fought bravely in cruel defeats like at Fort Wagner. Some, still slaves, served their Confederate masters in the war, digging, cooking, hauling, lifting and serving. Perhaps a handful did so willingly and believed in their cause.

Fourth, and not much known, he was constantly competing with Jeff Davis for foreign sympathy and support in England and France. They needed Jeff's cotton but hated his slavery. Lincoln hoped this would fool them and sway them to the Union side. It might not have been convincing to some overseas who saw through to its veiled purposes, but at least it kept them from swinging to Jeff Davis' side. Lincoln was walking a tightrope.

About that time, Lincoln came into his own. He had begun master-crafting those compelling words he needed. In his December message to Congress, a long fifty thousand words delivered by a moderator in his absence, it began with a blessing followed by well- wishing, a grieving about the war, and launched into a long host of boring humdrum matters. It was a dry beginning. After nearly losing them, it began to hit its stride at mid-point when the tone changed.

He wrote, "A nation may be said to consist of its territory, its people, and its laws. The territory is the only part which is of certain durability. 'One generation passeth away, and another generation cometh: but the earth abideth forever.' It is of the first importance to duly consider and estimate this ever-enduring part. That portion of the earth's surface which is owned and inhabited by the people of the United States is well adapted to be the home of one national family, and it is not well adapted for two or more.... There is no line, straight or crooked, suitable for a national boundary upon which to divide. Trace through, from east to west, upon the line between the free and slave country, and we shall find a little more than one-third of its length are rivers, easy to be crossed and populated, or soon to be populated, thickly upon both sides; while nearly all its remaining lengths are merely surveyors' lines, over which people may walk back and forth without any consciousness of their presence."

What he was getting at and talking about here was his own native, interior, land-locked, region needing access to seacoasts and ports for the good of the nation.

He added further that, "Our national strife springs not from our permanent part, not from the land we inhabit, not from our national homestead.... Our strife pertains to ourselves – to the passing generations of men; and it can without convulsion be hushed forever with the passing of one generation."

This brought him at last to the heart of the matter in his mind when he wrote, "Without slavery the rebellion could never have existed; without slavery it could not continue."

His last words to the Congressmen on this occasion were, "..... The fiery trial through which we pass will light us down, in honor or dishonor, to the latest generation. We say we are for the Union. The world will not forget that we say this. We know how to save the Union. The world knows we do know how to save it. We – even we here – hold the power and bear the responsibility. In giving freedom to the slave, we assure freedom to the free – honorable alike in what we give and what we preserve. We shall nobly save or meanly lose the last, best hope of earth. Other means may succeed; this could not fail. The way is plain, peaceful, generous, just – a way which, if followed, the world will forever applaud, and God must forever bless."

The cost for what Mr. Lincoln was requesting was immeasurably great. Of course "we here" would not be able to do anything to assure anything. It would have to be done by young men who are farmers or teachers or merchants and follow old generals into battle.

Jeff Davis, as the President of the Confederacy, his country, had his own views and demons to deal with also. On the occasion that he came back home to Richmond on January 5, after an extensive, exhaustive trip to the west of his country and review of his

Generals' performances, he just wanted to rest and be with his family. But the people were anxious to see him, grateful for his return and wanted to celebrate his appearance.

And so he mustered up the energy from his meager reserves, was invigorated by the people and spoke to them. He told them: "Every sound is the voice of my child and every child renews the memory of a loved one's appearance, but none can equal their charms, nor can any compare with my own long-worshipped Winnie", he had written home from Tennessee but believed he could not ignore the adoration from the crowd of his people and the courtesy they tendered.

"I am happy to be welcomed on my return to the capitol of the Confederacy – the last hope, as I believe, for the perpetuation of that system of government which our forefathers founded – the asylum of the oppressed, and the home of true representative liberty."

With his strained and exhausted voice which usually gathered in strength when he continued, he reverted to the deeds of olden days in the Old Dominion, where the earlier Revolution had been proclaimed, begun, and finally won. And so now he told these new Virginians, "anticipating the overthrow of that government which you had inherited, you assumed to yourselves the right, as your fathers had done before you, to declare yourself independent, and nobly have you advocated the assertion which you have made. Here, upon your soil, some of the fiercest battles of the Revolution were fought, and upon your soil it closed by the surrender of Cornwallis. Here again our men of every state; here they have congregated, linked in the defense of a most sacred cause. They have battled, they have bled upon your soil, and it is now consecrated by blood which cries for vengeance against the insensate foe of religion as well as of humanity, of the altar as well as of the hearthstone.

It is true, you have a cause which binds you together more firmly than your fathers were. They fought to be free from the usurpations of the British crown, but they fought against a manly foe. You fight against the off-scourings of the earth.

Every crime which could characterize the course of demons has marked the course of the invader … from the burning of defenseless towns to the stealing of silver forks and spoons."

Whether the price for that war was worth it is incalculable. After all I have seen on the ground, it pains me to consider it glory. I still believe it is right, but there is no glory. No glory whatsoever.

The commanding officers talked about glory. They were doing their job – what they were trained to do – getting us to march, to entrench, to stand up to withering fire from artillery and muskets, to charge with clashing bayonets, to staunch the bleeding, to bury the dead. There is no glory, just aggression meeting aggression.

Some called us killer angels. I never saw it that way. It may be honor. I do not know. It is not noble. Josiah tried to help me understand it and bring me peace through his God. I am not a Godly man.

I met Josiah Ashford, a just-freed slave, at the dockside of the Mississippi at Natchez. He had walked the fifteen miles over there from his former plantation, Savannah Oaks nearby that same day he had been freed. I had walked for many days from Andersonville in Georgia. We talked as strangers and became friends. I went with him all over Mississippi and Alabama looking for his lost wife taken from him. We set our fortunes together.

When we found she had been killed on another plantation, we had an altercation. I shot and killed the overseer. We stole two horses and headed north. He was a master cabinetmaker who made furniture. I was a master carpenter who built buildings. As I said, he became my brother.

The American

Two – Ohio

Josiah and I finally found our way to Hamilton, Ohio late in ’65. We had made our way north on horseback, the one’s we stole in Alabama, up the Tennessee and along the Ohio to Cincinnati. Hamilton is just north of Cincinnati and it seemed like the right place to stop and figure out what to do.

When Joe had learned that he had a lost daughter from his killed wife Josena, he was doubly heartbroken we couldn’t find her. So we decided to give up on the South and head north. He consoled me when we visited Shiloh and I consoled him for his great personal losses also. The war had cost us both plenty.

We did carpentry jobs for the farmers and town folks until we had enough money for Josiah to buy a small farm. He had no intention of being a farmer. Joe wanted to start a furniture making business. I stayed with him and we renovated the old barn to begin his humble factory. Before you knew it, we had been there for years and I guess it was home.

Joe made beautiful furniture and soon established a reputation for his work. His business took off and very quickly he was selling his fine furniture to farmers and town folk all over southwestern Ohio. I helped him build a proper factory in place of the renovated old barn.

I was always inventive with my work once I had developed the skills with my tools and hands. Starting back in Ohio with Joe’s factory, I had begun to think like an engineer or an architect. To do it, it needs you to visualize and then build it the way you see it in your mind. It is the same with carpentry or machinery.

He met a fine woman, Mary Custis, whose people had come there years ago from Virginia. She was a 4th generation freeborn Negro from Martha Curtis Washington's slaves. They married and had twins. The girl was named Josena after his first wife who was killed. The boy was named David after me. I was honored and stayed close to the growing family as the twins grew up.

Joe was so popular, he got elected to the Ohio legislature up in Columbus. He spent time up there when they were in session. I was so proud of how far my friend had come since I found him in Natchez as a newly freed slave all those years ago.

Back in Ohio, Joe developed an extensive library. His might have been bigger than my father Morgan's. Once Joe learned to read, his intellect and knowledge on all manner of things grew at an incredible rate. We had many discussions our years together. Sure, I taught him some history, but he taught me philosophy and law. We both were concerned about the direction of the country. That's where all these subjects came together. We both wanted the common man, be he Negro or poor white, to have an equal chance for a fair share if he worked for it. Joe's special interest was for the next generations of Negroes to get a good education.

For me, I stayed in town and ran a small carpentry business. It kept me busy building new houses and repairing old buildings for the area which was growing fast. I eventually hired two men to help me. I was getting a little older and it was good to have a couple young bucks to help with the heavy lifting.

I had my one chance for a wife and love of my life, but it didn't work out. Jim Culpepper wouldn't stand for me marrying his daughter Estelle. She was a colored woman and me marrying her was taboo in those days. It broke my heart and I went back to drinkin'.

Joe tried to get me through it, but after a while, I decided to start over. I still reflect on my lost youth and innocence.

I remember Estelle while I think about our fight for the freedom of colored people. After so many years living in Ohio, I just didn't seem to notice color anymore. I was very attracted to some colored women the same as any other shade of skin. It was such a liberating feeling compared to all the preconceptions and feelings everybody had back in Baltimore before the war.

After Lincoln was killed, that son-of-a-bitch Andrew Johnson took over and messed up most of what so many of us had fought and died for. Lincoln never would have picked him as his Vice President. His own Republican party did that even though Johnson was a Democrat from Tennessee of suspicious southern sympathies. The war still kept going, but now we were fighting it in our minds.

When General Grant picked up the reins, I think he did a fair job. He was a man from Point Pleasant, Ohio you know. He was born there along the Ohio River in 1822, not more than fifty five miles from where me and Josiah settled in Hamilton in 1865.

Everyone said he was a failure at everything in his life with the exception of his military career. They said he was a lousy President and administrator and couldn't resolve the scandal of the spoils system rampant all about him.

That may be true to some degree but I know his heart and it was certainly more genuine than McClellan or Sheridan or Sherman. At least President Grant tried to finish up what the war was for – he understood it – and improve the country by mitigating the many hateful actions in the South and selfish political nonsense in Washington.

But he sent the red headed Ohioan Sherman – his old friend and colleague who he had spent so much time talking to and strategizing and commiserating with, smoking cigars, while the newspapers called one a drunk and the other a lunatic - out west to kill Indians. Sherman stayed there and managed that for 15 years.

It was sort of like the time long before when General Andrew Jackson was President and did the same to the American native peoples back in the East.

As far as politics go, I still try to steer clear of it as much as I can. Unlike my father, I don't enjoy debating it or the party factions. But like him, I think historically as the best means to understand the present state of affairs. I guess I am a Jacksonian Democrat, the founder of that new view of democracy. Old Hickory did some despicable things at the beginning of this century that are shameful to our history. He was an Indian killer, a slaveholder and a self-made wealthy man who challenged the eastern elites. He believed strongly in States rights and acted to close down the national bank.

But he was a rugged frontiersman and a Scots-Irish fighter. Like me, he believed in the common man. Nobody is my superior and I am free to live my own life as I please within the limits of the law.

President Grant made William T. Sherman the Commanding General of the Army which Cump was from 1869 to 1883. That's all Cump ever wanted to be. He had said he would never stand for political office under any circumstance and I respected him for that.

All Sherman knew was that war was hell and he knew how to fight it. He just wanted to follow orders and use his genius for the invention of modern warfare. It was for him the Esprit de Corps – all he ever wanted to have, be and do. When he died years later in 1891 – a few years after I left for the West - he had lived in New York City and they held his funeral there. Confederate General Joe Johnston came and served his former enemy as his pallbearer.

For these men it was always about the Esprit de Corps. I was just a lowly foot soldier and most often despised the senior officers and thought them heartless and incompetent. We all did. But I understand their Esprit de Corps and dedication.

Then President Hayes oversaw the end of Reconstruction, after Grant did what he could, and tried to reconcile the divisions still in the country. Now it is Benjamin Harrison in 1891. Who knows what he will be, stand for or do? While I respect some men, I hate politics as a general proposition. There have been so many disappointments in the past and there will be again in the future.

Three – The Trip

I always like to travel light. Other than the practical convenience of that, I think the measure of a man's character is not how he acts when he has everything, but how he acts when he has nothing.

Does he jealously covet what the other man has? Or does he wish him well when he has more? With less, a man is freer. With more it is a burden worrying about losing all you have. All I need is a good horse, a rifle and a blanket roll.

That is not exactly true. When I left I carried a gunny sack with two clean shirts, some socks and a toothbrush. These were modern, more civilized times. But my blanket roll was like my old friend I had carried all over my travels in the South. And of course I carried my Army Colt.

It has been decades since I had rode the train. Back in '64, I rode the Confederate prison train from Richmond to Andersonville and swore that would be my last. But I knew that this trip was impractical to attempt on horseback. The railroad was the only way to do it.

The trains had been around the East a long time and were an important part of the war. For me though, the trip out West would be a new adventure.

From Cincinnati, the Baltimore and Ohio line went east which was no good. There was a local line between Cincinnati, Lebanon and Dayton, but that wouldn't get me very far. I figured I needed to find some way to Chicago. It was a major crossroads from the

East to the West with all the cattle, slaughterhouses and meatpacking going on there. From there I could easily go west out to St. Louis or Kansas City or places in Wyoming, Montana or Colorado – most anywhere I wanted.

Josiah told me I couldn't get there from Cincinnati, nearby where we lived in the village of Ashford, in the town of Hamilton. So he offered to give me a ride in his buggy carriage northeast up to Columbus. I agreed to this, his last kindness, and he followed his familiar route up to Columbus, the capital where his legislature was.

He came into the train station and stood by me while I bought my ticket. We sat outside on a bench quietly watching the tracks, waiting for the train. After a while we saw it coming up the track going west, almost right on time. We stood up and faced each other in silence.

Joe looked at me with sad eyes brimming over with tears, that face forever full of resolve and said "I will never forget you. We have shared together so much of our lives. I will think of you always. God speed and be well my brother."

I felt inside that same sadness he showed on his face and told him you know me better than anyone in my life. You know I have to go. I will think about you and wish you were with me for all the new things I will discover and do. You are the best friend I have ever known and I will miss you the rest of my days.

We clasped forearms in the old Roman way as men do that have great respect, admiration and affection for one another. We stood facing each another moment and I began to turn away as the conductor called "All aboard." I walked a few steps and turned back once again looking at the man I had loved and respected for so long.

Later, after we were apart for some years, I thought about Joe and our long time together. It was true what he said. He always spoke truth to me. My friend Joe was only three years older than me and came from a lowly place as a slave. But in many ways he was like my father Morgan, steering me toward a better and safer path.

I had left him my old journals to keep, thinking they might mean something to him as a keepsake to remember me. Maybe his wife Mary would enjoy reading about those olden times long ago in my youth. Maybe his grown children David and Josena would want to read about their Uncle David. With a sadness in his eyes, Joe humbly accepted them.

Now I have no further interest in keeping them. There is no need. I have no family or kin. The rest of my life, I will learn how to live in the moment. Whatever tomorrow brings, I will be there to see.

Joe cared for me and saw when my adventuresome spirit got too risky and close to danger. It could be self-destructive. He saw that and I knew it too. I couldn't help but notice that Joe could see it. He found ways to stay out of trouble and work with troublesome people and it made him happy. I just couldn't and never have been happy.

He was my safe harbor, like the lighthouse showing me the way out of troubled waters. It reminds me of storms on the Atlantic when I was a young Merchant Marine.

But I couldn't follow his beacon, any more than I could my father's, and kept looking for new ways to get into trouble, not really on purpose, not consciously, but true all the same. Trouble always found itself in front of my road and I couldn't or wouldn't walk around it.

It was true the last words I said to him and I never forgot them. I really missed him and wished he had been here with me these times. But that is my fault, not his. I had to leave him for whatever it is that drives me onto the next thing.

He was the older brother I never had. I will always love that man. He told me we would be together again someday in this life or the next. I sure hope he was right.

The Columbus Chicago and Indiana railroad was there. It had been leased to the Pennsylvania railroad since 1869. It went right from Columbus to Chicago, stopping to transfer in Fort Wayne.

Chicago in 1887 was a peculiar mix of wealth and squalor. I never cared for either of those things about cities. That's why I preferred steering clear of them as much as I could. The new local electric streetcars and elevated railway systems joined together with steam railroads making it easy to get around and in and out of that steaming mass of humanity. Doubting I would ever see this place again, I decided to stay for a short while and explore the city.

Even though I am put off by the crowds and squalor in big cities, I couldn't help but admire the architecture in the Windy City. It is the fastest growing city in the United States. It was a wonder to see the way they are planning and rebuilding the core of the city, after the fire in 1871, inside the beautiful river loop that comes in from Lake Michigan on the east and curves south. The arched stone bridges rising up and over to cross that pretty river were impressive.

Folks told me they are planning to build grand hotels along Michigan Avenue. State Street is booming with new life. Beautiful municipal parks are being planned and built along the great lake, starting with the new Lincoln Park. They have big plans and dreams I can appreciate. It was plenty worth it to see it all for a couple days.

But the heartbeat of the city is not its new architecture emerging from the aftermath of the fire. It is the Union Stockyards, the South Work steel mills and the Pullman railway-car plant. These are the places where the people work, where things get built, where dreams are turned into reality.

Before long, I naturally gravitated to the working class people and their neighborhoods. In a big city these are the darkest, filthiest and most crowded streets with tenements packing people densely together.

Their gathering places are the saloons – the centers of their working poor communities. They are served friendship and comradery there, just as I had known in Baltimore a life ago. These are the workingman's clubs, their trade union halls and guilds. The patrons look out for each other, discuss politics, and assist each other in finding employment – a working man school for both the working man scholar and the working man teacher. The saloons are the common ethnic ground without the shame of charity or the outside rules and restrictions of organized clubs. I felt at home.

(David would never know it, but just a few years later Josena and David Ashford would visit the magnificent Chicago World's Fair and Columbian Exposition in 1893 as wide-eyed young adults just after graduating from Oberlin College.

And in 1900, the year he was killed, progressive temperance reformers believing that saloons seduced customers into lives of drunkenness, crime and debauchery, studied them to find solutions to the perceived problems. Prominent sociologist Royal Melendy began a serious academic study of this social problem with this same premise. He learned that he was wrong and that saloons served their communities better than any institution available at the time. Reluctantly, he reported his findings to the doubting intelligentsia of his time.

Melendy had an opportunity for a further life lesson learned if he took it; that is to never accept the premise on the face of it from your opponent or anyone for that matter. If you do, it will lead you unavoidably to their conclusion.)

From Chicago there was railroads going every which way, to anyplace you wanted to go to by the late 1800's. There was a funny disconnect though back by the Mississippi. East of the Big Muddy there was railroads everywhere and for a long time, like I have told you. The West had railroads too. What was needed was better connections across the big river in the northern continentals and the southern ones as well.

Actually the term transcontinental railroad is misleading. They weren't one continuous road like it sounds. They were many separate links joined together sometimes in a roughshod manner.

While we traveled on the train the few days to Denver, I watched out the window at the rapidly passing scene as the land changed in its shape, color, and texture. The landscape from the Midwest to the West, across the prairies to the mountains, took on a moving panorama of diverse beauty. I couldn't help but be moved by how great and vast was our land – America. It was so new, so sparsely populated; almost still pristine in its breathtaking, awe inspiring barrenness.

The Mississippi River is on the west side of Illinois and forms the boundary with the next state west – Iowa. Chicago is on the east side of Illinois along the shore of Lake Michigan. So the railroads heading west of Chicago are all confronted by the challenge of getting across the Mississippi. That Big Muddy, the Mississippi Delta, makes me think about the Nile in Egypt – all that rich silt piling up and creating a vast area of fertility.

As we crossed that great river on a new railroad bridge, I remembered Lincoln's words – what he said about our enduring land and its rivers dividing it and that they were soon to be crossed. So the division was a temporary thing and we the people of this nation would conquer that too. I hoped this would portend greater things for our people as a symbol or omen of unity.

I was traveling in relative comfort, in a peaceful time with friendly, forward-looking hopeful people. It was so completely different and positive than my ride decades ago in the prison train from Richmond to Andersonville. The people traveling with me on the trip were just regular people – maybe teachers or engineers or hopeful businessmen – but with enough means to take the train.

The very poor, maybe alone or with families, couldn't afford this modern, comfortable, fast way to get across the country. They had to come in wagons with all their meager possessions and face the hardships and dangers to make their way that I didn't. I had saved some money and I felt lucky even sitting on these hard seats and eating cold sandwiches for many long days.

Oh, I know there are a few back there in freight cars taking their chances the conductor or porters won't catch them. They have only the food and water they can carry until they hop off when they get where they want to go.

And there are the rich in the private cars with sleeping berths and fine dining surrounded by mahogany and brass appointed accommodations like a moving mansion or palace.

Still I'm fortunate I have the means to travel like I do. I do prefer to keep my own company and avoid crowds and numbers of people herded together like cattle in any case. But despite all the layovers and inefficiencies, I'll be on the other side of the country real quick. In the meantime, I have seen the new towns springing up along the path of the railroads and the development across all the places in this American century.

West of the river, there was railroads springing up like crazy and catching up fast to the East. But railroads crossing that river boundary made for some difficulties and covered strange geographical directions and peculiarities that were inconvenient and not very sensible.

For my time here in the American country, they called it the Gilded Age and the railroads were at the heart of the country's social and economic history. It was full of corruption from the managers of the big railroad companies and their partnership with government.

This was the time when we started to use the word corporations and that word was synonymous with railroads. So the Gilded Age had more to do with wealth gained from rotten means than it did about finding gold.

We built the western railroads faster than we needed them and they failed as businesses one after another while their leaders and planners and money managers got rich. It was about operating on credit with government, not about profit and success, and walking away with other people's money when the companies went bust.

I think the Gilded Age is so much about the railroads. The greed, corruption and shenanigans we learn about were all about the railroads in one way or another. Like the Civil War itself, the railroads brought some good and some bad to my country, but at a great price.

There were reformers who constantly tried to rein in the power of the railroads. That power as always was about what some men did to others, not about the locomotives, equipment or tracks.

The railroad men had power that reached out to so many aspects of our economy and men's lives. They could extort favor from a community to run their rails close by to it or bypass the community and place their rails far away to cause one community to wither and another to grow. America had never seen anything like it before.

For me it wasn't anything I could do about it. I just see it and know what is happening.

The railroad companies competed with other business activities and with themselves as well. They lobbied the government and curried favor to pass regulations to hurt the competition and favor themselves. In a perverse way they were part of the reform themselves.

That Economic Panic of 1893 was caused by the railroad men and their corporations and the relationships they formed as groups of friends with our government. It was because they wanted to develop our country out here in the West at all costs. The waste of money, treatment of native peoples and foreigners (new immigrants) was all part of that driving American motivation – our self-belief in Manifest Destiny. The development did come but again, like my war, the cost to human lives was horrific.

Most of the railroad buildin' was done by 1890 for the West. The sound and the fury of it was in the 60's, 70's and 80's. But the economic and physical damage to some Americans would take a bit longer to end.

Anyway, The Union Pacific headed west from Chicago to Cheyenne, Wyoming, stopping for transfer. Then another leg, already part of the Union Pacific, continued to Ft. Collins in Colorado and due south on to Denver City.

While we slept in our seats at night, we stopped at the changeovers and got off the train a while to stretch our legs. Standing still once in a while for a brief time, we got to see the towns as places fixed in their positions. This was another perspective.

I talked with some of my fellow travelers on the many long legs of the trip, but most were lost in their private thoughts or taking all the time to read their books. I did get to read Mark Twain's The Gilded Age, first published in 1873, about what was happening in the country.

One lady sitting next to me saw me reading it and struck up a conversation with me. She asked me what I thought about Twain's condemnation of the western railroad industry and our government's participation in the crime. I told her he wrote it like it is with his own unique brand of humor about American life.

She was coming west from Virginia. I told her I was from Maryland and knew the East – the North and South of it – but had never been west of Ohio, let alone Chicago and parts west of the Mississippi.

People were going west to seek a new life for all kinds of reasons. There were even some mail-order brides. What a desperate thing that seemed like, but who am I to know or to judge?

One woman I spoke with was planning to go out to the prairie near Topeka, Kansas and open up a schoolhouse. She had been offered a position as a teacher by the townsfolk there. Somehow they had sought her out and she decided to pick up from Massachusetts and do it. I could not but wonder how brave and dedicated she must be to strike off alone into the unknown and certainly face the hardship and deprivation that would surely come to her. Her true grit was admirable. Other courageous and dedicated women like her have helped build this country.

When I finally arrived in Denver, I found it was a crazy western town. It ended up for reasons that happened later, I stayed there for quite a long time.

The city was growing up and down and sideways, hectic with new people rushing around and anxious to hit the hills for gold or silver. Usually it has a very dry high-desert climate, but occasionally flash floods or more often the spring melt-off, drown it in water and mud. When I got there, the streets were ankle deep in mud and the sidewalks were covered with wooden board planking to dry off muddy boots. There were far more saloons than churches. I don't think I saw a church.

I knew soon as I got there I would need a horse. Just like the old days with Joe in the South, it was the only way to get around. We had kept them up in Ohio too. We loved them for the fine partners they were. I found me that good horse. The way that it happened was this.

In Denver City, I met a fine young woman, too young for me, name of Darcy Farrow in a saloon in town. She was friendly and we got to talking. After some moments, we moved from the bar to a table off to the side and shared some whisky and talk. After some whiskey, we got mellow and the talk turned sentimental.

Darcy was a wonder to see. Her voice was the sweetest ever to land on my ear. Her eyes shone like bright lights. She had this way of touching my arm when we talked close. Her touch was as soft as a feather. I could tell right from the first, when I brought it up, she was a horsewoman.

She was a Scot like me. It surprised me how many came out West as pioneers. Mostly I thought they had settled down the spine of the Appalachians and into the South, with a few up into the remote areas of Maine. But we have an adventuresome spirit, so it makes sense how many had come out here.

She came from the Carson Valley Plain, from Yerington near Carson City, Nevada. The Walker River runs by there. It's fed from Sierra Nevada snowmelt and empties to the south in Walker Lake.

She told me all her stories about that territory. It had become a new state in 1868. There its people were mining for gold and silver before this new rush to Colorado for silver. Just after the war a lot happened out there that had begun well before it. Silver mined from Virginia City helped finance and may have saved the Union. It was known all over the country in the 19th century for its mining boom.

Carson City, Nevada, named after Kit Carson, was over on the eastern edge of the Sierra Nevada. The Virginia and Truckee Railroad ran from there in 1864. The railroad was named after Virginia City and the Truckee River. Nearby Yerington, Nevada was named after Henry M. Yerington, Superintendent of the Truckee Railroad since 1868. The Truckee carried a lot of bullion from the rural highlands of Virginia City to Carson City. Mark Twain reported news about it later in 1868 as reminiscence of his journalism career there in Nevada.

Darcy knew horses and she loved to talk about them. She was looking for something better just like I was. Like I told you, saloons are the places where folks come together to meet, talk, drink, gamble, dance and maybe fall in love. Sometimes they are the places where people argue and get into a fight, but not usually. Usually it is a place of relaxation and community.

She had moved to Denver City just four years ago after her betrothed jilted her. I cannot imagine how that could have happened.

When we got ready to leave and walked out, I saw she had a limp in her leg like me. She said her pony stumbled and fell on her a few years back and she felt lucky to have survived it. I told her I did too with my war wounds and time in the prison camp in Georgia.

Out on the boardwalk in front of the saloon, we paused a few moments to say goodbye. She knew I had been looking for a good horse to travel west, so she suggested I go see the McAuley ranch just outside town toward the west. She pointed me in that direction even though we were both lookin' that way at the sunset.

We gave each other a long embrace. That was the last time I ever saw Darcy Farrow for a dozen years. She was always on my mind for all that time.

To be honest about our self-view of resolute strength, there is an opposite side too. Probably from the Irish, it is a sad melancholy fatalism. In moments of weakness, when our guard is down, we don't always believe everything will work out for the best.

But we draw from this sadness, this fatalistic romanticism, also as a source of our strength. It flows out of us in our poetry, often released with our whiskey.

Four – The Gilded Age

While I *saw changes and development in my country after the Civil War, I was aware of the parallel changes in the world in the late 19th century. We called it the Gilded Age sardonically with a taste of bitterness. Certainly, as its name implies, it was about getting rich - getting rich quick if you could. Much of our development was about thievery from investors going on between the railroad corporations and their friendly allies in government to accomplish that end.*

In England it was the Victorian Age. Queen Victoria's reign from 1836 to the end of the century brought a new Renaissance of elegance and a blend of old world style with modern conveniences as the industrial world began to bloom in full. This was certainly not the first time this change came, but merely another cycle and a higher iteration of science, engineering, comfort and ease.

In my country, America it meant that the affluent adopted an affected ornate and elegant style of living and its trappings in their fine homes, including their furniture and decorations. Some would say it was over-decorated with every wall plastered with expensive paintings on a backdrop of vivid colored paint or deeply finished premium wood paneling, every fancy table or breakfront, in fact every horizontal surface, covered with coveted curios collected from exotic places. It was pretentious bragging if ever I have seen it.

It was big and dark while warmly lit with gas lamps and emerging electric lighting. Deep plush velvet, reds and browns, dominated the feel of the homes of the wealthy and those that could afford its pretense. It was an opulence fabricated to showcase the arrival of the successful.

It may have begun in London, but we saw it in Boston and New York and the French influence of it right down to the whorehouses in New Orleans and even out in the West. The extravagant excessiveness of it was apparent on the special railroad cars, ornately outfitted and well serving to the nouveau riche as they were conveyed west in the extreme of comfort.

I saw it emerging in Chicago and Denver City. There were pockets of such people and places in the midst of the dust, desolation and deprivation of the western desert and its settlers. There it was the land grabs, the cattle barons and the railroad barons.

The outward visible ostentatious opulence of the rich was offensive to me. I knew where they had got it, who earned it for them and who they stole it from.

On the surface of it, it was an age of grace and graciousness just like the Antebellum South was for its aristocratic planters and city merchants who factored cotton. But it was neither of these things in the truest senses. It was neither God's grace of benevolent love and protection, nor man's courtliness, manners or kindhearted care for his fellow being.

My early life in Baltimore with my father Morgan was comfortable and upper-middle class. It was not pretentious, just at ease for want of nothing. I have nothing against him. He was honest and never stole from anyone.

But my ideas of ease were not like his. I never wanted ease; I wanted adventure. I started that life as early as sixteen and never turned back. It led to working and living with the working class people, the common people and sometimes the poor. That was where I was felt comfortable and where I fit in. That was where I was at ease.

Five – Fannie

I hitched over there and met Fannie McAuley. She was alone with no sign of a man there at the ranch house. She greeted me friendly and we talked for hours. She did most of the talking and finally she showed me her horses.

She had come from Scotland, near the Borders in the lowlands, to Kentucky just at the end of the war. Her husband Angus and her settled in there to raise horses. Funny thing though, they had been Reivers and horse thieves back in the homeland, yet they came to raise horses in America legitimately.

So they learned how to raise Kentucky thoroughbreds on their land, in their new country. But the troubles and the turmoils there in Kentucky from the war were too much. They picked up and moved to Colorado. Here they learned to crossbreed thoroughbreds with western mustangs.

Fannie looked at me sincerely and told me none of that war meant anything to Angus and me. We didn't grow tobacco, or rice, or cotton, or sugar cane in Kentucky; we raised fine horses. We owned no slaves. We didn't appreciate Grant's or Sherman's Army of the Tennessee, or Morgan's Raiders from the Confederacy either.

Like all Scots, we just wanted to be left alone on our land and not see it destroyed by outsiders. We had no great army to protect ourselves, so we moved west. Even fighting Scots can recognize when a fight is not worth it. You may know our history and that we are the most feared in battle but this was not our fight.

If we had not moved quick, soldiers would have stolen our thoroughbreds and used them to haul caissons for cannon or supply wagons, starved them or blown them up in battles. That we could not abide. They would have to get their horses and mules elsewhere.

When they came there, just like back in Kentucky, Fannie and Angus McAuley together were a formidable force to be reckoned with. On her own now, Fannie was still a fierce, strong personality to deal with as well.

It ended up I stayed with Fannie. Angus had died a couple years ago when his heart gave out. We kept company and I helped her arrange her bed. Like every Scot, this Lassie, actually an older strong Scotswoman, couldn't pass up something for free, especially if a good bargain was struck for the benefit of the giver and the receiver. She was hard-bitten, hard-scrabble, but with mirth and satirical.

We spent our time together living in the moment. We didn't care what tomorrow might bring. It is poetic but true to a man's heart in love that while today the blossoms still clung to the vine, I tasted her strawberries. I drank her sweet wine. A million tomorrows may pass away, but I'll not forget the joy that was mine those days. She knew I was a rover, discontented with yesterday's glory and who I am from the song that I sang. Today was our moment. Come to bed she had said. We laughed and we cried and we sang. We had a powerful and poignant two seasons together.

I hadn't planned to, but I decided to stay a while with Fannie. Delaying my idea to get to Aspen, I thought this might be home. After all, this might have been what I have been seeking all the years since the war.

Fannie was younger than me and had no children. I had grown up without a mother but had always been fond of women. There was something going on here beneath the surface and beyond our recognition. She was always teaching me things – things about me my father never did. She intuited things about me. It was like nurturing in a way but not exactly like that. I found it sensually attractive. She was a plain woman compared to some, but pretty enough. I was drawn in in a way I had never felt before.

Although I was older than she, it was sort of a mothering she gave me. She was a comfort I had never known. Come lay beside me and just rest your weary bones she would say on more than one occasion. Fold me in your arms and rest your troubled old head on my bosom lad and let the troubles of the world melt away.

As I lay enfolded in Fannie's arms, I cried for all the years of war I had seen and for the guilt and pain and loss I had carried for such a long time. It was a forgiveness for what I had done and a release from the tortured memories. I forgave myself for having survived it when so many thousands had not, so many lives cut short in their youth, lying dead still, torn apart on the fields the last I saw them and have been dreaming about them just as they were only a moment ago.

She got up and picked up a small book from her shelf above her davenport desk in the parlor. She walked back over toward me extending it forward in two hands, as though making an offering, her azure eyes smiling sadly, glistening with emotional sympathy. She sat back down on the sofa next to me, so close I felt her warmth.

This old book has poems in it I have enjoyed and that helped me get through the loss of Angus, she said. I want to read you selected parts of one by Wordsworth that deeply affected me and I have read it many, many times. It is about immortality and recollections of early childhood. I want you to know it.

Enfolded in Fannie's arms, she read me the parts that were important:

There was a time when meadow, grove, and stream,
The earth, and every common sight,
To me did seem
Apparelled in celestial light,
The glory and the freshness of a dream.
It is not now as it hath been of yore
Turn wheresoe'er I may,
By night or day.
The things which I have seen I now can see no more.

The Rainbow comes and goes,
And lovely is the Rose,
The Moon doth with delight
Look round her when the heavens are bare,
Waters on a starry night
Are beautiful and fair;
The sunshine is a glorious birth;
But yet I know, where'er I go,
That there hath past away a glory from the earth.

But there's a Tree, of many, one,
A single field which I have looked upon,
Both of them speak of something that is gone;
The Pansy at my feet
Doth the same tale repeat:
Whither is fled the visionary gleam?
Where is it now, the glory and the dream?

Our noisy years seem moments in the being
Of the eternal Silence: truths that wake,
To perish never;
Which neither listlessness, nor mad endeavour,
Nor Man nor Boy,
Nor all that is at enmity with joy,
Can utterly abolish or destroy!
Hence in a season of calm weather
Though inland far we be,
Our Souls have sight of that immortal sea
Which brought us hither,
Can in a moment travel thither,
And see the Children sport upon the shore,
And hear the mighty waters rolling evermore.

Thanks to the human heart by which we live,
Thanks to its tenderness, its joys, and fears,
To me the meanest flower that blows can give
Thoughts that do often lie too deep for tears.

We are not alone, no matter whatever our trials, disappointments or horrors. We are born with an unburdened soul – pure and immortal – able to see God's glory all around us in everything in nature and the world we behold. As we live life our soul becomes burdened and we cannot see His glory as we once could. It is difficult to put down our burden and be as authentic as we were born.

Enfolded in Fannie's arms, I told her I see the graves and worse still the dead unburied. The souls gone and untarnished have left behind the earthly pain. All the sorrows have been shed. Only those who still live shall carry it until it is our time.

Enfolded in Fannie's arms, she told me that all had found peace after they gave their last full measure of devotion and I must also.

After all these years, let us say the words that we were taught David. It is for them David, for their immortal souls and for ours. Say them with me:

Our Father which art in heaven,
Hallowed be thy name.
Thy Kingdom come.
Thy will be done in earth, as it is in heaven.
Give us our daily bread.
And forgive us our debts, as we forgive our debtors.
And lead us not into temptation, but deliver us from evil:
For thine is the kingdom, and the power, and the glory, for ever.

Amen

Enfolded in Fannie's arms, she told me it is goodness, light illuminating the darkness. It is the way out of our troubles. We are not alone.

This hard woman, so strong resilient and wise, she was the one who gave me the gift of peace of mind. It was a great dark thing had gone. We lay quietly together and looked into each other's eyes. It was peaceful. I slept better than I had in many years.

While she lived alone since Angus had died, she did have two young hands come in through the week to tend to the horses and do some general handiwork needed at the ranch.

Fannie's best hand Mike had designs on her which I could tell by the way he looked at her when she wasn't watching. After Mike saw what was happening between me and her, he kept to himself. There were never any hard feelings between me and Mike.

She told me Angus had taught her to load and shoot a double-barrel shotgun and a repeater Winchester rifle. They had coyotes, and sometimes a wolf or a bear coming down from the mountains, pesterin' their horses. She had got pretty good with long guns but she had not used a revolver.

Turns out she did have to fend off a couple raiders in the past with her long guns. They were two old Confederates from Quantrill's men from over in Missouri who had lived out their lives as bandits and desperados. Some men never learned how or when to stop the selfish takin' from others, or the dishonor in killing of innocents, after the war.

So we practiced and I taught her what I could about how to hold it steady and squeeze the trigger, not pull it. She would need to get used to the kick. Then I worked with her on gettin' faster, figurin' a hand gun would usually be needed if troublesome men showed up when I wasn't around.

We practiced with my Colt at first. We shot bottles off the top of fence posts at about thirty feet and she got better with practice. Fannie got pretty good at it after a while once she got used to it.

Then we went to town and I bought her a Colt 44 six gun. She knew I was thinking of her since someday I might be leavin'.

One time we were shootin' bottles out on the back lot when out of nowhere Fannie told me she loves the name David. It is heroic she said. It reminds me of the Valley of Elah. In the bible, there is the story of the great battle fought there between the Israelites and the Philistines. Goliath was the champion of the Philistines and a fearsome giant. David was a young boy who offered to the

Israelite King Saul to go fight him. David faced Goliath without armor, just his staff, a sling and some stones from a brook.

Without fear he launched a stone from his sling which hit Goliath in the temple and smote him dead right there in his tracks. Surely the Lord was standing by David's side. David cut off Goliath's head and took it to Jerusalem to show the people. He grew up to become Israel's greatest king, or perhaps the one God loved the most. His son was Solomon, the wisest king.

I heard that story too Fannie. He was a great musician and a poet. He wrote the Psalms, some beautiful words. I sure can't live up to all of that.

No, she laughed, you cannot. But you are here with me now. I smiled at her.

So with her blessing, I decided to stay a while. We were in love. She taught me about horses – how to raise them, care for them, break them and train them. All I had been before that was a rider. Remember, I grew up as a coastal man who sailed on ships and was a foot soldier during the war. It was only when Joe and I stole John Drish's horses and rode to Ohio, I had any experience with the beasts.

Fannie loved to talk about horses. She told me Cortez brought them on a sailing ship to Mexico in 1493. Many died on the way. But they have survived on this land now for over four hundred years. The Mexicans bred them and raised them. Mustangs ran wild in herds on the American plains. The Comanche broke them and rode them. They are still here.

When me and Angus crossbred the Mustangs with our Kentucky thoroughbreds, the result was both speed and endurance. They are beautiful, tough sons-a-bitches. Those of us who live with them prefer them to humans most of the time she said.

Don't you think that's carryin' it a bit far? After all there was Angus and there is me.

She smiled at me coyly. Maybe. She pushed me onto the bed. That was the end of the conversation about horses.

She sold me a beautiful coal black filly, two years old, strong and spunky, just like the women I always fall for, at a fair bargain and me and Fannie parted friends. I held Fannie one last time and left her, a man with a satisfied mind. There is more to say about this I'll tell you later.

My horse's name is Maxine and she proved to be a trusty and faithful stalwart steed. I named her after Maxine Elliott who is a stage actress I admire. Her play The Cowboy and the Lady reminds me if I want to be a cowboy, I need a lady.

When Fannie and me struck our bargain about me buying Maxine, I started riding her around Denver. I bought her a fine leather saddle and looked for any opportunity to ride her to town to pick up some provisions or tools for the ranch. We started to become working partners real quick.

By the time I had settled in for a season with Fannie, I grew a full beard. It was whiter than my head of hair which still had a tinge of dark brown. Fannie didn't mind it. She said I looked like an old daguerreotype of General Lee. I told her that was wrong; I looked like General Grant only taller like Lincoln, but more handsome than him.

I read in the Denver paper about the Smuggler Mine in Aspen and how it was a big strike. The thought of that pulled on me and drew me to go out there.

One morning as the sun was coming up, I felt full of energy and restless. As I saddled up Maxine, Fannie was watchin' me while I averted her eyes. She saw me fasten my blanket roll behind the saddle this time. She knew this was the day I was leaving. We smiled at each other as I held her in a last embrace, neither of us speaking.

I grabbed onto the pommel and put my right foot in the stirrup. She saw me wince as I swung my left leg over the saddle. I sat looking at her eyes at last and shook the reins as we waved goodbye and I headed west.

From Denver City it was back in the saddle and due west to Aspen, a ways east of the territorial line with Utah at Grand Junction.

I thought about Fannie constantly. I had never stopped long enough to consider I could have stayed right there with her. I could have lived with her and helped her raise horses the rest of my life. But I didn't. My restless discontent drove me on further west. She knew that. She didn't try to hold onto me.

I had promised I would come back one day. It was about the talks we had together, about our blood going back over two thousand years ago when we were clans huddled together for survival just north of Hadrian's Wall. Evidently the wall succeeded beyond the Romans' wildest dreams. For us, it was even better. It insured our isolation.

It was about our ceaseless journey, our unwavering courage. We face the world on our feet, never bowing down and kneeling before nobility. That was for the English spirit to admire, not us.

She helped me understand who I am and why I am. Our people had carried this country on our backs she had said. Our independent and self-reliant spirit is the American spirit she said. We are the hardest, toughest people on earth she assured me.

Fannie told me if anyone ever thought for one moment the Scots-Irish Confederates had fought to defend the plantation owners and their property, they were a fool. Without us, she said the Civil War would not have lasted a month.

She told me think of it this way David, the Scots-Irish had a fighting faith in America. I thought they certainly did.

Our all-but-invisible ethnic group has created the core beliefs of our American democracy; that our rights come from God, not the Government; all of us are born equal, and 'born aristocrats' don't exist, and if you tread on these truths, we will fight you down to the last broken bone, she said.

I looked at her face – full of resolve and purpose – and it was just like Joe's. But this was the face of a Celtic woman. Her long jet black hair was pulled back severely on top of her head and tied in a single braid in the back. Her piercing azure blue eyes were fierce and intent. There was no backing down or giving up in her. Hers wasn't a quiet, silent patriotism for certain either.

Centuries ago she would have been a warrior leader adorned with blue paint and tattoos, bare armed with a spear in her hand. Men would have feared her when she charged full force with her band of freedom fighters.

From what I know of my heritage and the history of my people in America, I knew for certain she was right. Still our spirit comes at a cost to others, like native peoples and Chinese immigrants. It is self-centered. But so what we say. Leave us alone to live our lives and we will leave you alone to live yours. None of it matters if I stay out of your way and you stay out of mine. Live and let live. It was then that I had had that conversation with Fannie about this.

I told her, I said Fannie, it is one thing to stick up for yourself and not let someone take advantage of you. But it is another to hold a grudge and never forgive after the disagreement's issue is long over.

Fannie, right now in the papers, all over the country, they are writing the story of the blood lust feud between the Hatfield family in West Virginia and the McCoy family right across the Big Sandy River in Kentucky in what is called the Tug Fork region.

While there were earlier stories of strife and killings, the real troubles all started near the end of the Civil War when two friends, later the family patriarchs, were together in a Confederate unit fighting the Union in the Tennessee western campaign of the war.

When the Union was overrunning their outfit, William Anderson Hatfield stayed to hold them off while Randolph McCoy and the rest of his comrades got away. Later that night Anse showed up at their campfire much to their surprise. He announced he was done with the war and the fighting and he was leaving for home. Ole Ran said he couldn't break his vow and quit the cause like that. Anse left and went home anyway. Randolph stayed and, after his troop was decimated in another battle, spent the remainder of the war in a Union prison in Ohio. He came home a broken man more righteous and pious than ever before. He hated Anse Hatfield and his family.

After the war the troubles continued and escalated as they fought over a pig, land ownership, timbering rights, courtships and unsanctioned marriages of the young-ins across family lines. There were murders back and forth with no resolution.

It became a battle in the courts, with a lawyer on the McCoy side, a local judge on the Hatfield's' side and the Governor of Kentucky involved. Eventually it looked like a civil war was brewing between two states and legal claims were brought to the Supreme Court.

There was a New Year's Night Massacre this year and the Battle of Grapevine Creek back in 1880 which was just like a war between governments or states, where more than a dozen members of the two families was killed. The Governors of West Virginia and Kentucky threatened to have their militias invade each other's states.

Anse wanted peace while Randolph ultimately broke down, rebuked God and drank himself to a flaming fire of an end by himself in his cabin. There were tragic ends for many of their next generation and half of their progeny had been killed on both sides. I told Fannie all this.

She agreed with what I had said. She added that ancestry is always more complicated than it seems. Her MacAulay kinfolk claimed Gaelic-Norse ancestry as early Celts, along with the Lewis's, as their origin went way back in the old country, but she was not fair-haired like the Norse people. The spelling of the names of the families took on endless variations as time passed.

Her people, she said, got caught up in the Highlanders' feud between the Campbells and MacDonalds which was easily comparable to the Hatfields and McCoys here. The fighting and killing went back and forth for hundreds of years as the clans fought over power, land, religion, loyalty to the house of Bruce or Scotland's rightful king, autonomy of the highlands over the lowlands, and any other matters that occurred to them. The Campbells were always loyal to the idea of a king to rule over all of Scotland. The MacDonalds wanted a separate country of the Highlands.

The hatred, she told me, escalated until Robert Campbell ordered the massacre of the MacDonalds, including their women and children, at Glencoe in 1692. The Campbell clan was loathed throughout the Highlands after that. Over time the Campbells swallowed up the lands of my MacAulays as they had before with the MacGregors after first persecuting them for their differences. My MacAulays had accepted the leadership of the MacGregors and one strain of my kin had even sworn fealty to England's King Edward I. - the Scourge of Scotland.

That was how it was there she said. It is no different here. Brothers have been killing brothers since Cain and Abel. It is in Genesis.

I hear you Fannie, I said. I know we have been fighting each other forever. For me, I'm done with it. I am sick and tired of it. I have had half a lifetime of it – shedding blood for what good purpose?

She just looked at me dumbstruck with astonishment. Then her eyes turned warm and kind and she told me David, my dear man, I wish that you could. But my love, you cannot avoid it. We are human beings. There will come a day again when you will have to fight or want to fight sure as hell.

Deep down I knew she was right. Another time would come.

I asked Fannie how it was that her McAuley name sounded Irish, not Scottish. She beckoned me over to her rough wooden table in the kitchen and pulled out an old sheaf of papers from a cabinet. I could see they were very old letters and documents passed on over the generations.

The story of my people is old she said. It goes back and forth from Ireland to Scotland for centuries. Mine is just one variation of the long divergent line of kin. It is the one we brought with us to the new country. As you know, it was my name from my marriage to Angus. I was a Campbell. We were loyal to the king and hated by the Highlanders.

My husband's name might have been Macaulay at its root. There have been family members who spelled it Macauley, Macallay, Macalley, Macaullay, Macaully, Maccally, Maccaulay and Maccauly. It was MacAmhalghaidh, son of Amalghaidh, may have started it as an old Irish personal name. It gravitated to Dumbartonshire and became Hebridean in the northern isles.

There is more, much more, I could tell you about our history she said. Let me just say this:

The clan Alpin's tradition claims MacAlpin or MacAlpine is the oldest and most purely Celtic of the Highland clans, of royal descent from the dynasty of Kenneth MacAlpin who united Picts and Scots into one kingdom from the year 850 and transferred his capital to Perthshire from Dun Add in Dalraida - beside Loch Crinan. However, no clan of the name survived into the heyday of the clan system, though individual MacAlpins are recorded from the 13th century, mostly in Perthshire. Clan Mac Gregor claims origin from that royal MacAlpin stock: as also do MacAulay, MacDuff, MacFie, MacKinnon, MacNab and MacQuarrie.

"Mac" just means son of – MacDonald was son of Donald. Sometimes it is shortened to "Mc" like the Irish do. Sometimes it is just "M'".

In the Celtic tradition she said, the clan would "ingather" any stranger – of whatever family – who possessed suitable skills, maintained allegiance and, if required, adopted the clan surname.

Anyway, when Angus and me come to this country, we coulda give a shit less about all that old world life. I smiled at her and, after a moment, said you mean you could not of given a shit less. She just looked at me speechless for a quizzical moment. Then she got it and broke out laughing. Right you are wiseass lad she said.

But in a more serious moment she said David, it was our spirit we could never change. We carry it with us everywhere we go, over all of time, through all our generations. I understand you Fannie I said. That is what makes you wander, move on and keep seeking a better life. Sometimes it means you have to fight and conquer and win or die trying. I feel it too. For this I love you.

I'll tell you Fannie, my father Morgan did not have much interest in our roots from the old world. All I could get from him was that there were Wexleys in Ireland, Wales and England.

He knew we had been here for many generations and probably came over after the two first early settlements of English, but before the first revolution. That would make us Ulster Scots – Scots Irish. He supposed we might have been Ulster Scots but didn't know for sure. He was too busy making money as a banker.

Fannie I said, you know as well as I do how our country began. In the very beginning two groups of English settlers, our first British immigrants, came here and formed too tiny settlements. After they persevered, survived and began to thrive, the settlements became two huge territories – Massachusetts and Virginia. Eventually these splintered apart for religious, political, economic and philosophical reasons and became thirteen British colonies. As British citizens, we rebelled against our foreign king, fought the Revolutionary War and became this independent United States of America.

She smiled at me knowingly and nodded as she said, "I know all that too David."

But this is the important part I want to tell you, I said. We formed a government – our Constitution - as the best we could even with some ugly compromise. After General Washington finished his term as our first President, John Adams took over. His Vice President, who was to become his lifetime rival, was Tom Jefferson. They were often civil to each other but spent some years not speaking to each other. It was because they had two different visions for our new American country.

Adams saw us as an urban mercantile society settling in small towns and cities which would become big cities in an urban country with manufacturing, trade and industry. For this he believed we needed a large powerful central government.

Jefferson saw us as a rural society, an agrarian one, with small yeoman farmers who owned their property and gradually settled the continent to the west. For this he believed we needed a very small and limited central government. The states would be more powerful and closer to the freedoms of the citizens.

In the end we became both of these things. At first the division was along regional lines – North and South. Eventually the rural and urban areas became mixed throughout the whole country. Many of us came out West, like you and Angus and me, for more freedom found on the rural frontier. We as Americans have always done that. But then most everywhere pockets of urban culture and society are formed and we become more crowded and less free. With too many people, I think America will always continue this way.

"I see what you mean and you have said it so simply and clearly. I agree that it is so.", Fannie said.

I also told her I heard the story about Hugh Glass who came from Pennsylvania and went to Montana and Dakota as an explorer and frontiersman in 1822. He went up the Missouri on a fur trading venture.

His parents were from Ulster and he was one tough son-of-a-bitch Scots-Irishman. He survived a grizzly bear attack and abandonment by his fellow company of hunters out near Fort Kiowa. It was reported in 1825 in *The Portfolio*, a Philadelphia literary journal and picked up by the newspapers. I read about it much later when I was a boy in Baltimore. It means so much more to me now than it did then.

Glass married a Pawnee and had a Scots-Irish-Pawnee American son. Both of them were killed and caused him a lifetime of sorrow. This is more evidence that we have always welcomed outsiders, or in this case they welcomed him, to join our clan and be part of our families. Glass spoke fluent Pawnee and witnessed the attacks against them by their enemies, the Lakotas and Cheyenne who eventually defeated them. They had fought the Comanche further south too. They nearly died out but by 1874 there were 4000 survivors pushed into the Indian Territory in Oklahoma.

Well you know who you are from the life you lead, she reminded me. I see through to your nature from the song of wanderlust you sing. You must see you are like me by now. I told her I do.

While I came from Baltimore, traveled to places throughout the South, lived in Ohio and finally came out here, I realized that wherever I wander, by chance and happenstance, that is where I end up. Everywhere I have seen my people living, working, building, moving forward, enduring and building a whole country all across and throughout this great American land.

We are, and always will be, warrior poets, never stopping, never contented.

But the spirit of my kinfolk lives as close as it can to its ancestral Highlands - its hills, its lochs, its glens - somewhere in the Smoky Mountains and along the Tennessee River valley. Their ghosts endure there floating in the mists that rise above the crags and hollows and flowing with the streams of the waters.

The spirit lives there, protected once again from an intrusive civilization, behind its wall, as the remnant of Southern Appalachian culture, restlessly awaiting the next thing.

I felt and knew it deep down inside. It wasn't just because Fannie and I talked and she told me about it. I knew myself it was true. All this talk of clan and kin gives us a sense of something bigger, something greater we belong to, I had told Fannie in one of our last conversations.

I said, and as you say it teaches us who we are by our heritage and forbearers. I love you for this blessing you have given me by teaching me all this. Only at the first and last moment, for one step, we walk alone.

No matter where we wander, whoever we love, marry, or be with, who we know or befriend, we do not walk alone. We are born alone. We die alone. So wander, love, marry, be and befriend. But most important, know yourself the best that you can, the soonest you can. Be comfortable with yourself – in your own skin - because you do not walk alone.

Six – Freedom

Now I understand. It has taken me almost sixty years. Once I think about it in this way, it is so obvious. Before feudalism there was tribalism. Man lived in a natural state on the Earth. He had no concept of owning the land. It was God's Earth and man lived on it as he pleased. The state of man was more about the time in his story than the place.

This is how it was for the earliest people in Africa, in North America and pre-medieval ancient Scotland. The people lived in tribes or clans. There were few people and the planet was spacious.

The people gravitated toward a strong member in their clan-tribe-family for leadership. They fought willingly for him to protect their group from outsiders.

There was no organized society or need for it. The people were free as God created them, without even knowing the name for it – freedom. There were no nations, no cities and no governments. It was the natural state of man.

When man began to organize society, he made two significant conceptual changes – the ideas of land ownership and nobility. The Romans created a civilization of land ownership and dominance of nobility. The English did the same later.

Tribalism was replaced by feudalism. The peasants lived on the land claimed by the lords. They owed their fealty and their lives to him. This is what my Scots and Scots-Irish ancestors fought against in the late Middle Ages. Feudalism was slavery – the antithesis of freedom. My people came to understand that fiercely and have never stopped fighting against it.

The system of slavery, as it became in the South in my country, was a modern manifestation of English feudalism. The aristocratic planters were modern noblemen. Their slaves were their peasants. For them, this became the new natural order. For me and my people, it would never be.

Fannie was right. The white southern Confederates were not fighting to protect the noblemen, or their land, or their slave property rights. They were fighting as poor white farmers and mountain-dwelling clansmen against an invasion threatening to destroy their families and above all their freedom. A large powerful industrial government in the North was imposing nationalism on free people and their way of life.

I see that now. I understand that most of the Confederates I fought against, to preserve the Union and end slavery, were just like me. I had picked the right side to fight against slavery, but most of the enemy before me were not fighting for the preservation of feudalism and slavery. In terms of the numbers that fought, they were for the most part not the nobles.

While I had fought in the eastern campaign of the war – the Army of the Potomac under Generals McClellan and Burnside against the Army of Northern Virginia under Generals Lee and Jackson – mostly in Virginia and Maryland, I had little idea of what was happening in the western campaign along the Mississippi River. I had learned that after the fall of Vicksburg in '63, many Confederates had deserted and gone back to their homes. They found their families in deprivation and desperation, starving from the rampaging and pillaging their own Confederate government had done to them to re-supply their cause. They had been invaded by their own countrymen.

Jefferson Davis and R.E. Lee should have known half way through it with the loss at Gettysburg that their cause was hopeless. Their stubborn pride kept them going for two more years while they destroyed their own country as much as the invaders did. Desertion rates increased dramatically as the foot soldiers saw what was happening and understood the reality.

Some poor white farmers, like Newton Knight in Jones County, seceded from the Confederacy and waged war against them in defense of their own farms. Like so many non-slaveholding yeoman, he had been forced to join the Confederacy and was a cavalry Captain who fought at the Battle of Corinth. After that he deserted and changed sides. With a band of like-minded men, he waged guerrilla war on the Confederates with his small army of farmers and runaways in the swampy area near Hattiesburg and Taylorsville.

These men viewed the war from their Southern viewpoint as a rich man's war fought by poor men. Mississippi had passed a law that Confederates who owned twenty or more slaves were exempt from the fighting. So some poor whites like Knight enlisted runaway slaves to fight with them in the rebellion of the rebellion.

It was true there were many in the South as early as the 18th Century who hated the slaveholders and the institution of slavery as the Aristocratic class that it was. They had no intent to fight for their cause. They were poor and lived in isolation and knew they were looked down upon as a sub-class of white Americans. But the Appalachians and other remote areas were their Hadrian's Wall.

Most likely they viewed the invasion of the Yankees from the North as a more direct threat to their hard-scrabble, independent livelihood than they did the aristocracy in areas nearer by their own region. Therefore most of them fought for the Confederacy and its upper class white authority and the evangelical moral authority of its churches. Their choice was simple.

Slavery was coming to an end in the North. It was all but over there. Its system never fit in like it did in the agricultural South anyway.

That war should have been resolved between the two disparate peoples in the South, much as it was in ancient Scotland in the time of William Wallace; resolved by a groundswell of leadership from the peasants – black and white together – to overthrow the nobles. Maybe that is what John Brown thought he was doing.

As I said, I fought a war for the freedom of some while fighting against others for their freedom. War and freedom are more complicated and intertwined than they seem. One man's freedom is another man's bondage. War is cruelty and fighting it is useless. It rarely solves a problem.

Self-defense is another thing than aggression. War may be cruelty as General Sherman had said, but it may be unavoidable sometimes. It rarely solves anything right then and there at its outcome. Usually the end of a war is when the solution to a great problem can begin. At least that was true for my war.

There have been wars fought over a period of years over one or more issues about freedom. But there have been other wars fought on and off for centuries over the subjugation of a people, like in the old world.

Freedom and war go hand in hand all the way back to man's earliest existence, just as soon as he formed civilizations.

The South may have started the Civil War, or got tricked into it by their own decades of recalcitrance over slavery, fooling themselves about States' rights, but they fought a defensive war all the same.

For some like William Anderson (Anse) Hatfield, they got sick and tired of it and the Southern cause and walked away from it. For others like Newton Knight down in Jones County and other adjacent counties in the region of southwestern Mississippi, it was desertion too, but much more than that. Newt was a farmer, soldier and Southern Unionist who had fought in the war for the Confederacy at Corinth. He left the war when he learned that the horses on his farm had been taken by Confederates and his family had been hard pressed to keep up their farm.

He was joined by other disaffected men and freed slaves to form a band of guerillas in rebellion of the Confederacy. He was chosen as their captain. The small army lived and survived together fighting skirmishes against Confederates soldiers sent by General Polk to suppress their rebellious actions. Their hideout in the swamp was called "Devil's Den."

When his wife Serena separated from him, he fell in love and married a former slave named Rachel. Together they sired many children before they died.

He had determined that no country wanted them, so he supposed they had formed their own country. He declared its rules of self-government to be just four. Two of these were that a man kept what he put in and grew in the ground for himself and that a man is a man if he walked on two legs – simple as that.

After the war, as a Republican, the Union Army finally acknowledged him and tasked him with distributing food to struggling families in the Jones County area.

His epitaph said that he lived his life helping others.

So I learned that freedom and war aren't simple and many strange things have happened in my country. Kinship and religious factors helped shape what we have done and became as Americans.

We should have left them alone and stayed out of their way. But we cannot change that now. What is done is done. All I want is to be left alone. Stay out of my way. I will do the same for you. Elsewise, I will pick a fight with you for my freedom.

Joe used to tell me, "Judge not, lest you be judged." I understand what he meant and where he learned it. So I can decide not to judge another person's actions, beliefs or treatment of me.

All the same, I can decide to demand that he leave me alone and get out of my way. That is not judging him. That is letting him live his own life and doing the same myself.

After the historic battle of Bannockburn, the Abbot of Arbroath declared to the pope in 1320:

> *For as long as one hundred of us shall remain alive we shall never in any wise consent to submit to the rule of the English. For it is not for glory we fight, for riches, for honors, but for freedom alone, which no good man loses but with his life.*

Such was their resolve. Such was their refutation of central authority, their insistence on self-autonomy, independence, self-reliance and individual freedom. Free men they were.

Seven – Aspen

When I first came unto this country, I was already an old man. While I still get around fine on old Maxine's back, I had started to use a cane in my left hand to support my bad leg whenever I walked a distance. I'm still doing fine, but it helps to relieve the strain on my bad knee and atrophied calf muscle.

My experiences in Denver had been powerful and were illuminating. I will never see life the same again. It was what I learned about the West, its country and its people. It was meeting someone the likes of Darcy, and loving Fannie, and the love and appreciation of horses as the partners they are in life's journey.

Aspen is a man's town with a scarcity of women if you don't count the prostitutes camped out here to make their livin'.

It is astounding how life waxes and wanes in intensity. At times it comes at you so fast and all at once. Other times it comes along slow and sedate. I had fallen in love with two women in Denver, one for just an extraordinary day and the other for a passionate half of a year.

I try to remember those happy days of my life when I was a callow youth and life was so simple. It is sad that those times pass by and away, becoming a distant hazy memory of myself and life then.

But it passes away in the mists of time. Like a butterfly, it flutters before you a brief moment and is gone forever. War and hardship, cruelty and selfishness comes to us all after callow innocence is gone. With our clear-eyed harsher view as adults we still search for the goodness and try to remember.

John Donne said it so well. I have to give the English their due. He wrote in the 1600's that the bell tolls for us all. We are all connected. No man is an island.

It has been a while since I came out to Colorado in 1887. The East is far away and long ago. Out here everybody's a cowboy, even me a silver mine architect. I changed and adapted to the West and its people. It is wilder and freer – more breathing space.

If you want to understand Colorado, you got to go to the rodeo. This is how cowboys relax, show off, let off steam and compete. The circuit comes through here every year with traveling professionals and local hopefuls competing. They started the tradition in Mexico. The cattle drivers in Texas latched onto it.

There is calf roping, bull riding and steer wrestling. It's popular in Denver and they have been holding the Stampede over in Greeley for years now. The cattlemen there like to take a break between spring calving and summer haying to come to rodeo and test their riding and roping skills for prizes and braggin' rights.

I tried it figuring I've been riding horses for decades. It ain't so easy and certainly is a younger man's sport.

Colorado is a rugged mountainous place. I knew it would be before I came out here. But compared to where I came from back east, everything is bigger, sharper, clearer, fresher and more dramatic. What I did not expect was its connection to the New Mexico territory to its south and the Spanish speaking country below that border.

Out here it is about God, guns and country, maybe more about guns and less about God. What I like about it is the freedom. With no license or law, freedom is complete for the individual. But it is anarchy for the society. With too much law, there is no freedom. That is tyranny. I fought in a war for the freedom of some and against it for others, so I think about it some. Out here in the West, freedom leans mostly toward the anarchy side.

But the guns are necessary, particularly in a mostly lawless, wild place like this. Around here the Comanche will kill you if he is feeling mean-spirited and catches you alone. Further south in Texas and New Mexico, it is the Apaches to watch out for. If you can't take care of yourself, you are a goner. You have to be mindful of rattlesnakes everywhere in the open. Their bite will kill you if you don't pay attention. If you go out in the desert and are not well provisioned, you can die of starvation or thirst when there is no game or water. There are too many ways to die in the West.

I have my Army Colt from the war. Men like me in the infantry didn't have them. We had the old muzzle loaded muskets fixed with bayonets. But after the war, it was easy to buy the left-over revolvers the officers and cavalry had used.

I also bought a Hawken 50 caliber muzzle loaded, percussion cap, black powder, rifled carbine out here. They started making them back in 1820 before the Mexican War, but we were still using them near the end of my war, before the repeater carbines made by Henry and Winchester came out. They still make the muzzle loaders and my Hawken is about four years old.

I carry it in a saddle holster when I'm ridin'. We don't have any buffalo around here like out on the plains, but there are plenty of buck deer and goat, and sometimes wolves or mountain lion, to hunt in the hills up the mountains.

It is finicky though. Mine wasn't all it was cracked up to be. Half the time the percussion cap won't ignite the powder. I worry about that since I can't trust it will fire when I need it. It scared the hell out of me once when a Grizzly got too close to me. He ran off sure enough. Thank God.

On one trip south through the desert flats in New Mexico, I ran into an Apache war party. It was along the Rio Grande just north of Las Cruses. I spotted the six of them sitting horse on a mesa watching me ride through. I was close enough to see two of them had rifles set up on their legs and pointed toward the sky. I tried to look friendly while Maxine rode along, not making any moves toward my carbine in the saddle holster.

One of them, without a rifle, rode down toward me easy like without indicating his intentions. It was either his curiosity about a stranger or a feint with intent to attack. That is what the Apache do. They come at you one at a time if you are a lone rider. I guess it is their sense of honor or pride in their warrior abilities.

This was an attack. When he got a hundred yards from me, he changed from a trot to a full charge, whooping and wielding his tomahawk above his head. I didn't want to appear scared or put Maxine in harm's way, so I stopped and faced him.

When he got about twenty yards close, I pulled my Colt and fired at his chest. He dropped from his pony to the desert dust and I knew he was dead in his tracks.

I looked up at the others watching from the mesa and could see they were stirred up. They were all whooping and started moving down the mesa toward me. Forgetting their pride I guess, they all came after me together. The two with the carbines started firing.

Maxine figured out what was happening and took off at a sprint. I reined her toward an outcropping of rocks and she covered the quarter mile so fast the Apaches couldn't begin to catch up or get a bead with their rifles on the fast moving target.

We settled in the cover of the rocks and I dropped the first rider with my Hawken. The boom of the report from that 50 caliber big game rifle was so loud, and the sight of them losing their second brave, it took the spirit out of them. The remainder of the war party pulled up, turned around and charged off in the other direction. My war experience came in handy a few times out West.

Just east of here is the prairie. Settlers had been pouring in all the decades after the war, looking for land they could call their own to make a life as hard scrabble farmers and raise their families on their homestead. The problem there was the Indians. It was their land. But our government figured they could give it away to white pioneers to settle the rest of our country.

And we believed we could do whatever we wanted to the land as our Manifest Destiny. We cut timber, drilled mines and built railroads all over the West to make the travel across the whole country a practical reality.

The mighty Sioux Nation inhabited this land once- the Santee, the Yankon and the Yankonai, and the Lakota. Of these, the Lakota dwelled on the prairie as the great horsemen, buffalo hunters and mighty warriors.

We fought them in the Dakota War of 1862 north of here where 303 Santee Sioux were tried for their offenses against white settlers. President Lincoln commuted death sentences for 284, while 38 were hanged in Minnesota. Treaties and annuities were suspended. Some moved to the Crow Creek Reservation in Missouri.

Red Cloud fought the United States in the Wyoming and Montana Territories from 1866 to 1868. Again in 1876-1877 the Great Sioux fought the U. S. Military with the Cheyenne as their allies.

In 1890, just after I came out here, the Lakota were massacred at Wounded Knee. At the end of the century, I have seen the hired hunters, working for the railroads, slaughter the Buffalo to near extermination. They did it for sport and as a strategy to starve out the Indians and make them give in to our will.

The Santee and Lakota, proud Sioux people, starving and defenseless, were driven off the prairie and forced to move to reservations.

It was our Manifest Destiny that motivated us to believe we were entitled to this whole hemisphere. We knew the completion of the western railroads would make it all possible once we got the Indian problem resolved.

It began when Jefferson pushed them out of the East across the Mississippi. Then Jackson pushed them out of the South. Harrison herded them into Oklahoma which the white man had defined as Indian Territory. The Dawes Act and Homestead Acts gave 160 acres to settlers and removed land from tribal ownership under Federal authority. Lincoln and his successors finally destroyed them in the West.

Back in 1880, the reservations were established under the Treaty of Fort Laramie in 1868. It was so heartbreaking and sad, I have no words. We destroyed the once proud indigenous people of this land. And it was all unnecessary. There was plenty of room for everyone.

The many years that drifted by in Aspen, I ran my business and traveled south whenever I could.

But when I was in Aspen, I began to withdraw from people and just watched over my crew when I had to. So in 1891 I bought some land up the slope and built a cabin. Aspen appeared below me like a bowl or a saucer.

Maxine liked it up there. She had her own corral to run around in. We still needed to ride together, more her than me. I built her a quarter mile track around the corral and gave her a race when she wanted it.

I made a small stable and barn for her, secure from wolves or coyotes at night. There was a water trough and some extra space for her feed and grooming. Once I had civilized and outfitted my little plot for her and me, I made some creature comforts in my cabin for my solitary self.

I ain't touched a drop of whiskey in ten years, just a beer once in a while with my boys in town. For too many years Lady Whiskey kept me company and I loved her so well. She damned near destroyed me. My excuses for it had been lost women and the cruel war. Finally, I chose to live and it worked out better to part company with her.

Over time I collected a library of books shipped in from Denver or the east. These were my friends I needed the most. I contemplated mortality and the verities of humanity and was pleased. The life of solitude and the outdoor beauty around me was enough – more than enough.

It was time to settle up and sum up what it had all meant. It had meant Morgan and Josiah and Fannie most of all. These spirits were of the past.

William Blake was a peaceful comfort by the fire on cold winter nights. The Songs of Innocence and the Divine Image brought gentle thoughts. The Songs of Experience rang truer to life – Tiger, tiger burning bright – life and death if I die.

I read the poets Tennyson, Donne, Milton, Whitman, Yeats and Twain. Browning and Dickinson were too sloppy sentimental for me. I read Herman Melville's Moby-Dick and remembered the smell of the sea and that my old friend Josiah had read it when he was a slave.

Melville had spent years at sea like me and had said, "Faith, like a jackal, feeds among the tombs, and even from these dead doubts she gathers her most vital hope."

Joe had my journals so I had to remember my life as a sailor best I could without them. It was better he had them to remember me by. I could still smell the salty brine.

Reading and contemplating in the quiet tranquil solitude of the evenings at home in the 1890's, I saw that life is incongruity, inconsistency, and contrast if I stop to think about the unknowable connection between the people on Earth now at my time and times before –like the sootbleakened night under the gas lamps of Victorian London where the sandstone on the buildings has become chemically bonded with the smoke from coal burned in homes and spewed from chimney stacks of the infancy of man's early industrial age, or the clarity of the air and the light at sunrise and the way the face of the Rockies look from Aspen just after the spring runoff of snowmelt from its peaks in the same 1890's, or the savanna grasses vast across the plains of Africa when man first contemplated life on this Earth millennia before; contemplated his immortal soul and place as a speck in the cosmos for the first time.

I had seen most of my country and learned from my Love those important parts of the old country I had never seen- but seen enough through her eyes for me. I know who I am.

As I have spent time alone in my cabin, the quiet evenings have given me time to think. In reflection, in trying to understand the meaning of my life, I have turned back to the study of history once again as I did in my youth with Morgan.

From reading I have learned to put in perspective what I have experienced in my own life. Historiography has taught me what different historians have thought about an historical event or person over time. Different historians have viewed these things differently over time – perspective.

With the reading of exegesis books I have learned what different writers have thought about the writing of the great writers – perspective.

I have learned to embrace perspective to gain understanding. At first we are repulsed by perspective since the shallow view of it is that it is opinion and we always dislike the opposing opinion of others. We call it bias, prejudice or other derogatory names when it is really just a range of viewpoints.

I believe the more we look at the perspective of others and consider the variety of viewpoints, the more we learn. In the end, when we consider the actions of humans, we see that the truth is the sum of all of it. The understanding of it, with all its acrimony, has brought me more peace as ironic as that seems.

For example: *War is cruelty. There is no use trying to reform it. The crueler it is, the sooner it will be over.* When General Sherman said that he understood the nature of war, its inevitability and how to fight it better than the rest of us. The newspapers called him a lunatic – perspective.

Some have said that learning is a process like peeling back the layers of an onion – the deeper you go, the more you learn the truth. Others have said that all it is is an onion – all the way to its core. Maybe it is the layers that are the truth and the goal is not to get to the core. The truth is simpler than we imagine.

Fannie's truth was a settled truth in her mind. She had no doubts. There were no conflicts in her view of who she was or what her life meant to her. God bless her for her assuredness in her beliefs.

Eight – Sonora

After some time, whenever I needed a change of scenery, which for me was often necessary, I would saddle up and slide down into the New Mexico territory. It was still a territory then. It might become a state after a few more years.

The ride is an easy time, just 250 miles south down along the Continental Divide and parts of the Santa Fe Trail to Santa Fe, about a six-day ride. The El Camino Real de Tierra Adentro is near Santa Fe and connects to San Juan, New Mexico all the way south to Mexico City along the Rio Grande River.

When a lone western man travels around like I do, he gets to see the vast natural beauty of the deserts and the distant vistas of the mountains. It is a different beauty than the East and different from the South as well. You get to love the rich bright oranges, yellows and browns as a change from the greens of the grasses and forests back east of the Mississippi.

And the land is so open and un-impeded. You can see for miles across it to the horizon. The sky is bigger to the eye in the daytime that I could ever have imagined. In the black chill of night there are more stars in the heavens than anything I have ever seen. Guess that's why many become desert rats. This great land of ours is so big you can never see it all in its extent or diversity.

When you are standing outside on a clear night in Denver at a high elevation, or more so in Santa Fe which is a high desert with the mountains less a part of the panorama, the sky takes on a special difference. It is like you are alone on a flat platform with the sky full of countless stars. It is all and everything you can see. There is a sense you can feel, a vastness beyond belief.

The terrain has no obstruction of tall trees or buildings like in the East or even the South. There is no interference from other sources of light. It is you and the universe in the cosmos.

I remember it was like that on the ocean standing watch on my clipper ship as a boy. When the sea is calm, it was the same flat platform and the same Northern Hemisphere sky where rarely the colors of the Northern Lights – Aurora Borealis – appeared. It is then you know how small we are as an immeasurable speck of the whole thing. You cannot help but be humble.

The daytime is a different world and the differences in the West, the East and the South are apparent. Man must have known this same thing since the beginning of time in this world.

Maybe that is part of the attraction of the West for me, as it was for the ocean when I was a boy. Life is a circle as well as a cycle.

Santa Fe is in the mountains. You have to climb up a gradual elevation until you are on a high desert plateau. It is eight thousand feet above sea level – three thousand feet higher than Denver, the mile-high city.

It is the same with the diversity of the people as the diversity of the land; and I include in that the Indians and the Mexicans. It is their land and country just as much as or more than it is ours. Somehow I was taken in by their Spanish language and their descendants here in what is now our territory of New Mexico. The Mexicans are a lot like me – independent, self-reliant, capable people able to survive hardship. They have endured on this land longer than we have and I learn a lot about that from them.

That is truly why I consider so many of them in Santa Fe my friends. They have endured both the Spaniards and the Americans and they have the survival skills. They are still here. I enjoy the relaxations with my Mexican friends and I have come to have many. We sit back in the cantinas for their Tequila, my beer and some talk. We love to swap stories and tall tales, even if they are exaggerated and some not true.

They all know me in Santa Fe when I pass through. My friends there have names like Juan and Pedro. They have a sleepy, peaceful Spanish heritage there coming from Mexico, dating way back to the first colonists in 1610. The only other town coming from the Spanish that is older is St. Augustine in Florida. They came there to settle in 1565. Anyway, Santa Fe is the oldest American settlement I guess.

The people in Santa Fe, like the people in Mexico City and all of Mexico for that matter, are a mix of the high born Castilian Spanish and the indigenous native Indians. They have crossbred for hundreds of years but still have a caste system of two tiers.

In Santa Fe the old deep roots are evident. The Spanish high born descendants hold the provincial government positions and rule the territory locally despite the involvement of the United States since the Mexican American war and despite its independence from Spain before that.

So the people are a mix of low born Mexican Indians and high born Spanish nobles. It's another example of feudalism I see the world over. But I like the people and they are generally very friendly to Gringos like me when I visit. It was there in Santa Fe, because of the time I spent there with the locals, I learned the Spanish language. The people have more respect for an outsider when you speak to them in their language. Hell, the Indians had to learn it generations ago to get along in their own country.

They hold celebrations and fiestas all the time to celebrate their proud heritage. It will always be a part of the Southwest reaching way up into Colorado and across Texas.

The Mexicans were the first cowboys on the continent. There is much for me to discuss about horsemanship with my friends there. I'm knowledgeable now about breaking and training horses and share that with the Mexican people who have done that since the Spaniards introduced them to horses centuries ago. I have that in common with these horse people and the Indians as well. Their Gauchos were cowboys herding cattle before my people ever were.

If I had it to do all over again, I would have been in the cavalry, not the infantry, during the war. I couldn't then though because I was a city boy from Baltimore.

From there it is an easy drift into Mexico, another 250 miles down to the border at El Paso. I stay there for a day or two to look up some old friends.

I met James Longstreet once in El Paso. Old Pete had settled in New Orleans after the war but was out west trying to get investors for a new railroad from New Orleans to Mexico.

He was Bobby Lee's most brilliant tactician and strategist and I told him so. He was very gracious about it and thanked me for my service to the country. I had marveled at how smart he had been like a master chess player who could see six moves ahead. Old Pete could look at the events leading up to and the layout before a battle and almost see into the future. He was most always right. This made him too guarded and pessimistic for Lee's liking. But Lee respected him. He had to. His brains offset Lee's brashness and surely saved his chief commander's bacon on more than one occasion.

Unfortunately he had taken most of the blame for the Confederate loss at Gettysburg. He just knew Pickett's charge was foolhardy and he said so in no uncertain terms. He had been right.

Longstreet had been a lifelong friend of Grant's going back to their early days as cadets at West Point. They always had respect for each other's brains, grit and ability. The South grew to dislike Old Pete for selling out his southernness when he became a Radical Republican arguing for Reconstruction and equal rights after the war.

It was strange to meet General Longstreet in El Paso of all places. But it made sense. The big Georgian, Old Pete, had been dealing with the new post-war reality. El Paso was the major border town in Texas. Americans and Mexicans were crossing back and forth between the two countries all the time. Just across the Rio Grande was Ciudad Juarez in Chihuahua, Mexico.

The United States and Mexico wanted to do business. There was a growing cooperation for each country to gain a benefit. That is what we had begun doing in America the last hundred years. After conquering a region, maybe with a war to decide the more powerful, then we wanted to do business. We call that progress.

The Anglo and Mexican-Spanish cultures and languages were blending. Longstreet knew that. He was a smart man and always had been a forward-looking progressive thinker. Now he was fixing to build a railroad between the two countries. I'll bet Old Pete did it too.

Anyway, it had been an honor to meet the old General and I wished him well. I never minded talking about the war with anyone who had been in it since they understood what it was really like which no outsider ever could. When we talked about it he acknowledged that, for the common Confederate foot soldier, it was a rich men's war fought by poor men. I couldn't help but admire him for understanding that.

As for Texas, you know it became a Republic in 1836, having fought its own war with Mexico's Santa Anna. It was its own country, independent of Mexico and the United States, until it was annexed to the United States ten years later in 1846. Then it fought in the U.S.-Mexican War until 1848. Just twelve years later it joined the Confederacy in 1860 and fought for its independence once again.

So Texans are fighters and fiercely independent people. But they learned to cooperate and accept Spanish speaking Mexican people as part of their cultural heritage. Their language, food and traditions blended together.

Sounds like my people doesn't it? That's why I have always gotten along so well with them. In west Texas it is generally peaceful and friendly.

But I like to cross the border and travel deep into Mexico to immerse myself there with their people. My favorite town is Hermosillo – it means little brother - down Sonora way. It is just another 400 miles southwest from El Paso across some rugged country. That's the hardest part. I don't mind it. Hardship has been the story of the life I have chosen.

These are great distances to cover on horseback. I am gone from Aspen for weeks at a time. Fortunately my job and my crew allow me to do that. I can wander to my heart's content. It is the going I need. It has been so for some time. Fannie knew it.

The Continental Divide passes through Chihuahua in Mexico. I break off before that and swing west to Hermosillo. Hermosillo is a backwater of a desolate desert – if there is such a thing – with heat, dust, cactus, sunshine and quiet desperate poverty, horses and burros. It isn't much of a watering hole.

There aren't any ex-patriot Americans there. Probably there are some in Mexico City. Fact is the Mexicans are still sore at us from the Mexican-American War. They aren't very welcoming to gringos because they lost nearly half of their country from that war. We took a lot of new territory into the United States that would later add states to the Union – and the Confederacy.

I did get all the way down to Mexico City once. It is a huge city set in a bowl of a valley surrounded by mountains and always full of political unrest. I saw the ancient pyramid or temple there from when the city was called Tenochtitlan in 1325, right in the middle of town as a memorial to the mighty Aztec civilization before Cortes killed Montezuma and destroyed it in 1520.

I didn't know anybody there but met a group of Americans. They were living together in an enclave and I ran into them in the cantinas. They were mostly veterans from the Civil War down there to work together on that end of Longstreet's railroad. There they were, graybacks and bluecoats together getting along and putting the past behind them. It was gratifying to join them and see my Americans together as my countrymen.

The concentrated mass of humanity in Mexico City is impressive. Chicago pales by comparison. As you know, I'm not much taken by big cities and neither is Maxine. She gets jittery around so many people and so do I. We left after a few days and headed west into the desert toward the Baja.

For me the trip to Hermosillo is worth it though. They know me there and it feels like home. In Rosa's Cantina, I gather up my friends for some braggin' talk and a glass of beer. Rosa is smart as a whip – or at least cunning – and mean as a rattlesnake.

She has to be to handle that crowd in her cantina. Rosa is plump, average height, wears her black hair short and never changes the stern passive expression on her face no matter what anybody says or does. She looks like she hates all her fellow human beings. It takes some time to see through that mask and come to know she runs her place because she cares about people.

Rosa was about the same age as me, a little older than my Fannie McAuley. I visited her cantina every few months and conversed with her in her Spanish tongue. I came to know her and recognize she was a good person at heart, just tryin' to make a livin' and get by. I never saw a husband and figured he had been gone for some time. Rosa came to like me and see that I was a good man who could be trusted even though I am an Anglo.

So when I took a fancy to her daughter Maria, Rosa was fine with that. She knew her daughter Maria was strong, no wilting flower, and could take care of herself. Now for some reason Maria found an attraction in me. I don't know why. Maybe it was the curious love of a stranger, a mysterious cowboy from up north who was different and stood out from the men in town. Maybe she looked up to me like a father figure. Like me, without a mother, I could understand that. A fondness and affection grew between me and Maria while her mother Rosa watched.

Her daughter Maria is the finest example of sweet, Spanish womanhood my eyes have ever had the pleasure of gazing upon. Rosa's girl Maria is mi' amour *mi' corazon* - my heart and paramour. Spanish is a loving tongue.

It is peaceful, usually, but I got in a gunfight there once. The way it happened was this. But first, before that, Maria and I had been upstairs in her bedroom and living quarters above the cantina.

After a quiet dinner together - some tamales, chili con carne and rough red wine - we had looked into each other's eyes and knew we had a deep need, more than an itch, to go upstairs. I followed up the stairs behind her watching her loose dress sway from side to side from its gorgeous round pivot point at her waist. As I climbed the stairs, I looked down to the floor and saw Rosa busy at the far end of the bar pouring a customer a shot of Tequila. Our eyes came in contact, and Rosa gave me a faint smile – a quick knowing look with a subtle hint of acceptance - before she turned back toward the customer.

Upstairs in Maria's room, door closed tight, she threw her arms around me and pressed her soft flat belly and strong thighs against me hard. She moaned and looked at me with a painful expression. Clearly her need was as great as mine.

Now Maria is no child. I am not her first rodeo ride and won't be her last. We have an understanding when I come down Sonora way. She is much younger than me and may look twenty but she is a perfectly preserved much older woman than that.

Our time together is more than sensuous; she is funny. She points at this old cowboy's body while she caresses me gently with her infectious smile.

I look at her smooth brown voluptuous body with curly black hair in all the places where it is supposed to grow. It glistens at the sweet place between her charming thighs.

It doesn't take us long to get down to business when we are both feeling like that. I picked her up and bounced her on the bed, her hair flying away from her beautiful head. Her face is so gorgeous, I'm on the bed on top of her before the bed stops bouncing.

She had just enough time to throw her dress over her head and no need to remove underwear which she does not wear. I managed to kick off my boots, pull off my shirt and britches, including my underwear, but not enough time to worry about my socks.

We ride fast and together and before you know it we are lying side by side, her head tucked against my shoulder. Thank you David. Thank you Maria. Sweet Jesus she treats me so right.

She had a sit-up copper bath tub she kept in her room. When we got done she called for a family employee to bring up buckets of hot water. We took turns having a bath, washing each other and freshening up before dressing and going back downstairs. After we got situated at a table, that's when it happened.

Maria was sitting on my lap at a table sharing our beer and in comes a mean lookin' hombre. He was a big man carrying a lot of weight. I could see he was lookin' for trouble. Maria gave me that look with those laughing eyes that said 'David, stay out of it'.

The hombre' talked his way into the poker game at the big table. I knew trouble was comin'. Before long everybody started hollerin' at the hombre' for cheatin'. It was gonna' be a gamblin' fight.

He got red in the face and bolted up on his feet. He cursed at them and threw the table over. All the silver and cards flew around and bounced on the floor.

I set Maria down and got up to help. I said whoa there compadre, settle it down. He wheeled toward me and didn't say nothin'. He must have thought I was an easy mark, being a skinny gringo with a crippled leg. But I'm wiry and wily and I carry an equalizer too. I am an old man now, but still have a young man's spirit.

He started to draw and I grabbed my Army Colt fast as I could. His shot was first. He must have been nervous because it missed by a mile. Mine put a '45 right in the center of his chest. He dropped over onto his back on the floor. The blood began pooling around him on the rough planking.

Maria said I'd better beat it out of there fast before the sheriff comes. We stood up close together there in the middle of the room. All eyes were on us and it was quiet as a tomb. No one moved. It was like a daguerreotype still picture.

Rosa was slowly wiping the bar counter with a wet rag. She looked at me and nodded her head just slightly, almost imperceptibly. I touched the brim of my Stetson and nodded toward her in return.

Maria's sad eyes looked up at mine one last time. I looked at her beautiful face, and whispered, *dime porque lloras* (tell me why you're crying). She breathed into mine, *de felicidad* (of happiness).

She knew I had to go. She insisted on it for my safety. She loved me enough to let me go. My greatest loves had always done that when the time came. But her feelin's were of happiness for the thought of me. So were mine for the thought of her. So many of my loves were as much about an idea – romanticism - as they were about the reality.

That was the last I ever saw her, mi' amour *mi' corazon.* I often miss her, but I can't cross the line anymore. I strode out of the saloon, jumped on Maxine and she galloped out of Hermosillo heading northeast toward the border.

It is not nearly possible to describe how a man feels when he truly loves a woman - what he would go through, how far he would ride, what he would do to be with her – or more than one in a man's lifetime. My Maria is irreplaceable, one of a kind like Fannie. I would ride through hell itself, across the lonely desert with distant howling coyotes, from countless sunrises to sunsets, to find her and be with her.

In sleepy Mexico the deep religious Christianity in the people and their old missions in the dusty desert towns going back to the time of the Spanish is all part of these loving and passionate folks.

I'm not foolin' myself. She has had and will have other men. We can't be together all the time or forever. That changes nothin'. She loves me without any doubt. Our feelin's are strong and burnin' inside us. Her face is painted in front of my eyes when I ride with Maxine across the deserts and mountains to get there and hold her.

It is powerful and I wouldn't avoid these feelin's even if I could. She is a miracle, a dream and she is real – my Maria. I am a lonely dreamer but I love you.

As far as the women go, I guess I'm still thinking like a sailor. I have a girl in every port. I get to spend time with my special woman when I am in each town. I am a romantic wanderin' loner who falls in and out of love at the drop of a hat; or so I lead myself to believe. But I never forget a one of them. It is building up good memories to displace all the bad stuff from the war years that have taken me so much time to get out of my head.

The brown-eyed beauties like Maria in Hermosillo fairly take my breath away. And I must admit, my penchant for my big infatuations with the Senoritas is that loving Spanish language for the most part. Every girl I spend time with is my love for the time I am there.

But really this is just a fantasy feelin'. There have been only three women I have really truly loved in my life. There was Estelle Culpepper, my colored beauty back in Ohio, Fannie McAuley, my kindred spirit in Denver, and Maria my Senorita in Sonora.

Certainly though I am drawn to women with an intensity. It must be because I was raised without a mother. I must be always looking for her.

Fannie felt the closest I ever got. Estelle and Maria were younger and drove my man's passion for beauty. Darcy was just a beautiful idea – a picture in my mind like a beautiful sky, or mountain slope or a sunset.

As far as what I had done there in Hermosillo, as I remember Fannie, she had found the balance between the hateful mind and the loving heart. The hateful mind rails at the hypocrisy, and the irony of that, in human creatures. The loving heart forgives and forgets as it leads us forward through life. We must forgive, starting with ourselves. It must be so for us to die in peace.

And I believe she had taught me to do the same at the end. The mind sees the ugly in the humans of this world, but the heart sees the beauty in us all.

Anse Hatfield, Josiah Ashford and William Wordsworth all came to that understanding if only finally at the end. I can imagine that the commanders in the war and most of the rest of us did too ultimately.

Nine – The Mine

I came out here for a fresh start and a new lease on life. The rush was on for gold in California and silver in Colorado. Friends had told me Aspen was the place to go and strike it rich. It was a lawless, rowdy and dangerous place, but no more difficult for me than I had seen in the Merchant Marines or the war.

I figured my carpentry and architectural design skills would fit in somehow. Turns out the mining companies were in desperate need of help in designing, fabricating and installing wooden beam support structures in the deep tunnels.

The mining company wanted to hire me as an employee. But you know me and know I never could work for an employer for wages. So I hired a crew of seven men and started my own company. We had to cut timber and use it to fashion our beam and post structures. The timber is mostly soft wood out here and we had to factor that in to the load bearing capacity.

My crew had come out here from all parts of the country, some from the East and South and two nearby in Missouri. Jeff Grady and Frank Dell were my best hands. I could put Jeff in charge when I was away and didn't have to worry. He had the leadership skill and Frank had the best work skill. Both of them were younger than me and had the strength and energy we needed.

Jeff was average height and stocky-built with hard hands. He had tousled light sandy hair and a fair complexion. His pale blue eyes had a softness when he spoke to you. There was a kindness in his face and I knew he understood people almost intuitively.

Frank was taller and wiry with that black Irish look about his dark eyes. He reminded me of me when I was much younger and my hair was fuller and dark brown. He was serious and dependable. These were strong men who had seen some life and I was fortunate to have them.

I put Jeff in charge of the day-to-day activities and deployments, but in an effort to be democratic I met with both of them together every couple days at the saloon to have some fun and talk about our projects. We drank together but none of us had a drinkin' problem. That would have gotten in the way and I couldn't stand for it.

My crew were a good bunch. Sam McNabb had come out here on his own to speculate. When that didn't work out, he came to work for me. After about a year he left to go back to Missouri because his wife had turned ill and needed him back home.

Joe Johnson was a black man who had settled here with his wife and four kids. He was smart as a whip and strong as an ox. I left him in charge of the timbering operation.

Earl Thomas was not the brightest but he gave me an honest day's work, week in and week out. He was dependable.

When trouble came, I could count on Henry Wallace to be right by my side. As much as you know me, I would back down from a fight before he ever would. Sometimes that came in handy. I was too old to be the bodyguard for these young men in every situation.

I understand and expect that these young men are going to do some gamblin' and whorin'. That's fine, but the work we do is dangerous and we have to pay attention.

These men, like most of the rest, had come poor looking for gold. But the gold rush days were over and silver mining was different. You can't pan for it and if you don't have the money to finance a mine, you end up working for somebody. My boys understood that and understood my feelings about that authority thing too. We got along fine. Yep, they worked for me for wages, but it would never be a corporate thing.

Another of my crew was John Knowland. His family homestead was in New England. I learned later that his father had fought with the Massachusetts regiment under Burnside's Expeditionary Corps. His father had died in Andersonville while I was there. John had been just a boy when he lost his father. He wanted me to tell him everything I could remember about it. I told him I don't want to talk about it, but I'm sure his father fought bravely because we all did.

You see, I had no way or anything I could say to this man who had lost his father. First, I didn't know his father personally. Second, how would any description I could offer about my experience at Andersonville console him? Last, we who were in it could discuss it together in terms that made us feel better about it. That is because we were there and understood it. It was easier to share experiences with Confederates, common foot soldiers like me on the other side, than with anyone who was not there. No, I just had to tell this young man his father was brave and had an honorable death. That was a lie of course.

When I look at my men and think about how we work and relate together, it makes me remember something else Fannie and I talked about. It was important, more and different than our negative view of authority. It was the idea of the egalitarian view. Of course we are not all equal. No two men are the same in all regards. We all have different talents and gifts, souls and demons, strengths and weaknesses.

But we are naturally equal in our human rights. We are not given equality by some authority, just equal opportunity and treatment. Some men will rise to the top and some won't. Fannie often reminded me that our country was formed on that basis and that our ancient ancestors believed it too.

We agree with the egalitarian view looking up from the bottom. No man is our superior and we are no man's inferior.

Our Scots-Irish President Andrew Jackson believed in that. As a frontiersman, he had a pride in his capability and self-sufficiency city people back East would not understand. With their refined manner, they dismissed his value and looked down on him as crude and inferior. His was a new idea of democracy based on that populist egalitarianism.

Because of that – our egalitarianism – we have always included new members into our extended clan. The Scots-Irish have married outsiders. Our progeny has produced Americans with African and Indian blood mixed with our own. Like I said before, we were all tribal people. We all hold the same spirit. Now it is the American spirit.

For our work I needed to learn something about rock – geology – to figure out the loads, stresses and strengths required. There is mostly solid granite in these here mountains. It is only weakened by the silver veins and pockets running every which way at locations we couldn't identify. In Colorado we were called "hard rockers" because of this. The silver was the source of fault lines to consider, which we couldn't, for the pattern the explosions would produce.

South of here in Nevada, Arizona and other places like the San Juan's the rock composition is a softer mix and made up of volcanic igneous rock with maybe sandstone and limestone.

So with the variation of hardness, strength and weight, for us it was trickier and more dangerous.

While I had studied architecture and engineering back in Ohio, the physics of the geology involved with mining and mine safety was somewhere far afield. I read what was available and learned what I could, but most of it was experimental and based on experience and judgment. I did all I could.

They use Chinese immigrant workers to set the nitro when they blast deeper into the tunnels because no white man wants to handle that volatile stuff. I had to be responsible for certain aspects of mine safety. It was all tied together.

When they work deeper into the mine, they make planned explosions to break rock and open up the mine deeper in. The explosions yield broken rock they carry out with manual labor – the Chinese again – to bust it up further and examine for silver veins and content.

If busting up the rock doesn't reveal or release the silver, the rest of the process requires smelting. Furnaces heat the busted rock and also use a chemical reducing agent to decompose the ore. This drives off other elements as gases leaving the slag and separated metal behind. Coke or charcoal are commonly used as the reducing agent and produce carbon dioxide and carbon monoxide which kills more mine workers at the smelter.

That all works fine most of the time, but the stresses from the explosions travel beyond the site of the explosion and often cause unexpected cave–ins. This is where my structure supports come in. They are supposed to maintain the integrity of the tunnel.

It isn't foolproof. We don't have the information for the complex pattern of strengths and weaknesses throughout the veins in the rock. We are constantly rebuilding our structures and sometimes burying the dead – usually the Chinese.

The other problem we faced was a people problem. The owners would watch the workers for "high grading" which is where they steal and sneak out bits of silver in their lunchbox or concealed in their clothing. It is illegal theft and men have been hung for it.

I worked for the Smuggler Mine up on Smuggler Mountain. It had been the biggest and they took out a silver nugget weighing 2,054 pounds. We did find the veins of silver and the mine yielded rich deposits. In time the owner and his investors became filthy rich.

The kind of engineering I learned was hands-on, built from experience. It always got me in trouble with the corporate types. These were the men who sat behind desks far from the mining operations. That had fine academic educations and understood theory but never its practical applications. When I would argue with them and fight over what must be done, I never got anywhere. I couldn't change them. It was up to them they said. I didn't get to decide they told me. My only solution to this conundrum of communication was to move on when I got fed up.

When the Smuggler Mine had worked out and came to an end, I contracted out to other mines – the Sheep Mountain and Bear Mountain mines - and drifted along as the years passed.

It is so beautiful here in the Rocky Mountains. I like the springtime the best. After the snow melt off, it warms up and the colors are vibrant up in the hills and peaks contrasted with the azure blue sky and white billowing clouds.

But it became once again like my youthful years in Baltimore before the war. I kept occupied building things, and had friends, but it didn't feel like home. I was still discontented.

All those years in Aspen I thought about Denver but I never went back. The years rolled along and too soon it was too late. We walk alone. It was regrettable, and even inexplicable, but we come into this world alone and that is how we leave it. In the end we walk alone.

Ten – Revelation

After too many years, in the spring of 1899, I went back to Denver to see Fannie. For so long I had wanted to go back, but now it would be difficult to know what to say. How would I explain my long absence and my reappearance? She had willingly let me go. She had no intention of standing in my way to stop me. That's why I loved her. But how would she feel now? What would it be like between us?

We rode east toward the rising sun early in the morning after daybreak. Maxine sensed something as we headed toward Denver. There was something strange in the old girl's behavior. She whinnied and turned her neck as though to lead me in another direction. She was excited like the filly she was ten years ago.

About ten miles out the terrain looked familiar as an old habit. Maxine recognized the surroundings and began to gallop. Within sight of the ranch I said we are almost home girl.

When we arrived at the long straight entry road, with the white split rail fence along the side, she broke into a sprint. For the last mile, lathered up, heart pounding, she flew like the wind. I leaned into her bending forward as far as I could and buried my face in her powerful neck. Go old girl I told her. Give it everything.

As I raced with her closer and closer to our objective, my mind's eye saw her, anticipating the joy to hold her again. It was but a moment ago I looked back and left her, an eternity awaiting to see her once more.

We landed at her home in a whirlwind cloud of dust. At the ranch house gate, it didn't say McAuley. The name had changed. The people there told me she had passed away three years ago from a winter ague that turned to pneumonia. My heart fell in that moment and my mind was consumed in disbelief by its old companion melancholy once again.

They didn't know who I was but mentioned she had had a son. He lived in closer by town where a family close to Fannie had taken him in.

Darcy Farrow Wilcox had raised him with her husband Henry along with their own brood. They had been kind and caring. They said he was eleven now and doing very well. They hadn't adopted him and he had kept his mother's name.

Darcy had put on some weight and gray had taken over much of her long blonde hair, but her beautiful bright blue eyes still shone - as bright as city lights - with her whimsical and loving spirit. Her laughing smile was still the same. We remembered that day long ago in the saloon when we had found that extraordinary connection.

Her husband Henry was bald except for his dark red hair on the sides and back of his head. He was gregarious and had quizzical, kind brown eyes and I knew he was the good man she deserved. Henry Wilcox had made a success in real estate speculation during Denver's growth spurt at the end of the century. Their own property was spacious and a fine looking parcel of land.

As it turned out for reasons I am about to tell you, I stayed a few days at Henry and Darcy's place. I was a welcomed friend.

Darcy led me by the hand, her sensual touch still as soft as goose down, and said for me to come out back of the house. She wanted me to see the children playing out in the field. My mind was overwhelmed as the strong feelings I felt that day ago past surged in my heart again as though it had been a moment ago.

She explained how industrious they had been mowing a large area of the hay field, cultivating a fine lawn and building a wondrous green baseball field. Henry was a fan of the game and invested in his very own professional baseball park.

When she led me to the baseball field and spoke softly about the boy, I remembered again how I had thought about her and her voice as sweet as the sugar candy. I was so happy she had Henry. She was such a fine woman; she deserved not to go to waste.

Darcy pointed to a tall boy, with brown eyes and hair, playing center field. She motioned to him to come over to us. It was a practice game so he didn't mind and trotted over to where we were standing with his center fielder's glove on his left hand. She introduced him to me and he smiled at me quizzically. How fitting this was for both her and me.

So I found you David McAuley. That is the rest of my story – many parts my father Morgan, my brother in spirit Josiah and your mother Fannie never knew. I loved your mother better than any woman in my life. I have tried to live an honorable life and do the right thing.

Once in a lifetime if he is lucky, a man meets a woman like your mother. She was extraordinary in so many ways, I cannot tell you. But know that I loved her and knew her well. I can feel her with me always in spirit if never again in body.

Your mother told me that if you can have both love and duty, you have grace within you. I believe she had both of these things and did have grace.

I never could live up to the duty part, so I fell short of having the grace she had. Duty is washing dirty dishes or dirty hands and doing the things that are necessary and responsible. I had enough of that during the war when I didn't understand duty or what I signed up for would entail. But I have always respected the sense and action of duty in others.

I lived an outdoor physical life – building, making, fighting - which is a hard one but what I chose. I have always kept company with strong, vital men and women – strong in body and spirit. For most of my life, I tried to understand my nature.

My father couldn't explain it to me when I was young. He cared about other things. Your mother brought me to understand it finally in my old age. And now I have made certain that you can know it. It is important because you will understand so many things about yourself better someday.

There is more to this story you will know someday when you are older, but for now you know who I am and where I came from. Now you know that son.

All that you are, all you will ever be, comes from this story. It is your legacy, your heritage, the spirit of your future – your own story that will reveal itself to you one day.

There is one more thing I want to tell you before I go. It is getting dark now. There is just you and me on the field. Pick up your bat and look out at the field. The field lives and breathes just like we do. Men have met on the field to do battle for all of time. They are all there but you can't see them. Just look at the field.

Lay the bat on your shoulder and swing it at the ball. Doesn't matter if there is no ball coming at you. Feel it? Do you think you can hit the ball out of the park? Can you win?

You can if you find your authentic swing. Every one of us has one. Yours is just yours and no one else's. Swing harder. Give it all you got. Hit another one.

Your swing is yours alone and something that can't be taught or learned. It has got to be remembered. The world can rob you of it from all our woulda's and coulda's and shoulda's. Some of us forget what our swing was like. Inside every one of us is one true, authentic swing.

Just swing the bat. Feel the night breeze. Close your eyes. Feel the bat. Feel the weight of it. Don't worry about where the ball is going to go. You can't drive it over the fence. You have to let it. Keep swinging the bat until you are a part of the whole thing. It is something you were born with. That is good. Can you see it? They say God is happiest when his children are at play.

Have you ever watched the best hitter on your team, or opposing team or at a professional game, watched him take a practice swing? Looks like he is searching for something. Then he finds it. He settles. Feel his focus? He hits it right over the fence. He can choose from a lot of swings – strikes, whiffs, bunts, fouls. But there is only one hit in perfect harmony with the field. One hit that is his authentic hit. It chooses him. There is a perfect shot trying to find you. All you got to do is get out of its way.

Look at him. See how he is in the field. Not with intensity as if to slay a dragon. He looks with soft eyes. He sees the place where all the tides, the snow-capped mountains, the seasons and the turning of the earth come together. The place where everything is one, commensurate with your capacity to wonder.

You've got to seek that place with your soul David. Seek it with your hands that are wiser than your head. I can't do it for you. But I hope I can help you find a way- the harmony with the field, your authentic swing, that fence, all that you are.

Well it's getting full dark now and the stars are comin' out. We better go in the house. They will be expectin' us for supper.

Darcy and Henry had me stay a few days there. They wanted me to spend all the time with the boy I could. It was a blissful poignant time together with him. They were busy with their chores and their children.

David and I spent long hours on the porch staring at the Rockies. I gave him a pocket knife like mine and we whittled sticks for hours to pass the time. We made a lot of toothpicks and got to know each other warmly and comfortably.

It became time to go and I saddled up Maxine with my blanket roll and looked back a moment more at a loved one once again as I left Denver to go back to Aspen.

A while back before that I had been settled in my place on the slope out of town. The winter of 1898 had come on early and strong. During the storms I stayed snug and warm in my cabin with the woodstove stoked with firewood, isolated and secluded in my solitude – alone but not lonely. I began writin' a book – this one you are reading. I called it *The American: A Man's Life* and it was my story, what I had seen and done. Much of it is and will be about Fannie.

One day I received a letter from Darcy – long after Fannie had passed and just after I got back from visiting there. She wrote me:

June 18, 1899

Dearest David,

We didn't git to talk about this. The years you were gone me and Fannie became best friends. I loved her and looked up to her like an older sister.

You know I was with her when she got sick and agreed to take her son in when she was dyin'.

All the years you were apart, she had kept a diary. I'm sendin' it here to you, but please send it back when you are done with it. Your son David needs to have it to remember his Mama.

I think of you and her all the time, especially when I look at this growin' boy. He is becoming a handsome young man we can be proud of.

Stay well my dear man,

Darcy

Right now I had nearly finished my writin' about my Fannie and my heart leapt when I saw this. I put down the letter on the table and opened the rest of the package. There was a handsome, leather-bound book with a brass clasp. I held it in my hands spellbound, excited and so profoundly sad, my hands trembled and my eyes looked at this treasure through misty tears. I undid the clasp and opened it up.

Here was her story for her son and this part I want to tell you:

My life was a struggle and a joy. My husband Angus and me saw all the trouble in Kentucky and more than we wanted to handle. The Civil War wasn't our fight.

He was a tough son-of-a-bitch and I was no lady. The Lords and Ladies of the Manor, they stayed back in the old country.

As far as my folks, I got kin in West Virginia – they's coal minin' mountain people, and some in upstate New York of all things. They, the West Virginia ones, broke away from the Virginia people because they knew slavery was a sin before God. The Yankees in New York married Irish. It's a good thing my daddy back in Scotland never knew about those ones. He's got no love for Popery. So we's God lovin' Presbyterians by heritage, but now a lotta country Baptists here in America.

Angus's kin, the McAuleys, were close allies with the McGregors until the awful Campbells swallowed up both those clans. Angus's folks got no love for the English and they were cautious about the Irish too.

We can forget about all that old world rivalry. We got our own problems here in America. There are good and bad people everywhere, but we's good at sortin' them out. Now out in the West we call that horse sense.

We moved the hell out of there and come to Colorado. We worked our asses off and made a fine ranch raisin' thoroughbred mustang crossbreeds.

But he died and I was left on my own. At first I wanted to give it up. Then I decided there was no good reason on God's earth I should up and quit this. So I went it alone and hired a couple men to help with the ranchin' work.

Along comes this handsome older middle age man one day. He walks right up to me and says Darcy sent him to look at horses. I had been grievin' for Angus for a long while, but my heart went all aflutter. It had been many years since I felt like that from the sight of a man.

But this man was extraordinary. Not just the sight and scent of him standing there in his sweaty shirt and dusty boots, but even more I sensed a quality.

David Wexley stayed. I showed him horses and we talked. He stayed longer until we fell in love. We talked, we made love 'til the cows came home, ate together and talked some more.

His experiences had been even tougher than mine. I tried to console him, cradle him, mother him. We needed each other.

He stayed. He taught me how to shoot. I taught him how to raise, break and train horses. We loved and loved with our whole selves for two seasons.

He read me poetry. I read him the bible and taught him to pray. He learned he was forgiven. He learned he was not alone.

But this lonesome cowboy couldn't sit still for too long and I knew it. He had dreams and always had this faraway look like he wondered what was over the horizon. I could see it comin'. I knew someday soon I would have to let him go. He needed to fly with his healed wings. I needed to raise my two hands to the sky and watch him climb away out of my sight and my life.

He saddled up and went one day. The sight of him will never leave me as long as I live.

In the spring I had his baby boy. Darcy come over and helped me manage the baby and keep my place runnin'. She had her brood growin' up and the older ones come and helped too.

I told Darcy I miss David. It was the toughest Goddamn thing I ever did in my life lettin' him go. I loved him that much – lettin' him leave, leavin' him his freedom. Still do. Always will.

But I have his son and mine and that is a blessing from God. I haven't lost my faith in Him.

I gently put the diary down on the table next to the letter. There was much more to read but this was all I could bear today. I would treasure her words, see her face in front of my mind's eye, love her forever and pray to the Lord we could be together someday again.

Another day I read the rest of the pages. And then the pages were blank for half of the book. I closed it and held it on my lap for the rest of the afternoon and stared out the window at the cloudless blue sky fading as the sun settled down over the west of the slope. There was a brilliance, like a lambency, almost like gold.

I prayed a prayer of thanksgiving to Him who made us.

Never believe an old man if he tells you he has no regrets about the life he lived or the things he done. We have to do the best we can and answer for the rest of it on the day of reckoning.

end

Epilogue

In June of 1900, with the foothills of the Rockies in full bloom and snow capping the peaks, the explosion at the Bear Mountain mine rocked the solid ground in the yards and dropped tons of rock into the mine shaft one hundred feet away from where David and his crew were rebuilding some buttressing members in the tunnel. It caught them completely by surprise since no detonation had been scheduled for that morning. They were located closer to the mine entrance than the point where it occurred, and so they had a slim chance to escape. There were seven of them in all.

Three managed to dash outside to safety and four were crushed by the flying rock and concussion of the explosion. David couldn't run as fast as the younger men but his position was fortunately closer to the entrance than most of his crew. He was the third and the last, after Frank and Henry, to get outside. Fortunately Joe was in the forest cutting timber.

Dazed and blinded in the bright sunlight, David watched to see if anymore would come out behind him. None did.

A man watched from a spot on high ground about one hundred fifty yards from the tunnel entrance. In the confusion, no one noticed him standing alone as a stranger. He was a Mexican and a big man. He had come all this way from Sonora because his brother had been killed years ago in Hermosillo.

The Mexican was surprised to see David come out. He had planned for the explosion to kill him. But he had waited and watched for the result and had a contingency plan. He took careful aim with his repeater rifle and fired a 30 caliber bullet through David's back. It pierced his heart and David fell instantly. No one heard the rifle report or realized what had happened in those chaotic moments of noise and confusion.

He had died in summertime as he had wished but not by the peaceful means he had hoped for. There was no heir to carry on the Wexley name but there was a son all the same.

David passed out of his body and floated toward the bright light. The faces of Darcy and his young son standing beside Josiah, Mary, David and Josena Ashford faded as they waved goodbye. Fannie stood before him bathed in white light, smiling and beckoning him toward the place where he was welcomed. We do not walk alone.

Mary, Josiah's wife, had read about it in the newspaper back east in Ohio. All the report said was that there had been an accident at the Bear Mountain mine in Aspen, Colorado. When she told Josiah, they contacted the mining company for they had known it was the last mine he had worked for. They learned that David had been killed there but the circumstances were not clear.

Grief-stricken and shocked, Josiah arranged to bring his body back to Hamilton for burial on his land. It took a few days before he met the train in Cincinnati and brought the casket home in his wagon.

Josiah dedicated a cemetery and memorial park in Ashford, Ohio. He had provided a vast parcel of cultivated land for the internment of former slaves and Union and Confederate soldiers of the Civil War and their descendants.

He gave the eulogy for David's re-internment memorial service there after moving his remains from the back lot of his home. He, and members of his family, would follow them and him to this place in the future.

It was a peaceful, beautiful green space with rolling hills, tree-shaded valleys, babbling brooks and monuments of forgiveness, understanding, remembrance and healing for all the American people.

Frank, Henry and Joe, David's men that had survived the tragedy, took Maxine into their care. She was kept at the town livery. Folks could tell she was grieving; knew David was gone. She left most of her feed. Folks were waiting and trying to decide what to do. They were good people and nobody was going to steal her.

Darcy and Henry Wilcox heard about it and immediately agreed to go to Aspen and get Maxine. When they arrived in town they found her right away and explained to those who cared what they intended to do. They would bring her home.

The old girl was past middle age but still had a lot of life in her. They brought her back to Denver to their place, not very far from where she was born. Maxine recognized that.

Maxine had a sense, maybe from smell or somehow, that young David was David. She followed him all around the corral inside the paddock and David understood too the meaning of this. He fed her carrots and apples. They grieved together and had each other. She lived out the rest of her days happy there with young David riding her around their paddock.

Old Josiah died later in 1906 and Mary followed him in 1917.

David had written a letter from Aspen to Joe in the late fall of 1899, after many years had passed in their correspondence.

November 10, 1899

My Dear Brother Josiah,

I have found a son I never knew I had. He lives in Denver with a dear friend and her husband. He is an eleven year old spittin' image of me. My love, his mother, had died some few years before, but I was in Aspen and lost touch. My woman Fannie McAuley named him David.

It was best that my friends raised him instead of me after Fannie died. They had been caring for him so well and faithfully for so long.

As one who loves you, I have always remained grateful that you had your Mary, your woman who healed your sorrows. My Fannie did that for me and I have forgiven myself for my past.

The melancholy that remains is that I could not stay with her forever. I had to remain true to myself. But my love remains forever and in her next life she knows that.

You can rest assured the weight of your concerns for me can be lifted from your heart.

I still miss you and your family, our days in the South and all those years together up in Ohio.

As you would know, I have had a lot of years to think about our past. The true emancipation that followed the war, not the Emancipation Proclamation before it which was a political artifice to help the Union war effort, was the change to the Constitution which was a sin. It was a shameful sin because there was no effective plan or actions before it or after it to put the Negro on a footing where he could survive and thrive as a human being in America.

I blame the politicians and the American people for that. The Abolitionists and the Firebrands made no accommodation. The Freedman's Bureau was too little too late. It will be a problem for the black man and the white man for the next hundred years. I know you understand this as well or better than I. You have spent your life as a legislator trying to find a path forward for all Americans.

Joe, I wrote a book out here in Aspen. It is about my life in the West and my whole life before that including my time with you. I called it "The American: A Man's Life" and I found a print shop in town to bind up a few copies. I began writing it up here in my cabin before I ever met my son and then I finished it up after that and meant it for him. Darcy Farrow Wilcox in Denver has it for him for when he is grown up.

I still see the starved spirits of the apparitions from thirty five years ago. Not from the long marches or the fighting, the waiting in camps or the prisons, but the dead that haven't crossed over still, their spirits not resolved, their work undone.

I tell them now to be at peace as I am. There is beauty yet undiscovered, its cause worth the toil and the sorrow, its love the promise kept. I no longer regret it, my life the richer for the discovery of the child born from its passion, from the love of a woman, from the sight of God through her eyes and her promise of the life thereafter, the truth in immortality assured. My soul is full of love just as I know yours is. I can see it now Joe. It had been a grand time and the glory is not in the past. It is yet to come.

Be well my brother until we meet again,

David

Joe wrote back later that month with a tenderness of understanding:

November 30, 1899

My Dearest David,

I understand the mixture of your grief and happiness more than you can possibly know.

We were together when we looked for my Josena. We were together when we learned she had been killed. We were together when we learned of my lost daughter but couldn't find her.

But we were apart when my grown children found her in Mississippi and brought her home a middle aged woman – my daughter Hanna Drish.

Our lives have continued to follow together in Providence's divine path.

Your insights about our country have a depth very few can appreciate or understand. But you know I do brother.

Please send me a copy of your book so that my children will always remember you.

Forever your brother,

Joe

The strong bond of their lives had continued to entwine them and connect them together after the visible connection between them had been broken over time and distance, but had been replaced by the invisible hand.

Josiah's son, David Ashford had read David Wexley's journals left for his father's safekeeping and the book he had left as his legacy. He had known his father's friend when he was young and David Wexley had lived beside them. David Ashford showed the journals to his son, Josiah Ashford II and explained what this man had meant to his grandfather, what these two men had meant to each other, what it had meant to their family, that David Wexley had left behind a son, that while his grandfather and David Wexley were gone, there was a part of them still left behind.

In 1955, in Montgomery, Alabama, a forty year old man from Hamilton, Ohio named Josiah Ashford II, met a sixty-five year old man from Denver, Colorado named David McAuley. They marched down the street locked arm in arm together.

Martin had told them, "The time is always right to do what is right."

Josiah and David were free men who learned about their human connection. Their common ground had begun ninety years ago by the Mississippi River in Natchez when one's grandfather had met one's father. The ancient tree of their family history had common roots tracing way back to Africa and Scotland.

They had come from the same place as hard-bitten, God loving freedom fighters. They knew where they came from and knew their purpose. They knew their authentic selves. They faced the world on their feet, never bowed down or backed up.

The circle is unbroken and the American story continues.

There is no need to pray for the forgiveness of the sins of those that came before. He has forgiven them. There is no need to pray for their protection or safety. They have been gathered together with all those who love them, enfolded in His loving arms. We need only to remember them and honor them with our love and gratitude for their just duty and sacrifice.

So that we may never forget him or the many others who have served and have given their last full measure of devotion, who lived on to the end of the time given them, or died in the moment of service, who must be honored and remembered to the end of our time, and by all those who follow us, here are words better than I could ever express them from the old book:

All these were honoured in their generations

And were the glory of their times

There be of them that have left a name behind them

That their praises might be reported

And some there be which have no memorial

Who are perished as though they had never been

And are become as though they had never been born

And their children after them

But these were merciful men

Whose richeousness hath not been forgotten

With their seed shall continually remain

A good inheritance and their children are within the covenant

Their seed standeth fast and their children for their sakes

Their seed shall remain for ever

And their glory shall not be blotted out

Their bodies are buried in peace

But their name liveth for evermore

Ecclesiasticus, chapter 44, excerpt

Author's Footnote

I owe a special debt of gratitude to Canadian musical artists Ian Tyson and Sylvia Fricker Tyson. Their evocative voices told the emotional stories that helped me visualize and internalize the American West and its people back in those days. They deeply influenced my insights and made it feel as though I was there with my characters.

When I visited Scotland in 2006, we went to the Edinburgh castle on top of the hill, overlooking the modern city and the Firth of Forth toward the North Sea. It was noon at the end of May and a warm day. The Sargent-at-Arms ordered the firing of the cannon at the parapets on the top of the castle.

It was a tradition kept for all the years of their history. The cannon was fired every noon as a small ceremony. The guide told us it was to insure that the cannon was in good working order so that if the English come, we will be ready. Despite their loyalty to the U.K., their avowed British citizenship, the years of peaceful cooperation, the centuries of growth to their modernity, they would never be English and their Scottish spirit would never be lost.

This pride in tradition, this self-reliant, independent spirit is the same that built my country. The pioneers that built America brought this spirit and its ancient traditions with them. They were the men and women that conquered and settled our continent and they are the people who gave us our American spirit. We face the world on our feet, we never bow down to nobility; we endure; we never back down; we do what is right.

We fiercely hold to an egalitarian view toward our fellow man based on the idea that no man is our superior or our authority. We are Americans.

Characters in order of appearance

David Wexley

Josiah Ashford

Darcy Farrow

Fannie McAuley

Maxine

Rosa

Maria

Jeff Grady

Frank Dell

John Knowland

Sam Mc Nabb

Joe Johnson

Earl Thomas

Henry Wallace

James Longstreet

Henry Wilcox

David McAuley

Josiah Ashford II

Locations

Hamilton, Ohio

Chicago, Illinois

Denver, Colorado

Aspen, Colorado

Santa Fe, New Mexico

El Paso, Texas

Hermosillo, Sonora, Mexico

Montgomery, Alabama

Timeline

1832 – Born in Baltimore, Maryland

1848 – Sailed topsail schooners

1862 – Fought in battle of Antietam

1864 – Fought in Battle of the Wilderness

1864 – Imprisoned in Andersonville, Georgia

1865 – Came to Ohio with Josiah

1873 – Economic Panic, Grant's 2nd term

1887 – Left Ohio (age 55) to go west, stopped in Chicago

1888- Met Fannie and stayed in Denver

1889 – Moved to Aspen

1889- 1898- Travel through New Mexico, Texas, Mexico

1893 – Chicago World's Fair and Columbia Exposition

1893 – Economic Panic, railroad over-speculation

1896- Gunfight in Hermosillo

1899- Visited Denver

1900 – Killed at the mine (age 68)

1900 – Casket brought back to Cincinnati on the train

Review of books by Mr. Jennings

Hanna's Promise

It's a heartfelt and inspiring story of love, devotion and faith. One that the author weaves the sorrows, the triumphs, and the majestic harmony of God's grace through the wonderful and heart wrenching circumstances. Hanna sees the world through her own eyes, and sees the goodness in all people no matter of race or of circumstances. She sets out to bring hope and grace to everyone.

The author is a gifted writer and story teller. Hanna's Promise is more than just a book. It's a work of grace itself, one that every person should slow down long enough to read and enjoy it.

Toni House, author
Baton Rouge, LA

Hanna's Promise is David Claire Jennings second historical fiction novel. It is the sequel to After Bondage and War published last year. Intertwining historical events and sometimes little known facts within the story of Hanna, an orphaned slave girl, makes for fascinating reading. The reader enters the post-Civil War era and follows the life and times of Hanna Drish and the family she never knew.

The end of the Civil War finds 8 year old Hanna newly orphaned and suddenly a freed slave. Fortunately she is loved by John and Sarah Drish, who although her masters, love her as their own. With the threat of invading Union armies, they take Hanna to live with their friends in Mobile. We get a different view of slave owners than the usual stereotype as we come to know the two former slave owners who raise Hanna and care for her as a member of their family.

Hanna never knew her father, as he never knew of her until after the Civil War ended. He had gone on to become a renowned state representative in Ohio, remarried and had twins, one named for his dead wife, and one for his best friend, a Union soldier he met after the war. The novel After Bondage and War tells the poignant story of these two men and their search for happiness and peace.

Hanna's Promise is filled with the spiritual relationship she has with the Archangel Michael who helps her achieve a life of hope and grace through her relationships with everyone she meets. As she travels through life she meets many challenges as any Negro in the post-Civil War south would. But her serenity and kindness always shine through and help her overcome the negativity she encounters.

The reader is thrilled when she is finally united with the family she never knew and goes on to lead a blessed life affecting everyone she meets.

This is a book that engages the reader in the lives of the characters and leaves them with a feeling of hope for the future of mankind.

Irene Havekost – 6/4/16

I bought *Hanna's Promise- A Story of Grace and Hope* because the title intrigued me. As I began to read the characters came to life, perhaps because I am an adopted child who was reunited with his siblings. The twins David and Josena were described so that I felt that I could see them in my mind. The journey they took to find their sister was hauntingly familiar to my own journey. Hanna's struggles and her devotion to her promise to God often brought tears to my eyes.

David Claire Jennings writing was easy to understand, yet the words he used were powerful and capable of evoking strong emotion in the reader. The history was fascinating and full of things that I never learned in school. It gave me a better picture of life in the south after the Civil War.

I became so involved with the story and the characters that I wanted to know more about what had happened prior to the time of this book, so I purchased *After Bondage and War* by Mr. Jennings. I can't wait to start it and find out what happened.

I heartily recommend this book to anyone who has an interest in history, and likes characters that show the goodness in people and who lead lives of importance to others.

Thomas David

Hanna's Promise by David Claire Jennings was a very touching story for me; if you like historical fiction with a spiritual twist, you'll like this book. It's not a very difficult read, and it flows very smoothly between the stories of David Ashford and his twin sister Josena, who are secondary protagonists and second generation returning characters from David's first novel, After Bondage and War. The time period is post Civil War and Reconstruction.

David and Josena are son and daughter to Josiah Ashford, also a returning character; unlike David's first novel, Josiah plays a secondary role to David and Josena. Josena and David have spiritual and intellectual similarities, albeit one was trained as a historian and war correspondent and the other as an anthropologist. However, the physical characteristics and personality differences between the two are charmingly demonstrated: "Together they reminded you of Abraham and Mary Todd Lincoln, had they not been a brother and sister of color from a more modern time."

The meat and potatoes of this novel is David and Josena's quest to find their long-lost sister, an enigmatic woman who was the child of their father Josiah Ashford, when he was still in bondage, and his then wife, also a slave, named Josena, from whom his daughter from his second marriage is named after. We revisit the tragic slave revolt, briefly mentioned in After Bondage and War, and learn more details about how Josiah's wife Josena was killed. David and Josena's quest for their long-lost sister compels the reader to read on as both the reader and David and Josena learn more details about their sister: they find out her name is Hanna.

Hanna is the third-introduced, but main protagonist of the novel. Hanna's upbringing is skillfully portrayed: she is raised by two benevolent white families, the first, named the Drishes, had to give her up when the Civil War came calling too close to and even threatened their home, and the second, the Blanchards. Both families loved her like a daughter. The idea that a slaveholding white family could love and care for Hanna as a daughter is the first glimpse of racial harmony in the book. This theme of racial harmony is apparent throughout the book, especially with the character of Hanna, and it is a theme so desperately lacking in today's modern time.

Hanna's character is revealed to have a very spiritual mission. Her impetus in life is to promote racial harmony and further it through love, caring for all people, kindness and as the author puts it: "act justly, love mercy, and walk humbly with her God." Hanna's mission is introduced through a visit from an angel early on in the novel, in her childhood; she is asked to make a covenant, a promise to God to further racial harmony. It is this covenant, this promise that lends the book its name, Hanna's Promise.

All in all, this is a very good read. The language is easy to read, not highfalutin, but the concepts and themes are very deep and spiritual. Civil War and Reconstruction historical references abound. The characters are a joy to discover. God Himself even plays a role. And the quest of David and Josena to find their long-lost sister draws the reader in and compels them to feel the joy of their discovery. Hanna's spiritual quest for racial harmony is also very deep and her vision of a better America through spirituality, kindness, sympathy, empathy, love and caring is a quest that we all would do well to emulate today.

Edwin Smith

After Bondage and War

I first met David Claire Jennings when he was a student in my History 121 course at Columbia College. I soon discovered that I had much more to learn from him than I could ever possibly teach him. Much like the characters David Wexley and Josiah Ashford in After Bondage and War, David and I were at two different places in our lives. Yet, like Wexley and Ashford we discovered a bond and formed a lasting friendship.

David's passion for writing, combined with his very practical understanding of history and his life experiences all come together in his first book: After Bondage and War. David tells the story of slavery, war, and reconciliation with a level of emotion often absent from writing; he tells the human side.

James Giannettino, Jr., adjunct history professor, Columbia College

---

After Bondage and War is David Claire Jennings first historical fiction novel. It is the poignant and touching story of two men from entirely different backgrounds who meet after the Civil War, form a bond of friendship and brotherhood which last a lifetime. Josiah Ashford is a slave in Alabama, while David Wexley is an outspoken and adventurous Union soldier who had just endured the horrors of captivity at Andersonville. The war is over, but for these two men, the journey is just beginning.

Through fate or divine intervention, they meet in Natchez, are immediately drawn to each other, and begin a life-long adventure as they struggle to find the peace and happiness they both so desperately want and need.

Aside from their color, the main difference in Josiah and David is their faith. Josiah is filled with it, and David is searching for it. Looking for their place in this new world, they travel through the south looking for Josiah's wife Josena and when the search ends in tragedy, they head north to Ohio to make a new life.

For the reader, the fictional story is set in and among historical events, all true but with added insights into the hearts and minds of many famous men of the time. For a history buff, the story only adds to the history told throughout the book. For the fiction buff, the history only adds reality and interesting and many unknown facts to a wonderful story.

The book is an easy read, the reader is never mired down in long historical diatribes, and the fictional characters stories flow effortlessly from one situation to another.

Irene Havekost

Dave has a unique gift for writing history. He also has great perspective on life in general.

Dave is one of those people who has not only seen life, managed to live through those many ups and downs which we humans share but taken the time to observe and chronicle his perspectives.

William Burak, adjunct history professor, Columbia College

Not being a fan of history**, After Bondage and War** is not a book I would have picked off the shelf. However, a friend recommended it and to make him happy, I bought the book.

Surprisingly, I found it to be very good. There was just enough history with many things I had never known, to keep me reading on to discover what happened to the many characters in the story. Having been born and raised in the north, but spending the majority of my life in the south, it was easy to see the truth in the descriptions of places, attitudes and actions in the story.

I found myself relating to David Wexley's search for happiness and faith and envious of Josiah's deeply ingrained faith. The story was interesting, the characters likable or unlikable enough to keep my interest from beginning to end.

I look forward to the sequel Hanna's Promise to see where the story leads.

Dennis Owen – 6/4/16

I read *After Bondage and War* because I wanted to find out the story behind Hanna Drish, the heroine in *Hanna's Promise*. David Claire Jennings first book lived up to the challenge. I enjoyed it as much if not more than *Hanna's Promise*. As a replanted northerner, I think that I now finally understand the strong feelings surrounding the Civil War that still exist in the south. The history was fascinating, there was so much detail about historical figures that I knew them personally, how they thought and how they felt.

As I followed the life stories of the two main characters, Josiah Ashford and David Wexley, they became my friends. I suffered with them in their defeats and celebrated with them in their triumphs. I have always believed in the goodness of people, and to see two men from different walks of life, bond together as brothers to survive and succeed in the world, made my heart sing with happiness. Their story was touching, poignant and a testament to the concept of brotherhood among all men.

I am not an avid reader, so it is unusual for me to have quickly read and thoroughly enjoyed two books in a short period of time. Both books by Mr. Jennings had an easy reading style. Not too filled with long descriptive sentences, but with a structure that gave me as a reader many an "aha" moment. I felt treated as an intelligent reader who would understand the nuances of what was going on without being hit over the head with the information.

I heartily recommend *After Bondage and War* to any reader who enjoys a great story, truly believable and likable characters, and thought provoking ideas all mixed in with interesting historical information. I look forward to any future books by David Claire Jennings.

Thomas David

David Claire Jennings' novel After Bondage and War deals is a very touching story that deals with the underlying theme of racial harmony, as evidenced by the friendship of two characters from very disparate backgrounds, a white Union soldier with post-traumatic stress after the Civil War and a newly freed slave from a Southern plantation.

The two main characters and protagonists in this novel are Josiah Ashford and David Wexley. Josiah Ashford is poignantly described as having an "insatiable curiosity and an African respect and reverence for the wisdom of his elders...As an adult, he came to the view that he was the master of his fate. Free will permitted him to take charge of his life and strive for his own betterment."

David Wexley was born into a well-to-do family, but longed for adventure. Not wanting to continue in his father's business, he worked as a merchant marine for a while, in order to fulfill his wanderlust. Under a romantic view of war, he later joins up with the Union army during the Civil War, having viewed slavery as an injustice. The thrust of his character is a passion for fighting injustice due to his Scots-Irish temperament. Briefly, and beautifully, describing David's temperament due to his Scots-Irish roots: "They had a long history of hating the English but would pick a fight with anybody if the cause was right..."

The main antagonists in this novel are Marcus Taylor and Rebecca Stanley, slaveholders of the South. Exquisitely written, we learn of their ensuing courtship, marriage, and establishment of a plantation. Marcus and Rebecca acquire Josiah as one of their slaves; we learn of his harsh treatment on the plantation by Marcus' overseer, and Josiah's tender love for, and subsequent marriage to, another slave named Josena. We also learn of Josena's tragic fate.

As a historical fiction novel, After Bondage and War is about a 50/50 percent blend of actual historical events and characters versus fictional events and characters. Fans of Michael and Jeff Shaara and John Jakes will enjoy this novel. The 50/50 blend makes David Claire Jennings rather unique as an author, as the Shaaras and John Jakes have a higher percentage of either actual historical or fictional events and characters.

Civil War historians will enjoy the military strategy and history depicted in the chapters devoted to David Wexley's battles in the Civil War. But the humanity of the War is never lost:

"As darkness fell, he lay on the field with the thousands of the dead and wounded. It was quiet after the cannon and muskets had ceased firing. The ghosts kept company with the wounded and suffering. It was so still. There was only the sounds of the moans and cries for help from the living and those still to die."

It is a chance – or was it God's Divine Providence? - meeting in Natchez between the newly freed slave Josiah Ashford and the newly released from Andersonville prison Union soldier David Wexley that forms the critical turning point in the novel. Each side has to overcome their fear of how they will be received by the other, and the eventual outcome is a great success – they become fast friends and travelling companions.

The novel ends with the subsequent generations of Josiah's offspring, and David Wexley leaves to go out West. What happens to Josiah's children? – stay tuned for David Claire Jennings' second novel Hanna's Promise! What happens to David Wexley? – stay tuned for the third book in the saga, The American!

Edwin Smith

www.ingramcontent.com/pod-product-compliance
Lightning Source LLC
Chambersburg PA
CBHW070538030726
47505CB00001B/82
9780997460186